# 1,000,000 Books
are available to read at

# Forgotten Books

www.ForgottenBooks.com

Read online
Download PDF
Purchase in print

ISBN 978-1-331-75269-1
PIBN 10230216

This book is a reproduction of an important historical work. Forgotten Books uses
state-of-the-art technology to digitally reconstruct the work, preserving the original format
whilst repairing imperfections present in the aged copy. In rare cases, an imperfection in
the original, such as a blemish or missing page, may be replicated in our edition. We do,
however, repair the vast majority of imperfections successfully; any imperfections that
remain are intentionally left to preserve the state of such historical works.

Forgotten Books is a registered trademark of FB &c Ltd.
Copyright © 2018 FB &c Ltd.
FB &c Ltd, Dalton House, 60 Windsor Avenue, London, SW19 2RR.
Company number 08720141. Registered in England and Wales.

For support please visit www.forgottenbooks.com

# 1 MONTH OF FREE READING
## at
## www.ForgottenBooks.com

By purchasing this book you are eligible for one month membership to ForgottenBooks.com, giving you unlimited access to our entire collection of over 1,000,000 titles via our web site and mobile apps.

To claim your free month visit:
www.forgottenbooks.com/free230216

\* Offer is valid for 45 days from date of purchase. Terms and conditions apply.

English
Français
Deutsche
Italiano
Español
Português

# www.forgottenbooks.com

**Mythology** Photography **Fiction** Fishing Christianity **Art** Cooking Essays Buddhism Freemasonry Medicine **Biology** Music **Ancient Egypt** Evolution Carpentry Physics Dance Geology **Mathematics** Fitness Shakespeare **Folklore** Yoga Marketing **Confidence** Immortality Biographies Poetry **Psychology** Witchcraft Electronics Chemistry History **Law** Accounting **Philosophy** Anthropology Alchemy Drama Quantum Mechanics Atheism Sexual Health **Ancient History Entrepreneurship** Languages Sport Paleontology Needlework Islam **Metaphysics** Investment Archaeology Parenting Statistics Criminology **Motivational**

# The Doomed City

By

JOHN R. CARLING

Author of " Shadow of the Czar," "By Neva's Waters,"
"The Viking's

Illustrations by

A. FORESTIER

New York
Edward J. Clode
Publisher

# The Doomed City

By

## JOHN R. CARLING

Author of "The Shadow of the Czar," "By Neva's Waters,"
"The Viking's Skull"

Illustrations by

A. FORESTIER

New York
Edward J. Clode
Publisher

COPYRIGHT, 1910, BY
EDWARD J. CLODE

Entered at Stationers' Hall

# CONTENTS

| CHAPTER | | PAGE |
|---|---|---|
| I. | A Mysterious Wedding | 1 |
| II. | The Banquet of Florus | 18 |
| III. | The Queen of Beauty | 30 |
| IV. | The Dream of Crispus | 48 |
| V. | Simon the Zealot | 60 |
| VI. | "Delenda est Hierosolyma!" | 71 |
| VII. | The Journey to Jerusalem | 83 |
| VIII. | What Happened in the Royal Synagogue | 95 |
| IX. | "Let Us Go Hence!" | 112 |
| X. | The Vengeance of Florus | 124 |
| XI. | "To Your Tents, O Israel!" | 135 |
| XII. | "Væ Victis!" | 147 |
| XIII. | A Good Samaritan | 160 |
| XIV. | "Thou Wilt Never Take the City" | 170 |
| XV. | The Triumph of Simon | 181 |
| XVI. | The Ambition of Berenice | 198 |
| XVII. | The Making of an Emperor | 210 |
| XVIII. | The Preliminaries of a Great Siege | 228 |
| XIX. | The First Day's Fight | 241 |
| XX. | Circumvallation | 258 |
| XXI. | The Dying City | 266 |
| XXII. | The Rescue of Vashti | 290 |
| XXIII. | Closing In | 306 |
| XXIV. | "Watchman, What of the Night?" | 325 |
| XXV. | "Judæa Capta!" | 341 |
| XXVI. | Justice the Avenger | 354 |

Τῶν στρατιωτῶν τις ΔΑΙΜΟΝΙΩ ΟΡΜΗ ΤΙΝΙ ΧΡΩΜΕΝΟΣ ἁρπάζει μὲν ἐκ τῆς φλεγομένης ὕλης, τό δὲ πῦρ ἐνίησ θυρίδι χρυσῇ τοῦ ἱεροῦ.

*A certain soldier,* MOVED BY A DIVINE IMPULSE, *seized a blazing torch, and set fire to a golden window of the temple.*
*JOSEPHUS. Jewish War* vi. 4, 5.

# THE DOOMED CITY

## CHAPTER I

### A MYSTERIOUS WEDDING

THE purple light of evening had fallen upon the Syrian shore as Crispus, with a quick, swinging pace, trod the well-paced road that led southwards to the stately city of Cæsarea, the Roman capital of Judæa.

Evidently he loved the exercise of walking, since, had it pleased him to do so, he could have ridden, for at a respectable distance there followed, led by a couple of slaves, his two-horsed rheda, a traveling-car of sculptured bronze, provided with a leathern hood and silken awnings, and containing such necessary luggage (aptly named *impedimenta* by the Romans) as a man of simple tastes would require on a long journey.

Crispus, whose age was perhaps twenty-five years, had a powerful yet graceful figure, eyes of a deep gray, crisp hair of a bronzed hue, and a handsome face, as clear cut as if sculptured from marble, a face whose pure complexion spoke of pure living—a rare virtue in that age!—a face whose keen, ardent look gave promise that its owner was one born to achieve distinction, if indeed he had not already achieved it. "An antique Roman," one would say on seeing him, since he still adhered to the wearing of the stately toga, which in the first century was fast becoming superseded by the Grecian tunic; moreover, the ring on his finger was not of gold, but of iron, in accordance with ancient usage.

In journeying along he had caught sight, by the wayside, of a stone pillar engraved with letters which told that the said pillar was distant from Rome by the space of one thousand five hundred miles. Thus far, yea, and hundreds of miles farther, did the Roman power extend in this, the twelfth year of the reign of the Emperor Nero. Crispus' stern smile gave the keynote to his character—pride in the Empire founded by his forefathers, determination to maintain that Empire, though it cost him limb and life.

And in truth Rome counted few sons more patriotic than young Crispus Cestius Gallus, distinguished alike by feats of arms and by beauty of person; by noble birth, and by high office—for he was secretary to his father, the elder Cestius, who at that time held the dignity of imperial Legate of Syria, a dignity whose vast power and splendid emoluments made it a prize coveted of all Roman statesmen.

It was a lovely evening. A faint breeze came from the sea, whose waves, wine-dark in color, flowed with a sort of velvety ripple upon the yellow sands. To the east at the distance of a mile or more rose the Samaritan hills, mysterious and still in the evening light, their rounded summits clearly defined against the deep violet of the sky.

Now, as Crispus glanced ahead, he saw approaching a solitary figure, wearing buskins of purple, and a sleeved and embroidered tunic of the same color, cut to the latest fashion. He walked, his eyes set upon the ground, with a somewhat slow and pensive step, and would have passed by unheeding but for the cheery, rousing voice of Crispus.

"Ho, Titus! Is it thus in a strange land that you pass by your oldest friend?"

He who was thus addressed started, looked up, and, recognizing the speaker, dropped as if by magic his melancholy air, and advanced with smiling face and extended hand.

"By the gods, 'tis Crispus," he cried in a tone of genuine delight. "Now doth Fortune favor me. To think of meeting you in this barbarian province, a thousand miles from our Sabine farms! Whither are you bound? For Cæsarea? Then will I return with you."

Titus Flavius, destined in course of time to attain the imperial purple, was the senior of Crispus by one year: keen of eye, and with an aquiline nose, he looked every inch the soldier that he was, in spite of his perfumed and fashionable garb. A certain ruddiness of features showed him to be likewise a sort of "Antony, that revels long o' nights."

"What do *you* in this Jewish land?" asked Crispus.

"Rejoice at my presence here, for 'tis proof that I am restored to Nero's favor."

"I did not know that you had lost it."

"What? Have you not heard that when Nero—what a delightful buffoon he is, to be sure!—was singing on the stage at Corinth, my sire Vespasian was so little appreciative of good music as actually to yawn, and even to fall asleep and snore, with the result that not only *Pater nocens* but even *Filius innocens* was forbidden to appear in the imperial presence."

"I marvel that you did not both lose your heads."

"So do I. Though banished, however, I did not lose heart, but in the spirit of a true courtier I sacrificed every day to Nero's heavenly voice; and, on learning this (for I took good care it should reach his ears!), he recalled me to court, and marked his approval of my piety by sending me on a mission to Cæsarea."

"A mission? Of what nature?"

"Why, you doubtless know that yon fair city of Cæsarea is peopled both with Greeks and Jews, each claiming precedency of the other. Let procurator Florus post up an edict beginning, 'To the Greeks and Jews of Cæsarea,' and the Jewish mob will tear it down. Let him word it, 'To the Jews and Greeks,' and the

Greeks will not suffer it to remain up. The Greek high priest of Jupiter demands that on state occasions he shall sit upon the right hand of the procurator; the high priest of the Jews, when he comes to Cæsarea, claims the same privilege. The Greeks wish their language to be used in the law-courts to the exclusion of our own stately Latin—there's taste for you! the Jews clamor for their own tongue. This feud is productive of continual rioting and bloodshed. Therefore Nero, appealed to by deputies from both factions, hath pronounced his decree, dispatching it from Greece by my hand."

" And in whose favor hath Cæsar decided? "

" Nay, I know not. The decree was contained in a sealed letter addressed to Florus, who hath not yet made it public. As for me, instead of hastening back to Nero to show him how quickly I can transact his business, I, like a fool, tarry in the neighborhood of Cæsarea."

" There being a woman in the case," smiled Crispus; " otherwise the usually sensible Titus would not be garbed like a fashionable dandy. What would your stern republican father say to this perfuming of yourself? "

" A woman in the case? Say, rather, a goddess. No lovelier face hath ever been seen since Helen lured the Grecian ships to Troy."

" Fickle Titus! Last autumn he was vowing eternal fidelity to Lesbia, the hetæra; it was the Greek dancing-girl Lycoris in winter; this spring it is—who? "

" Lesbia and Lycoris! Pouf! " said Titus, as if blowing these nymphs away in air. " Do not mention them, I pray you, in the same breath with this splendid eastern beauty. I am serious now, if ever I were so. I would marry her to-morrow, were she willing; nay, more, to win her I would even repudiate the religion of my ancestors, and worship her Jewish God."

" Titus must indeed be smitten! So your fair one is a Jewess? "

"Ay, and in rank far above poor plebeian me," said Titus, sighing like a furnace.

"You talk thus! you who are a quæstor, tribune of a legion, and a messenger of imperial Cæsar?"

"And the son of a man who was once a horse-doctor; forget not that."

"You were brought up in the imperial household with Britannicus, enjoying the same luxuries and the same instructors as he."

"And very nearly drinking of the same fatal cup," commented Titus, grimly.

"The gods reserved you for a nobler destiny. But as to your fair lady—who is she?"

"A princess, beautiful, proud, scornful. Berenice her name, the daughter of that Agrippa who, some twenty years ago, was King of Palestine. He left her so much wealth that she is called 'Golden Berenice.' You know her?" added Titus, as he saw an odd look flit for a moment over the face of Crispus.

"I have seen her."

"Then you know how beautiful she is."

"Yes, she is certainly beautiful," replied Crispus, in a tone as if grudging the admission.

"You speak coldly. 'Tis clear I shall never have *you* for a rival."

"True, O Titus. When I mate it shall be with pure maid. Hath not your Berenice already had one husband?"

"She was wedded, when quite a girl, to Polemo, King of Pontus, who divorced her two years afterwards."

"Polemo?" ejaculated Crispus, in some surprise. "Polemo?—one of my father's friends. Why did he divorce her?"

"Nay, ask that of others. He was elderly and serious; she was youthful and gay: *there*, I suspect, lay the reason."

"Their separation," remarked Crispus, "does not appear to have left much bitterness behind, for, at a banquet given by my father to all the kings of the East, Polemo and the Princess Berenice sat side by side, seeming to be on excellent terms with each other. And, what struck me as strange, their glances were so often cast in my direction that I could not help wondering whether *I* were the subject of their talk. Were there any children born of this marriage?"

"One—a daughter, said to have died in infancy."

"And you would woo this Herodian princess? Do you frequent this lonely shore in order to sigh out vows to Venus?" said Crispus, pointing to love's planet that sparkled like an eye in the blue depths above.

"I come here hoping to have the pleasure of a few words with her as she returns to Cæsarea. An hour ago, so I am told, she drove this way in her chariot."

"You do right, then, in retracing your steps, for I can certify that no chariot has passed me."

"Then she must have turned aside, and gone inland," said Titus, looking to the left as if meditating a diversion among the hills in quest of the fair princess.

With a sigh he resigned the project, and strode onward beside Crispus, whose frequent questions on all that fell within the sphere of his vision showed that he was treading the shore of Palestine for the first time.

"How name you yon house?" he asked, pointing ahead to an edifice perched upon a crag that overlooked the shore road.

"I am told that it is called 'Beth-tamar.'"

"And that, being interpreted, meaneth 'The House of Palms,'" remarked Crispus, and smiling at Titus' look of surprise. "O, I know something of the speech of these barbarians, having learned it in childhood from one of my father's favorite slaves, a captive Jew; and so long as the fellow kept to his language, well and good, but when he tried to make me a proselyte to his superstition, he was promptly scourged, and put at a distance from me."

"Hebrew!" commented Titus. "You have the better of me. Would that I could speak it, for then it might dispose Berenice to look with a more favorable eye upon me. As it is, I have to say with Ovid:

'*Barbarus hic ego sum, quia non intelligor ulli.*'"

What more he would have said was checked by a command delivered in an authoritative voice:
"Halt!"
Instinctively the two friends paused, and glanced aloft. Standing upon a lower spur of the crag above them, and clearly defined against the star-lit sky, was a tall figure in a flowing robe.
"Who are you that bid two Romans halt?" demanded Titus, haughtily.
"The servant of a king," was the answer, delivered in the Latin language, though not with the true Latin accent.
"Your master's name?" asked Titus, suspiciously.
"Polemo, King of Pontus."
At this Crispus and Titus looked at each other, deeming it odd to be brought thus in connection with the monarch about whom they had just been talking.
"I have a message," continued the stranger, "for one, Crispus Cestius Gallus."
"My name," said the bearer of it. "What would the king with me?"
"My royal master bids you tarry an hour with him ere journeying on to Cæsarea."
"Where is the king to be found?"
"Within the walls of his mansion, Beth-tamar."
"And should I pass on my way neglectful of the king's bidding——?"
"Pass on, and miss a high destiny."
"Haste thee, and tell thy lord that Crispus comes with his friend, Titus Flavius."
The man had appeared suddenly; just as suddenly did he now disappear. Bidding his two slaves await

his return, Crispus turned from the maritime road, and began to climb the rough ascent. His ready acquiescence with the stranger's wish was viewed with some uneasiness by Titus, who was, however, quickly reassured by Crispus.

"Polemo, in this matter," said he, "acts as his own messenger, for it was he who spoke with us."

"The king himself?" said Titus, greatly surprised.

"Even so," replied Crispus. "We can enter Beth-tamar in perfect safety. I am not altogether unprepared for this meeting. As I was setting out from Antioch my father spoke thus to me: 'On your way to Cæsarea you may meet with King Polemo, who hath a proposal for you. I leave you free to accept or decline, but, if you will be guided by me, you will do his bidding, however strange it may appear.'"

Language such as this moved Titus to wonder, and he became almost as eager as Crispus for the meeting with the Pontic king.

Arrived upon the platform that formed the summit of the crag, the two Romans saw before them a rectangular edifice, massive and spacious, formed like most of the buildings in that region from blocks of limestone—a bare dull-looking structure; but then the Oriental house is not to be judged by its outside, for a costly exterior suggests wealth, and in the East, wealth, then, as now, is a temptation to the powers that be.

Within the arched entrance stood a slave, who, with a profound salaam, invited the two friends to follow him. Traversing a stone passage, they quickly emerged into a spacious court, open to the sky: rooms with latticed windows looked out upon this court, and to one of these the slave conducted the visitors, and there left them. The room was Oriental in character: a cushioned divan ran round the marble walls that gleamed with gilded arabesques and lapis-lazuli. In the middle of the tesselated pavement was a fountain, whose waters played with a golden sparkle in the soft radiance shed by the many lamps pendent from the fretted roof above.

As the two Romans entered, there came forward to greet them the same man that had spoken from the crag, a man of grave and stately presence, whose classic features can still be studied on the extant coins of the kingdom of Pontus. He had cast off the coarse garb he had worn without, and appeared now in a majestic robe of royal purple. On his finger glittered a gold ring, decorated with a cameo sculptured with a miniature head of Nero, a fact of some significance, since the wearing of such a ring was permitted to those only who had the high privilege of free access to the Emperor's presence.

"Welcome to Beth-tamar!" were the monarch's first words. "Aware that you were drawing near to Cæsarea," he continued, addressing Crispus, "I have ventured thus to intercept your journey."

"To what end?"

"Hath not your father told you?"

Crispus answered in the negative. Polemo seemed surprised at this; he hesitated, and glanced at Titus as if his presence were an embarrassment. Divining his thoughts, Crispus spoke:

"Titus is my *fidus Achates*. Let not the king take it amiss, but whatever is said must be said before him."

"Be it so," said Polemo, after a brief pause. "You must, however, both give pledge, that the proposal I am about to make, whether accepted or declined, shall be kept a secret till such time as I shall choose it to be known."

"The character of the noble Polemo," returned Crispus, "is a sufficient guarantee that he will require of me nothing dishonorable or nothing detrimental to the interests of the Roman state."

"Far be such thoughts from me. My aim is to add to its strength." Assured thus, both Crispus and Titus promised to hold sacred whatever the king were minded to reveal.

"Good! To come at once to the question, for I love not many words, you are doubtless aware of my misfortune in having no son to succeed me on the throne. I am," he added mournfully, "the last of my race. In these circumstances our lord Nero has graciously conceded to me the favor of nominating a successor, with the necessary proviso that my choice must fall on a man loyal to the Empire. Such a one I have found."

He paused and looked at Crispus, whose head began suddenly to whirl with a daring hope. Could it be that he himself was——?

"If," continued Polemo, "if loyalty to Rome be the first qualification in my successor, who more loyal than a Roman himself? who more likely to meet with the approval of the Senate than one of the Senatorial order? For these reasons, then, and because your past deeds have shown you to be worthy of the dignity, I am minded at a date three years from now to confer upon you the scepter of Pontus. What say you to this?"

At first Crispus could say nothing for very amazement. Then, recovering somewhat, he began eagerly to question the king, and found him to all appearances sincere in making the offer.

Now, although Polemo had made a special point of Crispus' worthiness, Crispus himself had nevertheless a secret belief that the king was actuated by some ulterior motive. He recalled a saying of his father's: "There is fire within Polemo for all his cold exterior. To me he seems a man who, having received a great wrong, is meditating a scheme of revenge—ay, and devoting his whole life to it. The weapon may take years in the forging, but when forged it will fall, swiftly, terribly." Recalling these words, Crispus began to wonder whether the offer just made was a part of the king's scheme of vengeance. Was he, Crispus, to be elevated to the throne merely to bring gall to some scheming and ambitious enemy? Crispus had a reasonable objection to be utilized for such a purpose; but still, what mattered? Here was an opportunity of gaining a splendid dignity, and it would be foolish to let his scruples as to the other's motive interfere with his ambition.

A king!

" All things," said Porus, " are comprehended in that word."

What fancies crowded thick and fast upon Crispus' mind as he tried to picture the future!

He would be a father to his people; would regulate their finances; foster their commerce; increase the army; promote the use of the Latin language and encourage Greek culture. In the glens of the Caucasus, bordering upon his kingdom, were wild tribes that had never yet acknowledged a conqueror. He would curb their predatory incursions, and augment his territory at their expense. Nay, he might even pass that mighty mountain-barrier, and carry his arms over Scythia, a region that had defied the attempts of the Persian, the Grecian, and the Roman. Why should he not be in the North what Alexander had been in the East, and Cæsar in the West? Then, when his kingdom had become enlarged and Latinized, he would act the patriot, and transfer his dominion to the Senate, making it a province of mighty Rome.

Dreams, perhaps, but it is in such dreams that empires have sometimes had their beginning.

" What answer do you make? "

" At present, none," replied the cautious Crispus. " Is your gift accompanied by any stipulation? "

" One only. He who chooses the king of Pontus must also choose its queen."

" In other words, I must take a wife, a wife to be chosen by you."

"That is so."

"And failing to do this—no scepter?"

"Truly said. The gift of the kingdom is dependent upon your marrying the lady of my choice. The two go together."

"And what date do you fix for our nuptials?"

"This very night—nay, this very hour."

"*To-night?* Ye gods! You hear that, Titus?"

"The lady is at hand, for in the reasonable belief that you would not refuse a throne I have had her brought here."

"Her name?"

"Call her Athenaïs, since that is the name she will take as queen."

"I am not to know her real name! What is her rank?"

"Superior to your own, for she is of royal blood."

"She is of fair shape, I trust?"

"Zeuxis never delineated a face and form more lovely."

These words served to whet Crispus' curiosity. He expressed a wish to see his prospective bride.

"See her you will not; she will be veiled during the ceremony. Nor will you hear her voice, for she will not speak. When the rite is over you will resume your journey to Cæsarea."

"Without seeing the face of my wife!" gasped Crispus in amazement. Was there ever so strange a marriage proposal?

"It is my will that you shall not know whom you have married. The lady is beautiful, high-born, and brings a crown as a dowry. Is not that enough?"

"And when will my bride be made known to me?"

"On the day when you assume the scepter."

"And the date of that event?"

"As I have said, at the end of three years."

"The word of Polemo is his bond," said Crispus, "but seeing that—*absit omen!*—you may be dead ere the three years be past, what warranty shall I then have of the due execution of this, your promise?"

"This," replied the king, producing a parchment-scroll and unrolling it. "'Tis yours as soon as the nuptial ceremony be over."

Crispus ran his eye over the scroll, and saw that it was what Roman lawyers would call an *instrumentum*—in other words, a legally-executed document, constituting him the heir of Polemo in the sovereignty of Pontus. It was subscribed with the signature of the king, and, what was of far more weight, with that of Nero himself.

"Do you assent?"

"I assent."

"Consider well; remember that you are to pledge yourself to remain faithful to Athenaïs, who in turn pledges herself to remain faithful to you. Should you in this interval be found breaking your vow by offering love to any woman—yea, even though it be to your own unknown wife"—Crispus smiled at the supposition—"you lose the crown of Pontus."

"Your terms are strange, but I abide by them."

"You are ready to wed?"

"This very hour."

"You promise not to lift her veil? You are content not to hear her voice? You are willing to depart as soon as the rite is over? You promise with your friend to observe secrecy as touching this night's work?"

There was a light as of triumph in Polemo's eyes when the two Romans gave assent to these terms. It confirmed Crispus in his belief that the king was using him as an instrument of vengeance. But, as before, he said within himself, "What matters?"

"With what rites do we wed?" asked Crispus.

"With the words customary in your own Roman nuptial ceremonies, confirming them by placing this token upon the finger of the bride," returned Polemo.

He handed to Crispus a gold ring. It was set with

a ruby, upon whose surface there was graven, with beautiful and marvelous art, a device that caused a quick look of surprise to pass over the face of Crispus. As he slowly and mechanically turned the ring over in his hand the ruby darted forth sparkles that caused what was sculptured on the gem to vanish as if in a blaze of fire. At that sight Crispus gave a great start, and darted an inquiring look at the king, who replied by a smile full of a hidden meaning. Titus, who took due note of all this, was naturally not a little puzzled; he refrained from comment, however, believing that Crispus would enlighten him later.

"Follow me," said Polemo, and, lifting a curtain, he led the way to another chamber so dimly illumined by one lamp only that the parts remote from the light were scarcely discernible, an arrangement obviously due to Polemo's determination that Crispus should see as little as possible of his bride.

In the semi-darkness two waiting figures, both deeply veiled, were faintly visible.

Of the one that stood a little in the rear Crispus took no note, she being obviously an attendant. It was the other upon whom his eyes were set. Slender and of medium stature, she wore the usual dress of a Roman bride, the *tunica recta*, a long white robe with a purple fringe, and girt at the waist with a zone. The *flammeum*, or veil, which effectually concealed her features, was bright yellow in color, as were likewise her dainty little shoes. The bride's hair with the point of a spear, was dispensed with on this occasion, her head being covered with a coif, so well disposed that not a single tress was visible. So completely was her person hidden that, let her dress be changed, and there was nothing by which he could identify her, if he should meet her again that same night.

Though Crispus could not see her eyes, he knew full well that she was watching him as keenly as he was watching her, a scrutiny in which the advantage was all on her side. She stood, wordless and motionless, evidently awaiting the king's pleasure.

"Athenaïs," said he, "this is your husband."

She made a little obeisance to Crispus, a simple act, yet performed with a grace that charmed him.

He did not know in what relation Polemo stood to the bride, but his way of speaking implied a quasi-authority over her, and since it was the fashion in those days for parents and guardians to arrange marriages with very little regard for the feelings of the two most concerned in the affair, Crispus could not help wondering whether pressure had been put upon this Athenaïs to induce her to consent to the union. He would find out.

"Lady," he said, "I am willing to marry, but only on the understanding that you come to me without compulsion. Therefore, if you take me of your own free will, testify the same—since you are forbidden to speak—by coming forward two paces."

Athenaïs hesitated, but only for a second. Giving him what he felt to be a grateful glance, she advanced two steps.

"A mutual agreement," smiled Polemo. "This is as it should be."

He whispered in the ear of the bride something that Crispus could not catch. Whatever it was it evoked from her a little ripple of laughter, so sweet and silvery, that Crispus was put into sympathy with her at once.

"If her face be as witching as her laughter!" thought he.

But her laugh, however charming to Crispus, had a very different effect upon Titus. An attentive spectator would have seen him start violently, and turn pale. He seemed on the point of breaking out into words, but checking himself, he stood mute, his whole attitude expressive of dejection, a feeling that seemed to increase as the nuptial ceremony proceeded. Crispus, occupied with the matter in hand, did not notice his friend's agitation.

At a sign from Polemo Crispus drew near to Athenaïs, Titus acting as paranymph, or, to use the modern phrase, "best man," the veiled attendant performing a similar office for the bride.

Athenaïs, directed by the king, put forth a white and prettily-shaped hand, which Crispus took in his own.

If her feelings bore any resemblance to those of Crispus she must have felt like one in a dream, for he could scarcely believe the scene to be real. An hour ago he would have laughed had anyone prophesied for him an early marriage, and yet here he was on the point of marrying a woman of whose past history he knew nothing, a woman from whom, as soon as the ceremony was over, he must part, without seeing her face, without receiving so little as one word from her, part for a space of time to be measured, not by months, but by years! What would his friends at Rome think of a marriage contracted under auspices so strange? "Weddeth Crispus as a fool weddeth?" would surely be their comment.

Thus much, however, could be said for his act: it had his father's sanction, and with this thought Crispus tried to suppress all misgivings.

Mechanically he found himself repeating after Polemo the final words of the rite that was to unite him for life with the unknown Athenaïs.

"Leaving all other, and keeping only to thee, I, Crispus Cestius Gallus, patrician of Rome, do take thee, Athenaïs, to be my lawful wife, to be openly acknowledged as such when it shall please thee to claim me by this token."

So saying, he slid upon her slender finger the golden ring given him by Polemo.

No sound came from the woman who was now his wife, but her agitation was shown by her trembling hand, by her accelerated breathing, by her attitude, half-reclining, in the arms of her attendant.

Her hand seemed to close voluntarily upon his own. The thrilling pressure of those fair fingers imparted to him somehow the belief that, originally reluctant to come to the ceremony, she now viewed it with pleasure, a thought that gave him pleasure in turn.

The sweet laugh that had come from her, the clasp of her pretty hand, her willingness to trust her whole future to his keeping, so moved Crispus that he began to feel a keen regret that he must immediately part from her. He became almost angry with himself for having submitted to the hard terms prescribed by Polemo.

As he released her hand she sank back half-swooning in the arms of the other woman, who, at a sign from Polemo, proceeded to draw her gently from the apartment. Till the last Crispus kept his eyes upon her, hoping that, in spite of Polemo, she might raise a corner of her veil, and give him just one glimpse at least of her face.

It was not to be, however. She melted away into the shadows around, and he saw her no more.

The two Romans walked again by the star-lit shore with Beth-tamar far behind them.

"What," asked Titus, who, since the wedding ceremony, had been strangely silent, "what was engraved on the stone of the nuptial ring that you should start so?"

He received little enlightenment from the reply of Crispus:

"*The image of a temple in flames!*"

# CHAPTER II

### THE BANQUET OF FLORUS

EARLY on the morning after his arrival at Cæsarea, Crispus was waited upon at his lodgings by Gessius Florus, procurator of Judæa, who, apprised of Crispus' coming, lost no time in calling upon the son of the Syrian Legate, that Legate whose word was all-powerful in the East.

Previous knowledge had disposed Crispus to take an unfavorable opinion of Florus, an opinion that became strengthened on seeing the man himself. A shallow-minded Greek of Clazomenæ, and no true Roman, he had gained the procuratorship of Judæa, not through merit, but by the influence of his wife Cleopatra, who was a close friend of the reigning Empress Poppæa.

Florus, though born in Ionia, had little of the grace that is usually associated with that region, and had Crispus not known otherwise he might have taken the governor, with his round bullet head, furtive greenish-brown eyes, and heavy brutal jaw, for a member of that pugilistic fraternity whose feats with the cæstus were the delight of the lower orders among the Romans.

He was desirous that Crispus should form one at a grand banquet, to be held that night in the Prætorium, or procuratorial palace.

Crispus was about to decline the honor, when he thought of Athenaïs. For all he knew to the contrary she might be a resident of Cæsarea, and if so, her " royal blood " would certainly entitle her to an invitation. She might be among the guests. He would go, though it would be difficult, if not impossible, to recognize her.

## The Banquet of Florus

Florus withdrew in apparent delight.

As for Titus, he departed that same day for Rome, embarking on the good ship *Stella*.

"There is no hope of my ever winning Berenice," he said, though without assigning any reason for coming so suddenly to this lugubrious conclusion.

Before his departure, however, he did Crispus a good service by introducing him to a brave and worthy Roman, Terentius Rufus by name. He was the captain of the garrison stationed at Jerusalem, and had come with his cohort to Cæsarea to aid in the work of suppressing the riots that were almost certain to arise upon the coming publication of Nero's edict relative to the precedency claimed by the Jews and the Greeks.

Terentius Rufus, like Crispus, had received an invitation to the banquet of Florus, and so, at the appointed time, the two presented themselves at the Prætorium.

Upon making their way to the hall appropriated to the feast, a hall called Neronium after the reigning emperor, they paused a moment at the entrance to contemplate the sight. The marble saloon, supported by porphyry columns and blazing with the radiance of a thousand lamps, was a scene of glitter, movement, and color. Sweet spices burned in gilded tripods; the rarest flowers glowed from sculptured vases; the ivory triclinia with their purple cushions, the lavish display of gold and silver plate, the rich dresses and jewels of the ladies, made a picture destined to live long in the memory of Crispus.

He marveled to see such splendor in the hall of a provincial governor.

"Whence does Florus obtain the wealth that enables him to make such a display?" he asked.

"There are others who would like an answer to that question," replied Rufus, mysteriously.

"Where *is* Florus?" asked Crispus, glancing around, and not seeing the procurator.

"Probably tickling his throat with a feather to produce a vomit," answered Rufus, referring to the disgusting custom practiced by many Romans of that age for the purpose of creating an appetite. "You may trust him to do full justice to the banquet."

Crispus was not slow to recognize among the guests that type of physiognomy which, graved on Egyptian monuments long ere Rome was founded, has continued almost unchanged to the present day.

"There are many Jews here to-night," remarked he.

"And Jewesses, too," replied Rufus; "and here comes the fairest of them all, leaning upon the arm of Florus. For a wonder he's sober!"

There was a sudden cessation of tongues as a curtain that draped a certain archway was lifted by two bowing slaves to give entrance to the procurator.

Glancing around, Florus immediately caught sight of Crispus, and advanced to give him welcome. He was accompanied by a lady, none other than the Princess Berenice, and as Crispus quietly surveyed her, he thought it no wonder that Titus should have fallen in love with her at first sight. She had dark hair and dark starry eyes, and a face which, when radiant with a smile as it was at that moment, was perfectly dazzling in its loveliness. Her figure, which was as beautiful as her face, was appareled in a robe of purple silk, embroidered with flowers of gold and adorned with the costliest pearls.

She greeted Crispus with a sweet smile of recognition.

"Do not neglect me to-night as you did at Antioch," she said half-jestingly, and then giving him a witching glance she passed on, with Florus, to her place at the banquet. While the procurator reclined at full length upon the triclinium, Berenice sat erect beside him, for the posture assumed by men at the banquet was deemed unbecoming in women.

Crispus and Rufus had places assigned them at the triclinium adjoining that of Florus, and upon the same couch with them reclined a shrewd-looking, keen-eyed man, who, so Rufus informed Crispus, went by the name of Tertullus, and was a distinguished forensic orator.

"Mark well his noble name," said Rufus, laughingly. "Tertullus, thrice-Tully! What could be more suitable for an orator? Take my advice, Crispus," continued he, "if you have a lawsuit while at Cæsarea, fail not to employ my friend Tertullus, who never undertook a case he did not win."

"Save once," corrected Tertullus. "Paul of Tarsus escaped the stoning we had marked out for him."

"Ah! I am forgetting him. The dog, it seems, is a Roman citizen. He appealed to Nero, who let him off."

"And what was the result?" commented Tertullus. "A few months later Rome was in flames, lit by the hands of his disciples. The wretches! Haters of mankind! I know of only one class of men more vile than they, and that is the sect of the Zealots, whose latest victim I am."

"How mean you?" asked Rufus.

"Have you not heard? No? Well, a few days ago I was journeying from Jericho to the Jewish capital. Knowing the state of the country, I traveled in the company of an armed caravan that was going the same way. We took a long circuit northwards to avoid the dreaded Pass of Adummim; all to no purpose. Manahem and his Zealots, like vultures scenting their quarry afar, swooped down upon us. I was one of the few that escaped. When is Florus going to dispatch an expedition against that robber crew?"

"Did you lose aught?"

"Some gold plate, and—what I treasured above all earthly things—a myrrhine vase, so precious that I weep when I think of it."

"Don't think of it, then," said Rufus. "Turn to a more pleasant theme, the Princess Berenice. She looks more charming and more youthful than ever to-night.

Now, how old should you take her to be?" he continued, addressing Crispus.

"Not much past twenty," he hazarded.

Rufus laughed pleasantly.

"Why, 'tis sixteen years ago since she married Polemo. She cannot be a day younger than thirty-eight."

Crispus was surprised to hear it.

"There is many a young girl here to-night," said he, "who looks older than the princess."

"Berenice takes extreme pains to preserve her beauty," remarked Rufus. "'Tis said that, like Poppæa, she bathes daily in asses' milk to render her skin soft and supple."

Florus now gave the signal for the feast, and there entered a train of pretty Greek maidens with baskets containing wreaths of flowers, for to dine ungarlanded would have been a departure from fashionable usage. Berenice chose a wreath of violets; Florus made a similar selection.

"The flower honored by a princess must be *my* choice, too," he whispered.

This little by-play did not pass unnoticed by Crispus.

"Florus is madly in love with her," commented Rufus. "For the matter of that, who isn't?"

"I thought that Florus already had a wife," said Crispus.

"That's no obstacle in these lax days, when a man takes a new wife with each year. It is whispered that Florus contemplates divorcing Cleopatra."

"Where is Cleopatra at this present time?" asked Crispus.

"In Rome," answered Tertullus, as he fixed a garland of roses upon his head, "looking after her precious husband's interests. He takes advantage of her absence to pay court to Berenice, who cares not a whit for him, and intends no hurt to Cleopatra. Berenice is not to be too hastily condemned," he continued, observing Crispus' frown. "Her action in this matter, as in all others, is guided by two motives—love of her people, and love of her own superstition. Now, Florus, in the exercise of his procuratorship, can, if he be so minded, inflict injuries upon the Jewish people, and can also, though to a limited extent, interfere with the administration of their public worship. 'But,' argues our fair Berenice, ' he is not likely to adopt these courses while seeking to win *me*, who am a Jewess. Therefore, for the good of the Jews I will amuse him with hopes.' Now after this long speech," added Tertullus, "let me eat. I can see the lampreys coming, and they are my favorite dish."

And the delicacy being set before him, Tertullus applied himself thereto. After a time he raised his voice and addressed the procurator.

"I have myself, O Florus, given great attention to the breeding of lampreys, but I confess that I can never get them to attain the delicate flavor of those bred by you."

Two or three other guests made similar remarks.

Florus smiled with the air of a man who, having discovered an excellent thing, is determined to keep it to himself.

"Now, it is precisely because I happen to know *how* the delicate flavor is acquired," whispered Rufus, "that I avoid partaking of that dish."

"By the trident of Neptune," said Tertullus, "I wish you would communicate the secret to me, for I am mightily fond of lampreys."

"Well, keep it a secret, for Florus may not thank me for telling it. Whenever one of his slaves commits a fault worthy of death, the poor wretch, instead of being hanged, is flung into the piscina to feed the lampreys. By the gods, I do not jest," he added, as he noted Tertullus' look of incredulity. ."Get his chief piscinarius into a corner, put a dagger to his throat, and he'll confess that what I say is true."

As the Roman law gave to a master the power of

life and death over his slaves, Florus' peculiar practice did not evoke from Crispus the abhorrence that the man of the twentieth century would express at such a deed. As for Tertullus, he even went so far as to intimate that he might adopt the practice himself.

"If a slave *must* die," argued he, "let him die in a way that will add to his master's enjoyment."

Crispus sought to change the subject of conversation by asking Rufus the name of the richly-clothed man who reclined on the left of Florus; he was a majestic-looking, dark-skinned personage, with hair and beard finely dressed. At the beginning of the feast he had drawn forth a little ivory casket, from which he had produced an asp that had immediately twined itself around his bare arm, and there it remained partaking occasionally of such morsels as its master chose to give.

"That," replied Tertullus, "is Theomantes, the priest of Zeus Cæsarius, and a skilled diviner."

"And the serpent he carries with him, if you are fool enough to believe it," remarked Rufus, "is an incarnation of the great Zeus himself. You can see by the place assigned to Theomantes how highly he is esteemed. Every Roman governor nowadays must have a soothsayer in attendance upon him, and Florus would not be out of the fashion. It is this Theomantes who supplies our procurator with the liquid for his daily bath."

"The liquid? What liquid?"

"Well, not water, which is good enough for common mortals like you and me, nor yet milk, which the fair Berenice finds so excellent a cosmetic. Florus' taste runs in favor of blood."

"*Blood!*" ejaculated Crispus.

"Even so. Do you not know that by some physicians blood is deemed very efficacious in strengthening the human frame when exhausted by debauchery? So our dear governor bathes daily in a sanguinary fluid drawn from the veins of oxen slain in sacrifice, his superstitious fancy disposing him to believe that there will be more virtue in blood of that sort. Oh, it's not an uncommon practice, I assure you. We've even drawn from the Greek a name for it, calling it taurobolium."

"Every man to his taste," commented Crispus, dryly; and continuing his inquiries as to the guests, he asked, "Who is that fierce graybeard reclining next to Theomantes?"

"Ananias, son of Nebedeus, at one time high priest of the Jews," replied Rufus.

"And a cheating knave!" commented Tertullus. "In his prosecution of Paul of Tarsus before Felix he employed me as advocate, and hath never yet paid me my fee. But I'll be even with him."

"Do you mark," continued Rufus, "how, from time to time, Ananias glowers at Theomantes? He considers that he himself should be sitting next the governor."

"He is welcome to the place for me," laughed Crispus. "And who is the fair damsel beside him? His daughter?"

"Daughter me no daughter, forsooth!" returned Rufus. "That is Asenath, a Syrian dancing-girl, and his latest favorite."

"I must reluctantly confess he hath a pretty taste," said Tertullus; "she is a delicious armful."

"And she is desirous, you see, that we should observe the fact," remarked Rufus.

The girl in question was a lovely brunette, attired in a Coan robe which, even in that decadent age, was deemed a trifle too extreme, consisting as it did of silk so transparent in texture that the shapely limbs of the wearer could be seen as through colored glass.

And, be it observed, she was not the only female at the banquet thus diaphanously clad!

"That's the girl," continued Rufus, "to please whom he burnt in his own house the incense that it is not lawful to burn anywhere save upon the altar of the Jewish temple. And as she was once curious to view the Jewish worship, Ananias had the way from his house to the temple carpeted for her pretty feet, and canopied to shield her from the sun. And he himself was so fastidiously minded that he was accustomed to wear silk gloves at the altar to avoid soiling his dainty fingers with the blood of the sacrifices,[1] though why a Sadducee, such as he, should want to worship God at all is a mystery to me. In the opinion of Ananias man dies as a dog dies. It seems to me that a God who creates man from dust merely to turn him into dust again is scarcely deserving of worship. What say you?"

"Old Homer could have taught him better doctrine than that," returned Crispus.

The conversation, it will be seen, was taking a theological turn; something of like sort was happening at the adjoining triclinium of Florus.

"I hate these Christians as much as you do," remarked the procurator to Berenice. "But Nero hath taught us how to deal with them. And you say there are still some of this sect at Jerusalem? I had thought that my predecessor Albinus, in slaying James, the brother of this Christus, had put an end to these fanatics. You shall have your way, princess. Within a week of my coming to Jerusalem there shall not be a Christian left alive."

"Now the gods confound these Christians!" said Tertullus aloud. "They grow daily wilder and madder in their blasphemies. They have now the effrontery to affirm that this Christus of theirs, who died in the eighteenth year of Tiberius Cæsar, was something more than a man, that this Galilæan peasant was in very truth a manifestation of the supreme deity, the creator of the universe, and the great To Pan spoken of by the divine Plato."

At these words there was on the part of Crispus a start as of surprise.

## The Banquet of Florus

"When do you say this Christus died?" he asked somewhat quickly.

"In the eighteenth year of Tiberius Cæsar," replied Tertullus.

"In what month?"

"On the fourteenth of Nisan, according to the Jewish calendar."

"Which in our style would be the seventh of April," explained Rufus, after a rapid mental calculation.

Crispus' surprise seemed to deepen.

"And you say the Christians call their founder To Pan? Strange!" he murmured.

"Why so?" asked Florus.

"I could tell a curious story of that month and year. But there! let it pass."

"No, we must *not* let it pass," cried Florus, and thinking to do honor to Crispus, he said to those within his immediate vicinity, "Silence, friends, for the noble Crispus' story."

All eyes were bent upon Crispus, who hesitated for a moment, and then, seeing expectancy written upon the faces of the guests, he began:

"Well, since you will have it: At the time just mentioned, namely the month of April in the eighteenth year of Tiberius, there chanced to be upon the Ionian Sea a merchant vessel bound for Italy. It was eventide; the breeze had died away, and the ship lay becalmed off the Isle of Paxos. Suddenly the stillness that lay upon land and sea was broken by a voice coming from the lonely shore—a voice clear and solemn, and one that carried awe to all who heard it, for it seemed scarcely to belong to earth. '*Thamus!*' it cried. Now the pilot of the vessel happened to be one Thamus, an Egyptian, a man of humble and obscure origin, and not so much as known by name to those on board. Full of fear, he let himself be called twice ere he would answer. At the third cry he found courage to ask, 'What want you?' And thus did the voice make reply: 'When thou comest to Pelodes, cry aloud that the great Pan is dead.' That was all; no more. The passengers, amazed and awed by the event, debated among themselves whether it would be wise to obey the mysterious voice. Thamus, himself, determined the matter: if on attaining the appointed place there should be wind enough to fill the sails, he would pass by in silence, but if not, he would proclaim the message. The breeze freshened, the ship glided on, but when they reached Pelodes it made no further progress, for the wind suddenly dropped again. Thamus, therefore, taking his stand upon the prow, turned his face to the land, and shouted in a loud tone, '*Great Pan is dead!*' Then from the hitherto silent shore there arose a sound like the voice of a multitude, a sound as of weeping and wild lament."

Such was the story told by Crispus, and he finished with the odd feeling that the telling of it had pleased neither the Jewish nor the Gentile portion of his auditors.

" Whence do you derive this story? " asked Theomantes with a somewhat supercilious air.

" From my father, himself a passenger in this same vessel."

" Who were they that made these sounds? "

" Beings more than mortal; of that he is convinced."

" Gods and demons? "

" It may be so."

" In a lamenting mood? "

" A wailing as of despair, so my father describes the sound."

" Gods in despair at the death of someone? And this happened in Greece in the eighteenth year of Tiberius? Would you have us believe that the Christus crucified by Pilate and the ' Great Pan ' of your story are one and the same, and that his death has caused the downfall of the gods? "

"I am hardly likely to adopt that explanation, believing as I do in the eternity of those gods by whose worship Rome has grown so great. The story is true, let the meaning be what it may," added Crispus in a tone whose sharpness deterred Theomantes from making any further comment.

# CHAPTER III

### THE QUEEN OF BEAUTY

Now, while telling his story, Crispus had become suddenly alive to the presence of a very beautiful girl sitting at an adjoining triclinium. It was not so much her beauty, however, that attracted him as the attention she had paid to his words. She was by far the keenest and most attentive of his listeners, seeming to hang breathless upon his lips during the whole recital; of all the assembly, she seemed to be the only person to receive the story with pleasure.

"Rufus," whispered he, "who is that girl with the lovely golden tresses? To the left of us—on the next triclinium?"

Rufus turned in leisurely fashion to survey the maid in question.

"I know not her name, or who she is. She came hither accompanied by him who reclines beside her. As I see no likeness betwixt the two, I take it he is not her father."

The man referred to was evidently a Hebrew, and distinguished both by his noble features and rich attire.

"Her father? Not he!" said Tertullus. "That is Josephus, a Jew, and yon damsel, I'll swear, is no Jewess. There is a grace and beauty about her that is quite Ionic."

"Who is this Josephus?" asked Crispus.

"He is a priest of the first of the twenty-four courses," replied Tertullus, "and a rabbi so wondrously wise from his cradle upwards that when he was only fourteen, aged priests and venerable sanhedrists would consult him on points of the law too hard for their own understanding."

"What's your authority for that story?" said Rufus dryly.

"The best authority—his own.' He hath told me so many a time. At the mature age of seventeen he had exhausted the whole course of philosophy, and had decided that Pharisaism is the road to heaven. But though a Pharisee, he cultivates Grecian literature, has literary aspirations, and is said to be writing at the present time a treatise that shall prove us Greeks and Romans to be in the matter of antiquity mere children of yesterday when compared with the Jews."

Josephus did not much interest Crispus, but the young girl did, and he continued to watch her. This was probably her first experience of a Gentile banquet, and she seemed ill at ease amid her new surroundings. And no wonder! If the naked statuary and voluptuous paintings to be seen around, the immodest Coan robes worn by the women, and the shameless license of their language were distasteful even to the pagan Crispus, how much more so to a young maiden trained in the pure and lofty principles of Judaism? Berenice, alas! reared in the atmosphere of a decadent court, could learn in the Prætorium of Florus little that was new in the shape of wickedness, but the case was far different with a young and innocent girl.

"If this Josephus be her guardian, he is not exercising much discretion," thought Crispus. "The banquet-hall of Florus is not the place to bring a young girl to."

At this point Ananias, the ex-high pontiff of the Jews, and Theomantes, the priest of Zeus Cæsarius, created a diversion.

"Ay, ay," muttered Rufus, "I knew that they'd be quarreling ere long."

The two representatives of antagonistic religions were holding an animated dispute; as the controversy waxed hotter their voices rose proportionately, till at last they attracted general attention. Everyone else in the assembly left off talking to listen to the disputants.

"Mercury a thief?" cried Theomantes. "So be it, then! And is it not written in your foolish scriptures that while Adam slept God stole from his side a rib which He fashioned into the first woman? What else, then, is *your* God but a thief?"

Ananias' reply was anticipated by the Princess Berenice, ever quick to defend her ancestral religion.

"I will answer you," said she to Theomantes. "Last night some thieves broke into my house, and stole a silver vase." She paused for a moment, then added, "But they left a golden one in its stead."

The Jewish guests greeted Berenice's little parable with loud applause.

"Jupiter!" laughed Florus, "I wish such thieves would come every night."

Theomantes returned to the attack. Holding his serpent close to the face of Ananias, and causing the reptile to give a hiss that made the Hebrew priest start, he laughed and said:

"My God is greater than yours."

"Prove it," sneered Ananias.

"Is it not written that when your God appeared in the burning bush, Moses drew near, but when he saw the serpent, which is my god, he fled?"

"True," replied Berenice, answering for the silent Ananias, "and a few steps sufficed to put him beyond reach of the serpent. But how can one flee from *our* God, Who fills all space, Who at one and the same time is in heaven and in earth, on sea and on land?"

Theomantes, about to continue the dispute, was checked by a gesture from Florus, so the heathen priest, with a somewhat dark look at Berenice, subsided into silence.

"You have here," commented Rufus, "a specimen

of what is always happening in Cæsarea when Jew and Gentile meet. But, ah! here cometh the wine."

Now, it was the fashion of that day to begin the drinking with an invocation to the reigning emperor, and hence Florus, looking around upon his guests, lifted his cup as a sign for them to do the like, saying at the same time:

" Friends, a libation to the god Nero!"

The *god* Nero!

Though to the pagan portion of the assembly the words conveyed no impiety, the case was otherwise with the Jews, but those present were of the worldly-wise class that sacrifices religion to policy, and hence most of them, including the Sadducee Ananias and the Pharisee Josephus, shamelessly prepared to join with Florus in offering to the wickedest man of that age a libation as to a god.

Now, pagan though Crispus was, there was one thing in the Roman religion that he, in common with many others, could not approve, and that was the deification of the living emperor, especially when the deification extended to such a one as Nero. And yet to refrain from joining in the libation was dangerous, being tantamount to the guilt of *læsa majestas;* and of all crimes, the greatest, in the eyes of the buffoon then at the head of the empire, was the refusal to acknowledge his divinity.

Come what might, Crispus determined to have no part in the libation, and while there was on all sides a preparatory lifting of cups, his own remained untouched. He found a companion in Rufus, and some others, including the unknown maiden, whose eyes were eloquently expressive of abhorrence.

He and those of like thought were rescued from an embarrassing situation by the action of the Princess Berenice. With a pale face and agitated air she had risen to her feet, and in a voice trembling with suppressed emotion she addressed the wondering assembly.

"There once reigned," she began, "and in this very city, a king who, on a set day, made an oration to his people; and they cried, 'It is the voice of a god, and not of a man!' And because he rebuked not their words the hand of heaven smote him there that he died. And that king," she added, with a catch in her voice, "that king was my father!"

The fate of Agrippa the Elder was well known to all the guests, some of whom, indeed, had been present at that divine judgment—pronounced by the smitten king himself to be divine—and the memory of the event, added to the impressive words and solemn manner of his fair daughter, caused a thrill to pervade the assembly.

"And now, O Florus, do you desire the like fate for Nero? To call him god is to draw upon him the wrath of that eternal One, Who will not permit His glory to be given to another."

As she sat down amid a murmur of approval from the better-minded, it became suddenly apparent to Florus that he had made a big blunder. All-desirous as he was of winning the favor of Berenice, he had strangely overlooked the fact that the libation in the form proposed by him might be distasteful to the religious ideas of the Jewish princess. He gladly seized the opportunity of extricating himself from an awkward situation by endorsing the words of Crispus, who said:

"The princess hath spoken well. Let us, O Florus, not give to a mortal, however highly placed, the honor that belongs only to the immortals."

"Be it as the princess wishes," said the procurator. "We will change the phrasing to one in which all may join." With that he added, "To the health of the Emperor Nero!" and plashed upon the tesselated pavement a few drops of the ruddy wine, an example in which he was followed by the rest of the guests, Jew and Gentile alike.

"A beautiful cup, O Florus," remarked Tertullus, attentively eyeing the goblet from which the procurator had made his libation. "I am quite charmed by it. May one ask for a closer look?"

The cup in question was one of those myrrhine vases imported from the far East, vases whose delicate semi-transparent material was as much a mystery to the ancient Romans as it is to the modern antiquary.

"Mark my word," whispered Tertullus to Rufus, "if we shall not find on one side of that cup a natural vein of purple curving into something like the shape of a Grecian lyre."

Florus, always glad to have the excellency of his treasures acknowledged, addressed a slave.

"Girl, pass this cup to the noble Tertullus. A judge of art, he will know how to appreciate such a work. By the gods, have a care how you carry it!"

The girl, thus bidden, conveyed the vessel to Tertullus. Its chief beauty consisted in the great variety of its colors, and the wreathing veins which here and there presented shades of purple and white, with a blending of the two. As Tertullus had said, one of these veins bore considerable resemblance to a lyre.

"I never thought to see thee again," muttered Tertullus to himself, apostrophizing the cup. "How come you here in the hands of Florus? A rare work of art," he added aloud, as he returned the cup to the procurator. "You have had it long?"

"These seven years."

"Seven days, you mean," murmured Tertullus; then aloud, "It must have cost an immense sum."

"Thirty talents," replied Florus with a careless air, as though the amount were a mere trifle. "There are but two vases of this kind in all the empire; they were brought to Rome by a Parthian merchant. Petronius purchased the one, I the other."

"What a liar you are!" thought Tertullus; and

then, as if dismissing the matter altogether from his mind, he said in a low tone to Rufus:

"Doth Simon the Black still linger in his dungeon?"

Rufus replied in the affirmative.

"May one ask," smiled Crispus, "who is this Simon the Black?"

"You are a stranger in Judæa, or you would not have to ask that question," returned Rufus. "Simon the Black was till lately the chief of a robber-band of Zealots, whose haunt was among the almost inaccessible crags that overhang the Red Way, the famous pass that leads from Jerusalem to Jericho. The Jew was allowed to traverse the pass in safety; the ordinary Gentile was taken captive and held to ransom; but as to the Roman, woe to him if caught!—it being the way of Simon to hang all such without the alternative of a ransom. Hence he is called by those of the Jews who hate our rule, 'The Scourge of the Romans,' and is regarded by them as a patriot.

"The curious part of it all is that Florus, though often appealed to both by the Romans and Greeks of Cæsarea, refrained for a long time from sending a military expedition against this nest of robbers, and when at last he yielded to public pressure, and dispatched my Italian Cohort on the errand, his parting words to me were, 'I do not want to be troubled with prisoners.' I declined to take the hint, however, and brought back Simon alive, much, it would seem, to the mortification of the procurator. And here at Cæsarea the fellow lies in a dungeon, Florus strangely refusing to put him on trial.

"It's galling to think," added Rufus, "that my work will have to be done all over again. The pass hath been seized by another bandit—Manahem, a son of that notorious Judas of Galilee, who drew away much people after him in the days of the taxing. More catholic in his views, he plunders and slays Jews and Gentiles alike. And now again Florus—odd, is it not?

—is thwarting me in my wish to proceed against this new malefactor."

"Not at all odd," remarked Tertullus, "if my suspicion be correct; and, by Castor! I'll try to verify it before twenty-four hours be past." And then, speaking aloud, he turned and addressed the procurator.

"O Florus, do you take your place on the bema tomorrow? 'Tis a court day."

The governor frowned at this introduction of business into the midst of pleasure.

"What cases are there to try?"

"There is the case of Simon the Black. The Romans and Greeks of Cæsarea are clamoring for his trial."

"Let them clamor."

"The long delay over this matter hath so enraged them that they swear if Simon be not brought to justice by the next court day, which is to-morrow, they will storm the prison, and will themselves bring him forth to execution."

"And should they make the attempt," remarked Rufus gravely, "I doubt very much, O Florus, whether we can depend upon the fidelity of our cohorts to prevent it. This Simon hath slain so many Romans that military and civilians alike are desirous of seeing him brought to justice."

Florus, looking very ill at ease, was silent for a moment.

"You are convinced that our captive is really the Simon the Black, and that he hath committed the crimes attributed to him?"

"Quite," replied Tertullus. "I have documents and witnesses enough to prove his guilt twenty times over."

"Why, then, need we go to the trouble of a public trial? Since you are certain of his guilt, I will do as did Antipas with him that was called 'The Baptist'— send an executioner to his cell. How say you? Speak the word, and within an hour you shall have his head here upon a charger."

"Antipas' act is a bad precedent," returned Tertullus. "Your predecessor Festus, as Ananias there can testify, was more equitably minded. 'It is not the manner of the Romans,' said he, 'to deliver any man to die, before that he which is accused have the accusers face to face, and have license to answer for himself concerning the crime laid against him.'"'

"Words deserving to be written in letters of gold," commented Crispus, to the manifest displeasure of Florus.

"Moreover," observed Rufus, "the people will never believe Simon dead if he be secretly executed."

"They will, when they see his head over the Prætorium gate."

"His crimes have been open and public," said Tertullus, "let his trial be so."

"To-morrow?" said Florus. "Why not the next day?"

"The day after to-morrow is a sabbath," replied Tertullus. "The Jewish witnesses will refuse to attend court on that day."

"The sabbath! the sabbath!" repeated Florus pettishly. "Why is the sabbath greater than any other day?"

"Why are you greater than other men?" asked Berenice gently.

"Because, princess, it hath pleased Cæsar to make me so."

"Well, then, it hath pleased the Lord to make the Sabbath a greater day than any other," smiled Berenice, never at a loss for an answer where her religion was concerned.

"Will not the noble Florus," said Crispus, "state the reasons for his delay in bringing this prisoner to trial?"

The noble Florus did not reply to this pointed question. He frowned, and hesitated; but, with a son of the all-powerful Legate of Syria present as a witness of his irregularities, he felt he could not do otherwise than grant the just request of Tertullus.

"Have, then, your way," said he. "In the morning Simon shall be put upon his trial."

And with that he resumed his conversation with Berenice.

"He'll be sorry for that concession," laughed Tertullus quietly; and then, turning to Rufus, he added, "See that Simon's guards sleep not to-night. Florus is quite capable of taking him off secretly."

"You mean——"

"I mean," whispered Tertullus, "that the deferring of the trial is due to the fact that this Zealot, if brought into open court, could say something to the detriment of Florus; what, I would fain find out. Therefore, I say again, look well to the prisoner to-night."

Rufus promised that he would see to the matter.

At this point the ears of the guests were attracted by a sound like that of cords passing over pulleys, and looking whence it came, they saw a curtain that draped a wide archway ascend, revealing behind it a stage.

And now, while the palate of the guests was being regaled with the choicest of wines, their eyes were gratified by a series of beautiful tableaux drawn from the domain of classic mythology. The last of these represented the Judgment of Paris; by a trifling departure from the original story, the prize of the fairest goddess was to be a golden zone.

Paris, apparently unable to come to a decision as to which of the three diaphanously-attired goddesses was the fairest, made the award dependent upon their dancing. At this there followed *pas seuls* of such a character that the modest maiden who sat by Josephus was compelled to avert her gaze.

Venus, having received the award from the hand of the Dardan shepherd, advanced to the edge of the stage, and surveyed the audience.

"Alas!" she cried with a sudden sigh, "Paris has

made a mistake, for I see one here more lovely than
myself. Let the gift be hers, and let her be hailed as
Queen of Beauty."

With that she unclasped the golden cestus and flung
it into the middle of the hall just as the curtain was
falling upon the tableau.

A slave, picking up the fallen zone, carried it to
Florus.

"'ΚΑΛΛΙΣΤΗ'—'for the fairest,'" said he, reading
the sapphire letters set in the golden cestus. "The
question is," continued Florus, looking round upon a
bevy of ladies who had drawn near to view the zone,
and it was well worth viewing for its beautiful workmanship, "the question is, who *is* the fairest?"

But, however fair each lady might secretly deem herself, as there was not found any bold enough to come
forward and claim this title, it became clear that, if
the zone must be bestowed at all, it would be necessary
to appoint an umpire to decide this ticklish matter.

The ladies, entering with a zest into the scheme, were
quite willing, so they averred, to submit their charms
to adjudication.

"A pretty little tableau, this," whispered Rufus to
Crispus, "prearranged by Florus for the purpose of
flattering the vanity of Berenice. His liking for her is
so well known that whoever is appointed umpire—unless he be a very independent character—will lack the
courage to decide for any but the princess."

A proposal on the part of Tertullus to appoint the
umpire by lot was received with acclamation. Crispus,
somewhat against his will, was forced by Rufus to take
his place among the candidates for the office, and, what
is more, when his turn came for putting his hand into
the balloting urn he drew forth the tessera inscribed
with the decisive word, "*Judex.*"

He compressed his lips, much preferring that the
honor should have fallen upon some other.

Rufus now made a proposition.

"Methinks it is but fair," said he, "that the lady round whose waist the zone is clasped should bestow a kiss upon the adjudicator."

This was laughingly made one of the conditions of the contest.

And now, amid much mirth, about twenty of the ladies began to prepare for the event. The rest, either from modesty or distrustful of their charms, drew aside, content to look on.

Among those who would fain have withdrawn, not only from the contest, but also from the palace itself, was the young girl who had so much attracted the notice of Crispus.

"Let us go," she whispered in a distressed voice to Josephus. "This is no place for me."

But he sought gently to persuade her, by dwelling upon the value and beauty of the jeweled zone, the ease with which it was obtainable, the pride and pleasure she would feel in being hailed as the Queen of Beauty.

"The zone will not fall to *me*," said she. "Look, and see how many beautiful women there are around."

"None so beautiful as you, Vashti."

She shook her golden tresses at what she deemed his partiality. In the end, however, she consented to let her will be overborne by his.

The fair contestants were now moving to the place of judgment, a spacious hemicycle at one end of the banqueting hall. Among them were the Princess Berenice, and the Syrian Asenath, the favorite of Ananias.

As Vashti moved forward, her air of innocence and purity seemed to give secret offense to the wanton dancing-girl; her lip curled with contempt, and resolving to strip the other of her veil of modesty, she came out with a proposal of a malicious and daring character.

"How can it be told," cried she, "who is the loveliest, so long as we remain clothed? The robe may hide deformities. Let it be a condition, O Florus, that in this contest we appear naked."

Speaking thus, she laid both hands upon her swelling hips ready to fling off her robes at the least encouragement.

Now, seeing that in the Floralia at Rome women were accustomed to dance quite naked, and that at Etruscan banquets the ladies often showed their fair forms without any clothing whatever, the proposal of Asenath was not quite so startling as it would be at the present day.

There were, of course, screams of dissent from the fair contestants themselves, but to the gilded and decadent youth of that assembly, Gentile and Jew alike, living only for sensuality, Asenath's suggestion met with a ready approval. Not even the high priest, Ananias, lifted his voice against it. The Princess Berenice stood like a statue, stately and still, neither assenting nor dissenting. As for Vashti, her cheeks had become of a deathly white, her whole air and attitude were eloquent of a vivid horror at finding herself amid a circle of gilded youth who stood by waiting only the word of Florus, to assist her, *volentem, nolentem,* in the task of disrobing.

" What says the excellent Florus? " cried Asenath.

" The proposal seems to me to be fair, for the robe, as you say, may hide deformities. But," he continued, becoming secretly conscious that Crispus did not favor the idea, " the question is out of my hands; it rests with the adjudicator."

" And *he*," replied Crispus, " decides that the ladies shall remain clothed. This is a contest for beauty, and there is no beauty where there is no modesty."

" O good and pious youth, ascend to heaven! " said Asenath with a mocking laugh; and realizing that *her* chance of winning the zone was gone, she stepped from the contending circle to the side of Ananias, who looked by no means pleased with the decision of Crispus. He, the priest of a religion that claimed to be purer far than any of the pagan systems, had received a tacit rebuke from a pagan—a mortifying experience, the more so as he secretly felt it to be deserved.

Compliant with the directions of Florus, the contestants took their station upon a low marble seat that lined the hemicycle; and, when so placed, presented a variety of faces so dazzling in beauty as to make the adjudicator's task a hard one.

As if to enhance his difficulty, Crispus received at that moment a piece of news somewhat startling in character.

Touched upon the shoulder by a hand, he turned, and, to his surprise, found Polemo by his side. If the Pontic king had been present at the banquet Crispus had certainly missed seeing him, nor could he now tell from what corner he had sprung.

"*Athenaïs is among the contestants!*" whispered the king; and ere Crispus could put a question to him, Polemo had slipped among the crowd that was standing around to watch the sight, and had vanished as mysteriously as he had appeared, leaving Crispus in a whirl of amazement.

His wife among the contestants!

Stern justice required that the prize should be given to the fairest, but still, for all that, it would be a graceful compliment to let his wife have the honor; it would certainly please her, who was now the one women whom it behoved him to please. But how to identify her?

There was additional embarrassment in the fact that the chosen lady, on receiving the girdle, was to bestow a kiss upon the judge that had so honored her. To be kissed, in the presence of his unknown wife, by a lady adjudged by him to be the fairest of all present! If by some good fortune the lady chosen should happen to be Athenaïs, well!—but if not, what would her feelings be? No wonder Crispus shrank from the task of selection, and thought for a moment of retiring in favor of some other umpire.

The contestants were now ready awaiting the judgment.

Permitted to adopt whatever attitude they pleased, the majority posed as if for a sculptor. A few stood or sat, but the greater part assumed a reclining posture, as being the better adapted to display the grace of their figure. Extraneous ornaments were allowed; and hence one lady, lyre in hand, posed as the muse Polyhymnia; a second, toying with a golden vase, assumed the character of a Danaïd; a third, for the purpose of showing the curve of a graceful arm, held aloft a silver lamp; while a fourth displayed a snowy limb in the feigned operation of tying her sandal; and so on of the rest, each forming in herself a living picture that would have charmed the eye of an artist.

Midway in the hemicycle sat Berenice, who, neglecting all adventitious aids, merely sat erect, as if relying solely upon her beauty, and next her came the timid Vashti, taking that place as being the only one left vacant.

Holding the girdle in his hand, Crispus went very slowly along the semicircle, passing from one fair form to another, and studying each with a critical eye.

The behavior of the ladies during this severe scrutiny offered a variety of contrasts. Some blushed, as did Vashti; others, like Berenice, sat with serene dignity, as if unconscious of the matter in hand; some sought to win favor by a caressing glance; others used the witchery of a sweet smile; and one or two there were that could not refrain from laughter.

The completion of his survey left Crispus undecided, and disappointed: Athenaïs, if she were really among these ladies, was evidently determined to keep her secret, since she had given no sign by which he might recognize her. Among the many sparkling rings worn by that fair bevy, there was none that he could identify as

Crispus went very slowly along the semi-circle

the pledge placed by him upon the finger of his bride twenty-four hours ago, the ring set with a ruby sculptured with the likeness of a temple in flames.

Since his bride chose to hide her identity there remained nothing for him but to act in the spirit of strict impartiality by awarding the zone to her whose beauty in his judgment was most deserving of it, a difficult matter where all were so beautiful. Even that *arbiter elegantiarum*, Petronius (of whose friendship Florus had boasted), had he been present would have found the question a perplexing one.

Crispus recommenced his survey, amid the breathless excitement of those most immediately concerned.

"He has seen us all," was the general thought; "now he will make his choice."

Half-way along the line he paused—hesitated—stood still. Directly facing him were the Princess Berenice and the maiden Vashti. His glance, divided between them, showed that one of these two was to be his choice, and a little sigh of envy went up from eighteen disappointed hearts.

For some moments Crispus stood in doubt. Their beauty was equal, or nearly so.

The Princess Berenice, with her raven hair, dusky eyes, and majestic bearing, seemed like the incarnation of dark and starry night; the other, with her soft violet eyes, tresses like sunbeams, and gentle mien, was like fair Aurora sweetly stealing upon the eastern sky.

"If there were but two prizes!" murmured the unhappy Crispus.

"Why does he hesitate?" growled Florus. "Is it not plain to be seen that Berenice is the fairer?"

That girdle had cost him thirty thousand sesterces, and he did not want to see it bestowed upon a person for whom he had not intended it.

Berenice met the scrutiny of her judge with a proud glance, betokening a confidence that Crispus, who loved modesty, did not like to see; on the other hand, Vashti ventúred but once to raise her eyes with a sweet, timid, wondering air that moved him strangely.

That glance decided the event!

"Lady," said he, "what is your name?"

"Vashti, daughter of Hyrcanus," was the reply, delivered in a low, trembling voice.

"Then Vashti, daughter of Hyrcanus, as the fairest of all present, receive this golden zone."

Vashti was but human; it was a sweet little triumph for her. There leaped into her eyes a sudden look of pleasure, a look that was succeeded by one almost akin to fear as she glanced at the humiliated princess, whose beauty, long supreme in Judæa, was now publicly relegated to a second place.

Half pleased, half frightened, scarcely knowing what she was doing, Vashti rose to her feet, an act that gave Crispus the opportunity of girding her waist with the zone, and securing it with the clasp.

The conferring of the prize upon a Jewess occasioned dissatisfaction among some of the Gentiles; a few, too, of the Jews resented that the Herodian princess should be excluded in favor of an unknown maiden. In both parties there was, however, a majority which, more generous in sentiment, or perhaps thinking that Berenice and her beauty had queened it too long over other women, expressed its approbation by the shout:

"All hail to Vashti, the Queen of Beauty!"

"Is not the umpire, too, entitled to a reward?" asked Crispus.

Vashti started back with a burning blush that made her look the more beautiful.

"Nay, I must not forego it."

He was so completely dazzled by her loveliness as to forget for the moment that his unknown bride was watching him. Taking Vashti by both hands he drew her gently towards him, and momentarily pressed her warm, red lips to his own, an act greeted by the company with another round of applause.

## The Queen of Beauty

All very pretty, but what would Polemo think of it?

Becoming suddenly alive to the existence of that monarch he looked around for him, and saw him at a distance surveying the scene with a sphinx-like expression that gave no evidence as to what thoughts were passing within him. Crispus took a step in his direction, but the king, as if wishing to avoid him, vanished among the crowd, and was seen no more that night.

A little later Rufus addressed a question to Crispus.

"Did you notice Berenice's look when you bestowed the prize of beauty upon Vashti?"

"No; how did she look?" asked Crispus absently.

"She looked—she looked," said Rufus reflectively, as if casting about in his mind for some image to express his thoughts, "she looked the picture of sorrow. She looked—well, don't laugh if I use this comparison—she looked as a wife who loves her husband might look when she sees him fascinated by another woman."

Crispus started, stared strangely at Rufus, then walked away.

"Now what have I said to offend him?" muttered the wondering Rufus.

# CHAPTER IV

#### THE DREAM OF CRISPUS

TEMPTED by the beauty of the starry night, as well as by the wish to be alone with his thoughts, Crispus passed from the banqueting hall, and sought the spacions gardens attached to the Prætorium, gardens that with their variegated parterres and smooth lawns, marble fountains and shady walks, differed little, if at all, from the aspect presented by a modern pleasaunce.

There is nothing new under the sun! Even the practice of forcing shrubbery to assume artificial shapes was not unknown to the ancients, and the boscage of these gardens presented at different points a variety of figures, graceful and grotesque.

Now, as Crispus walked meditatively along a quiet path he caught sight of a distant and solitary figure standing by a marble seat that gleamed white against a background of dark cypresses. Her face was turned from him, but there was something familiar in her form; the stature and shape suggested Berenice, and as he drew nearer he became certain of it. At the sound of his footsteps the figure turned, and dimly, beneath the gloom cast by the cypress leaves, he saw the face of Berenice—Berenice, yet with golden hair! He stopped short in surprise. Then in a moment the likeness that he had seen, or thought he had seen, vanished, leaving in its place—Vashti! He looked, but the resemblance was no more. A mere fancy wrought by his imagination and the dim light.

Vashti greeted him with a shy smile, and a blush due to the memory of the kiss that he had bestowed upon her.

## The Dream of Crispus

She was awaiting, it seemed, the return of Josephus. He had left her there for a moment while he ran off to speak a word with Ananias, whom he had beheld in the distance.

Crispus looked round, but could see neither Ananias nor Josephus; in fact could see no one save the beautiful maiden beside him.

"I'll act as your guardian till his return," smiled he, as he seated himself and invited Vashti to do the like.

It was a beautiful night, with nothing to disturb its stillness save the far-off sounds of music and revelry coming from the Prætorium.

Their position, on ground slightly elevated, gave them a full view of the sea, a purple mirror reflecting in broken sparkles the light of a thousand stars.

To their left, and looking like a long white ribbon flung out upon the dark water, was the mole of Cæsarea, its far end adorned with the Drusion, a noble tower upon whose top a fire was flaming for the guidance of ships sailing into the harbor.

It was not, however, upon the Drusion that Crispus' eyes were set, but upon Vashti. He longed to know something of her personal history, and the present occasion afforded him an excellent opportunity. The difficulty was how to begin. A patrician of Rome, who had in his time conversed unrestrainedly with princesses and queens, and even with the Empress Poppæa, he actually found himself embarrassed in the presence of this Hebrew maid of seventeen. There was something about her, a spirit of innocence and purity, that marked her off as altogether different from the women of that age.

However, having once contrived to begin a conversation he found it easy to maintain it, and ere long he succeeded in eliciting something of her parentage and history.

Her mother, it seemed, was a widow, Miriam by name,

who had one other child only, an infant. Her father, Hyrcanus, had been a wealthy rabbi of some distinction. ("Clearly Tertullus was wrong," thought Crispus, "in giving her a Grecian origin.") Hyrcanus, at his death, an event of the previous year, had by will left his family and effects to the care of his friend Josephus, who thus exercised in relation to Vashti the office of guardian. She and her mother were staying for a brief space only at Cæsarea, their usual home being at Jerusalem, in the street of Millo. Miriam, a strictly orthodox Jewess, had been much opposed to her daughter's going to a Gentile feast, but had finally yielded to the wishes of Josephus.

All this was told, not in her native Syro-Chaldaic, but in Greek; and Crispus did not know which was the more charming, the melody of her voice, or the grace and purity with which she spoke the beautiful language of Hellas.

"I learned the Greek from my father," she explained in answer to Crispus' question. "He trained me in it from infancy."

Crispus marveled to hear of a Jew with views so unorthodox.

"According to my friend Rufus, your rabbis have said, 'He who teaches his son Greek is as if he reared swine.'"

"*Some* rabbis have said that. But my father belonged to the school of Gamaliel, who taught us to appropriate whatever is good among the Gentiles. The Greek language is good, and Josephus and I are availing ourselves of its treasures."

"In what way?"

Instead of giving a direct reply, Vashti asked a seemingly irrelevant question.

"How old should you take our nation to be?"

As Hebrew history formed no part of the study of Roman youth, Crispus was fain to confess his ignorance.

## The Dream of Crispus

"Well, how old is Rome?"

"More than eight hundred years," he answered with conscious pride.

"Which proves your nation, when compared with ours, to be but of yesterday. We Jews were a people a thousand years before Romulus drew his plow along the Palatine."

Crispus, jealous for the antiquity of his nation, was disposed to question Vashti's statement.

"Why, you are as skeptical as Apion. You have heard of Apion?"

"No," laughed Crispus. "Who was he?"

"A grammarian of Alexandria, and the author of a work intended to show that we Jews are quite a recent nation in the history of the world, a libel that has so wrought upon the spirit of Josephus that he is writing a reply, whose title is to be '*Contra Apion.*'"

"And you are aiding him in the work? Come, deny it not!"

Vashti smiled assent.

"I act as his amanuensis," added she.

A Hebrew maiden of seventeen versed in Grecian literature was a novelty to Crispus. Curious to know whether her learning was anything more than superficial, he ventured, with her own consent, to subject her to a catechism derived from the reminiscences of a two-years' curriculum in the schools of Athens, but soon relinquished the task on finding her knowledge far more extensive than his own.

"You have been questioning me," said she with a smile, sweet yet grave, when he had finished. "Now may I claim a like privilege?"

"In order to demonstrate my ignorance," laughed Crispus. "Well, I'll put myself under examination. Be not too hard with me."

Thus adjured, Vashti began.

"Why does your Greek poet Bianor, in commenting

upon the fable of Arion, who was cast into the sea by the sailors but saved by the dolphins, say it is meant to teach us that '*By man comes death, but by the Fish salvation*'?"'

This, Crispus thought, was a very odd question. He had merely heard of Bianor as a poet living in the days of Tiberius; and that was the extent of his knowledge concerning him. As to the passage quoted by Vashti, it had no meaning for him. The words, however true of the fabled Arion, were scarcely applicable to mankind at large.

Over Vashti's face there passed a shade as of sadness, momentary only, but it did not escape Crispus' quick eye.

"I thought perhaps you might have comprehended," said she. "Your story told to-night at the banquet, the story of 'Great Pan,' led me to hope that—that— no matter! I see now that I was wrong," she added with a sigh.

Saddened because she found him unable to explain an obscure line of a Greek poet! Why, what an odd maiden was this! And the curious part of it all was, she refused to enlighten him; and hence he could not but conclude that Vashti had some secret to which the poet's words were the key.

The conversation flowed on, and soon touched upon Jewish antiquity again. There were Jews, so Vashti averred, Josephus for example, who could carry back an authentic ancestry over a space of two thousand years. Crispus was wont to pride himself upon his ancient family, but what was its antiquity compared with such as these?

"And can *you* show so long a genealogy?"

"My father Hyrcanus could."

Crispus thought this a somewhat odd reply.

"But if *he* could, so can *you*, seeing that you are his daughter."

"Only those genealogies are deemed authentic that

are inscribed on the public rolls. *My* name is missing from them."

"How is that?"

"Nay, I cannot tell, but such is the case. I discovered it but a few days ago. I was in the Archeion —the House of the Rolls, we call it—with its keeper Johanan ben Zacchai, who has always regarded me with fatherly affection. Moved by curiosity, I asked to be allowed to see my own name in the public genealogical records. 'Well, to please you, my daughter,' said he. So he brought out the rolls of papyrus and parchment; and after a long time, and much searching, he found the names of my father Hyrcanus, and my mother Miriam, but *my* name he could not find, though my little brother Arad's is recorded. So you see——"

The sound of approaching footsteps checked her utterance. On turning, Crispus and Vashti saw at a little distance a stately and beautiful figure that for a moment stopped short, apparently in surprise, at seeing the pair in such friendly converse. It was the Princess Berenice. Some instinct told Crispus that she was looking for him, and he beheld her with a sort of self-reproach. In spite of her half-jesting reminder that he should not, as at Antioch, neglect her, he had repeated his indifference; his only dealing with her had been to depose her from the proud position of being the first beauty of the land. What wonder, then, if she should feel somewhat hurt?

"I will leave you now," murmured Vashti, making as if to rise.

"Nay, do not go," said Crispus, venturing, all unconsciously, to lay a detaining hand upon her wrist.

Crispus wondered at her heightened color, and at the new light that came into her eyes. Was she pleased to think that he would not dismiss her, even in favor of a princess?

He withdrew his hand, but not before Berenice had

noticed the action. Observant woman is doubly observant at such times.

"Will the Queen of Beauty," said the princess with a slightly disdainful air, "permit me to share the conversation of the noble Crispus?" And, without waiting for a reply, she seated herself, as she spoke, at the left side of Crispus, Vashti being at his right.

"What is passing in the palace?" asked Crispus.

"The wit of Florus," replied Berenice. "The wine hath got into his head. Like Nero, he thinks he can sing. But I was very good, and kept a grave face the while; nay, I even asked him to sing again, which pleased him hugely. I cannot say the same of his hearers."

She laughed so pleasantly that Crispus was fain to laugh too.

And now there began on the part of Berenice a flow of talk that, sometimes witty, sometimes wise, was always interesting. She touched on topics grave and gay, from the government of the empire to the latest fashion in sandals, never failing tó illumine the subject in hand with some subtle observation. She had the field all to herself, for Vashti was content to be a listener, while Crispus put in a remark now and again. It seemed almost as if Berenice, surmising that Crispus had found a fascination in Vashti's conversation, had determined to display her own brilliancy. And certainly the character of both was a revelation to Crispus, who, accustomed hitherto, in the haughty and exclusive spirit of his race, to regard the Jews as an inferior nation, was agreeably surprised to find among these "barbarians" two women who, while equal in beauty to any Greek or Roman lady known to him, were certainly superior in intellect and charm.

"'Tis the first day of the new moon," observed Berenice, suddenly.

"I see her not," returned Crispus, glancing over the face of the sky, and thereby missing Berenice's little frown. A foe to paganism, she did not like to hear personality ascribed to the moon.

"Its slender crescent is visible at Jerusalem, if not from here," said Berenice. "*That* tells me so."

She pointed to a far-off peak upon the southern horizon, a peak upon which there had appeared a light no larger than a star. The sparkle was repeated at a point northward of the first; a third followed; and soon a whole line of fires was twinkling upon the hill-summits of Judæa.

"Our way of announcing the first day of the month," explained Berenice. "So soon as the new moon is seen from a certain hill near Jerusalem by watchers appointed of the Sanhedrim for that purpose, the tidings is flashed by fire-signals throughout all the land. 'Tis an old custom lately revived by the high priest Matthias. But I will not weary you with matters in which a Roman can take no interest."

"There you err, princess. My visit to Jerusalem— for thither am I bound—is undertaken for the sole purpose of seeing your temple."

"You wish to see our temple?" exclaimed the princess in great surprise, "you, who at the banquet avowed yourself a worshiper of the gods of Rome! What interest can our temple have for *you?*"

"My interest is the outcome of a—a———"; he hesitated for a moment, and then added, "a dream."

A statement so singular naturally evoked Berenice's curiosity, and she begged him to tell the dream. Vashti, though she said nothing, was, as Crispus could see by her looks, equally curious to hear it.

"I wish now that I could recall my words," said he, "for though it was but a dream, the telling of it may cause me to fall into disfavor with you both."

That "both" was a distasteful word to Berenice, seeming, as it did, to imply that he thought as much of Vashti's opinion as of her own. Evidently he did, for it was not till Vashti had added a persuasive word that he would begin his story.

"A few nights ago," said he, plunging at once *in medias res*, "I seemed in my sleep to be standing in what appeared to be the court of some magnificent temple. This court, colonnaded on its four sides, was a spacious one and open to the sky. It was night, and the stars faintly twinkled. Before me at some distance rose the temple itself, an edifice constructed of pure white marble.

"The place was not quiet—far from it. Singular to relate, although no one was visible, the court seemed to be thronged with men. There was a running to and fro over the pavement, the clash and clang of arms, and the sound of warriors engaged in deadly fray. I laid hand to my sword, desiring to range myself on the one side or the other, but how could one take part in a combat like this—a combat of ghosts?

"Suddenly I became conscious of a glow; in front of me, upon a low balustrade, lay a flaming torch. As I looked at it a voice, seeming to come from the sky, cried in the Hebrew tongue, 'Burn!' and the flambeau shook itself as if impatient to be grasped. I hesitated. Again the voice cried, 'Burn!' in a tone so awe-inspiring that I durst not disobey. I lifted the burning brand, and tossed it through a golden window of the temple. A shower of sparks rose from within; next came a tongue of fire, leaping forth from the window; a little while and the whole structure was mantled with flame and smoke. At the same instant I awoke."

Berenice's dusky eyes, eloquent with a nameless fear, were set full upon the speaker's face.

"Can you describe the temple seen by you in the vision?"

"I can shut my eyes now," said Crispus, suiting the action to the word, "and recall every feature. I am standing on the north side of the temple; it extends

## The Dream of Crispus 57

east and west for a length of perhaps two hundred and fifty cubits. To enter it one must first pass a low balustrade of marble, curiously wrought, upon which stand little pillars engraved with a notice in Greek and Latin letters. I have a distinct remembrance in my dream of reading the notice. It forbade the Gentiles on pain of death from entering the shrine."

Both Vashti and Berenice gave a faint cry of surprise.

" Did you speak, princess? "

" No, no! Go on. What next? " she asked breathlessly.

" After passing the balustrade one has the choice of four gates, each ascended by a stately flight of stairs fifteen in number. Of these gates, three, situated near the western end, are near each other; the fourth stands far remote towards the eastern end. Each gate consists of two folding doors, crusted with gold and silver, and is flanked by massive towers." He paused for a moment, and resumed: " I related this vision to my father, who was as much startled, princess, as you appear to be. ' What you have seen,' said he, ' is the temple at Jersusalem.' Can you wonder, then, that I desire to take a view of it? "

" And did you know nothing of the interior of our temple till the time of this dream? " asked Berenice.

" Absolutely nothing, I pledge you my solemn word. I was, of course, aware that Jerusalem contained a notable temple resorted to by devout Jews out of every nation under heaven, but that was the total extent of my knowledge. Not a single detail of its architecture was known to me."

Berenice seemed perplexed, even troubled.

" Strange! whence comes this dream of yours? " she murmured.

" You do not doubt the vision? "

" How can I, since you affirm it to be true? "

" You admit that my description is correct? "

"It cannot be gainsaid."

"Well, then, since it is beyond the power of the human mind, whether sleeping or awake, to gain such knowledge as I gained at that time, shall I offend you by saying that the vision was directly vouchsafed to me by the immortal gods?"

"The gods?" returned the princess with a touch of disdain in her voice. "The gods? The gods of you Gentiles have no existence. There is but one true and living God."

"Have it so," replied Crispus, who seemingly could tolerate reflections upon his religion much more easily than Berenice could upon hers. "Shall we say, then, that the vision was sent by your own deity?"

"Impossible! Would He Who has enjoined upon us the perpetual worship of Himself give command to destroy the one and only temple in which that worship is carried on?"

"He might," observed Vashti, "if He purposed to make His religion more spiritual. Pure religion requires neither temple nor altar."

"There speaks one who is no true daughter of Abraham," retorted Berenice.

"Nay, princess, it is because I *am* a daughter of Abraham that I say it, for what temple did Abraham have?"

Berenice, about to make an angry retort, was checked by Crispus.

"We are drifting from the primary question," said he, "which is, whence came my dream? That dream was plainly a supernatural one."

"Whence?" returned Berenice. "Whence but from the kingdom of evil? There are wicked spirits as well as good, and the prince of them is named Satan, who would rejoice if he could but persuade a Roman to destroy the temple. I pray you, noble Crispus," she continued, with considerable emotion, "dismiss this dream from your mind, lest by dwelling overmuch upon it you should come to believe that you have a Divine mission to destroy the temple."

"It may be that I have."

Crispus spoke with the grave air of one who believes in the truth of his words. For a moment the princess gazed at him, speechless with consternation. Recovering her voice, she cried indignantly:

"What good could come from such a deed?"

"Much—to Rome!"

"How?"

"That temple," said Crispus, speaking in a cold, deadly tone that set Berenice shivering with terror, for she loved her temple more than her life, " that temple draws annually to its courts three million Jews, all animated by a fierce hatred of Rome, and all fanatically persuaded that One born in Judæa shall obtain the dominion of the world. You know it is so, princess; you cannot deny it. Your temple is a perpetual menace to the safety of the empire. Destroy the temple, and we put an end to these annual gatherings with their vain and treasonable hopes."

## CHAPTER V

### SIMON THE ZEALOT

EARLY on the morning after the banquet there flew through Cæsarea the surprising news that the notable Zealot, Simon the Black, was to be put on his trial on the noon of that same day.

Eager to witness the scene, a motley crowd, composed of Jews and Greeks, Romans and Syrians, flocked, long before the appointed time, into the basilica, or court of justice, till the numbers were such that the building would hold no more.

A Roman basilica presented an appearance very similar to that of a modern parish church, consisting as it did of a nave, and two aisles divided from it by a row of columns. At one end a portion, elevated like a daïs and railed off like a chancel, formed the *bema* (the word had passed from the Greek into the Syro-Chaldaic) or tribunal, where the judges sat and orators pleaded. The whole of the interior was further surrounded by an upper gallery raised upon the columns that divided the aisles. The ground floor and the galleries were for the accommodation of the public.

In the middle of the bema, which was paved with tesselated marble, stood the governor's curule chair, and on each side of it were rows of seats intended for the assessors, it being the custom for a provincial governor to be assisted in his judgments by a sort of informal council consisting of distinguished citizens.

Shortly before noon there was a movement on the bema, caused by the arrival of persons interested in the trial. Among them was the priest Theomantes, who, in virtue of his dignity as priest of Jupiter Cæsarius,

## Simon the Zealot 61

proceeded to ensconce himself in the seat immediately upon the right of the curule chair, an act that caused murmurs among the Jews and applause among the Gentiles.

Ananias now entered, and seeing his own action anticipated, scowled, hesitated for a moment, and then deliberately sat down upon the lap of his rival.

" 'Tis mine to sit upon the right of Florus," he cried.

Thereupon, Theomantes, exerting all his strength, flung him off, amid mingled laughter and hooting from the two factions.

" Even if the high priest of the Jews *had* the right to this seat, it is not thine, seeing that thou art not high priest."

Now, it is not at all improbable that in their struggle for precedency these two graybeards might have come to unseemly blows before a delighted audience, but for the intervention of Terentius Rufus, who, with a body of spearmen, was stationed in front of the tribunal for the purpose of preserving order among the spectators.

" I never thought my services would be required upon the bema," said he.

And mounting the tribunal, he threatened unless Ananias settled down quietly in some other seat that he would remove him, as having wantonly and purposely created a disturbance in a court of justice.

" Let Ananias possess his soul in patience," he cried, " till it shall please Florus to make known Cæsar's decree on this matter."

The humiliated Ananias made as if he would retire altogether from the court, but finally, thinking better of it, sat down upon the left-hand seat, just as Florus made his pompous entry.

Crispus appeared about the same time, and, as being a distinguished visitor, was assigned a place among the council.

Florus, having seated himself in his curule chair, demanded to know what business was set down for the day, and as it appeared that there were many cases requiring his judicial decision, he announced that he would begin with the trial of Simon.

A thrill of excitement ran through the basilica when the order was given, "Go, lictors, bring hither Simon, surnamed the Black."

Without delay the prisoner was brought.

Walking between two guards, his hands tied behind his back with a cord whose end was held by a third soldier, came the terrible Zealot, who had hanged so many Romans that men had lost all count of the number. A man, tall and muscular, and having a singular breadth of chest, with black hair, black eyes, and black beard. Clothed in the dress he wore when captured, a gabardine all slashed with sword-cuts, and black with dried blood; with face unwashed, and beard and hair long and unkempt, he made a wild and savage figure. Captivity and darkness, chilling damps and meager diet, had failed, however, to tame his spirit; he stood, dark, scowling, defiant, the living incarnation of enmity to Rome.

Florus, after a brief and (as it seemed to Crispus) uneasy glance at the captive, turned to a table where sat the advocates, and asked:

"Who conducts the prosecution?"

Tertullus arose.

"Be brief. No oratory," said the procurator.

In a Roman trial proceedings usually began with the questioning of the accused in the endeavor to prove out of his own mouth the charge brought against him. Should this procedure fail, or should the prisoner, through obstinacy, refuse to answer, it became necessary to call upon witnesses.

Tertullus turned to question the captive, while the clerk of the court, with lifted pen, sat ready to record the dialogue; for, be it known, there were in that age scribes who, by a system of abbreviations, were capable of writing as fast as a man could speak.

"Your name?" began Tertullus.

"You ask me my name?" said the Zealot with a laugh of scorn. "You ought to know, seeing what fear it has put into the hearts of you Romans. I am Simon, son of Giora, of the tribe of Benjamin."

"Your birthplace?"

"Gerasa, beyond Jordan."

"Your calling?"

"Slayer of the Romans."

"Consider! You desire the clerk to write down that answer?"

"Let him write it twice, yea thrice, and in his largest characters."

"You confess, then, that you are of the sect known as the Zealots?"

"A curse on your Gentile terms; I am of the sect of the Kenaïm."

"Zealots or Kenaïm, 'tis much the same. What are their tenets?"

"These: call no one king but God; pay no tax save to the temple; slay every Roman who presumes to exercise authority over the holy seed."

"'Call no one king but God'? Then you do not acknowledge the authority of Cæsar?"

"Cæsar!" It is impossible to describe the contempt with which he spoke the name. "Cæsar! I spit at the name of Cæsar."

And he did, there and then, upon the pavement. This repudiation of imperial authority was received by the servile Græco-Syrian mob with a roar of execration.

"*Læsa majestas!*" was their cry. "Fling him over the rails!"

"'Assassinate every Roman'?" continued Tertullus. "Then you would assassinate Florus, if you could?"

The very suggestion caused the face of the Zealot to mantle with ferocious joy.

"Place a dagger in my freed hands, set me within three paces of him, and you shall see."

"The court will take the will for the deed," observed Tertullus dryly. "Attend to the indictment. You are charged with being the chief of a band of Zealots, or, if it please you, Kenaïm. Stationed among the heights in the Pass of Adummim, it was your wont to issue forth, and to rob and to hang every Roman that came that way."

"A marvel! A lawyer speaks the truth!"

"How many Romans have been put to death by you?"

"Put that question to the vultures. I kept no register of the slain. Thus much I know, that, give me my freedom, and you shall see me repeat the work with a new band."

"Traitor to the empire, do you glory in your guilt?"

"The guilt is yours who presume to exercise authority in a land that God sware with an oath should be ours forever. Out of this land, then, ye Romans, with your legions and your lictors, your taxes and your idols! It is contrary to the will of God that Cæsar should bear rule in Judæa, and the Jew that acknowledges him breaks the law of Moses. For it is written therein, 'One from among thy brethren shalt thou set king over thee; thou mayest not set a stranger over thee which is not thy brother'; whereof let due note be taken by that smug Ananias there, who fraternizes so comfortably with his country's enemies!"

"As it was your custom," continued Tertullus, "to plunder, as well as to kill, you doubtless gained considerable wealth?"

"Wealth? Ay, stores of it," said Simon, his eyes sparkling as if at the recollection.

"None was found in the place of your capture."

Simon laughed exultingly.

"It exists, for all that, in a place where no Roman

can lay hand upon it, reserved for the great day of vengeance."

" Or, in other words, it is to be used in fomenting war against Rome? "

" Lawyer, thou hast said."

" It is rumored that several persons of high station have been in communication with you? "

" The highest in the land. I can see now upon the bema here some of my past accomplices. Why are they not placed beside me to be judged? "

The uneasiness that had never been absent from the face of Florus seemed now to increase. It was noticed by Tertullus, who smiled to himself with the quiet satisfaction of an archer who, after many trials, has hit the mark at last.

The crowd of spectators, hitherto restless and murmuring, became suddenly hushed. Florus' long delay in bringing Simon to trial had given birth to sinister rumors as to the relations previously existing between the procurator and the robber-chief. Was the dark story about to be confirmed? With breathless interest they awaited the issue.

" The court will be pleased at having these accomplices named," said Tertullus with affected carelessness.

" I name them not, unless I have a promise that they shall be arrested without delay."

" The court will have no hesitation in arresting them, provided that you can prove your charge."

" Good! If it be a crime to plot against the life of a Roman, bid the lictors go and bind the hands of Ananias."

Tertullus' face fell somewhat. Ananias was not the name he wanted.

" Lying Zealot! " exclaimed the priest; and, forgetting for the moment that it was not a Jewish court in which he could do according to his own pleasure, he cried, " Strike him on the mouth! "

" O Ananias! Ananias! " said Simon, shaking his

head with mock gravity, " were you not once an aecomplice with me in a plot to slay a Roman citizen? 'Tis clear you have forgotten my face: let me recall it to you. Did there not once come to you—'tis eight years ago now—forty Sicarii,⁶ of whom I was one, offering to slay Paul of Tarsus, a Roman citizen, mark you! and freeborn? Did you not readily join in the plot? And now do you disavow your old friend Simon? Nay, verily, be honest, and take your trial with me."

Over the face of Ananias there had suddenly crept a look scarcely compatible with the idea of innocence.

" Will no one stop the mouth of the lying knave? " he cried, trembling with passion.

" Your looks sufficiently show who is the lying knave," answered Simon coolly. " If ye desire proof of this, my accusation," he continued, addressing the court, " send to Jerusalem for Paul's nephew; he will confirm what I say. Does the court agree that Ananias shall take his trial with me? " added Simon, looking around him with a sardonic smile. " No? And yet 'tis the fashion of Romans to boast of their justice!—justice, forsooth! "

" Prisoner," said Florus, " be not so free of tongue, and you may find that our Roman justice, whose purity you seem to question, can be tempered with mercy."

" Now, let the court carefully mark that little speech," said Simon coolly, " for, being interpreted, it meaneth, ' Keep quiet as to *my* doings, O Simon, and I will endeavor to procure your release.' But in vain do you offer me the bribe of life, O Florus, in order to stay my tongue. Welcome torture, scourgings, death, if I do but succeed in hurling you from power."

Simon was not to be appeased, and Florus, catching sight of Tertullus' smile, suddenly realized the lawyer's motive in pressing for the public trial of the Zealot. It was to ruin him—Florus!

It was out of the question either to gag the prisoner or to declare the court closed; either alternative would

## Simon the Zealot 67

expose him to suspicion. He, the judge, must sit and listen to an accusation, which, even if it were untrue, would be greedily believed by nine out of every ten, so unpopular was he with the people over whom he ruled. And when the story should reach Rome, as it undoubtedly would—his enemies would take good care of that!—it might mean the loss, not only of his procuratorship, as Simon had said, but even of his life.

"The brazen effrontery of this knave!" said he, assuming a stern bearing. "Knowing that his doom is certain, he seeks to delay sentence by vilifying the character of his judges. Go, lictors, bring hither the flagellum."

"And, when brought, apply it to the shoulders of the robber Florus," said Simon.

"Ye see for yourselves," said Florus, turning to the assessors, "what an incorrigible villain this is!"

"Listen to a story that is no fiction," continued Simon. "Florus sent a secret messenger offering me free license to plunder and slay Roman and Gentile alike, on condition of his receiving half the spoil."

"A lie as black as Erebus!" thundered the procurator.

"It is one thing to accuse, another thing to prove," remarked Tertullus quietly, secretly delighted at the turn events were taking.

"I have no proof in writing. Florus is too artful a fox to employ ink and parchment on such a matter. His intermediary in this business was his freedman, Nymphidius."

"Is it worth while sending for this Nymphidius," asked Tertullus of Florus, "that he may deny this allegation?"

"It is useless sending for him," observed Rufus, "for he died this morning—suddenly."

"Who helped him to die?" asked Simon. "For it appears to me that his death has occurred at a time very convenient for Florus."

A significant question, this! Men looked at each other, little doubting that Florus had by foul means removed an awkward witness from his path.

"Bear with me, noble Florus," said Tertullus, "if I assume for a moment the truth of this knave's story. What answer," he continued, addressing Simon, "what answer did you give to Nymphidius?"

"This was my answer: 'Tell the uncircumcized dog of a Florus that Simon will plunder without asking *his* leave. Let him send to Manahem, the son of Judas, who will doubtless be glad to purchase license on such terms.'"

Tertullus now dropped his mask and became, like Simon, an accuser of the procurator.

"It was this Manahem, O Florus," said he quietly, "who a fortnight ago robbed me of a myrrhine drinking-cup, which last night appeared upon *your* table."

Now, during all this time Crispus had been listening with a strange conflict of emotions. Hatred of Simon's crimes was mingled with admiration for his daring spirit. He was also compelled to admit that the existence of the Zealots was, to a certain extent, justified by Roman misgovernment, a fact very unpalatable for a patriot like Crispus, ever striving to believe that Rome and justice were convertible terms. From the rule of wicked and rapacious governors like Pilate and Felix, Albinus and Florus, what other spirit could develop in Judæa but a burning hatred of Roman rule, combined with a determination to throw off the yoke whenever a favorable occasion should arise?

Though Simon was doubtless deserving of death, yet nevertheless Crispus' sense of justice revolted against his condemnation by judges like Florus and Ananias, themselves guilty of malefactions. He resolved to disassociate himself from the council.

"Since the prisoner," said he, "questions the integrity of two of his judges, and, as it seems to me, with some show of reason, I herewith decline to take any further part in this trial."

Suiting the action to the word, Crispus rose from his seat and withdrew from the bema.

" And I do the like," said Theomantes, moved in his action mainly by his feud with Ananias.

" And I! "—" And I! " exclaimed several other members, rising and descending from the tribunal.

Florus sat, full of impotent rage, on perceiving that the statements of Simon and Tertullus were believed in, not only by the common people, but also by the majority of the council.

" The trial is adjourned," he cried. " Let the prisoner be carried back to his dungeon."

The command came too late. Simon had perceived among the Jewish portion of the spectators certain disguised Zealots, who, both by eye and by gesture, were secretly inviting him to make a dash for liberty.

Acting on the hint, he suddenly wrenched himself free from his guards, darted to the edge of the tribunal, and, taking a flying leap over the line of soldiers that guarded its front, he alighted among his friends, who, struggling desperately, began to push him towards the open doors of the basilica.

The soldiers, attempting to follow, were at once opposed, not only by the whole Jewish body, but also by the Græco-Syrians, who in this matter were actuated not out of any love for Simon, but from a desire to thwart and disappoint Florus, whose rule was hateful to them. The court of justice became immediately transformed into a wild tumultuous pandemonium.

" Down with the wicked Florus! "

" Death to old Ananias! "

Stones and other missiles, discharged by men of both factions, now came whirling into the tribunal. Ananias, gathering his robe about him, fled to a place of safety. Florus, as he was lifting his hand in the futile attempt to quell the tumult, received a sharp-edged flint upon his temples. Down his quickly-paling face flowed a stream of blood, a sight welcomed by both factions with a huge roar of delight.

"Guards, hither to me!" cried the alarmed procurator.

Four stout soldiers sprang forward and screened him with their bucklers, that rattled again and again to the pelting shower of stones as the procurator, following the example of Ananias, fled amid hootings, cursings, and derisive laughter.

At the command of Rufus the soldiers, by threatening the people with leveled spears, soon cleared the courthouse. They failed, however, to recover Simon, who, dragged off by his friends, contrived to make good his escape.

"He'll harass us again," grumbled Rufus, a prophecy destined to meet with ample verification.

# CHAPTER VI

"DELENDA EST HIEROSOLYMA!"

"Then you will not marry me, princess?"

Such were the words addressed by Florus to Berenice, as he walked beside her in the sunlit gardens of the Prætorium.

The ugly gash he had received that morning from the well-aimed missile had not enhanced his personal beauty. Berenice, as she watched him from beneath the fringe of her dark, silky eyelashes, shivered, and thought how like a satyr he looked! She mentally contrasted the bloated coarseness of his visage with Crispus' clear bronzed healthful complexion.

"Marry *you!*" she said, emphasizing the last word. "My lord Florus, you have a wife already!"

"So had my predecessor Felix, but that did not prevent your sister Drusilla from marrying him."

"Poor deluded Drusilla! she would never have so acted but for the spells and sorceries of Simon Magus."

"Would that I knew where this Simon were to be found," sighed the governor, "for then would I, too, employ him in the like office!"

"You have the great Theomantes," laughed Berenice. "Cannot he weave spells for you? or has he already done so, and failed? But, my lord Florus, have pity on your wife. Why do you desire wicked Berenice in place of the good Cleopatra?"

"Fairest of women," began the governor gallantly.

"Nay," said the princess, somewhat darkly, "Crispus hath openly deprived me of that title."

"A fool, who hath no eyes for real beauty."

"Is it Berenice the Fair or Berenice the Golden that you are seeking to woo?"

"Mine," answered Florus with a fine air of virtue, "mine is not a mercenary character."

"Except where the spoil of Zealots is concerned," laughed Berenice. "I fear greatly that this morning's revelation will deprive you of office."

The procurator, too, was very much of this opinion, but it was not pleasant to hear it from her. Masking his anger beneath a hollow smile, he said:

"To gain you, princess, I would—yes! I would willingly turn proselyte, and that is more than Felix did for Drusilla."

"'Tis a tempting offer," said Berenice, with a sweet mocking laugh that charmed while it maddened the procurator. "How the Jews would joy in their new convert! Picture me leading Florus by the hand to the temple, there to present him to Matthias as a pious neophyte!" Then, becoming grave again, she went on, "My father Agrippa was king of Judæa, and it has ever been my aim to control the destinies of this same land, an aim foredoomed to failure were I to marry you."

"Why so?"

"O dullard! You have ruled because your wife was the friend of the Empress Poppæa." ("*Was?*" thought Florus, wondering why she should use the past tense; he was soon to learn!) "Had you divorced Cleopatra to marry me you would have set the empress against you, and then where would have been your procuratorship?"

This view of the case had often occurred to Florus himself. Still, what was the loss of his office compared with the handling of Berenice's gold?

"And," continued Berenice, "even supposing that the empress, overlooking the slight to her friend Cleopatra, should be willing to maintain you in office, she can no longer do so, seeing that she is dead."

"Poppæa dead?" gasped Florus incredulously.

"So saith my freedman Sadas."

## "*Delenda est Hierosolyma!*"

"Whence did he learn it?"

"A ship from Rome has just arrived in harbor with the tidings. Everybody on board is talking about it. Our greatest proselyte is dead, killed by a blow from Nero's foot, and she with child! Kicked to death by him whom you would have had us worship last night as a god," she added, her lip wreathing in scorn.

Florus was thunderstruck at the tidings, foreseeing a quick end to his rule now that there was no Poppæa to stand between him and the punishment justly due for his misdeeds. He knew full well that as soon as the Jews received the news they would send to Rome an embassy praying for his removal. They would certainly mention that little deal with the Zealots, not to speak of various other little peccadillos.

"And in ceasing to be procurator," said he, wrathfully, "I, of course, cease to be of interest to you?"

"Unless you should become Cæsar, in which case send for me, and I will come to you—yea, fly! As empress of the world I could do the holy nation better service than as queen of Judæa."

Empress of the world! She spoke lightly, little dreaming how narrowly she was to miss gaining the imperial throne.

"You think only of your people, and of your superstition," muttered Florus.

"Only of my people, and of my—superstition. You have hit off my character."

"You have been playing with me for your own ends," said he, his great coarse cheek reddening with anger. "And now you cast me off as one casts off a sandal that has outlived its use."

"O Florus, have done!" she said with a wearied air. "We have both been acting. Let us drop the mask. 'Tis not Berenice herself that is the charm, but her gold with which you hope to cancel past debts and to continue your infamous orgies. And I, divining your motives, have likewise played the hypocrite, feigning a love I never felt, if by so doing I might benefit Judæa. Strangely have you mistaken my nature in thinking that, apart from your procuratorship, you could ever have held any interest for me. My lord Florus, I bid you farewell."

And with that she left him.

The face of Florus was as the face of a demon as he watched her walking scornfully away with never a backward glance of pity or remorse. Love for her had now altogether vanished from his heart; no other feeling there but a big black hatred that transformed him to the elemental savage. His only thought now was to revenge himself upon her. But how? Death? It were a somewhat difficult matter to compass the end of a Jewish princess. True, he might hire the daggers of the Sicarri, even as the procurator Felix had hired them to assassinate the high priest Jonathan—he fell at the very altar—but suspicion would attach itself to him, and this was a thing to be avoided, if possible.

Besides, a death like that were too light a punishment; one sharp pang, and all would be over. His vengeance must take a more subtle, a more protracted form. How to accomplish it was the question, and thus thinking, he walked meditatively back to the Prætorium.

On entering, he learned that King Polemo—Berenice's ex-husband—was awaiting an interview with him in the Ivory Hall, a saloon so called from its paneling.

Florus received the news with something like a frown. "What wants he with me?" he muttered, darkly. "'Tis he who has brought me to this." But in a moment his face cleared again. "A friend of Cæsar! Ha! he may be of help to me in this crisis," and he accordingly directed his steps to the Ivory Hall.

"Bring wine," commanded he; and this being done, Florus was left alone with his visitor.

The friendship—if, indeed, it deserved the name—existing between the two men, had begun a year previously at Rome at the time when Florus was about

## "*Delenda est Hierosolyma!*"

to proceed to Judæa in the character of procurator. The king's sudden attachment was a fact somewhat puzzling to Florus, who, however highly he might think of himself, was nevertheless secretly conscious that his character was not such as to appeal to a man of Polemo's stamp. However, there the fact was: Polemo was evidently anxious to ingratiate himself into Florus' good will, for, finding that the Roman was ill-provided with money, he supplied him with a sum sufficient to enable the new procurator to make a splendid entry into Cæsarea. Since that time Florus had received additional sums from the king. Never was there a more willing and a more charming lender than Polemo. Content with receiving written acknowledgments of the amount, he did not press for repayment. Let not Florus disturb himself; he could pay at his leisure. Delighted at this easy way of obtaining money, Florus had, in the course of one short year, recklessly borrowed again and again, till in his more sober moments he trembled to think how great was his debt. If suddenly called upon to refund the whole at once, he would be a ruined man.

Of late Florus had grown very uneasy; the suspicion, nay, the certainty seized him that the king was trying to establish a sinister hold over him. There was in Polemo's grave air and peculiar smile something that seemed to say, "What I bid you do, you will do!" And Florus, feeling himself chained hand and foot, durst not resent the other's quiet air of mastership, for these were the days, be it observed, when the Roman law ordained that, whatever his rank (unless he belonged to the imperial family, who, of course, were above all law) the debtor unable to meet his liabilities must become the bond-slave of his creditor.

That Polemo had some end in view was certain, but what it could be, Florus had, so far, not the least inkling.

One fact, however, became increasingly clear. Polemo, who in days gone by had submitted to the rite of circumcision in order to gain the hand of Berenice, had now no love either for Judaism or the Jews, and spoke of the latter in terms of scorn and hatred.

Florus, disposed by nature to be harsh in dealing with the people under his rule, seemed to receive a tacit if not direct encouragement from Polemo; at any rate, he never left the king's presence without a determination to adopt new methods of repression, even though by so doing he should run the risk of losing the favor of Berenice. It seemed almost as if Polemo had set himself to counteract her influence; and in truth Florus, swayed first by one and then by the other, had vacillated strangely between right-doing and wrong-doing. His own natural disposition, however, inclined him to follow the sinister suggestions of Polemo, to such an extent as to make his procuratorship more infamous in character than any that had preceded it.

Florus had often wondered what was the attitude of Polemo's mind towards Berenice, but on this point he could never quite satisfy himself. When he had ventured, not without some diffidence, to intimate his intention of wooing the king's one-time wife, Polemo smiled, bidding him succeed—if he could! And after that, whenever the two met, Polemo never failed to inquire, not without a suggestion of sarcasm, how the other's suit was progressing.

He did the like on the present occasion.

" May her own Jewish devil, whom they call Satan, carry her off to Tartarus," was Florus' elegant rejoinder.

" Ah! stands the case so? I thought 'twould have that ending. 'Twere unwomanly of her to accept the love of a man already wedded, especially as she herself——"

Florus wondered what was coming next, but Polemo had checked himself as if about to say too much.

## "Delenda est Hierosolyma!"

"I came not, however, to talk of Berenice," he continued, "but of your own desperate position."

"A position for which you are in some measure responsible," said Florus.

"Nay, this secret league with robber Zealots is a folly all your own. I have advocated severity, but unfortunately your severities have never gone far enough for my purpose."

*His* purpose? thought Florus. Did he think, then, to govern Judæa through him? It would seem so.

"Your shafts have galled the animal merely without causing him to turn and fight."

"Be plainer with me."

"My desire has been to see the Jews rise in revolt by reason of the harshness of your administration. Your timid leniency has foiled my aim. The Jews have *not* risen."

Florus grew secretly angry to think that he had been a tool alternately to Polemo and Berenice, the more so as he had succeeded in giving satisfaction to neither.

"'Twere better to carry out my policy. To goad the Jews into rebellion is now your only hope of salvation. Your harsh dealing in the past will then have some justification. You can plead that the character of the people forced you against your will to be severe. Repressive measures are required by a people always on the verge of breaking out into war. Their revolt at this juncture will serve as a cloak to cover your former misdeeds."

Now, while Polemo was speaking thus, a new feeling came over Florus. He found his anger giving place to a tingling sensation of pleasure, as he recalled Berenice's words that she cared for nothing but her people and her religion. Here in the suggestion of Polemo was the opportunity of striking at her through these twin idols of her affection. Among all his schemes for hurting Berenice he had not thought of this. The very thing! What a splendid vengeance it would be if he could successfully goad the Jews into war, and then utilize that war as a means for destroying both nation and temple!

There have been monsters in history; Florus was one of them. His malevolence could contemplate with equanimity the extermination of a whole people provided only that he could hurt Berenice by the action; and if the groan of every dying victim should send an additional torture to her heart, why then, the more that died the better!

But, as he fell to reflecting, his ardor cooled somewhat.

The scheme was all very fine, but, in spite of Polemo's opinion to the contrary, seemed likely to recoil upon his own head. How could the governor that had purposely provoked a war hope to escape punishment at the hands of Cæsar? He put the question to Polemo, who received it with secret satisfaction, perceiving that Florus was quite willing to do the work, if only he could emerge from it with safety.

" Fear not. Having performed your task, you disappear for a time. My kingdom of Pontus shall afford you a safe asylum till the counselors who surround Nero shall have persuaded him that you have in reality done a good work."

" Humph! will they be able to do so? " asked Florus, dubiously.

" They will," answered Polemo. " Am I not the friend of Cæsar," he continued, exhibiting the ring whose stone was engraved with Nero's portrait, " entitled to stand at his right hand. I will show him that you are a keen patriot; that all your outrages so called, even your alliance with the Zealots, have been but the development of a profound and subtle policy, all directed towards one aim only—the good of Rome."

Florus, whose actions were never directed by anything but his own self-interest, grinned at the notion of being taken for a patriot.

## "*Delenda est Hierosolyma!*"

"The Jewish superstition," continued Polemo, "is spreading, not only among other nations, but also among the Romans themselves. The captive is taking captive the conqueror. The Roman Senate sees in this wide diffusion of Judaism a menace to the safety of the empire. How is it to be stopped? There is but one way: destroy the temple at Jerusalem, and you destroy the superstition. And since war is the only means of accomplishing this end, Roman statesmen would be grateful to Florus for initiating the war. Why should we show a false mercy to the Jew? Consider Rome's past policy towards him, and the return he makes for it.

"Rome does not seek, nor even wish, to impose her own gods upon any of the subject nations. But how different is the case with the Jew, who compasses sea and land to make one proselyte, and in the person of Poppæa has all but captured the imperial throne itself. Not a city of the empire but has its synagogue, though, forsooth, the Jew will not permit a single Gentile temple to be erected on the so-called holy soil of his own land—nay, would fly to arms should the thing be attempted.

"This people are seeking to Judaize the empire, and should this proselytism continue at its present rate of progress, Rome is doomed."

"How so?" asked the startled Florus.

"Because mankind, when Judaized, will turn, not to Rome, but to Jerusalem, as the capital of the world, and the seat of ideas. The high priest, and not Cæsar, will wield the scepter of empire; and, since toleration is unknown to the Jew, Oriental barbarism will triumph over Western civilization. Three times a year shall we be compelled to appear at Jerusalem. The laws of the Twelve Tables will give place to the precepts of the rabbis. Homer will be burnt in the market square; the philosophy of Plato superseded by the Pentateuch of Moses. Our circus games, Olympian contests, and theatrical plays will cease. Sculpture will be forbidden; the fairest masterpieces of Phidias will perish beneath the hammer of fanatics. The beautiful temples of Greece will be given over to the flames—there must be but one temple only, that of the jealous Hebrew God. All that gives to life brightness, and beauty, and joy, will vanish forever from the world, and we must find our chief pleasure in circumcision and the synagogue, in fastings and Sabbaths."

"By the gods, Polemo, you frighten me!" exclaimed Florus, contemplating with dismay this picture of a Judaized world.

"I trust I do, for then you will the more readily carry out my designs against the hateful race of fanatics, who will do all I have said, if they be not checked. The existence of the Jew and his proselyte ought not to be tolerated by the Roman; their very creed teaches them disloyalty."

"In what way?"

"How is the power of Rome maintained? Only by its army. Abolish the legions, and how long, think you, would it be before the Northern barbarians would come pouring over the Rhine and the Danube bent on our overthrow? What part do the Jew and his proselyte take in our common defense? None! Let a Roman subject become a disciple of the synagogue, and though called upon, he obstinately refuses to serve in the army, on the plea that he may have to march or to fight on the Sabbath day, a thing forbidden by his religion. Rome has had to yield to them, and hence the unwritten law exempting Jews and their proselytes from military impressment. The Gaul and the Greek, the Spaniard and the Egyptian, must be told off to defend the empire: you and I, dear Florus, must shed our blood, in order, forsooth, that the Jew may have leisure to trade upon us, and grow rich."

"A piece of injustice, the very thought of which makes one savage," commented Florus.

## "Delenda est Hierosolyma!"

"The Jew is *in* the empire, but not *of* it; he enjoys its advantages, but refuses to pay for them. The wealth made by him in huckstering is not employed to benefit the province where earned, but is sent to the temple at Jerusalem, there to lie dormant. The drain of gold and silver to the temple is so serious a matter as to have affected at times the currency of a province, compelling its governor to forbid the export.[7]

"Why this piling up in the temple of treasure, amounting to millions of aurei? Why? Because war cannot be carried on without gold. This hoard, which the Jews would have us regard as merely the religious offerings of pious souls, is in reality being accumulated for the purpose of waging war against Rome."

"I have often thought so myself," said Florus, who had never thought anything of the kind.

"You heard Simon the Zealot say that he had put his gold where no Roman could touch it; what place did he mean if not the sanctuary of the temple?—a sanctuary to which even Cæsar himself is denied access. I warrant that the escaped Zealot will find asylum there, for before he took to the mountains he was known to be the friend of Eleazar, the captain of the temple, an officer whom you know to be outspoken in his hatred of Rome. But to return from individuals to the nation. When they deem the occasion ripe, they will of themselves declare war, a war certain to begin at the passover time; for, on the pretext of coming up to the feast, the Jews and their proselytes can be conveniently summoned from every quarter of the empire. Rome hath never liked these gatherings, and with reason. Their numbers grow year by year: at the last passover the pilgrims swelled the population of Jerusalem to the number of three hundred myriads. Ye gods! Think of it! Three million fanatics all burning with a hatred of Rome allowed to assemble in a city, said to be the strongest in the world! What can the Senate be thinking of? Why should we wait till this nation be grown more powerful? Even now there are rumors of alliances with nations outside the borders of the empire—with Parthians beyond the Euphrates, and with the Arabs of the desert. Every year increases *their* strength, and *our* peril. But let their city and their temple be given to the flames—which is what must happen in the event of war—and their religion comes to an end; the day of proselytism is over; the pilgrimages cease, for who will have faith in a deity powerless to protect his temple? ' The gods of Rome,' 'twill be said, ' are more potent than he of Judæa.' Judaism once destroyed, the empire is safe. It is in your power, Florus, to do this, and I——"

"*Satis!*" cried the procurator. "You have said enough to convince me that the destroying of this nation is a patriotic and righteous deed."

But Polemo had still another argument left, more powerful than any other. He had purposely kept it to the last.

He drew forth a small roll of parchment notes, which Florus recognized as his own monetary acknowledgments.

"On the day that the Jews declare war, I shall burn these without asking for repayment."

# CHAPTER VII

### THE JOURNEY TO JERUSALEM

THE first rays of morning sunlight were gilding the stately towers of Cæsarea as the soldiers of the Italian Cohort filed through the southern gate of the city.

They were marching on foot to Jerusalem, a journey of some sixty miles, marching by the military road made by the Romans themselves, a highway so well and durably paved that portions of it still remain after the lapse of nearly two thousand years.

A little in advance of these troops, and justly proud of their fine and martial appearance, rode the tribune Terentius Rufus, and at his side was Crispus, mounted likewise upon a curveting steed.

On the previous day Nero's edict had been posted up in the public places of Cæsarea; it gave the precedency to the Greeks.

Now, though it was plain to the least observant that the city was seething with excitement caused by the triumph of the one faction and the mortification of the other, Rufus and his cohort had been commanded by the procurator to return to Jerusalem on the ground that all was quiet at Cæsarea!

" And Florus himself," remarked Rufus, " is withdrawing to Sebaste with his legion, so that the city will be entirely denuded of troops. Pluto take me!" he continued, knitting his brows in perplexity, "if I can understand his conduct save upon the supposition that he wants to kindle the torch of war."

The two rode on in silence for a while. Then Crispus, who from time to time had been glancing back at the marching troops, said, with a somewhat perplexed air:

"Rufus, there is something lacking in thy cohort. What is it? Ah! I have it. The eagle! Where is it?"

"Purposely left behind in the Prætorium at Cæsarea."

"Name of Mars!—why?"

"In going through Judæa we have to pay respect to the Jewish superstition, which, as you know, regards all images with abhorrence."

Crispus was for the moment dumb with indignation.

"What!" cried he. "We must not carry our standards in a country conquered by us? Doth Rome rule Judæa, or Judæa Rome?"

"Judæa doth, in this matter at least, rule Rome."

"I pray you, Rufus," said Crispus, reining in his steed, "bid a centurion return for the eagle."

But Rufus shook his head.

"Pontius Pilate was of like mind with you. He made his first entry into Jerusalem with figured banners. For three days and two nights the Jewish populace howled, raged, and wept round his Prætorium. At the end of the third day he sent his troops among them with drawn swords. The Jews flung themselves prostrate, bared their necks, and cried that they would rather die than see their laws broken.

"What could dismayed Pilate do? He couldn't massacre a whole people in the first week of his government. Compelled sullenly to yield, he sent the ensigns back to Cæsarea. Since that day no troops dare venture into Jerusalem save with plain banners."

"Forbidden to carry the eagles," muttered Crispus wrathfully. "How long shall this be?"

"Till our next war with them, when we shall more thoroughly vindicate the supremacy of Rome, and be masters in our own house."

"When will that be?"

"'Tis but a matter of days, in my opinion."

## The Journey to Jerusalem 85

Days! To Crispus this was startling news, and yet not unwelcome.

"I carry with me a sealed letter," continued Rufus, "addressed to King Agrippa, who is at Jerusalem. He is, as you know, the brother of the Princess Berenice, the nominator of the high priest, and the supreme guardian of the temple treasures. The purport of the letter I know not, but if I may judge from Florus' sinister smile as he handed me the missive, it contains some command which Agrippa will be loth to execute. Should the Jews of Jerusalem support the king in his attitude, it may prove the beginning of an outbreak whose end no man can foresee. I may be wrong, Crispus, but I have a presentiment that in this letter we are carrying the fate of Judæa."

Crispus frowned. He loved fighting, but it seemed to him there would be little honor and glory gained in reducing to submission a people goaded to war by the deliberate oppression of an unjust governor.

The road traversed by the Romans wound southwards through the flower-enameled meads that constitute the Plain of Sharon, never more lovely than when seen in the soft sunshine of a May morning.

Now and again in their march the Romans would pass a gayly-clad group of Jewish country-folk, many of them accompanied by asses and mules, laden with timber.

"Pilgrims bound for Jerusalem," explained Rufus in answer to Crispus' inquiries. "Within a few days comes the Festival of the Xylophoria, or the Wood-offering, when the Jews are accustomed to bring to the temple supplies of timber sufficient to keep the sacrificial fires going for a year."

At a wayside spring a somewhat numerous caravan had made a brief halt to refill their water-skins, and to refresh their beasts of burden. The air was lively with the sound of timbrels, of songs, and of dances.

The approach of the clanging cohort, with its swinging martial stride, put a sudden stop to the mirth.

"The Romans! the Romans!" was the cry.

Silent of tongue, but with eyes that looked unmistakable hatred, the pilgrims drew aside to let the legionaries pass. One fierce-looking Jew, bolder than his fellows, cried aloud: "To Gehenna with all Gentiles!"

Rufus rode past with a smile of contempt.

"Yon fellow knows full well," said he, "that if I choose, I can hang him to the nearest tree, and yet the knowledge of that fact cannot keep him from expressing his hatred of the Romans."

"What is the Gehenna to which he would consign us?" asked Crispus, who was not so well versed in Hebrew matters as Rufus.

"The Jewish Tartarus, a place of flame and torment, to which you and I, no matter how virtuous our life, are destined to be sent, according to the saying of the rabbis, 'The Gentiles are only so much fuel for Gehenna.'"

"They don't love us, these Jews," laughed Crispus.

"Hatred of the Roman is drawn in with the maternal milk. You see now the necessity for maintaining so large a military force in Judæa. Africa, once the seat of the Carthaginian empire, is kept in order by a single legion. One legion, too, suffices for warlike Spain. Greece, once so great in deeds of arms, hath no legion at all within her bounds. These turbulent Jews require three legions. Think of it! Thirty-six thousand men perpetually under arms in a province no larger than our native Latium, so restless are these Jews, so hostile to our rule."

"Why that stoppage in front?" said Crispus, glancing ahead at a group of distant pilgrims who had come to a sudden stand-still in a way that threatened to impede the march of the on-coming Romans.

"That," replied Rufus, "is another proof of Jewish

# The Journey to Jerusalem

contempt for the foreigner. The stone you see by the roadside marks the border of two provinces. At present we are in heathen Phœnicia; pass that stone, and we are in holy Judæa. Your Hebrew, on arriving at the frontier, takes off his sandals and carefully wipes them, lest he should pollute the sacred soil of Judæa by bringing upon it the profane dust of other lands."

Crispus looked, and saw that it was even as Rufus had said. Every Jew, upon coming to the frontier-stone, removed his shoes, and either wiped or shook them, a somewhat useless cleansing, seeing that a minute afterwards the six hundred men of the Italian Cohort were bringing in Phœnician dust with them.

"You are a patrician of Rome," said Rufus, addressing Crispus, "proud of your pure and lofty lineage, but know this, that if the vilest beggar in Jerusalem should be touched by you on the eve of the passover he would deem himself so unclean as to be unable to keep the feast. Purification by bathing would entitle him to the privilege of the supplementary passover held seven days later to meet such cases."

A march of some twenty-five miles brought the cohort to Antipatris, a military station guarding the line of communication between Cæsarea and Jerusalem. Within the barracks of this town Rufus found ample accommodation for his troops. At nightfall he and Crispus ascended to the battlements of the Roman castle; from their lofty position the two could see the whole extent of Sharon, from the mountains to the sea, whitened by the silvery moonlight.

Far and wide over the landscape gleamed the fires of the Jewish pilgrims, camping for the night under the leafy terebinth or by the wayside spring.

"List!" said Rufus, with uplifted finger.

Floating upward from the valley below came the sound of many voices conjoined in a mournful melody. Now and again Crispus could faintly catch some of the words of the refrain.

"If I forget thee, O Jerusalem, let my right hand forget her cunning!"

As the breeze wavered, the voices rose and fell with a weird and plaintive effect, and Crispus thrilled as he listened. There was, to his way of thinking, a sob in every cadence—"How long, O Lord, how long?"—a wild appeal to heaven for vengeance against their present oppressor, the Roman.

A spirit of profound melancholy fell upon Crispus as he contemplated the character of this strange Eastern nation. In his journey that day every face seen by him, every incident that had happened, gave proof that though Jew and Roman touched each other at a hundred points, they were nevertheless as far apart as if seas rolled between them.

While all other nations of the empire, including even Greece, so renowned in arts, arms, and learning, were content to live peaceably, nay happily under the shadow of the eagle-wings of Rome, the Jew maintained an attitude of sullen hostility to his conqueror.

How long was this antagonism to last? Was the Jew to remain forever a thorn in the side of the empire, or must the solution of the problem come, as Rufus was convinced it would, in the shape of an exterminating war?

Next morning at sunrise the march was resumed. The road, that had hitherto followed a line parallel with the coast, now turned inland, and leaving the maritime plain behind them, the Romans began to ascend the picturesque ravines that wind towards the rocky tableland upon which Jerusalem is built.

Gophna, another military station, fifteen miles distant from the holy city, was their second stopping-place.

At daybreak they began the third and final stage of their journey, along a road dazzlingly white and dusty.

At the ninth hour of the morning the cohort was toiling through an upland ravine. In front of them

## The Journey to Jerusalem 89

at some distance was a numerous body of wood-bearing pilgrims. Suddenly, as their van gained the highest point of the road, a thrilling shout broke from it, followed by a precipitate hurrying forward on the part of all of those in the rear.

"Yerûshalaïm! Yerûshalaïm!" was the cry that rang out on the morning air, the cry of the Jews.

"Hagiopolis! Hagiopolis!" exclaimed the Greek proselytes.

"Hierosolyma!" said Rufus quietly.

Impelled by a natural curiosity, Crispus pressed forward his steed, and, as he gained the northern height of Scopus, the whole city at one flash burst full upon his view.

He drew rein, and, with a lively interest, gazed upon the famous city—"*longe clarissima urbium Orientis*" —whose origin was lost far back in the night of antiquity, a city gray with age ere ever a stone of Rome was laid!

A century earlier Jerusalem had presented a dull and even squalid appearance; but, thanks to that magnificent despot, Herod the Great, a monarch distinguished by his taste for Grecian architecture, the city was now a dream of beauty, with its imperial mantle of proud towers; its marble palaces gleaming through the clear, transparent air of a Syrian morn; its stately colonnades and triumphal arches, interspersed with the foliage of the tall and graceful palm; and, above all, the pure, white temple, "a mount of alabaster, topped with golden spires," flashing in the morning sunlight with a splendor that forced the eyes to turn aside.

Crispus looked at it, and thought of his dream.

"Mark me," said Rufus, "it will never be well with Rome till yon fair city be leveled with the dust, and the plow passed over it."

Prophetic words!

If those Jews, among whom Crispus and Rufus were now making their way, could but have foreseen the future, their daggers would have flashed in the sunny air, and the two Romans would have been no more!

The supreme emotion evoked among the peasant pilgrims by the sight of the holy city was expressed in characteristic fashion. Some laughed aloud in the insanity of joy; others, with clasped hands and tears in their eyes, sank upon their knees, and not a few among the women fainted. Some pulled off their sandals, and walked barefoot towards the city, as though the way were hallowed ground; others assumed their richest robe, as if they were about to enter a holy synagogue. One member of the throng, a Levite, lifting up a sonorous voice, began the chanting of a psalm, appropriate to the occasion; and the refrain was immediately taken up by the whole multitude, slow-moving towards the city:

" The hill of Zion is a fair place, and the joy of the whole earth; upon the north side lieth the citadel of the Great King."

" Now, if by the Great King is meant Cæsar, which is to be doubted," remarked Rufus, " these fanatics are right. Thou seest yon edifice, Crispus, towering high above the temple. 'Tis my Roman citadel, of whose hospitality you must partake."

Making their way through a region of groves and gardens, adorned with the mansions of the wealthy residents, the Roman troops entered the city, and threading its narrow, winding streets, came to their quarters in the citadel Antonia, so named by Herod the Great in memory of his friend and patron, Marc Antony, its usual name among the Jews being Baris, or the Tower.

This fortress occupied the summit of a lofty rock, separated from the mount on which the temple stood by a deep ravine, crossed by a line of arches. As the temple—in itself a stronghold—dominated and looked down upon the city, so did Antonia dominate and look

## The Journey to Jerusalem

down upon the temple. Far above the golden roof of the sanctuary towered its haughty battlements, adorned with the standard bearing the significant letters, S.P.Q.R. Upon that proud banner, the visible symbol of Roman dominion, no Jew ever looked save with a wrathful curse.

Leaving his men in their quarters, Rufus, losing no time, set off, accompanied by Crispus, for the palace of Agrippa, bent on delivering to that monarch the letter of Florus.

It was still early morning, and the streets, thronged by pilgrims, new-arriving, presented an animated and busy aspect, which would disappear later, when the heat of noontide would usher in the quietude of the siesta.

Suddenly, high above the sounds produced by the restless throng, there rose a voice, and one so weird that Crispus had never before heard the like. At its hollow tone, voices, sounds, footsteps, ceased. A hush as of death fell over all.

Along the middle of the street, and moving at a pace that never changed from its slow and measured uniformity, came a wild-eyed, melancholy figure, clad in a single robe of camel's hair, and tied at the waist with a leathern girdle.

His arms were raised to heaven; he glanced neither to right nor left; his face was like a mask of stone, set in one unchanging expression of woe.

No man stopped him; no man questioned him; all knew the uselessness of it.

He was a familiar figure to the people, but familiarity had never lessened one thrill of the awe felt by them whenever he appeared.

"A voice from the East, a voice from the West, a voice from the fours winds, a voice against Jerusalem and the holy house, a voice against the bridegrooms and the brides, and a voice against this whole people. Woe, woe to Jerusalem!"

The people stood, as they always stood when he passed by, immovable, silent, wondering. Did they behold a madman, or one in whom was the spirit of the ancient prophets?

"Who is yon fellow?" asked Crispus, watching the figure as it receded in the distance.

"Jesus, the son of Hanan. 'Tis four years since he began to appear at the yearly feasts, traversing the streets and uttering the woe that we have just heard. Brought before the tribunal of the procurator Albinus, and questioned, he would answer only, 'Woe, woe to Jerusalem!' Though scourged till his bones were laid bare, he maintained during it all a dry eye and a stony countenance, uttering the while his weird plaint. He seems to be, not a man, but a voice."

"The voice of some god, it may be," muttered Crispus, upon whose mind the incident had left a singular impression. "Doomed Troy had its Cassandra, whom none would believe until too late. So, too, Jerusalem seems to have its prophet, to whom this foolish people, that dream of war, would do well to give heed."

Resuming their walk, the two friends ascended the slope of Mount Zion, and came to the old Asamonean Palace, the residence of King Agrippa.

"Aren't you coming in with me?" asked Rufus, as Crispus hesitated. "We may encounter the Princess Berenice."

Crispus turned away, saying he would await his friend's return in the Xystus close by. Rufus looked after him in some wonderment.

"For the future," he muttered, "I had better refrain from mentioning Berenice's name; it seems to trouble him."

Rufus, on being admitted to the presence of Agrippa, found him seated at a table. In person he was tall and slender. Delicate and refined in features, and dressed in the height of Jewish fashion, he presented, at any rate in the eyes of the sturdy Roman, a some-

# The Journey to Jerusalem

what effeminate appearance. On one side of him was his sister Berenice, who had arrived at Jerusalem the preceding night; on the other was an elderly man with a hooked nose, thin lips, and a yellow polished forehead, who looked like a typical rabbi, as indeed he was, being none other than Simeon, the son of the celebrated Gamaliel. Before him lay an ink-horn and a parchment scroll; between his fingers was a calamus or reed pen. Evidently he had been composing some document with the aid of his royal friends, and all three were looking as if very well pleased with their work. Rufus wondered whether they would look so well pleased after reading the document that *he* was bringing for them.

"This prayer," said Simeon, laying his hand upon the parchment-scroll before him, "this prayer will serve as a fan to winnow the chaff from the wheat."

The three looked up as Rufus entered. He, being the commandant of Antonia, was a great man in Jerusalem, and they therefore received him affably.

"And what would the excellent Rufus with us?" asked Agrippa.

The excellent Rufus handed the letter to the king, who took it between his delicate jeweled fingers and broke the seal. While he was doing this Berenice rose from the table, and drawing near to Rufus addressed him in a low tone.

"Did you leave Crispus at Cæsarea?"

Her tone and look, betraying more than ordinary interest in the absent Roman, came as a revelation to Rufus.

"As I live," he thought, "this woman loves Crispus." Aloud he answered, "Nay, princess, he hath accompanied me to Jerusalem."

"Where is he now?" she asked eagerly.

And Rufus, knowing that it would bring trouble into those beautiful eyes were she to learn that the phlegmatic Crispus preferred the miscellaneous crowd in the

Xystus to the attractions of the Asamonean Palace, replied, " I left him in Antonia."

What other question she might have asked was interrupted by Agrippa, who, having mastered the contents of the epistle, was frowning terribly. He called his sister to his side and handed her the letter. She knit her brows as she read, and in turn passed the missive to Simeon, who, after duly perusing it, seemed to be more angry than his royal patrons.

They were quiet for a time, all thinking.

" Submit not to this demand," said Berenice passionately, addressing her brother, " since submission will be quoted as a precedent; we shall be virtually acknowledging his right to make such claim. One oppression will lead to another."

" True, but on the other hand," returned Agrippa, " if he should seek to make good his demand by force of arms 'twill lead to tumult and bloodshed—nay, even to open rebellion, for at this present time the popular mind is strung to a high state of tension by prophets who predict the near advent of the Messiah's kingdom."

Turning to Rufus he said aloud:

" You know the contents of this letter? "

" Indeed, no. I was told no more than to press for an immediate answer."

" I will defer my reply till to-night."

Rufus bowed and withdrew.

" *I* am the cause of this," said Berenice sorrowfully.

" You, princess! How? " exclaimed Simeon.

" This is Florus' way of taking vengeance upon me because I have declined to listen to his wooing."

# CHAPTER VIII

#### WHAT HAPPENED IN THE ROYAL SYNAGOGUE

THE heat of noontide had passed, and Crispus, under the guidance of Rufus, was spending his time in viewing the city. It might be thought that the Temple would be the first place visited by him, but this Rufus reserved for the night, when, by virtue of his office as commandant of Antonia, he would be able to exhibit that edifice—or as much of it as was permissible for a Gentile to see—by the tender light of the moon, and freed from the crowds that frequented its courts during the day.

" And what place is that? " asked Crispus, pointing to a quadrangular edifice of white stone, over whose portal was written in Hebrew characters the word " *Shalom,*" or " Peace."

" The Royal Synagogue, so called," answered Rufus, necessity here compelling him to break a certain injunction he had laid upon himself, " so called as having been raised by the Princess Berenice at her own private expense. Among the Jews, if you would gain a character for piety, build a synagogue."

" Is the worship going on? "

The proximity of a sun-dial enabled Rufus to give an answer. " It is a little before the ninth hour, which constitutes the *Arabith,* or time of evening prayer. Worship will begin shortly. You see the pious are already hurrying thither."

" I have never yet seen a synagogue service," said Crispus, " and would fain see one."

" I deplore your taste, but for friendship's sake I'll accompany you. 'Tis the fashion of the Jews, as you see, to run to their synagogue, by way of showing their eagerness for divine worship. But we, who are dignified Romans, can take it more leisurely."

Discoursing thus, Rufus drew near the Royal Synagogue.

"A small edifice, this, but neat," he continued. "Now if you want to see something really splendid in a synagogic shape, go to Alexandria and view the Diapleuston, with its seventy golden chairs for the seventy members of the Sanhedrim; and as for size, so vast is it that the signal for the 'Amen' has to be given by the waving of a flag. 'Tis a striking scene!"

As they stood upon the threshold, Rufus addressed the decurion that was in attendance upon him. "It is forbidden to wear arms in the synagogue; therefore, Quintus, take charge of my good sword, and tarry here till I come again. Doff we our sandals, Crispus, for 'tis the custom to enter barefoot."

Access was gained to the interior of the synagogue by a vestibule. Here stood the doorkeeper. He recognized in Rufus the commandant of Antonia, and at the latter's desire conducted the two visitors to a place at the rear, where, screened by a pillar, they could see without being seen.

The interior of the synagogue was very similar to that of a basilica, being oblong in shape and divided by pillars into aisles.

The worshipers were ranged, the men on the one side and the women on the other, a partition about four feet high running between them—a striking contrast to the modern synagogic usage of placing the women in side galleries, screened with lattice-work.

At the farther end of the building was a platform or daïs, on which stood the ark, or coffer, containing the rolls of the sacred books. Before it rose a golden candlestick, with seven branches.

"A copy of the one in the temple," observed Rufus.

# What Happened in the Royal Synagogue 97

In front of the platform was a line of seats, whose occupants, mostly aged rabbis, sat facing the congregation. These were the places of honor, the " chief seats " so much coveted by every Jew; and here, by special privilege, as being the foundress of the synagogue, sat the Princess Berenice.

" Who is that sitting on the right of the princess? " asked Crispus.

For reply Rufus drew forth a golden coin, and pointed to its obverse, which bore the legend, " Agrippa, the Great King."

Crispus, knowing that Agrippa's realm of Chalcis was of less extent than many a Roman estate, asked:

" In what is he great? "

" In his own esteem, and in the knowledge of his own law, being expert ' in all customs and questions which are among the Jews.' We shall perhaps have the pleasure of hearing him read from the Law and the Prophets, since he is fond of so doing."

" And what is that short marble pillar at one side of the daïs? "

" That is the Red Column. Offenders against synagogic discipline are tied to it and scourged."

Rufus had scarcely said this when the people rose to their feet, the customary attitude for prayer.

The shelîach, or " angel," who presided over this part of the worship was Simeon, the son of Gamaliel, and he began with an announcement that caused no little surprise among the members of the congregation.

There was to be made, beginning with that very day, an addition to the current liturgy of the synagogue, an addition necessitated by the conduct of those impious sectaries, the Nazarenes.

" Who are the Nazarenes? " whispered Crispus.

" The Christians," replied Rufus.

It was well known—so ran the tenor of Simeon's remarks—that in spite of their changed faith, these apostates, being in no way recognizable, since they preserved the outward semblance of orthodox Jews, were in the habit of resorting to the synagogues, and of joining in the worship, thus defiling the holy people by their presence. As such mixed worship could not be acceptable to God, the true Jew must take steps to preserve himself from such defilement. Therefore for the future the initiatory prayer would be of a character such as no Nazarene could join in without at the same time abjuring his faith, since it contained curses directed against Jesus, the son of Panther.' That prayer he would now proceed to recite, and let each member of the congregation mark well his neighbor, and take due note of him who should refuse to ratify it with the customary " Amen."

" Who is Jesus, the son of Panther? " asked Crispus.

" The same as he whom we call Christus. His disciples say that he was born of a pure virgin—a manifest impossibility. The Jews, with more reason, assert that his mother committed adultery with a soldier named Panther."

Now, as Crispus was passing his eyes over the congregation at this juncture, he happened to see what had hitherto escaped his notice. Vashti was standing among the worshipers. She was pale, very pale; the expression of her face, the very attitude of her figure, were suggestive of mental distress.

For a moment Crispus was puzzled to account for her agitation; then the truth like a flash of light darted into his mind. Vashti had a secret, and one that could no longer be kept hidden by her unless she chose to play the traitress to her conscience, and that, he felt certain, she would not do.

" Cursed be Jesus, the Son of Panther! "

A shiver passed over Vashti; she compressed her lips tightly, while from every other Jewish mouth there flew an " Amen!" uttered with a vehemence that spoke of a fierce and vindictive hatred.

## What Happened in the Royal Synagogue

Ere Simeon could come to his next sentence, a man by the partition—it was Sadas, Berenice's freedman—who had been intently watching Vashti, suddenly raised his arm to attract attention, and cried in a voice that penetrated to every corner of the congregation:

"Holy rabbi, here is one who refuses to say 'Amen' to that anathema."

Amid the breathless silence that followed, all eyes turned, first upon the speaker, then upon the person pointed out by his accusatory finger.

The congregation doubted. This maiden, so regular in her attendance at the synagogue, daughter of the rabbi Hyrcanus, and ward of the orthodox Josephus, an apostate? It could not be.

"Vashti, daughter of Hyrcanus," said Simeon gravely, "do you refuse to join in the common voice of the synagogue?"

Vashti was silent.

"Cursed be Jesus, the son of Panther! Do you not say 'Amen' to this anathema?"

At this, which to her mind was blasphemy, the girl's spirit took fire.

"I do not. It is our duty not to curse, but to bless."

"Are you wiser than our fathers and the prophets who were wont to curse the enemies of the faith?"

"They belonged to a covenant that is past. Besides, even they did not curse the dead."

"Then curse we the living!" cried Simeon angrily. "Cursed be the whole tribe of Christians! Do you say 'Amen' to that?"

"In doing so I should be cursing myself."

From the age of twelve, her time of joining the synagogue, Vashti, by reason of the sweetness of her disposition and of her liberality in alms-giving, had won the favor of the whole congregation. But now, all in a moment, that favor was withdrawn. Jewish bigotry asserted itself. The knowledge that she had become a

Christian converted friends into enemies. She found herself surrounded by dark and scowling faces.

"Judgment!" cried Sadas, the man who had accused her; and a hundred voices took up the cry, "Judgment!"

In the Hebrew word for synagogue—Beth-din, or House of Judgment—is expressed one of its peculiarities; besides being a place of worship, the synagogue was also—and this with the sanction of the Romans themselves—a judicial court for the trial of such offenders as were accused of violating the precepts of Judaism.

"Let the damsel be brought hither," said Simeon in cold judicial tones.

The many hands put forth to push her forward were needless; of her own free will she walked from her place to the front of the congregation.

Her girlish figure standing all alone before the crowd of wrathful spectators failed to elicit their sympathy; the gray-haired elders, who were her judges, had likewise hearts of marble; neither youth nor beauty had power to influence them in the matter of a person apostatizing to the hateful creed of the Nazarenes.

"Damsel," said Simeon, "we require no witnesses of thy guilt. Out of thine own mouth thou standest condemned as being a Christian. Yet are we minded to give thee time for reflection. Thou mayest, if thou wilt, withdraw thy statement."

"I cannot withdraw the statement, for it is true. I am a Christian."

Fierce cries broke forth from the assembly: "Traitress! Apostate! Nazarene!"

"How long hast thou been a Christian?"

"'Tis a matter of a few weeks only."

"You have received the baptism prescribed by this heresy?"

Vashti signified assent.

"Who was he that baptized thee?"

# What Happened in the Royal Synagogue 101

"I may not name him."

"Doth our city contain many of this faith?"

"Very many."

"Name some," commanded Simeon. This he said, not believing that she would do so, but knowing that her refusal would add to the wrath of the assembly.

"Even among the heathen to betray one's friends is counted base. How much more, then, among Christians?"

"By revealing their names you will be doing much towards redeeming yourself from the punishment that otherwise will most surely come upon you."

"Not even to redeem myself from death will I betray my friends."

"Come, girl, be not obstinate. Who were they that persuaded you to adopt Christianity?"

"The Law and the Prophets chiefly."

"You blaspheme."

"Nay, give me leave to speak, and I will show you that our so-called new faith is but the fulfillment and and completion of the old."

"This damsel resembles her master Paul," sneered Agrippa. "With a little talking she thinks to make us Christians."

Simeon, seeking to prejudice her still more in the opinion of the narrow-minded Jews, to whom all Gentile learning was an abomination, continued:

"You have given much time to the study of the Greek writings?"

"As did your father Gamaliel," was the quiet reply. "If it were a virtue in him, why seek to make it a fault in me?"

"Hear, O Israel," said Simeon, addressing the assembly, "in my father's school were a thousand students, of whom five hundred studied the wisdom that is in the Law; and to-day they are all living, and held in honor. And there were five hundred who studied the Grecian vanities, and to-day there is not one of

them alive."' He paused for a moment, and then put
the customary question:
"Can anyone here present show just cause why punishment should not be inflicted upon Vashti, daughter
of Hyrcanus?"

Vashti looked round upon the assembly, but in the
words of the Psalmist she had become a stranger to
her brethren, an alien among her mother's children.
There was none that would speak a good word for
her.

"There are two persons here," said Vashti, "who
can testify, if they would, that my change of creed
is not deserving of punishment."

"Who are these witnesses?"

"King Agrippa for one."

That monarch, upon hearing himself appealed to,
regarded Vashti with a languid and scornful gaze.

"Thou callest upon *me* to testify in thy favor?"

"O king, after Paul of Tarsus had set forth his
tenets before your tribunal, did you not say, 'This
man doeth nothing worthy of death or of bonds'? My
faith is but the same with his. Since you pronounced
*him* innocent, how can you declare *me* guilty?"

These words put the king in a very awkward dilemma. Deny them he could not; to confirm them would
be equivalent to a declaration of her innocence. He
shrugged his shoulders, and, like the coward that he
was, took refuge in silence.

"And who is the other witness?" asked Simeon, after
a very awkward pause.

"Yourself," replied Vashti. "Will *you* not plead
for me, you whose grandsire Simeon held the infant
Jesus in his arms, calling him 'The glory of the people
of Israel'?—you, whose sire Gamaliel, speaking of the
apostles of Christ, said, 'Refrain from these men, and
let them alone'?"

Simeon's face darkened, and he turned away. Every
word spoken by Vashti did but increase the wrath of

## What Happened in the Royal Synagogue 103

her judges, who wanted, not argument, but submission and recantation.

No more questions were asked. The council, drawing together, conferred in whispers around the chairs of Agrippa and Berenice.

Having agreed in their verdict, the judges returned to their seats—all save one, a noble and gentle-looking elder, who said with a ring of indignation in his voice:

"I protest!"

But his protest availed nothing. Unable to save Vashti or to bear the sight of her punishment, he walked from the synagogue amid the somewhat angry murmurs of the assembly.

"Who is he?" asked Crispus.

"Johanan ben Zacchai, wisest and best of the rabbis. Though he himself is an orthodox Pharisee, his father Zacchai, or—to Grecize the name—Zacchæus, a wealthy publican of Jericho, is said to have been a secret Christian. Hence his sympathy for poor Vashti. Are you going to intervene on her behalf?"

"Anon. Let us first see what her punishment is to be."

Simeon now rose to pronounce judgment.

"Vashti, daughter of Hyrcanus, your punishment is a twofold one; you will receive forty lashes save one, and you will be shorn of your tresses."

The vindictive character of the sentence set Crispus' blood on fire. "To be shorn of her tresses?" he murmured. "Such a suggestion as that could proceed only from a woman's mind. Princess Berenice, your hand is in this."

Vashti, on hearing her doom, swayed, and would have fallen to the ground but for the officers who supported her on each side. She had expected some such penalty as the payment of a fine, or excommunication from the synagogue. But the loss of her hair—the glory of a woman! And *scourging!* The mere physical pain of this last was as nothing in her eyes compared with the horror of being stripped to the waist in the sight of all the congregation.

A mist swam before her eyes; her face, pale before, now became deathly white; she tried to speak, but her tongue failed her.

Looking for all the world like one insane, she turned her swimming gaze upon the assembly, but saw no pity in their set faces. What punishment could be too severe for a Nazarene? Nay, verily, let her be thankful that her doom was not stoning, as it assuredly would have been but for the humiliating fact that the death penalty required the sanction of the hateful governor, Florus.

And now appeared the executioner carrying the dreadful whip, a wooden shaft with three long ox-hide thongs, thirteen strokes from which made the conventional thirty-nine stripes. The Law allowed forty, but the Jews, affecting to be merciful, diminished that number by one.

"Pull off her garment, and bind her to the Red Column."

At these dreadful words Vashti, rendered strong by agony, broke from her guards, and moving swiftly forward fell on her knees before Berenice.

"Princess, you are a woman. Have pity on me. If I must be scourged let me—let me retain my vesture."

The two officers who had followed Vashti fell back at a sign from Berenice. Bending forward from her seat, she said in a whisper:

"*My hour of triumph now. It was yours at Cæsarea.*"

At her chilling tone Vashti shrank back. Her eyes became big with horror as the truth suddenly flashed upon her that the whole synagogue proceeding was a plot, formed by the jealousy of Berenice, who feared that Vashti was seeking to win the love of Crispus. Suspecting her to be a Christian, she had induced Simeon to compose the new prayer, purposing by this

## What Happened in the Royal Synagogue 105

means to wreak her vengeance upon the girl whose beauty had been preferred to her own.

This sudden revelation of the character of the princess, the subtlety of her plot, the wickedness of masking it under the guise of religion, came upon Vashti with a shock so great as almost to drive the scourging from her mind. For the moment her only thought was, how could the princess be so wicked?

"Officers, the lash!" said Berenice, spurning the suppliant girl with her foot.

"Hold, let the maiden be!" cried a voice coming from the rear of the synagogue.

There was a great start on the part of Berenice, who knew not till then that Crispus was in the synagogue.

Vashti started, but it was with joy. Gone in a moment was her sense of fear. She turned her eyes from the two men who held her to the stately figure of the Roman stalking up the floor of the synagogue, determination written upon his countenance. Her trusting and beautiful smile set Berenice's heart thrilling with pangs of jealousy impossible to describe. Her plot for the humiliation of Vashti seemed likely to end in creating another link of sympathy between the two whom she would fain keep apart.

Amid a death-like silence Crispus, followed by the faithful Rufus, made his way to the front. There was in his cold eye a gleam that caused the two officers to let go Vashti, who, released from their hold, would have fallen but for the supporting arm of Crispus.

He turned to face the angry assembly, who were beginning to murmur at seeing the hateful "apostate" snatched from their hands by an authority equally hateful. A stranger in Jerusalem, Crispus was unknown both to the congregation and to Agrippa, which last took him to be some meddlesome officer from Antonia, bent on exercising an authority to which he had no claim.

He started to his feet with an angry air.

"Who is this that seeks to interfere with the course of Jewish justice? Know you not that I am Agrippa, the great king? Who art thou?"

"My friend," said Rufus quietly, "is Crispus Cestius, son of the Syrian Legate, a maker of kings, and —an unmaker."

This answer completely confounded Agrippa. He recognized the wisdom of becoming immediately humble. The authority of the Proprætor of Syria, the Ruler of the East, soared far above that of Judæan procurators and Herodian kings. A hint from him to the Roman Senate that Agrippa was unworthy of his post would be quite sufficient to deprive him of his crown. Smoothing his brows, and assuming a smile that in no way harmonized with his inward feelings, he said:

"And what would the noble Crispus have of us?"

"The release of this maiden."

The politic Agrippa, on the point of granting the request, was stayed by his more strong-minded sister, who was not disposed to let the captive go without at least a protest.

"By whose authority do you make this demand?"

"By that of the Legate of Syria."

"Will you let us see in the Legate's own handwriting the order for the release of Vashti, daughter of Hyrcanus?" said Berenice, sarcastically.

"He acts by me, his secretary and deputy."

"How know we that he will confirm your act?"

"Should he refuse to do so I will restore the maiden to your hands," said Crispus, who knew that he was quite safe in giving this pledge.

Taking courage by his sister's example, Agrippa now ventured upon a mild protest.

"But, noble Crispus, you are infringing Jewish rights. The Legate hath no jurisdiction over the internal affairs of our synagogues."

Crispus gave a disdainful smile.

## What Happened in the Royal Synagogue 107

"The authority of Cestius Gallus is supreme over every matter, small or great, within the province of Syria; he has power to reverse any judicial sentence, whether of basilica or synagogue, that he deems unjust, as he will certainly deem this to be when it comes to his hearing. Do you question his authority, O king?"

Berenice answered for her brother.

"It is not to be doubted," said she, "that a fond father will ratify the action of a foolish son. Pronounce the damsel free, Agrippa. Cæsar at Rome may burn Christians alive, but we of Judæa must not even whip them. The great Crispus forbids it." And gathering her robe around her she swept out with a proud and scornful air.

The two Romans—no man daring to stay them—proceeded to remove the trembling Vashti from the synagogue, and, attended by the decurion Quintus, they conducted her to the gate of her house in the street of Millo.

"So, Vashti, you are a Christian?" said Crispus. "I think I understand now the allusion in the poet Bianor, 'By the Fish we are saved.'"

She smiled, pleased to think that he had remembered her words.

"Under the name of 'The Fish,'" said she, "we symbolize our Divine Master, who leads us through the waters of baptism."

As she spoke—they were standing at the time within the gateway of her dwelling—their ears were caught by the tread of numerous feet accompanied by fierce cries, and looking whence these sounds proceeded they saw, coming at a quick pace and with faces expressive of the wildest excitement, a mob of Jews, some carrying steel weapons and others wooden clubs.

In a moment the three Romans sprang within the stone passage, dragging Vashti with them, and closed and barred the gate.

They soon discovered, however, that they were not the objects of attack; it was doubtful whether they had even been seen. Like the rush of a whirlwind the crowd swept past the gateway, rending the air with their cries.

Similar sounds, proceeding from the adjacent streets, showed that these also were being traversed by excited throngs.

" Down with Florus! " shouted some.

" That's a saying with which I can very well sympathize," said Rufus.

" Death to the Romans! " cried others.

" Ha! that's a different matter. That touches you and me," he continued, addressing Crispus.

" The temple of the Lord! The temple of the Lord! Sacrilege! Sacrilege! "

Successive waves of people rolled along the street, voluble women among them, dragging their slow-moving children by the hand. Their fragmentary talk soon enabled the listening Romans to gather the cause of all this excitement.

Florus had sent to Agrippa demanding seventeen talents from the Corban, saying that he wanted them for Cæsar.

The Jewish mind was fired to wrath not so much by the amount itself—which was rather a small one for a man of Florus' rapacity, the sum being about £6,000 in modern English currency—but by the fact that the demand was made upon the Corban or Temple treasury. The gold deposited there was regarded as sacred to Jehovah, to be used only in His service; the diverting of even a single shekel of it to any other purpose was, in the eyes of the frenzied Jew, one of the greatest of crimes. It would be a crime if committed by the high priest himself; but when the demand came from a heathen, unclean, uncircumcized, rapacious, whose objcet, as all well knew, was not to transmit the money to Cæsar but to spend it upon his own sensual pleas-

## What Happened in the Royal Synagogue 109

ures, it was no wonder that the contemplated profanation should fire the blood of every Jew, and send him running with all haste to prevent the sacrilegious deed.

" It is as I have said," whispered Rufus to Crispus. " Florus is purposely trying to create a revolt."

" Vain is it for Rome to boast of her justice," sighed Crispus, " when she sends forth governors such as Florus."

" If there be an uproar in the temple," continued Rufus, " it is my duty to quell it."

As soon as the street of Millo had become comparatively quiet the three Romans stole forth, taking a wide circuit so as to arrive upon the north side of Antonia, the side farthest from the temple.

On their way they encountered a company of youthful and richly-dressed Jews, who, basket on arm, in imitation of beggars, were soliciting alms by way of casting ridicule upon the procurator.

" Give an obolus for Florus, he is so poor! " they whined in a mocking voice.

" Woe to them if Florus gets to hear of it! " muttered Rufus.

On arriving at the Turris Antonia he found that his centurions had taken all precautions for the safety of the fortress. Upon the roof of the cloisters facing the bridge that connected the fortress with the temple, the Italian Cohort was drawn up in all the glittering panoply of war, their silence and discipline presenting a striking contrast to the tumult and disorder that was raging not many yards distant.

The temple-courts were filled with a crowd so numerous that it seemed as if the whole city must have assembled there. To the mind of Crispus with his Roman love of order there was something peculiarly repulsive in the spectacle before him. It was an Oriental mob, and like all Oriental mobs when inflamed with rage, its units behaved like frenzied demons. They spat towards the Romans; they tossed their garments;

they shook their fists; they yelled out curses; they cast dust into the air.

The wilder spirits among them took to flinging stones, the rattle of which, falling upon the brazen armor of the soldiery, was audible above the tumult of voices; of all which the superbly disciplined Roman troops took no more heed than a man takes of gnats on a summer eve.

Rufus, advancing to the head of the stairs that descended to the temple-court, lifted his hand. The sign was perceived and understood, but it was some time ere the crowd quieted down to a listening mood.

Standing upon the very place where, eight years previously, Saint Paul had addressed a raging mob, and speaking in the same language—the Syro-Chaldaic—Rufus sought to pacify the fears of the multitude.

Florus, it seemed, had demanded seventeen talents to be taken from the Corban. He—Rufus—was not prepared to say that the Jews were wrong in resenting this demand; as the servant of Florus it was not his business to criticise the actions of his master, but the Jews were certainly wrong in their way of showing their disapproval. The lawful method was to dispatch an embassy to Florus to state why they considered the demand unreasonable. Let them do so without delay. If they were now assembling under the belief that he—Rufus—was going to invade their sanctuary for the purpose of seizing the seventeen talents they were in error; he had not received any such order from Florus, and till such order came he would be endangering his own head if he should venture to forestall the will of the procurator. They could, therefore, depart quietly to their homes in the full assurance that their treasures would remain untouched for that day, at least, and probably for several days to come. As to what might ultimately happen, well, it was not wise to anticipate evil.

Rufus had scarcely made an end of speaking when

*What Happened in the Royal Synagogue* 111

on the still air rose the chiming of the silver trumpets, blown by the priests as a signal that the hour had come for the closing of the temple.

The crowd murmured, hesitated, but finally departed in peaceful fashion, and the great temple-courts were left to silence.

# CHAPTER IX

"LET US GO HENCE!"

IT was the evening of Crispus' first day in Jerusalem, and Rufus, who, as the Roman overlord of the temple, had free access to its outer courts during any hour of the day or night, now suggested a quiet and contemplative walk around its cloisters.

"Come!" said he, "and I will show you THE STRONGEST FORTRESS IN THE WORLD!"

By the glorious light of an Eastern moon, that silvered the sleeping city and the peaceful hills around it, the two Romans crossed the arch connecting the fortress Antonia with the northern side of the Temple Hill, the hill anciently known by the name of Mount Moriah.

They descended a flight of stairs and entered the northern cloister of the temple, a cloister divided into two long aisles by lines of marble columns, forty feet in height, and formed of marble, beautifully polished.

"Each of these columns," remarked Rufus, "consists of a single block."

The roof of the cloister was of cedar, curiously graven, and the pavement a mosaic of many colors.

This magnificent colonnade was reared upon the very edge of the scarped cliff, and extended in a direct line east and west for a length of more than one thousand feet.

"The temple-platform," observed Rufus, "as you will see, after having gone round it, forms an irregular quadrangle, and occupies the flat summit of a precipitous rock. We'll inspect all four sides in turn. First, what think you of this, the northern side?"

Crispus turned his eyes upon Antonia, frowning white in the moonlight from the other side of the ravine.

"Throw down that arch," said he, "and you make this side of the temple practically unassailable, and— but whom have we here?" he added, breaking off suddenly.

Slowly making their way along the cloister came a band of men clothed in semi-military garb, and bearing spears. A few carried torches, whose yellow glare was reflected from the polished surface of column and pavement.

"Be it known to you," said Rufus, "that the temple has *two* captains, Roman and Jewish. While it is my duty from Antonia to keep watch *over* the temple, it is the duty of yon officer to keep watch *within* it. This is the Levitical guard going its round. Woe to the sentinel whom they find asleep. They'll beat him with clubs, or wake him by setting fire to his clothing."

"Who is the fierce-looking hero marching at their head?"

"That, my dear Crispus, is the rival captain of the temple, Eleazar, son of the ex-high priest Ananias, whom you have already seen at Cæsarea. Betwixt father and son is open war. Ananias, suave and polite, courts the good graces of the Romans; Eleazar, sullen and fierce, boasts his hatred of us. He is said to be secretly leagued with Zealot banditti, and to have known more than he ought of the doings of Simon the Black. Indeed, Quintus is of opinion that the fugitive Zealot, with the connivance of Eleazar, is at the present moment hiding within the sanctuary. If so, he is secure from arrest, for Cæsar himself may not enter there. So deep a scorn hath this Eleazar for Romans that he refuses to return their salutations. Be thyself a witness."

The Levitical guard had by this time reached the place where the two Romans were standing.

"Peace to you, Eleazar," said Rufus, raising his hand in salute.

But the Jewish captain marched past at the head of his guard, taking no notice whatever of the Roman.

Rufus laughed with good-humored contempt.

"What did I tell you?" said he to Crispus. "That was not well done, Eleazar," he called out after the receding figure. "Johanan ben Zacchai makes it his boast [10] that he never yet let Gentile forestall him in giving the salaam."

Speaking thus, Rufus led the way to the eastern cloister, which, extending in an even line due north and south, formed the second side of the irregular square.

"Now here we have a truly Titanic work," he said. "When the temple was first planned by an ancient king called Solomon, he found the summit of the hill too small for his architectural ideas, so what did he do but rear a wall sheer up from the valley below till it was on a level with the top of the mount; the vacancy betwixt the wall and the mount was then filled in with earth and stone, and on the esplanade thus formed was built this grand colonnade, which we now see; hence its name, Solomon's Colonnade. From the summit of yon pinnacle at the southeast corner the plumb-line falls a sheer descent of four hundred and fifty feet—at least so say the priests who have measured it. Cast your eye downward, and mark the depth!"

As Crispus leaned far over the stone balustrade, and ran his eye first to the right and then to the left along the vast mass of masonry, rising vertically in mid-air, he muttered: "The gods themselves would not dare attack the temple from this side."

Far down, scarcely visible, glinted a slender line of water.

"The brook Cedron," said Rufus, "flowing to-day, dry in summer. The name Cedron, or Black, is justly deserved, for into the rivulet flows the black blood of the daily sacrifices conducted thither by channels bored through the solid rock."

"How name you yon fair hill in front of us?"

"The Mount of Olives, so called from its trees. Come, view we now the third side."

They passed on to the southern cloister, which, like the eastern, was built upon a vast substructure of masonry rising in massive grandeur from the valley below.

"This," said Rufus, "bears the name of the Royal Colonnade, as being the grandest of all, for whereas the other cloisters have but two rows of pillars, this has four. And mark them! Each column is a monolith, fifty feet in height, and as to its thickness, three men with joined hands can scarcely encircle it."

This Royal Colonnade, open on the side towards the temple, was closed upon the other by a wall. The two, therefore, mounted a staircase and walked along its roof.

"Those houses whose roofs you see beneath us extending far to the southward, form the suburb of Ophel, the residence of the priests and their servants, the Levites and Nethinim, whose duty necessitates their living near the temple."

"It seems to me," muttered Crispus, as he gazed downwards, "that he would be a bold general who would venture to make his attack from the south side."

Walking onward, they came to the last, or western cloister, whose edge overhung the ravine known as the Valley of Tyropæon, a deep cleft that completely severed the temple-mount both from Acra or the Lower City, which lay due west, and from Zion or the Upper City, which lay to the southwest.

The temple-hill and Mount Zion were joined by a stone bridge, a magnificent structure, being in length 354 feet, and having a roadway 50 feet broad; in the center the depth of the valley beneath was 225 feet!

"Well, what think you of this—the fourth side?"

"Destroy the bridge, and you make this part of the temple inaccessible."

"Yet this was the side—there was no bridge then—that our great Pompey successfully stormed."

"It speaks ill for the skill of the defenders."

"But well for the courage of the Romans—eh? But I doubt whether even Pompey would have carried his assault had not Jewish superstition favored him."

"In what way?"

"He was told that the Jews had such reverence for the Sabbath that they would not fight on that day unless actually attacked. He therefore spent every Sabbath in raising huge mounds, and the rest of the week in guarding them; at the end of twelve months he made his triumphal attack."

"Would the Jews again act so supinely, think you?"

"I doubt it. Since then they have seen the folly of their ways."

Having walked all round the colonnades to the point whence they set out, the two friends now passed into the spacious court open to the sky. In the middle of this court rose the Sanctuary, or the Temple properly so called.

"It stands, if you will believe the Jews, upon the very center of the earth's surface," remarked Rufus. "In the adytum the stone upon which the high priest deposits his censer upon the Day of Atonement is regarded as the navel of the earth."

Crispus, approaching the edifice upon its north side, experienced a strange thrill as he beheld, just as it had appeared in the dream, the golden-latticed window through which he had flung the incendiary torch.

"Do you know, Rufus, to what room that window belongs?" he asked, pointing it out.

"'Tis one of the windows of the Hall Gazith, the chamber in which the Sanhedrim meet to try those accused on a capital charge. Among others condemned there, was the founder of the sect of the Christians, who worship their Master as a god; though, methinks, if he had aught of divinity in him he should have delivered himself from his enemies."

They walked round to the east, the quarter that gave them the finest view of the edifice.

It was a fabric of white marble, inferior, doubtless, in point of beauty to the graceful templès of Greece, but far superior to them in size and magnificence; and as for solidity, Rufus was careful to point out to the wondering Crispus that some of the blocks composing the external wall were no less than sixty feet in length!

" A fortress within a fortress!" he murmured, viewing the fabric with the eye of a soldier. " He who captures the cloisters has but begun his work."

But the glories hidden within the Sanctuary were not for the gaze of Gentiles. Around the whole of the edifice ran a low marble balustrade—the " middle wall of partition "—whose dwarf pilasters bore inscriptions in Greek and Latin, forbidding the alien to proceed further on pain of death.

Here and there, as Crispus could see, half-concealed in the shadows of the temple-wall, stood the dusky forms of sentinels, who, though to all appearances inert, were nevertheless keeping a jealous watch upon the two Romans.

The floor of the Sanctuary was not upon the same level as the floor of the Court of the Gentiles, but stood at an altitude of twenty-two feet above it, upon the summit of a solid platform of masonry.

This elevation was ascended by a stately flight of stairs leading up to a magnificent pylon, whose twofold gate was richly plated with Corinthian bronze, a composite metal, more esteemed in that age than silver or gold.

" The Eastern or Corinthian Gate," remarked Rufus.

Though access to the temple was forbidden to the Romans, there was not wanting even upon its very forefront the sign of the Roman dominion.

Over this gateway was the golden image of an eagle with extended wings, a surprising sight in view of the Jewish hatred of sculpture.

" Placed there by Herod the Great out of compliment to Augustus, and though many a fiery Zealot has climbed up there with intent to hew it down, our procurators have determined to keep it there."

Having taken as close a view of the edifice as was permissible, Crispus drew back to contemplate it from a distance.

He had all a Roman's reverence for antiquity, and the thought that the smoke of the daily sacrifice had ascended from this temple for the space of more than a thousand years was well adapted to impress his imagination.

Hallowed by the white light of the moon, the fabric rose with solemn and majestic air, the very stillness resting upon it seeming to have in it something of the divine.

He was tempted almost to believe in the strange miracles said to have occurred here—above all in the permanent miracle asserted by every Jew that the dark, central shrine, curtained off from mortal view, and never trodden by human foot save once a year only, was the dwelling-place of the deity himself!

A light touch upon his arm ended this reverie, and Crispus, on turning, found himself looking into the eyes of the Princess Berenice—very lovely eyes they were, too!—yet in them he fancied he could detect a light as of fear, due perhaps to the wild belief that he had come to take a clandestine view of the temple as a preliminary to the flinging of the incendiary torch.

" What do you here, princess? "

" Keeping watch upon you," she said with a laugh

that was not all a laugh. "It is my habit to walk at night in these courts."

Rufus at this juncture thought fit to slip quietly away, leaving the two together.

Crispus thought of the circumstances in which he had last seen the princess.

"Why look you so earnestly at me?" smiled Berenice, becoming conscious of a very attentive gaze on his part.

"I am wondering, princess, why eyes so beautiful and gracious as yours are now could look so pitilessly upon poor Vashti."

"My love for my religion is such that it makes me cold, even cruel, to all who oppose it."

Her statement was probably true in a general sense, but Crispus doubted whether she had been moved by religious zeal in the case of Vashti.

"Then you must hate me, who am likewise opposed to your religion?"

"Nay, you are not an apostate. You have never known the truth."

And then, as if anxious to get away from the synagogue scene, in which she was conscious that she had not appeared to advantage in Crispus' eyes, she pointed to the Sanctuary and said:

"Do you not think it beautiful?"

"'Twere wrong to think otherwise."

"Too beautiful to be wantonly destroyed," she said significantly.

"You see me without the fatal torch—as yet."

"As yet?" she repeated, with a touch of fear in her voice. "You are not—you are not letting that dream still hold a place in your thoughts?"

"Whatever opposes Rome must be destroyed, even if it be a temple."

"You would destroy our temple? You cannot," she said, speaking with a vehemence that surprised, and even startled Crispus, "you cannot. It is beyond the power of Cæsar and his legions. Let all the nations of the earth league together for that end, and they would fail. The temple is eternal, and cannot be destroyed, for our prophets have so assured us. The world was made for the sake of the temple,"—she was but repeating the doctrine of the rabbis—" and so long as the world shall stand, so long will the temple stand. When the last day shall come," she continued, her eyes shining with all the enthusiasm of a devotee, " there will still be seen the smoke of the sacrifice ascending from the altar. It is the place loved of God, the place where He has chosen to put His name forever."

So spoke Berenice, and perhaps never in the history of the world did words meet with a rebuke more startling and more significant.

For scarcely had she finished speaking when there rose upon the air a mysterious something that caused her to grasp the arm of Crispus with a convulsive start.

From the hidden interior of the Sanctuary there came a sound that bore—to compare it with earthly things—some resemblance to the rising of a wind; faint at first, its volume increased, little by little, till, issuing from the Sanctuary, what seemed to be a rush of air swept through the temple-courts.

A wind, and yet no wind! It had no effect upon external objects: not a fold of Crispus' toga waved; not a hair of the princess was stirred.

What was happening was like nothing earthly; the sense of a mysterious and unseen presence struck an awe to the soul of Crispus. If he had never before believed in the supernatural, he believed in it now; if he had never before felt fear, he felt it now. The hand which his first impulse had sent to his sword dropped powerlessly to his side again. What availed the might of a legion, or of ten thousand such, against invisible and spiritual powers?

Terror had laid hold of Berenice; half-swooning she sank upon her knees, her hands still clinging to the

## "Let Us Go Hence!"

wrist of Crispus; but for his detaining hold she would have fallen prone upon the pavement.

Closing her eyes as if to shut out some awful vision that was about to appear, she faintly gasped with blanched lips: "*The bath col!*"

She was not alone in her belief. From different parts of the temple-court persons, hitherto unseen by Crispus —priests, Levites, Nethinim—had suddenly started into view, and were gazing up at the lofty temple, whose long and magnificent façade gleamed like a bank of pearl in the moonlight. And one cry only broke from their lips, to die away in a feeling of mingled awe and terror:

"THE BATH COL! THE BATH COL!"

Crispus was sufficiently familiar with this phrase to know that it meant the voice of the deity.

Did this "sound as of a rushing mighty wind" really emanate from the Hebrew God who was said to ride upon the whirlwind, and to speak in the voice of the thunder?

That was the belief of the Jews assembled in the court; they were about to hear the awful voice that had spoken to their fathers from Sinai!

Slowly—very slowly—the quivering, continuous flow of sound died away. For a brief space there was a weird spell of silence; then came a sudden clangor, startling by contrast with the previous stillness, a clangor like that of hollow brass struck by a giant hand.

All eyes turned instantly upon the Corinthian Gate of the Sanctuary. That great gate, whose folding-doors of plated bronze were so ponderous as to require the united strength of twenty men to turn them on their hinges, was now slowly revolving inwards as if yielding to some invisible pressure from without.

Wider and wider grew the space between the two doors, till at last they had revolved so far back that they could revolve no farther.

The gate had opened apparently of its own accord! And now came an awe-inspiring sequel.

From the interior of the Sanctuary issued a solemn voice, crying in the Hebrew tongue:

" LET US GO HENCE! " [11]

All trembled at the sound; none more than Crispus. " The voice that spoke in my dream! "

This moment of supreme and thrilling terror was followed by a sequence of sounds suggestive of the departure of a vast multitude. It seemed as if ten thousand feet were descending the lofty stairs of the Corinthian Gate, and were treading the pavement of the forecourt. Yet neither shape nor shadow met the gaze of the appalled and trembling Jews, who had drawn together in one dense throng as if for protection against—they knew not what!

As for Crispus, had he wished to describe his feelings at this awful moment he might have employed the language of the sacred writer: " Fear came upon me and a trembling that made all my bones to shake. Then a spirit passed before my face; it stood still, but I could not discern the form thereof! "

For there was a flowing of air past him, as if some long procession were going by; he could detect the sound of rustling garments and of sighing voices; yet had his life depended upon the action, he durst not put forth his hand to test whether the unseen train that was gliding past were palpable to the touch.

The sounds passed on, taking their way through the eastern cloister; and, mounting upon the wings of the night, they melted away in the direction of Olivet.

Long, long after the mysterious voices had ceased, the Jews, filled with a divine awe, stood speechless and motionless, as if fearful lest their speaking should call forth the wrath of departing deity.

Among the group was the famous rabbi, Johanan ben Zacchai. He was the first to find tongue.

Pointing to the interior of the Corinthian gateway,

with its walls and roof fashioned from the cedar of Libanus, he cried in a solemn tone:

"The end of the temple hath come, for this is that which was spoken by the prophet, saying, 'Open thy doors, O Lebanon, that the fire may devour thy cedars!'"[12]

And at that word "fire," Berenice looked at Crispus and trembled.

# CHAPTER X

### THE VENGEANCE OF FLORUS

FLORUS was in Jerusalem, and—sinister omen!—an armed legion with him.

Following fast upon the dispatch of his letter demanding the seventeen talents, he had taken up his abode in the old palace erected by Herod the Great upon Mount Zion. This, as being the usual residence of the procurators while at Jerusalem, had received the Roman name of Prætorium.

Its two colossal wings of white marble, the Cæsareum and the Agrippeum, named respectively after Augustus and his great minister, were united by a long terrace, which, from its tesselated flooring, was called by the Romans the Pavement, but by the Jews Gabbatha, or the Elevation.

On the morning after the arrival of Florus, a vast concourse of Jewish citizens assembled in front of this terrace when it became known that the procurator had summoned the members of the Sanhedrim thither for the purpose of interrogating them as to the riot that had taken place three days previously.

Among those who came was the crafty Sadducean priest Ananias, who hoped, by reason of his private friendship with Florus, to dispose that tyrant to pacific measures.

Beside him, glooming within himself, was his eldest son, the fierce, dark-browed Eleazar, captain of the temple, whose wrath was scarcely to be restrained by the whispered admonitions of his more politic father.

Florus, disposed for reasons of his own to receive the Sanhedrim in the open air, had given orders for

## The Vengeance of Florus 125

his curule chair to be brought forth, and set down upon the Pavement midway between the two wings.

In the rear of this elevated tribunal and along its whole length glittered the brazen bucklers and crested helmets of the legionaries; they flanked the walls of the two wings likewise, so that the whole military force formed the three sides of a rectangle, the fourth being open to the view of the public.

These troops were the Twentieth Legion, a force drawn, not like Rufus' Italic Cohort, from native Romans, but from the dregs of the Syrian populace who were forced to a military service from which the Jew, by reason of his religion, was exempt. Hence the feeling of these troops towards the Jewish nation was one of fierce hatred, a hatred that had often shown itself in deeds of blood. Let Florus give but the word and they would not hesitate to massacre every man, woman, and child before the tribunal.

On this particular morning, as they stood awaiting the coming of the procurator, there was in their manner something so sinister and expectant that a secret misgiving, a sense as of tragedy to come, seized upon many of the Sanhedrim.

Florus appeared at last, and contemptuously ignoring the fawning smiles of Ananias stalked to the curule chair, dark, haughty, frowning.

The herald called for silence, an unnecessary order, seeing that a death-like stillness had fallen upon the occupants both of Gabbatha and the public square.

Florus' mood was shown by his first question to the Sanhedrim.

"Is it true that my person has been mocked by the youth of this city, who have gone about, basket on arm, and crying aloud, 'Give an obolus for Florus the Pauper?'"

The members of the Sanhedrim looked at one another in alarm. Finally they glanced at Ananias as if inviting him to be their spokesman.

Hiding both hands within the folds of his robe—an Oriental way of showing respect and humility—and making a profound obeisance, Ananias spoke:

"O Florus, live forever——"

("Now heaven preserve us from that calamity!" muttered Eleazar.)

"That certain youth *have* behaved ill is but too true, and we cannot deny it. But——"

Florus cut him short.

"Ye see in me the representative of Cæsar——"

"None more worthy to represent him, O Florus," said Eleazar, caustically.

"And he who mocks me, mocks Cæsar," continued the procurator with a side glance at Eleazar. "I therefore demand of you, the Sanhedrim, who are responsible for the due maintenance of order in this city, that the youths who have affronted me be handed over here and now to be dealt with as their misdeeds deserve. And if ye fail to produce these malefactors, know that for many days to come ye shall have a tale of sorrow to tell."

Miserable Sanhedrim! Among the elder of them were some who, thirty years before, on an occasion never to be forgotten as long as time shall last, had said, and that, too, on the very spot where they were now standing, "We have no king but Cæsar." Thus had they made their choice. Verily, then, let them not repine if Cæsar, or his representative, should treat them in a manner not according to their liking!

The hapless Ananias, collecting with difficulty his wits, which had been somewhat scattered by Florus' fierce air, stammered out a deprecatory speech.

What he said amounted to this: that the people were as a whole peaceably disposed; some few had done amiss, and for these let pardon be granted, for it was no wonder that in so great a multitude there should be some more daring than they ought to be, and by reason of their youth foolish also. It was, too, a very difficult

## The Vengeance of Florus

matter to distinguish the innocent from the guilty; and seeing that all alike, those who had offended as well as those who had not, were sorry for what had happened, it would become the clemency of Florus to overlook the affair, lest a too stern application of justice should bring about disorders even more grave than those that had already taken place.

" That last is in the nature of a threat! " exclaimed Florus fiercely. " Yours is just the sort of speech one would expect from a man who has plotted against the life of a Roman citizen," he continued, with a fine forgetfulness of his own delinquencies. " Disorders more grave will undoubtedly ensue, if the guilty are allowed to walk unpunished. Say without periphrases whether you will, or will not, give up these malefactors."

Ananias hesitated, but Johanan ben Zacchai was bolder than the ex-high priest.

" We cannot," said he, " consent to give up these youths."

At this there came a shout of approval from the people assembled before the tribunal.

Florus glared at them for a moment, and then resumed:

" And yet refuse to make a grant to Cæsar of seventeen talents from the Corban? "

" Shall man rob God? " exclaimed Eleazar, fiercely. " This, too, we will not do."

Again a shout of applause, this time louder, from the populace. Florus accepted it for what it was meant, defiance of himself. Turning to the troops in his rear, he cried:

" Put these rebels to the rout. Plunder the Upper Market. Slay all who oppose."

Plunder! What more agreeable order for the soldier? They required no second bidding. Like tigers suddenly let loose they raced across the bema, sweeping the helpless Sanhedrim aside, and drawing their trenchant broadswords they precipitated themselves upon the defenseless people, striking out right and left, and using not the flat of the blade, but the point and edge.

It was all the work of a moment. Taken completely by surprise, and without arms to defend themselves, the front ranks, hideously gashed, sank moaning to the ground. The rest of the crowd, aghast at the sight, and suddenly realizing that a massacre was intended, strove to avoid the Roman blades. But for those nearest the bema flight was impossible owing to the density of the throng. Then began a horrible struggle for life; he who fell in that crowd never rose again, but was trampled to death, trampled out of all recognition; moved by the instinct of self-preservation everyone strove to thrust his body forward betwixt his neighbors, or failing this, tried to drag his fellow back in the attempt to interpose something between himself and the terrible swords that were steadily coming on from behind.

With the flight of those farthest from the bema, the mass became gradually loosened, and finally breaking into detached groups, fled in all directions, pursued by the shouting and triumphant legionaries.

But the Romans were not to have it all their own way. Many of the Jews, escaping to the streets adjacent to the square, took refuge in the first houses they came to, and having barred the gates, they ascended to the roofs and proceeded to assail the enemy below with tiles and stones. Others who had fled farther afield, procuring weapons or whatever implements might serve as such, retraced their steps, and favored by their knowledge of the narrow and winding streets, ventured to give battle to the Romans, and what is more, contrived for a time to hold them in check.

The streets of Zion rang with the clang of arms, and the shouts of the combatants.

News of what was happening came quickly to the

## The Vengeance of Florus

ears of Berenice, producing in her mind not only consternation, but an agonizing sense of self-reproach. She felt herself to be indirectly the cause of it all. It was Florus' revenge for her rejection of him. Her first impulse was to fly to the procurator, and appeal to him to stay his hand. Her pride revolted from this step. But, as the sound of the fray grew louder and fiercer, she became more agitated; casting her pride away she resolved to hasten to his tribunal and intercede on behalf of her people.

As a royal princess, she deemed herself secure from molestation by the Roman soldiery; but, forgetful of the fact that she was unknown by sight to the majority of them, she ran forth from her palace without a single attendant. Fortunately she was seen by her master of the horse, who, collecting as many of her household troops as he conveniently could at a moment's notice, went after her with all speed.

On coming within sight of the tribunal Berenice paused aghast. Hell itself seemed to be let loose that day. The Jews, captured in the neighboring streets, were being dragged into the square to be ruthlessly slaughtered before the very eyes of Florus. No distinction was made as to age or sex. Even infants, torn from the arms of shrieking mothers, were tossed aloft and caught upon the points of spears. Young girls, tied naked to stakes, were exposed to the brutal jests of the soldiery, who offered their captives liberty if they would but consent to taste a morsel of swine's flesh.

As Berenice, with reeling brain, stepped forward, she caught sight of a group of drunken soldiers, standing around a bright-eyed Jewish boy, whose age could not have exceeded twelve years.

" Tell us the name of your God? " exclaimed a soldier.

" He is called the Lord," answered the boy, nothing daunted by the ring of fierce faces around him.

"Well, curse the Lord and you shall live," said a second soldier, menacing the lad with his spear.

But the little fellow had been too well drilled in the shibboleths of Judaism to do their bidding.

"Cursed be all they that serve graven images," he replied defiantly.

"This wolfling will grow up into a brave wolf," laughed the first soldier.

"That shall he not," cried the second savagely; and, raising his pike with both hands, he drove the weapon through the breast of the boy, who, with the one word "Mother!" fell dead upon the spot.

"O God!" gasped Berenice, "canst thou look on and let these men live?"

Scarcely able to move for horror, she made her way up the steps of the bema, and drew near to Florus. With hands clasped at the back of his neck, and with one leg thrown carelessly over the other, the procurator was lolling at ease in his curule chair, amusing himself with the fears of a numerous body of richly-dressed captives, who were said, rightly or wrongly, by his spies, to be the very youths that, three days before, had gone about begging money for the indigent Florus.

"By the way," said he, "why don't you Jews eat pork?"

The question drew loud laughter from the senseless soldiers standing by.

One of the captives ventured the remark that there were some nations that did not eat lamb.

"And they are quite right," commented Florus. "Lamb is very insipid; but pork—ah! that is one of the choicest delicacies the gods have conferred upon mankind, and I swear by Pluto that if ye will not eat of it ye shall die."

"Florus, in the name of God I adjure you to have pity upon these youths," cried Berenice. "Refrain from further bloodshed."

The feeling of Florus was a strange mingling of love

## The Vengeance of Florus

and hatred as he beheld the distressed princess in all her wild beauty, her hair loosened, her feet bare.

His first mad impulse—he had been drinking heavily—was to clasp her in his arms and kiss her passionately regardless of the spectators; his next, as he recalled her scornful language at Cæsarea, was to spurn her with language equally scornful.

Hatred triumphed. He had gone too far now to recede, and since he could not have the sweetness of love, he would have the sweetness of revenge.

Among the captives was a beautiful youth, whose unmistakable air of fearlessness had given secret umbrage to the procurator.

" Marcus, you here? " cried Berenice in dismay. He was known to her as being a worshiper in the Royal Synagogue.

" Fear not for me, princess. *I* am safe."

Self-confidence such as this moved Florus to a frenzy of wrath.

" Lictors, crucify me this knave who considers himself so safe."

" Oh, no! no! " cried Berenice in an agony of grief.

The youth, with a proud smile, gave utterance to words that in every province of the empire, save one, had power to stay the hand of even Cæsar himself:

" CIVIS ROMANUS SUM—I am a Roman citizen! "

" Ah! So *that* is thy hope? Well, it shall not avail thee. A Roman citizen? Pah! How easy to become such nowadays! Damas the Jew is a knave, but he has two oboli to spare; so the prætor touches him with a wand, twirls him round, and lo! Damas the Jew becomes Marcus the Roman, and struts about in a toga."

And here Florus, leaping up, illustrated his words by strutting about with an air of mock dignity, amid the laughter of his satellites.

" I am a freeborn Roman; nay, more—I am of equestrian rank."

"A knight—eh? Well, we'll acknowledge thy dignity by giving thee a higher cross and painting it purple. Lictors, bring hither a stock."

In his mad desire to torment to the uttermost the soul of Berenice, Florus did not hesitate to defy Roman law by an outrage so great that Cicero confesses his inability to find a name for it. "It is an offense to bind a Roman citizen; a crime to scourge him; almost a parricide to kill him; what, then, shall I say of *crucifying* him?"

Such an outrage on the part of a Roman governor might be deemed incredible were it not attested by a contemporary historian.

"Florus," says Josephus, "dared to do what no governor before his time had ever done—to have men of the equestrian order scourged and nailed to the cross in front of his tribunal, who, although they were Jews by birth, were yet of Roman dignity notwithstanding."

Desirous of adding not so much to the agony of Marcus as to that of Berenice, Florus, with a cruel smile, issued a fresh order.

"Hold! before crucifying the knave we'll scourge him."

A strange thing is the heart of a woman! Berenice, who had been willing to subject a young girl to scourging, now shuddered when a similar torture was proposed for a young man.

As for the victim himself, vainly did he urge his legal right to be transferred from the tribunal of Florus to that of Nero.

"*Appello Cæsarem*—I appeal unto Cæsar," he cried.

"Cæsar's a long way off," laughed Florus. "In Greece, playing the fool. You'll have to shout a good deal louder, if he's to hear you."

Deaf to his protests, the lictors stripped the youth of his garments and tied his wrists to a column. He

## The Vengeance of Florus 133

tried to be brave, but where is the man that *could* be brave when subjected to the strokes of the " *horrible flagellum* "?

A thrilling scream burst from Marcus' lips as the leathern thongs, weighted with triangular pieces of lead, descended upon his naked, quivering flesh.

" O Apollo! How sweet a voice!" cried Florus mockingly. " By the gods, Nero must look to his laurels, for he hath a rival. Give him a second stroke. Ah! a higher note this time. Swing the flagellum again. We'll run him through the whole octave."

The rest of the captives, apprehensive of the same fate, looked on with blanched cheeks and terror-stricken eyes.

Berenice's distress of mind made her look like some wild thing. Her manifest agony was a luxury to the soul of Florus.

" There are twenty of these youths," he whispered, " and they shall all suffer the same fate, scourging and crucifixion. But you can save them, if you will."

" How? " gasped Berenice.

Florus' whispered reply was of a character so infamous that the indignant princess raised her hand and struck her open palm against his cheek; struck, too, with all her force.

Smarting with the pain, Florus started back with a very ugly look upon his face.

" Guards, remove this woman from the bema. What hath she to do with these matters? "

And the rough soldiery, paying little respect either to her womanhood or to her rank, drove her down the steps of the tribunal."

Night fell, calm and beautiful.

The Syrian stars looked down upon the tribunal, whose stones, could they have spoken, might have told how, thirty years before, a wicked populace had cried, " *His blood be on us, and on our children!* "

That self-invoked curse was working out its fulfillment.

There, on the very spot where those words had been uttered, stood a multitude of crosses, each lifting a ghastly victim to the midnight sky!

# CHAPTER XI

### "TO YOUR TENTS, O ISRAEL!"

DURING the massacre instigated by Florus, a massacre that numbered no less than three thousand six hundred victims, Crispus, by nature of the case, had been compelled to look helplessly on.

Side with the Roman troops he could not; to side with the Jews would have been unpatriotic. His attempt at mediation met, like that of Berenice, with an insulting repulse from the procurator. Burning with indignation, he retired to the Turris Antonia and addressed to his father a letter describing the disgrace that had been brought upon the Roman name by Florus, and urging the Legate to come at once with a legion and restore order in Jerusalem by the only method possible, the deposition of the wicked procurator. This letter, when finished, he dispatched to Antioch by the hand of a swift courier.

Florus, having given ample ground for rebellion, proceeded, in pursuance of the same sinister policy, to take his departure, withdrawing all his troops save one cohort, and that a divided one, half being allotted to the Prætorium, and half to Antonia.

Never did the baseness of Florus' character appear more than in this, the final act of his official career. He knew that, in the present excited state of the city, garrisons so slender would offer an irresistible temptation to the seditious. But what cared he for the Romans whom he was leaving behind? If the garrisons were massacred, why, so much the better for his purpose.

As Florus looked back upon the city he was leaving

he might have said with a nobler Roman than himself, "Mischief, thou art afoot; take what course thou wilt." [14]

Among the troops ordered to leave Jerusalem upon this occasion was the Italian Cohort of Rufus, who, however great his dislike of the procurator, had, as a loyal soldier, no other course than to do as he was bidden.

Crispus, determined to remain in the city, betook himself to the Prætorium, and offered his services to its commandant Metilius, who was glad to welcome any auxiliary, and especially one like Crispus, whose suggestions for the defense of the palace were not only original, but, what is more, practicable.

To Metilius' lament that, owing to the lack of the requisite missiles, the balistæ and other machines of like character would have to remain idle, Crispus laughingly replied:

"If it comes to that, we can discharge these statues upon the heads of the mob."

He was standing at the time in a magnificent hall decorated with sculpture, and, happening to cast a casual eye over the marble masterpieces around him, was so much attracted by one of them that he walked up to it and examined it with an attention that set Metilius wondering.

The statue represented a beautiful maiden clothed to the feet in a graceful stole. Upon the pedestal was sculptured the one word, *Pythodoris*.

"Pythodoris?" murmured Crispus. "Were not that name graven here I should have called it Vashti."

For indeed, the statue, both in face and figure, was so like the Hebrew maiden that anyone acquainted with her might very well have supposed that it was intended for no other person.

"Pythodoris?" said Crispus reflectively. "The name is new to me. Who is she, or perhaps I ought to say, who was she?"

# "To Your Tents, O Israel!"

Metilius confessed himself unable to satisfy the curiosity of Crispus. He, too, had never heard the name.

"This much I know about the statue," remarked he; "that it is a recent addition to this gallery, and was, I believe, a gift of King Polemo."

The introduction of the Pontic king's name added not a little to Crispus' perplexity.

"The lady evidently is, or was, a queen," observed Metilius, pointing to the Oriental diadem upon the head of the figure.

Surveying the statue more closely, Crispus saw engraved upon the sandal in minute letters, ΛΑΣΟΣ ΕΠΟΙΕΙ.

"'The workmanship of Lasus,'" said he, reading the name of a sculptor well known at the beginning of the first century. "'Tis fifty years ago since he died, so we may conclude that this is the image of a queen no longer living. How to account for her resemblance to Vashti? But," he added suddenly, cutting the matter short, "we do wrong to stand musing here, when there are graver matters to attend to."

Herein Crispus spoke truly. The seditiously-disposed among the Jews had noted with secret joy that Florus had left the city all but denuded of troops. What could the two slender garrisons of three hundred each do against the whole city? To neglect such a golden opportunity for the recovery of freedom was a contravening of the will of Elohim, who must surely have brought about this arrangement for the good of the holy seed.

Day by day affairs grew more threatening; in the temple-courts and in the synagogues, fiery Zealots from the mountains, and wild-eyed prophets from the desert, declared to the credulous multitude that all the signs of the times pointed to the near advent of the long-promised Messiah, when the Jewish nation should not only be free, but should reign supreme over all the children of the earth from the rising of the sun to the setting thereof.

Vainly did Agrippa and Berenice seek to deter the infatuated populace from a course certain to end in the ruin of the Jewish state.

"To your tents, O Israel!" was the answer of the Zealots. "What dealings have we with Cæsar, or what is our portion in Rome?"

It was eventide, and the silver trumpets were sounding the signal for the closing of the temple-gates, as two figures mounted the stairs leading to the roof of Solomon's Colonnade.

The one was Eleazar, the captain of the temple, the other Simon of Gerasa, who, during several days, had been living in a secret chamber of the sanctuary; for Eleazar could not refuse the right of asylum to a patriot whose stores of wealth, acquired by brigandage, had always been sent by secret and devious methods to the temple treasury.

As the two paced the roof they talked, and seldom in the history of the world has talk been more momentous in its consequences.

"The people are ripe for war," said Eleazar with a fierce, exultant smile. "We'll set them to attack the garrisons in Antonia and the Prætorium."

"Whence shall we obtain the necessary arms?"

"You know Masada?" asked Eleazar.

It would indeed have been strange if Simon had not known the name, at least, of the famous stronghold, emphatically named Masada—"THE FORTRESS"—built by Jonathan Maccabæus upon a precipitous cliff, fifteen hundred feet in height, overhanging the waters of the Dead Sea, a fastness in which the treasures of Jerusalem had been deposited for security during the troubled times of the Asamonean monarchy.

"It contains arms for ten thousand men," continued Eleazar.

"With a Roman garrison to guard them."

"Tush! the garrison is but a slender one, and, aware of this, I have sent off a band to attack the place."

Simon received this startling news with a grim joy.

"'Tis a declaration of war," remarked he.

"'Tis meant for such. One must make a beginning."

"But Masada!" remonstrated Simon. "Art mad? The fortress is impregnable."

"And therefore the more easily surprised. An impregnable fortress always renders its garrison careless."

"Who heads this daring expedition?"

"Manahem, the son of Judas of Galilee."

"The traitor who bought from Florus the license to plunder!" exclaimed Simon wrathfully; for he and Manahem had long been jealous rivals.

"Shall I repel a man who offers me his services?" answered Eleazar. "Four nights ago he descended from the mountains with his guerilla band, and sought me out, bidding me tell him to do something for the cause. I bade him go and take Masada."

"If he succeed, he will indeed be a Manahem," sneered Simon, playing upon his rival's name, which in Hebrew signifies Comforter.

Overhead hung a dark-blue firmament sparkling with stars, by whose light the nearer hills that "stand round about Jerusalem" were clearly visible; beyond them, appearing far off on the horizon, was the mount known from old time as Beth-haccerem, whose conspicuous peak had marked it as a suitable station for signaling tidings to Jerusalem by that primitive mode of telegraph, the beacon-fire.

Eleazar's eyes were set upon Beth-haccerem, and Simon, following his companion's gaze, was surprised to see a light springing into being upon the dark summit of the distant peak. No evanescent flash, but a light that continued to sparkle and glow; evidently a signal, the meaning of which was known to the priest, if one must judge by the satisfaction that gleamed from his dark countenance.

"Sooner than I durst hope," he murmured. "The impregnable fortress has fallen."

"*Masada?*" gasped Simon with a mingled feeling of amazement and jealousy.

"So is yon light to be interpreted," replied Eleazar. "The armory of Masada is now in our hands, and to-morrow a train of wagons will come rolling towards Jerusalem laden with weapons for the people."

"How will your father and the Sanhedrim take this deed of yours?"

"Leave me to deal with them," replied Eleazar with a hard smile.

On the next day a meeting of the Sanhedrim was convened by Matthias, the high priest, for the purpose of considering the course to be observed by that body, should the common people persist in their outspoken determination to take up arms against the Romans.

At this gathering—held in the temple within the walls of the famous *Lishcath Ha-Gazith* or Hall of Squares, so named from its checkered pavement—Eleazar came out with a new and startling proposition, upon which he desired a vote should be taken.

"It hath been the custom in our temple since the days of Herod," said he, "to offer daily a sacrifice for the safety and welfare of the reigning Cæsar. But why should we pray for our enemy? why pray for an uncircumcized heathen? why pray for Nero, who in claiming Divine honors insults the name of the Most High? In praying that the life of this blasphemer may be prolonged, what are we doing but praying for the continuance of blasphemy? Brethren and fathers, this must not be. My voice is that from to-day the sacrifice for Cæsar shall cease."

As soon as Eleazar had resumed his seat, Ananias rose to oppose the daring innovation propounded by his son.

"However agreeable this proposal may be to our secret inclination," said he, "the question for us is, in what light would Nero regard it, for it will not escape his knowledge. He would take it as an affront —nay, more, as a declaration of war."

"Let him take it as such," said Eleazar, boldly.

"Now you reveal your true aim," answered Ananias, "which is to act as a mover of sedition. You would have the Sanhedrim declare war against Rome."

"War is certain to come—nay, is here now—and there is no other course left for the Sanhedrim but to side with the multitude in their struggle for liberty."

"Not so," cried some, loudest among them being Ananias.

"O then, you will fight on the side of the Romans—a noble act for patriotic Jews!"

"There is a third course—to remain neutral," said Simeon ben Gamaliel.

"That way death lies. The people—the fight once begun—will have no neutrals among them. Their cry will be, 'He that is not with us is against us.'"

"We can leave Jerusalem," said Johanan ben Zacchai. "Not without cutting yourself off from God. The sacrifices through which He is alone accessible—can they be offered anywhere but in that place where He has chosen to put His name? Dare we as priests live apart from the temple? No! And, since we cannot prevent the war, we must seek to guide its course by putting ourselves at the head of the national movement, unless we would see ourselves set aside and relegated to obscurity, and even, it may be, given over to prison and to death. It is clear that——"

But at this point the council, at the instigation of Ananias, lifted up their voices in dissent, so loud and so prolonged, that the orator was compelled to come to an end.

At the first lull, Ananias bade Matthias put the

question to the vote, and, this being done, the proposition for the abolition of the Cæsarean sacrifice was defeated by a considerable majority.

"So ends your treason!" sneered Ananias, addressing his son.

Eleazar rose, somewhat pale, but with a defiant smile on his lips.

"The vote is of no consequence——" he began.

"Hark to him!" cried Ananias.

"As captain of the temple, I decree that from to-day no more sacrifices shall be offered on behalf of Cæsar."

"And how will you effect your decree?" laughed Ananias.

"Why, thus," replied Eleazar coolly, placing a ram's horn to his lips, and blowing one sharp, shrill note.

At that sound every door opening into the hall Gazith flew wide revealing a sudden blaze of arms. Then, marching with slow and majestic pace, there filed into the chamber a tall and stately band of Nethinim clad in glittering mail. Moving with admirable order, they ranged themselves along the four walls of the chamber, and then stood, shield and spear at their back, as silent and motionless as statues.

These Nethinim formed a part of the temple guards, servants of Eleazar, who, independently of their oath of obedience to their captain, were for other reasons devotedly attached to his person. Whatever he should bid them do, that would they do.

And what was his bidding to be? The silent Sanhedrim waited in wonder, indignation, fear.

"The vote of to-day has taught me," said Eleazar, "who are the friends and who are the foes of Israel. Let those who are on my side," he continued, "move to the right."

The invitation was accepted by not more than a dozen members, among them being Matthias the President, and Simeon ben Gamaliel.

"From to-day," continued Eleazar, "the temple becomes the seat of a holy war, the abode of the Lord's host, a citadel in the service of freedom. Henceforth, its gates open only to the true worshipers of Israel, whose foes ye are," he added, turning to his Sanhedrist opponents. "Withdraw, ere the scourges of the Nethinim quicken your steps."

The fierce storm of indignant protest that burst from Ananias and his party met with a savage laugh from Eleazar.

"You dare threaten us with expulsion from the temple?" cried Ananias, his eyes blazing with wrath.

"This is no place for the friends of Cæsar. What! ye will not budge? Guards, drive these traitors forth."

As if the command were a joy to them, the Nethinim rushed forward, at the same time drawing forth scourges and whips which they applied without more ado to the bodies of the immovable Sanhedrists.

Then ensued a strange scene. From the Sanhedrim came screams of pain and fierce protests, undignified scufflings and even oaths.

Their feeble resistance was soon overborne; without weapons, and inferior in numbers and strength to their more youthful opponents, they were thrust forth from the Hall of Squares, and driven across the wide court of the Gentiles.

A sight so unusual at once attracted the attention of the multitude, who were at first disposed to side with the struggling Sanhedrim, but the magical words, "Friends of the Romans," quickly turned their sympathies into the opposite scale, so that they readily joined the Nethinim in the work of expulsion; and the end of it all was that the venerable fathers found themselves outside the temple, indignant and breathless, disheveled and bleeding.

After a brief consultation, they took their way across the Tyropæon Bridge to the Upper City, and entered the palace of Ananias. From its flat roof they could see something of what was passing in the temple. Every part of the holy house was glittering with arms. Eleazar was making good his word; the temple was being garrisoned, in the interests not of Rome, but of Israel.

Aware of the hatred with which his pro-Roman sympathies were regarded by the mob, Ananias, in conjunction with a large body of Jewish loyalists, deemed it prudent, before the day was out, to take refuge with the soldiers in the Prætorium.

Late that same night, Berenice escorted by a small retinue made her way to this palace; and, while her guards waited without, she herself entered to take a farewell of Crispus.

She came with startling tidings. Simon the Black was in the city, and, resorting to a master-stroke of policy, had freed all the poor debtors—and they were a very numerous body in Jerusalem—by persuading them to set fire to the Archeion in Ophel, the building in which were registered all monetary loans contracted by private citizens, such official registration constituting the only legal proof of the transaction. Having thus involved the multitude in an irrevocable act of sedition, Simon had next led them forth to Olivet, where the Zealots of Manahem, returning in triumph from the conquest of Masada, were now engaged, by the torches' glare, in making a free distribution of arms to all who were willing to fight.

With signs of the liveliest agitation, the princess told how it was the intention of the mob on the following morning to storm the two Roman strongholds, and massacre the garrisons by way of retaliation for the butchery wrought by Florus.

" Will you not leave the city with me, ere it be too late? " she asked of Crispus in earnest tones.

" 'Tis not the fashion of Romans to desert their post, however numerous the foe," returned Crispus.

" Your departure will not be desertion, for no one

has ordered *you* to fight. Your station here is a voluntary one."

"I will not leave my fellow-countrymen to their fate! That your people have good cause for insurrection is, alas! but too true. But, for all that, my way is clear. I am a patriot and a Cestius, and it is my duty to keep the Roman eagle supreme in this city, or die in the attempt."

Berenice was silent for a moment; then, laying her hand upon his arm, she said in tender tones:

"Let me stay here to help you; you may become wounded, and who is there to nurse you? And if you die, which heaven forbid, I—I will die with you."

Crispus could not but be touched with this expression of sympathy on her part. Forgetting the incident in the synagogue, he felt that he could love her, if she were always like this. And as he had once thought Vashti's face to be like Berenice's, so now did he think Berenice's face like Vashti's, as he beheld it at this moment transfigured with a beautiful and heroic light.

"Princess, this is no place for you," said he gently.

He conducted the reluctant and sorrowful Berenice to her palanquin at the palace gate. As he parted from her some tempting spirit bade him whisper tenderly:

"Farewell, *Athenaïs.*"

He might not have pronounced that name had he foreseen its effect. Her sweet and lovable expression vanished in a moment, to be replaced by a cold, suspicious look that repelled him as much as the other had attracted.

"Why do you call me by that name?" she asked, seeming to shrink from him.

"Perhaps I am trying an experiment, princess," said he, significantly.

Evidently it was an experiment that did not please Berenice. She looked for all the world like a woman detected in a secret. With a glance that might be interpreted as one almost of fear, she sank back on the cushions of the palanquin, and, without another word to him, gave the order for the bearers to proceed.

In pensive mood, Crispus watched her departure. Whether she were Athenaïs, or whether she were not, it was difficult to see why the simple mention of the name should act so strangely upon her. That he had not lost her favor, however, was evidenced by the arrival, during the night, of three thousand Jewish cavalry. They were the troops of King Agrippa, and had been sent by him to bring his sister safely out of the troubled city; meeting them on the way, Berenice had bidden them go on to the help of the little garrison in the Prætorium. It can readily be imagined how gladly these new auxiliaries were welcomed by Metilius, but when Crispus suggested that one-half of them should proceed to Antonia, Darius, the master of the horse, declined, on the ground that the princess' orders were that he should fight for the Prætorium only.

# CHAPTER XII

## "VÆ VICTIS!"

EARLY next morning the Zealot chief Manahem, who, with his followers, had camped during the night upon Olivet, descended that mount, and, seated upon a chariot, entered the city with an air of pomp and state that moved the spleen of Eleazar, as he watched the procession from the roof of the temple-cloisters.

"Is this fellow a king?" said he. "Will he reign at Jerusalem?"

Manahem was welcomed with enthusiastic acclamation by the newly-armed populace, who demanded that he should at once lead them against Antonia, fully believing that he who had taken Masada would have no difficulty in taking a similar fortress. Manahem could not decline this task without risking his character for bravery; so, after plundering and burning the deserted palaces of Agrippa and Ananias, he advanced at the head of a tumultuous and disorderly throng towards the Turris Antonia, where, having procured silence, he—in very bad Latin—called upon the commandant to surrender the fortress.

"I am a Roman."

And the officer, deeming that answer sufficient, disdained to give any other.

"So was he who held Masada," replied the Zealot chief, giving the signal for the attack.

All day long under Manahem's leadership a fierce fight raged round the fortress, but when night fell, the Jews had nothing to show for their fiery valor except their heavy tale of dead and dying.

Manahem's wrath, arising from his failure, was enhanced by the remark of Simon, who, out of jealousy, had refrained from helping his brother-chief.

"You have caused the holy seed to be massacred."

"Thou shalt captain them thyself to-morrow," said Manahem.

"Be it so," replied the Black Zealot calmly.

Next morning when the multitude had again assembled for war Simon thus addressed them:

"Let him who had father or mother, son or daughter, killed in the day of Florus come forward."

Immediately hundreds of men pushed their way to the front.

"Behold the men who killed them!" cried Simon, pointing with his sword to the fortress.

This lie, for such it was—the garrison having taken no part whatever in the massacre—had a telling effect upon the crowd, filling them with new fire and new fury. Led on by Simon in person, they rushed forward with the scaling ladders and planted them against the walls, though it was only to be driven back again. For many hours the battle raged; nineteen times repulsed, they returned with spirit unabated to the attack; at the twentieth assault, which took place towards the close of the day, the Jews succeeded in effecting an entrance.

"Leave not one alive!" was their cry. "Did they spare us and our little ones?"

The little garrison, faced by overwhelming numbers, bravely maintained the honor of the Roman name; with never a thought of asking for quarter, they fought doggedly on, "each stepping where his comrade fell," till the blade glimmered in the grasp of the last man.

The standard that on the loftiest tower had so long flaunted before Jewish eyes the hateful letters S.P.Q.R., was hauled down and torn to shreds.

Thus fell, after two days' hard fighting, the great fortress of Antonia, an event that gave little pleasure to the victor of Masada, when he heard the people saying that night, "Manahem hath slain his thousands, but Simon his ten thousands!"

"To the Prætorium!" was the cry of the multitude next morning.

Manahem resumed his command; and, mounted on a prancing horse and followed by shouting crowds, he advanced to the open space fronting Gabbatha, and in a loud voice called for the surrender of the palace.

The reply to this was an arrow, which, as intended, went clean through the crest of Manahem's helmet.

"Your heart next time," said Metilius, "if you again propose treason to a Roman."

Manahem, swearing by Urim and by Thummim that the defenders of the Prætorium should meet with the same fate as those of Masada and Antonia, moved off to a quarter, whence, shielded from the missiles of the enemy, he could direct the operations of the siege.

The most pitiable object in the Prætorium at this time was Ananias. He had ventured to look forth from a window, and the crowd, recognizing him, yelled out their fierce hatred of the Sadducean hierarch, loudest among the shouters being priests themselves, whose words soon showed the cause of their fury.

"Who sent his servants round to collect the priests' tithes, and bludgeoned those that would not pay? Who but Ananias?"

"Who, when he had got the tithes, kept them to spend upon the harlot Asenath, so that many priests died for want? Who but Ananias?"

Before his terrified gaze they paraded the gory head of the Antonian commandant fixed upon the point of a lofty pike.

"Thus shall it be with thy head," they cried.

From that hour Ananias had the air of a man haunted with the certainty of coming down. With melancholy countenance, he wandered aimlessly through the splendid halls of the Prætorium, trembling at the din of battle outside its walls, and expecting at every moment to witness the fearful inrush of fierce-eyed, saber-brandishing Zealots, all athirst for his blood. His cowardice moved even his Jewish friends to contempt.

"Ananias, thy face is like a whited wall," laughed one.

A whited wall! Those words troubled him for the rest of the day, reviving, as they did, a saying that had long since passed from his memory.

"*God shall smite thee, thou whited wall:* for sittest thou to judge me after the law, and commandest me to be smitten contrary to the law?"[15]

Whence, and from whom, came these words? Evidently from some prisoner before his judgment-seat, whom he had ordered to be struck.

Yes; he remembered now; it was the indignant utterance of Paul of Tarsus—that Paul whose life he had sought to take by the daggers of the Zealots. And now, by the irony of a divine Nemesis, the daggers of these same Zealots were seeking to take *his* life!

Were there no secret chambers, he wailed, where one could hide? He had heard that Herod, in building this palace, had constructed such. Would no one point them out? But all were too busy with the siege to attend to his plaint.

That siege was conducted with cool skill on the part of the Romans, and with undisciplined fury on that of the Jews, who with that fanatical frenzy peculiar to Orientals, did not hesitate to fling their naked bodies upon the Roman pikes in the vain attempt to force a way into the Prætorium.

Every device known to the warfare of that age was tried by the Jews—escalade and fiery arrows, batteringram and secret mining—tried and made of none effect by the vigilance and ingenuity of Crispus. He, far more than Metilius, was the life and soul of the garrison, even as Simon proved himself more resourceful and valiant than his captain Manahem, who chose for the most part to sit still in a safe place, paying out five golden pieces for every Roman head brought to him.

King Agrippa's cavalry did excellent service at the first. Sallying forth at unexpected times they scattered the mob with their furious charges, and, sweeping the streets clear of the besiegers, they rode triumphantly round and round the palace. But Simon soon found a remedy for these tactics by sprinkling the ground with steel calthrops that lamed the horses and brought down the riders. After this the cavalry refused to make any more sallies. Simon marked their flagging zeal, and was quick to turn it to his own advantage. By the mouth of a herald he proclaimed that the Jewish defenders of the Prætorium should have full liberty to march out of the city with their arms and effects; some few, however, were to be exempted from this privilege, Ananias being one of the number. To his eternal disgrace, Darius, master of Agrippa's horse, accepted these terms; Metilius, owing to the paucity of his own band, was unable to prevent this defection, and accordingly, on the twenty-first morning of the siege, the Jewish contingent began to file through the front gate of the Prætorium, amid the jeers and curses of those whom they were leaving to their fate.

Death had reduced the number of the Romans to two hundred and fifty; and, as it was impossible with so small a force to defend the whole circuit of the Prætorium, Metilius seized the opportunity while the eyes of the Zealots were fastened upon the outgoing Jewish troops to withdraw quietly and quickly to the three great towers of Mariamne, Phasaelus, and Hippicus, erected by Herod the Great, and respectively dedicated to the memory of his wife, his brother, and his friend—towers situated upon the city-wall, which, at this point, formed in itself the northern and western sides of the Prætorium.

In the matter of military architecture, antiquity had

nothing to show more marvelous than these three towers. Each stood upon a base of stone without any chamber or vacuity in it, the base of Mariamne forming a solid cube of thirty feet, that of Phasaelus forty, and that of Hippicus sixty. The battering-ram was powerless against these enormous blocks, compacted with unequaled perfection, and bound together by iron cramps.

The Zealots, quickly discovering that the Prætorium had been abandoned by its defenders, entered, and a wild scene ensued. Never remarkable for discipline or for subserviency to their chiefs, they wrangled fiercely over the spoil, even to the extent of drawing swords upon each other. Upon one point, however, all were agreed—namely, that the beautiful sculptures adorning this old Herodian palace were a violation of the Second Commandment, and an insult to the Jewish religion.

"Idols!" they screamed.

Making no distinction between the statues of mortals and those of gods, they called for hammer and mallet, and broke all alike to pieces.

"Vashti's image among the rest, I suppose," muttered Crispus, as he watched the work of destruction. "I would have given much to preserve it."

The next day two Zealots, who had been exploring every corner of the dismantled palace, emerged with a shout, leading captive an old man. It was Ananias, who had lain during the night concealed in a subterranean aqueduct.

More dead than alive, the trembling priest, who had once held despotic sway in Jerusalem, was hauled amid contumely and blows to the presence of Manahem, who received him with a smile of savage satisfaction.

"What shall be done to this friend of the Romans? this traitor to his country?" said he, affecting to ask the advice of Simon, whom he secretly hated, yet dared not hurt.

And herein Simon behaved in very subtle fashion, for wishing Ananias to die, yet suspecting that if he said as much, Manahem, out of sheer opposition, would adopt a contrary course, he made answer:

"Let him live."

It was with a malicious smile that Manahem replied:
"It is my will that he dies."

And at his nod two Zealots buried their daggers deep in the breast of the one-time high priest.[16]

An hour afterwards Simon was in the temple-court conversing with Eleazar.

"Thy sire is dead."

Eleazar was startled, and to some extent grieved. Filial sentiment was not altogether dead in him, in spite of his recent quarrel with Ananias, and on learning how the latter had died, he exclaimed fiercely:

"God do so to me and more also if I make not the end of Manahem as the end of Ananias!"

The arrogant Manahem, unconscious of the forces secretly working against him, now entered upon a course that brought him to ruin.

In the sack of the Prætorium he had come across a purple robe and a golden crown, both belonging formerly to Herod the Great, and, putting these emblems of royalty upon himself, he began to assume the air of a king.

Leaving a strong force to watch the towers, Manahem, regally attired, marched with the rest of his followers to the temple, declaring his purpose to be a religious one; he came to offer a sacrifice as a means of obtaining further victories.

But Eleazar, suspecting that his design was to gain possession of the temple-fortress, without which Manahem could never be master of the city, closed the gates, set every available Levite on guard, and refused admission to the Zealot chief.

And now arose a dissension among the followers of Manahem; some were for obtaining ingress to the temple by force of arms, but others, sensible that Eleazar was as good a patriot as Manahem, were for withdrawing.

Then Eleazar, seeing the quarrel becoming great among them, fanned the flame by a speech that ended with the words:

"Men, zealous for God, you who out of a love of liberty have revolted from the Romans, do you now betray that liberty? You who have cast off the yoke of a foreign tyrant, do you now take upon you the yoke of one home-born?"

Simon, who was standing beside Eleazar, clenched the matter.

"Ten thousand gold pieces to the man who brings me the head of Manahem," he shouted.

Thereafter all was confusion.

Some of the Zealots, siding with Eleazar, turned their swords against their former chief, of whose tyranny they had already begun to weary; the rest, closing around, endeavored to defend him. Then, beneath the temple walls, there began a desperate fight, maintained for a short time with equal fortune on both sides; but when the armed Levites, under Simon and Eleazar, descended from the temple, the scale of battle turned. The defeated party fled through Ophel, within whose narrow and winding streets Manahem contrived to elude capture; but only for a day or so. Discovered in his hiding-place, he was dragged forth and slaughtered.

Thus ignominiously perished the last of the sons of the famous Judas, the Galilean, sons, who, like their untamable father, had spent their lives among the craggy heights of Judæa, waging guerilla warfare with the Roman.

Eleazar now took upon himself the captaincy of all the disorderly elements in the city. Simon was his second in command, and under their joint direction the siege against the Roman garrison in the three Herodian towers was pressed forward with vigor. But the fierce attack was met by a defense equally fierce; ten Zealots died for every Roman, since the garrison from the cover of their lofty walls could deal far more hurt to the besiegers than the besiegers could to them.

Yet, in spite of the fact that the advantage was all on his side, not many days had passed before Metilius, yielding to a strange and unaccountable spirit of cowardice, suddenly announced his intention of seeking terms with the enemy. Crispus, thunderstruck at this weak-mindedness, argued in vain. Metilius held the command, and it was his to do even as he listed.

Great was Eleazar's satisfaction to hear himself addressed from the battlements by Metilius on the question of capitulation.

An immediate armistice was proclaimed; and Eleazar, after a brief deliberation with Simon, declared that if the Romans would descend from the towers, and deliver up their arms, they should be permitted to go forth from the city free and uninjured. To this Metilius assented, and the compact was ratified by the reception into the towers of three Jews, distinguished in rank, who, giving their right hand to the tribune, swore "by the altar of God" to carry out the promised stipulations.

Placed in a disgraceful position by this coming surrender, Crispus determined at first that he would remain behind, though he should be the only one to do so; sword in hand he would die, defending to the last the Tower of Hippicus. But he soon relinquished this notion as a piece of splendid but useless heroism; he would be casting away his life without saving the fortress. It would be wiser and more satisfactory to live on, and take part in his father's campaign against the city, a campaign that would soon reduce the Jews to submission again.

At the hour fixed for the surrender—it was the Sabbath day—the Romans descended from the towers, and stood on level ground.

They were received by Eleazar and Simon, who pointed the way the soldiers should march. Metilius, on looking, saw that his band would have to pass beneath two spears set obliquely in the ground so as to form a kind of yoke; the Jews were adopting a Roman ceremony applied both to slaves and to captives taken in war.

At this sight the blood even of Metilius rebelled.

"This was not included in the compact," said he.

"Nor excluded," replied Eleazar with an insulting smile. "March!"

Opposition being, in the circumstances, futile, the Romans were compelled to submit to the humiliating ceremony. As each passed beneath the yoke he delivered his sword and buckler to certain of the Zealots stationed there to receive them.

But when the last Roman had been deprived of his arms, the Levitical guards of Eleazar, sword in hand, came crowding round the little band. Their significant looks sent a sudden suspicion to the hearts of the Romans.

"The end has come, Metilius," said Crispus. "'Twere better to have gone on fighting."

"Prepare for death, ye uncircumcized fools," cried Eleazar with a savage laugh.

"Death?" faltered Metilius. "Death, when ye have vowed by a solemn oath to respect our lives!"

"We swore by the altar of God, and such oath is not binding upon the conscience of a Jew. Here standeth Gamaliel's son, Simeon, master of all the learning of the scribes. Let him say whether I speak falsely."

And that rabbi, who chanced to be present, stepped forward to justify Eleazar's assertion.

"The elders have delivered it," said he, "that if a man swear by the gold of the altar he must keep his oath, or dread condemnation; but if he swear by the altar only, he is not guilty if he break his word."

But Johanan ben Zacchai, who happened likewise to be present, opposed this casuistry.

"Simeon," said he, "which is the greater, the gold, or the altar that sanctifieth the gold?" And, turning to Eleazar, he said:

"Will ye indeed slay these men?"

"Aye! Did they show us mercy in the day of Florus?"

"You will never get another Roman garrison to submit."

"Be it so."

"Defer the deed, for to-day is the Sabbath."

"A holy day and a holy deed—to exterminate idolaters."

Simon, although a party to Eleazar's guilty trick, was nevertheless willing to make an exception in favor of one of the captives.

"Give me the life of this man," said he, pointing to Crispus.

"That fellow?" said Eleazar, with a wrathful glance at Crispus. "He is the one who has done us the most hurt. Why do you seek to spare him?"

"Because at my trial he was the first to rise and rebuke the wicked Florus."

"He is the man," said Simeon ben Gamaliel, "who defied and insulted us in our own synagogue by snatching a Christian damsel from the punishment justly due to her."

"These heathen," said Eleazar, "when they get the opportunity, try to make us forswear our faith. Verily, we will do the like by them."

The bravery exhibited by Crispus throughout the siege of the Prætorium had created in Eleazar a feeling, not of admiration, but of rage; and this rage was now enhanced by the serene and fearless bearing of the captive.

Drawing his sword he walked over to Crispus.

"Cursed polytheist, what is the name of your chief god?"

"He is called Jupiter."

"Then curse the name of Jupiter, if you would save your soul alive."

Eleazar's sneering and insulting menace drove Crispus to a foolish, yet heroic, defiance.

"Men," said he, turning to the Romans behind him, "the end has come. Let us die bravely." Then, raising his hand aloft to heaven, he cried, "Sovereign Jupiter, all hail!"

"Swine that thou art!" exclaimed Eleazar; and, grinding his teeth with rage, he plunged his sword to the very hilt into the side of Crispus, who sank to the ground as one dead.

Quickened by Eleazar's example, the Levites and Zealots began a massacre of the defenseless captives. But Crispus' words had not been without effect upon the Romans. How bravely they died let that historian say who was contemporary with the event.

"They neither defended themselves, nor asked for mercy, but only reproached their slayers for breaking their oath and the articles of capitulation. And thus were all these men barbarously murdered, all excepting"—alas! that it should be written of a Roman!—"all excepting Metilius; for when he entreated for mercy and promised that he would turn proselyte and be circumcized, they saved him alive, but none else."

Thus was Roman rule extinguished in Jerusalem in the year 66 A.D., a little more than a century after its capture by the great Pompey.

On that same Sabbath, the high priest Matthias, in view of the great triumph, decreed that the evening sacrifice should partake of a thanksgiving character; and that, to enhance the dignity of the occasion, the water used in the service should be taken, not from

"*Væ Victis!*" 159

the ordinary draw-well in the southern court of the sanctuary, but from the hallowed Pool of Siloam outside the city wall.

But the Levitical train dispatched on that errand returned with dismayed faces and empty urns.

Siloam would take no part in the wicked thanksgiving. *Its waters had ceased flowing!*[17]

# CHAPTER XIII

### A GOOD SAMARITAN

"HE is opening his eyes! *He lives!*"

So spoke Vashti as she knelt beside the silent and recumbent form of Crispus.

The unmistakable rapture in her tone seemed to displease the woman standing beside her.

"Why should you be glad, child? He is an enemy to our race."

"Mother!" said the girl, reproachfully. "Did he not save me from scourging?"

"Is that any reason why we should imperil our lives on his account? We shall be stoned to death if the Zealots learn that we are hiding a Roman in our house. Better for us that he were dead."

"O, mother, hush! lest he should hear your unkind words."

Crispus, though awake, heard nothing of this conversation, being too faint and confused at first to understand anything. Gradually, with the clearing of his senses, he discovered himself to be lying upon the floor of a low-roofed chamber that had latticed windows, and was prettily furnished in Oriental style. He wondered what place it was, and how he came to be there. Then, as memory began to assert its sway, he recalled the scene in which he had last closed his eyes—Eleazar's glare of hatred, the swift sword-flash, the sharp pang of pain, and the sinking into darkness and insensibility.

He had expected sudden death at the hands of Eleazar; but clearly he was not dead yet. Some person must have removed his supposed corpse from the pile

## A Good Samaritan

of massacred Romans, and who could that person be but the lovely maiden that knelt beside him?

He tried to lift himself upon one elbow, but fell back exhausted by the effort. There was no strength left in him.

"Are you in pain?" asked Vashti.

"No; only weak—weak!" he said in a voice that startled him; he could not speak above a hollow whisper.

Vashti placed her left arm beneath him; and, lifting him, she put a cup to his lips.

"Drink!" said she.

Crispus drank, of what he knew not—some dark liquid—but it seemed to endow him with new life.

"Eat!" was her next command.

Submissive as a child, Crispus ate of whatever her hand offered.

"And now," continued she, "sleep, and sleep will give you strength."

He wanted to ask questions, but Vashti enjoined silence by placing her finger upon his lip in so pretty a way that he was fain to do her bidding; so, closing his eyes, Crispus, almost against his will, dropped off to sleep again.

His sleep extended over several hours.

On waking he found Vashti by his side again, ready to minister to his wants; and, as these wants included a desire for knowledge on certain points, she proceeded to enlighten him.

"You are in my mother's house," said she. "This is my own chamber; and there," she continued, pointing with pride to several tiers of shelves filled with papyrus rolls, "there are my Greek books."

She then went on to tell him how he came to be there. After the massacre of the Roman garrison, Josephus, at her request, went to the fierce Eleazar and asked for the body of Crispus, saying, "He is a Roman noble, known to me. I pray you, let me give him honorable burial." Eleazar's reply was, "Take him; I war not with the dead." When the supposed corpse of Crispus had been conveyed to her house Vashti sorrowed over it, but her grief suddenly turned to joy when she detected a movement of his lips.

By a happy stroke of fortune—the hand of God, Vashti called it—Eleazar's sword had passed through the ribs of Crispus without injuring the vital parts. His seeming death was a swoon due to loss of blood, a loss so great that a few more drops might have ended the matter. There was life in him, however—faint it might be—but still life, life that with due care might be preserved. And so—for they durst not call in a physician, lest the truth should become known to the outside world—she and her mother, who had some knowledge of the healing art, had dressed his wounds and carried him to this chamber.

Vashti smiled sweetly when Crispus murmured his gratitude. "Now, I pray the gods that the Zealots may not discover this, your kindness to me."

Then she told him of Metilius' base appeal for life, a story to which Crispus listened with scorn.

"Rightly named Metilius—little coward!" said he. "What became of him?"

"The Zealots dismissed him with contempt."

"What a life his will be! He'll never dare show his face among Romans again."

He attempted to raise himself, but, as on the previous day, found that he was too weak to do so.

"How long am I to lie here?" he said with something like a groan.

"Till your lost blood be made good."

"When will that be?"

And though pre-informed by her mother that Crispus' return to vigor was likely to be a matter of weeks, Vashti replied with a cheerful smile, "Not many days hence," justifying herself by the knowledge that to put a patient in a desponding mood is to retard his recovery.

Vashti's mother was named Miriam, an elderly dame, so hard and sour of visage, that Crispus could but wonder how she came to have a daughter so fair and graceful. He formed a somewhat adverse opinion of Miriam. True, she visited his chamber every day; but, as he could plainly see, her inquiries as to his progress were merely perfunctory; in spite of the fact that he was the son of the great Roman Legate of Syria, she looked upon him as an encumbrance—nay, more, as a positive danger, in view of Zealot rule, a person to be got rid of at the earliest opportunity; and Crispus inwardly chafed at being unable to oblige her in this respect. A Jewess of the orthodox, narrow-minded type, she was out of sympathy with Vashti's ideals; and Crispus mentally blessed the late Hyrcanus in that he was of a different character from his wife, and had given his daughter an Hellenic as well as an Hebraic training.

The dissimilitude betwixt mother and daughter had become accentuated of late owing to Vashti's conversion to Christianity. When questioned on this last matter, Vashti acknowledged, striving the while to hide her tears, that the change of faith had caused Miriam to become strangely hard and cold.

It was perhaps this growing spirit of estrangement on the part of Miriam that caused Vashti to find a solace in the companionship of Crispus, who, though a heathen, seemed more in sympathy with her than her own Judaic mother.

Crispus marveled at Vashti's care for him, marveled still more as the days went by without any slackening of her ministrations. An ideal nurse, she seemed bent on doing everything within her power to render pleasant his enforced inactivity. Tactful to a nicety, she was never in the way and never out of it. Responsive to the passing whims of her patient—and what patient is not whimsical at times?—she could recognize when he wished for solitude, and would leave him to himself;

if he were desirous of conversation, she was ever ready to meet his desire. On learning that he had a great liking for Herodotus, she drew that charming, old-world historian from her little library, and read to him day by day, seldom failing to illumine the subject with interesting comments of her own; and once, at eventide, she took her harp and sang in a voice so sweet that Crispus begged for a repetition of the pleasure; and, ever after that, as the shades of twilight fell, she would sing to him from that cycle of psalms which, though he knew it not, are destined to be sung till the end of time.

It puzzled Crispus that Vashti should so interest herself in him. Was this interest the expression merely of her gratitude, for the service he had rendered her in the synagogue, or was it the expression of a more tender sentiment? Was Vashti seeking to win his love? The thought troubled him. It was hard to be compelled to crush this rising desire on her part—that is, supposing it existed—for however pure, attractive, and beautiful Vashti might be, she was not for him; he must remain faithful to the unknown Athenaïs, not only because it was a point of honor for a Cestius to keep faith, but also because his ambition could not easily forego the kingdom dependent upon his mysterious marriage.

Vashti, it seemed, had a little brother, a child of eighteen months. One morning she brought him with some diffidence into the chamber, and, finding that Crispus did not object to his presence, but, on the contrary, derived considerable amusement from his infantine attempts at talking, she brought him every day; and though Vashti was " as learned as Minerva " —Crispus' own expression—she proved herself in other respects a veritable tom-boy, playing at " hide and seek," and romping round the room till the child fairly shrieked with delight. It was a new feature in her character, and one that pleased Crispus.

## A Good Samaritan

Tired at last of play the little fellow clambered upon his sister's knee, and nestled against her breast.

Vashti's remark that he was called Arad led to a talk upon personal names and their meanings; and, of course, Crispus soon fastened his attention upon her own name.

"Vashti is a Persian word said to mean beautiful," she replied with a little blush.

"You could not change it for one more appropriate," remarked Crispus, "unless it were———"

He paused. A wild suspicion had suddenly taken possession of him, a suspicion that set his pulses thrilling with a delicious pleasure.

"What new name would you suggest?" asked Vashti with a wondering smile.

"What do you say to Athenaïs?" he asked, watching her keenly as he spoke.

Was he mistaken, or did Vashti give a start as if she recognized the hidden purport of the question? Her surprise, if such it were, was quickly under control. She looked at him with eyes calm and unfathomable in their expression.

"No true Hebrew maiden would like *that* name."

"Wherein doth it offend?"

"It is derived from the name of a Grecian goddess."

"And therefore suitable for one as learned as Athene."

Vashti smilingly shook her golden tresses at the compliment.

"I do not like the name," she said, as she gently rocked Arad to sleep.

So far Crispus' experiment was a failure. There was nothing in her manner to suggest the hypothesis that she had been the veiled lady of Beth-tamar. Still, there seemed to be a sort of shadowy connection between her and the unknown Athenaïs. He reasoned thus:—
Vashti was very like the statue of one, Pythodoris; that

statue was the gift of Polemo; Polemo was he who had arranged the wedding of Athenaïs.

Crispus resolved to proceed warily.

"You appear to be well versed in Grecian history," said he. "Can you tell me who Pythodoris was?"

Vashti became lost in thought for a few moments, and then replied:

"There was a queen of Pontus who bore that name. She died about thirty years ago."

"Any relation to the present king, Polemo?"

"His mother."

"Was she a beautiful woman?"

"I'm sure I don't know," laughed Vashti. "Why do you ask?"

"There was a statue of her in the Prætorium."

"Then if you've seen it you ought to know whether she were beautiful."

"The statue was very like *you*."

"Oh! then she wasn't *very* beautiful."

"The statue was so like you that at first sight I thought it was meant for nobody else till the name Pythodoris, carved on the pedestal, corrected my error."

Vashti's eyes opened wide in wonder. She could assign no reason why the statue of Pythodoris should resemble herself.

"And she was the mother of the present king, you say? Have you ever seen this Polemo?"

Vashti replied in the negative.

"But he was present at the banquet of Florus."

"Then I suppose I must have seen him without knowing him," replied Vashti; and, having succeeded in hushing her little brother to sleep, she carried him gently from the room.

Something like a sigh escaped from Crispus as he realized that since Vashti did not know King Polemo she could not have been the veiled lady of Beth-tamar.

Next day when Crispus suggested that it might

## A Good Samaritan

hasten his recovery if he could breathe the purer air of the roof, Vashti and her mother, lifting the cords at the head and foot of his pallet, carried it, albeit with some difficulty, up the short staircase and deposited it upon the flat roof beneath the shade of a trellis overhung with vine-leaves, so placing the pallet as to prevent him from being overlooked by the occupants of the neighboring houses; while at the same time an opening in the parapet near by enabled him, whenever he chose to raise himself upon his elbow, to observe a good deal of what was going on in the streets below.

All Jerusalem was resounding with the preparations for war. Though the aged and the wise might shake their heads gravely and hold aloof from the revolutionary movement, the young and the unthinking, elated at seeing the last vestige of Roman rule swept from the capital, flung in their lot with the Zealots and spent a considerable portion of each day in the performance of military exercises under captains appointed by Eleazar and Simon. The city walls were being repaired and strengthened, the very women and children laboring enthusiastically in the task. The air rang with the beating of steel upon the anvil, the steel that was to be dyed deep in Roman blood! At night Ophel was one red glow with the light that came from the various forges.

"They have hewn down the golden eagle from the gate of the temple," said Vashti.

"They cannot take him from the sky, however," replied Crispus, pointing to a magnificent specimen that was sailing aloft with slow and majestic motion. Suddenly, this eagle drooped its pinions, and, descending like a plummet, alighted upon the parapet just above the head of Crispus.

Vashti started back with a little scream; then, by motioning with her hands, she tried to make the eagle fly off; he took no notice of her, however, but sat with unruffled plumage, the embodiment of majesty and gravity. Try as she would Vashti could not get the eagle to stir, but, finding that he remained quiet and showed no disposition to attack either Crispus or herself, she relinquished her efforts and resumed her conversation, timorously glancing from time to time at the eagle, which kept its post as though it were some faithful sentinel appointed to watch over the patient.

This little incident was not without significance for Crispus, whose mind, in common with other minds of that day, saw an omen in anything out of the common. At the very moment when Eleazar was threatening him with death, he had appealed to sovereign Jupiter. Now, the eagle being the symbol of that deity as well as of the Roman empire, he could not help interpreting its presence as a heaven-sent assurance that Jove and the legions would effect his safety. Aware, however, that Vashti had no faith in his gods, he kept this opinion to himself.

In the evening the eagle flew off. The two watched till it became a mere black speck upon the glowing gold of the western sky—watched till it faded from view.

"It will return on the morrow," said Crispus confidently.

Sure enough, next morning the eagle came winging its way eastward; and, as before, it alighted upon the parapet above the head of Crispus, as if bent on renewing its watch. Vashti, grown somewhat accustomed to its presence, viewed it now with less apprehension, and made no attempt to repel it.

"The money of the new government," said she, with a sad smile, exhibiting a shekel, one of those pieces known to the Jews of after ages as "The money of danger," and now, by reason of their rarity, eagerly sought by numismatists.

"If their fighting prove no better than their coinage, it will go ill with them," remarked Crispus, who,

## A Good Samaritan

on closely inspecting the supposed shekel, saw that it was in reality a Roman coin that had recently received in the Jewish mint a fresh stamp—namely, that of a palm branch encircled with Hebraic characters, whose signification was, "*The first year of the freedom of Zion.*"

So imperfectly, however, had the work been executed that the original effigy, the head of Nero, with its Latin inscription, was discernible beneath the Jewish impression.

"They try to efface Cæsar, but fail," said Crispus. "Good! I accept the omen."

At eventide the eagle flew off, returning again next morning. On the fourth day, however, it did not appear, nor on any subsequent day.

# CHAPTER XIV

#### "THOU WILT NEVER TAKE THE CITY"

THE moon of a lovely autumnal night silvered the sleeping Roman camp that lay at the entrance of "the going up to Beth-horon." Not a sound disturbed the silence, save the light tread of the vigilant sentinels pacing their rounds.

The array of black tents, glittering arms, and lofty standards, occupied a vast area, square in shape, and defended on all sides by an earthen rampart, and an outer trench filled with water from a neighboring stream—defenses made by a three-hours' labor with mattock and spade, the whole army having toiled at the task. No matter how short their stay in a place —and the camping on the present occasion was for one night only—the Roman legionaries would never, at least in a hostile country, take their sleep till they had secured themselves from attack in the manner just described. Four gates, facing the four points of the compass, gave entrance to the camp, whose countless lines of tents crossing each other at right angles looked with the intervening spaces like the streets and squares of a well-planned city.

This military force was under the command of Cestius Gallus, imperial Legate of Syria, and its object was the restoration to Roman rule of the rebellious city of Jerusalem, sixteen miles distant.

The tent of the general-in-chief, or, to employ the Latin term, the prætorium, was pitched, according to immemorial custom, by the gate nearest to the enemy, in this case the southern one, as being on the side towards Jerusalem.

This tent, furnished in the simplest fashion and

## "Thou Wilt Never Take the City" 171

lighted by a lamp pendent from the roof, contained but one occupant, the Legate.

He was a man of about sixty years, grave and soldierly; his face at ordinary times had a look that showed him to be, in spite of his military profession, a man of a humane and kindly disposition; but now, and for many days past, there had been in his aspect something so stern and cold that the soldier about to ask a favor of his general shrank away, reserving the matter for another time.

The sudden entering of a man unannounced caused the Legate to look up with a frown.

"Who comes here?" said he, shading his eyes with his hand.

"A wise man and a fool."

"How can that be, royal Polemo?" said Cestius, smoothing his brows as he recognized his visitor.

"He who is not a fool at times is never a wise man," returned the Pontic king, taking his seat with an air that proved him to be on familiar terms with the Legate.

"You have returned from Achaia very quickly," said Cestius.

"Twelve days on the sea going and coming. I doubt whether the double voyage were ever performed in so short a time. I found the god"—this with a sneer—"at Olympia."

"You told him of the revolt?"

"All that I knew of it."

"And his commands?"

Polemo drew forth a scroll of papyrus, secured with red wax and impressed with a seal which Cestius knew to be that of Nero. Breaking the seal, the Legate read the missive, first silently, and then, for the benefit of Polemo, aloud.

"Our faithful servant, Cestius Gallus, is herewith granted full liberty to deal with the rebellious city of

Jerusalem in whatever way he deemeth best for the interests of the Roman republic.

"Given on this, the eighth of the Ides of September, in the twelfth year of our reign.   NERO AUGUSTUS."

"Liberty to deal with the city as I please?" exclaimed Cestius, a fierce fire sparkling from his eyes and a color lighting up his hitherto sallow cheek. "*Delenda est Hierosolyma!* Not a man in it shall live. Its women and children shall be sold into slavery. I will give their temple to the flames and the city to destruction. Not one stone of it shall be left standing upon another. Jerusalem shall be blotted from the face of the earth."

This threatened doom being the very end for which Polemo had been clandestinely working during a space of many years was received by him with secret rapture; nevertheless he could not help wondering why Cestius, usually humane in his dealings, should have become animated by a spirit so merciless. But now, as Polemo noticed, what he had not noticed before, namely, that the Legate was wearing a black pallium, the emblem of mourning, he was seized with a sudden suspicion.

"I am the last of my race," said Cestius, answering the question expressed by the other's eyes. "There is no son to carry on my name."

"Say not that Crispus is dead!" gasped Polemo, whose look of grief could not have been keener if he, and not Cestius, had been the father. "Crispus dead! Then my plan for the humiliation of—Oh, it cannot be! How? When?"

"You shall learn. 'Tis the time for it," said the Legate with a glance at a clepsydra that stood on the table before him.

"The time?" repeated Polemo wonderingly.

"Every night at this hour I strengthen my spirit in its purpose of vengeance by hearing anew from the mouth of an eye-witness the story of a massacre wrought by the lying oath of a cowardly priest."

Even as he spoke the curtain draping the entrance of the tent was lifted, and there entered two spearmen leading between them a captive whose dress and physiognomy bore unmistakable evidence of his Jewish origin.

"A deserter from the city. Now, fellow, tell thy tale."

Frequent repetition had made the captive fluent in his narration, so with an unfaltering voice and in a simple style he gave a full account of the calamitous ending to the brave defense of the Prætorium.

"Art certain that Eleazar's was a fatal stab?" asked Polemo.

"It could not have been otherwise; he dealt stroke upon stroke," replied the Jew, who saw no reason why he should not heighten the story of Eleazar's cruelty. Lives there a man who can relate an event exactly as it happened?

"Woe to Eleazar!" said Cestius. "'Twere better for him had he never been born."

"What became of the bodies of those that were massacred?" asked Polemo.

"They were taken outside the city to a place called Aceldama, where it is the custom to bury strangers. A trench was dug, and the corpses were flung into it, one upon another."

"You saw the body of Crispus treated thus?"

And the man stating, not what had happened, but what he fancied had happened, answered in the affirmative.

"Flung into a common grave! Lost to me forever!" murmured Cestius. "I am denied even the melancholy consolation of taking home his ashes."

With the morning light the Roman army, having breakfasted, prepared to resume its march.

At the first shrill sound of the trumpet the tents fell flat to the ground; at the second, which followed at a measured interval, they were piled with other baggage upon wagons and beasts of burden; at the third signal the march began, the vanguard filing off in stately order, eight abreast. Soon the whole of the vast army was in motion, winding like a glittering, scaly serpent up the mountain pass that led towards Jerusalem. Mounted scouts pushed on ahead for the purpose of forestalling those ambuscades which are the delight of an Oriental people.

Cestius, who rode in the center of the host with King Polemo by his side, became annoyed at the irregular movements on the part of the columns composing the vanguard, who for a time would maintain a march so brisk as to leave a long interval between themselves and the central division, and then, without any apparent cause, would come to a dead halt, moving on again a few minutes afterwards. At last a stop was made of such duration that it brought the whole of the army following to a standstill, thus tending to create a degree of confusion not often witnessed in the Roman ranks. Unable any longer to control his impatience, Cestius, setting spurs to his steed, galloped forward, bent on administering a sharp reproof to the tribune in charge of the vanguard.

On being questioned as to the cause of this long halt that officer referred his angry general to the tall and stately figure of a priest, standing a few paces in front of the first rank and bearing in his hand the short *lituus* or augurial staff. It was Theomantes, priest of Jupiter Cæsarius, the one-time councilor of Florus, but now acting, and that at Cestius' own wish, as the official augur of the Roman army. The Legate had a high regard for him, but when Theomantes, presuming on this regard, ventured to check the advance of the whole army, he was undoubtedly usurping the authority of the general, an act not to be tolerated.

"How now, Theomantes?" cried Cestius angrily. "Why this delay?"

"Seest thou yon eagle?" said Theomantes, pointing to an eagle in front of them, poised apparently motionless in the air.

"I see it. And what then?"

"'Tis the divine director of our march. When it advances, we advance; when it stops, we stop; for so will it be to our advantage."

"And when it retreats, I suppose we must retreat," sneered Cestius. "Shall a father, bent on the sacred duty of avenging his son, be stayed by a fowl of the air? Fellow, thy bow and arrow," he cried, addressing a Cretan archer that stood by; and, having received what he had asked for, Cestius fitted a shaft to the string, and, taking aim at the eagle, let fly.

The shot was a good one; pierced by the arrow, the eagle dropped to the earth like a falling stone.

"Fools!" exclaimed the Legate scornfully, as he noticed the dismayed looks of the superstitious soldiers, "exercise your reason. If yon eagle had the power of foreseeing the future, would it not have kept far hence, and not have flown hither to meet its death by the arrow of Cestius?"

"Cestius Gallus," said the augur, solemnly, "thou hast slain the messenger sent by Jove to direct our march. The wrath of the gods will be upon thee for this. *Thou wilt never take the city.*"

With this he broke his augurial staff in two, and cast the pieces at Cestius' feet; then, walking to the roadside, he seated himself upon a crag; and, covering both head and face with his mantle, in token of grief, he added: "Here will I abide till I see thee returning in headlong confusion."

"I will prove thee a liar," said the Legate fiercely. "Forward!" he continued, addressing the vanguard.

The Jews, gazing from the lofty ramparts of their city, beheld with secret fear the drilled legions of Rome ascending and descending "the hills that stand about Jerusalem," and stationing themselves at every strategic point; their eyes, turn them which way they would, saw nothing but the glitter of the eagles; all retreat was cut off; the city was girt with a ring of steel.

As the house of Miriam, widow of Hyrcanus, was one of the highest on Mount Zion, and as Mount Zion was the highest of the four hills on which Jerusalem was built, it follows that the military display outside the city could not escape the notice of Crispus as he lay upon the roof. The sight filled him with patriotic pride, a pride enhanced by the knowledge that it was his father who led that mighty host; *he* would not fail in the work; Rome would again vindicate her supremacy; and Eleazar and the false, cowardly crew that had taken part in the barbarous massacre of the garrisons would receive their merited doom. A pity he, Crispus, must lie here, unable to join in the coming fight!

Beside his pallet sat the gentle Vashti, her eyes on the Roman host.

"Your father will not take the city," said she quietly; "at least, not at this time."

Crispus, almost startled by her air of certainty, asked what reason she had for her belief.

"There are in this city," replied Vashti, "a multitude of Christians over whom our Divine Master watcheth, for He is not dead but liveth eternally. Think you that He will permit His saints to fall by the sword of the Romans? I trow not; those guilty Jews who have hardened their heart against Him will receive their just doom; but of His disciples He saith, 'There shall not a hair of your head perish.' And therefore that we might know when the time is come for us to quit the city, He, while on earth, gave us this sign."

## "Thou Wilt Never Take the City" 177

Vashti drew from her bosom a scroll of papyrus written in Greek characters, and read from it the following sentence: "'*When ye shall see Jerusalem compassed with armies, then let them that are in the midst of it depart out.*'"

"How can they depart out with a hostile army camping all round?" asked Crispus, captiously.

"How, indeed? Therefore it is necessary that this hostile army should be withdrawn for a time."

"In order to give the Christians the opportunity to escape!" said Crispus with a touch of sarcasm in his voice.

Yes, that was her belief, and she had no other reason for it than a supposed prophetical passage in a book she called the Evangel! This was not the first time (for she had often talked to him about her religion) that Vashti had sought to connect her Divine Teacher with the course of contemporary events. In her view He was the central figure of the world's history; old times pointed to His coming; new times were to flow from it. Present events were taking place for no other reason than to advance the interests of the new religion. The general Cestius was merely a passive instrument in the hands of the deified Galilæan; his march to Jerusalem was not to vindicate the majesty of Rome, but to serve as a Divine sign to the Christians, and, having played the part allotted to him, he was to march back again without taking the city! Crispus could scarcely listen with patience to a theory so fantastical.

A Cestius to retreat? Go to!

However, as Vashti quietly remarked in answer to his arguments, the event would decide.

"Is your father a cruel man?" continued she.

"Quite the contrary; for a soldier he is said to be too merciful."

"Yet he has vowed to slay every man in the city, and to sell the women and children into slavery."

"How know you that?"

"It is shouted at us by the enemy whenever they draw near the wall, and not by the common soldiers only: the centurions mock us with the same doom."

"He thinks me dead, and hence his wrath. 'Tis a pity he should be in error. How it would gladden him to know that I am alive! Is there no way of communicating with him?"

Vashti reflected.

"I think," said she, "I can contrive to let him know that you are living."

"How?" asked Crispus, eagerly.

"If you will write a letter I will try to have it conveyed to him. I know a Christian youth, Heber by name, whom I have but to command, and he will perform this service for me. His house is upon the city wall. To get to the Roman camp he has but to lower himself by a rope. He can carry your message, but whether he can bring one back——"

"No. 'Twill be a dangerous business to be seen returning. Let him remain in the Roman camp. And tell him that whatever reward he likes to ask for—in reason—my delighted father will give. And now for stylus and papyrus."

Vashti flew to procure writing materials, and Crispus, sitting up, proceeded to indite the following epistle:

"To the most excellent of fathers, greeting.

"Cast off your black pallium, and make a sacrifice to Jupiter the Saviour, for I, your son Crispus, am not, as you suppose, in Hades, but am lodged with the widow Miriam, whose house is in the street of Millo, abiding secretly for fear of the Zealots. That I have not sought to escape to the Roman camp is due to my enfeebled frame, which would not be living at all, but for the care and attention of a sweet maiden named Vashti."

"You must delete the word *dulcis*," said Vashti.

But this Crispus declined to do.

"Therefore should you take the city"—he put this hypothetically in deference to Vashti's belief—"you must, as owing your son's life to her, deal leniently with the nation to which she belongs, and show the mercy that pertaineth to an honorable Roman general. May we soon meet. *Vale!*"

He added the date, together with a strange sign that puzzled Vashti.

"A private mark," he explained. "'Twill convince him of the authenticity of this little epistle."

Later in the day Vashti went off with the letter; and, returning after an interval of two hours, was able to announce that Heber had undertaken the charge, but from due regard to safety he would not make the attempt till after nightfall.

Evidently he kept his word, for when Vashti visited his house next day his mystified kinsfolk declared that he had vanished during the night, deserting apparently to the Roman camp, since they had discovered a rope hanging from the window of his room.

Crispus from his place on the roof continued to watch with a lively interest the doings of the Romans.

Three days were spent by the Legate in perfecting his arrangements for the taking of the city; on the fourth day he advanced, delivering his attack from the north.

For five days the fighting went on, very much to the advantage of the Romans; at the close of the sixth day they had captured certain strategic points—a capture that made it manifest, even to those citizens least experienced in military affairs, that the morrow would bring with it the fall of the city.

Crispus, who had watched the operations with the trained eye of a soldier, remarked with filial pride: "My father will do in one week what took the great Pompey twelve weeks."

But Vashti shook her pretty head mournfully.

That same night the remnant of the Sanhedrim and the captains of the Zealots met in the hall Gazith to deliberate upon their desperate situation. There was scarcely a man among them but believed the doom of the city to be a matter of a few hours only.

The once fierce Eleazar trembled now, remembering that it was *his* hand that had struck down the Legate's son. Though Cestius should be never so merciful to the rebels, there was one person at least whom he was certain not to spare.

Gloom and despondency marked every face but that of Simon; he alone maintained a bold front.

"To-morrow about this time," said he, "Cestius will be in full retreat."

"Yes, if the Messiah should descend from heaven to help us," said Matthias, the high priest.

"Earthly means will suffice."

"What is your plan, for you evidently have one?"

"Simply this; I shall go to Cestius and shall say to him, 'Cestius, withdraw your legions,' and he will withdraw them."

"Have we need of madmen?" said Matthias, turning scornfully to Eleazar, "that you admit this fellow to our councils?"

# CHAPTER XV

#### THE TRIUMPH OF SIMON

NIGHT melted into the golden light of a lovely morning.

The Jewish multitude, pale-eyed and anxious, trooped to the city walls.

To their surprise the encircling lines of legionaries that had been posted to the east, and to the west, and to the south, of the city were all in motion, taking their way to the camp at Scopus.

Conjecturing what this new movement should mean, the Jews came to the conclusion that Cestius was massing all his troops for the final assault, to be delivered from the north.

This was likewise the opinion of Crispus; his father was purposely leaving three sides of the city unguarded in the belief that the Jews would fight with less desperation, as knowing that a way of retreat was open to them both on flank and rear.

By noontide all the various sections of the Roman army were seen to be concentrated upon the northern heights of Scopus. Not a cohort, not a maniple, not a single legionary, was visible elsewhere. Even those strategic points which on the previous day had been won at the cost of so much toil and blood were all relinquished, the troops that held them having withdrawn to join the common host.

This last movement was, in the eyes of the Jewish multitude, a very mysterious one. What did it mean? They looked on in silent and breathless wonder.

Suddenly, the shrill note of a trumpet rang out upon the morning air. The distant notes were borne by the breeze in faint cadence to the ears of Crispus. With a sudden thrill at his heart he listened, doubtful as to whether he could have heard aright. Again the trumpet sang out. The same strain as before. There was no mistaking its meaning, and Crispus sank back with a groan of despair.

*It was the signal for retreat!*

The great army that had set out from Antioch burning to redeem Roman honor by recovering Jerusalem was now actually moving off again, at the very moment when it might have successfully accomplished its work; moving off—to quote the contemporary historian—" without any reason in the world!"[18]

Silently the people stared, scarcely able to believe their eyes. Then, as each successive evolution made the truth more and more plain, there burst from a hundred thousand voices a yell that seemed to rend the very firmament.

" THE ROMANS ARE RETREATING! "

" It's a stratagem to lure the Jews from the city," said the bewildered Crispus, trying to delude himself with false hopes. " They will follow, and he will fall upon them."

He was right in saying that the Jews would follow.

The gates of the city clanged wide, and an armed multitude, Simon at their head, poured forth with intent to harass the retreating foe.

Crispus, watching with mournful and rueful visage, took his last look at the soldiers of the Roman rear-guard as they stood in glittering splendor upon the sky-line. They had faced about on the very summit of Scopus to discharge a flight of arrows at the foremost column of the pursuing Jews; a few moments afterwards and they had disappeared behind the heights.

Their parting shots had no effect upon the advance of the Jews, who in a wild, tumultuous mass swept forward up the broad, white, dusty road and over the brow of the hill; in course of time they, too, like the Romans, became lost to view.

Crispus fully expected to see them ere long come surging back in headlong flight; but no! Sounds as of tumult and fighting reached his ears, but these sounds becoming more and more distant showed that it was *not* the Jews who were fleeing.

Sorrowfully he lay down, and while vainly trying—for he would not accept Vashti's explanation of the matter—to devise some theory to account for a retreat so strange, he fell asleep. Vashti seized the opportunity to steal quietly off, and making her way to the temple turned into the Eastern Cloister or Solomon's Colonnade. Here the Christians of Jerusalem were wont to meet, drawn thither by the knowledge that this place had been a favorite resort of their Lord while upon earth. As Vashti made her way along this arcade she came upon a little group—men, women, and children—whom she recognized as adherents of the faith, the holy band that had survived the persecutions alike of Jewish Sanhedrim and Roman procurator. Their air, sad yet sweet, and the character of their attire—for they were habited as if for a long journey—told her that they were taking their last farewell of the temple. Some were gazing wistfully around, as well knowing that they would see the place no more; a few knelt reverently upon the pavement, and kissed the stones that had once been trodden by the hallowed feet of the Saviour.

Among them, exercising a mild and paternal authority, there moved one, dignified and saintly in aspect, Simeon, son of Cleophas, revered as being the cousin, according to the flesh, of the crucified Master. A pillar of the church, and a witness of the truth, he had already lived seventy years, and was destined, either from the pure and temperate character of his life or from being specially favored by heaven, to live yet fifty more, terminating his long life by a glorious martyrdom."

It was his hand that had baptized Vashti, whom he now greeted with a gentle smile.

"You are quitting the city?" said she, sorrowfully.

"Even so," returned Simeon; "at intervals, and in small groups, that we may not attract the attention of our enemies. We have seen the sign foretold by the Lord while He was yet with us: 'Jerusalem compassed with armies.' Therefore do we obey His voice and hasten our departure, lest the Zealots should return to intercept our flight. The door is open; who can tell how soon it may be shut? We have a further sign in the Messianic fountain of Siloam that has withdrawn its waters from this wicked city."

"And whither are you going?"

"Beyond Jordan to the city of Pella among the mountains. My daughter, are you not going with us, seeing that upon this city, that hath shed the blood of the saints, there is coming utter destruction?—yea, *Tribulation such as was not since the beginning of the world to this time; no, nor ever shall be.*'"

There was in the bishop's words that which set Vashti's heart thrilling with a nameless fear. She yearned to accompany the little band to Pella, but durst not run contrary to the will of her mother, who, she well knew, would never be persuaded to quit the city. And there was little Arad. And the good but heathen Crispus, for whose conversion she daily prayed, ocenpied also a place in her heart. No! she could not bear to part from these, and so she resisted the persuasive words of her new-found friends.

"Why will you make me weep?" said she. "If it be the will of the Lord can He not protect me here equally as well as at Pella?"

"Daughter, thou hast well said," returned Simeon. "Is it not written: 'Who ever perished, being innocent? or when were the righteous cut off?' We leave thee

# The Triumph of Simon 185

in His hands. Be sure that we shall not fail to pray for thee daily."

"Your blessing, father," said Vashti as she knelt upon the pavement.

"You have it, my daughter," replied the good bishop, laying his hands upon her head.

The little band now turned sorrowfully away, casting many a lingering look behind. Vashti, gazing from the pillared arcade, watched them as they quitted the Shushan or Beautiful Gate, and made their way down the hillside to the brook Cedron. Crossing the dark stream by a bridge they ascended the leafy slope of Olivet; arrived upon its summit they paused to take one long, last look at the city, and then, disappearing one by one over the brow of the mount, they became lost to view.

With a sense of desolation at her heart, such as she had never before known, Vashti went home again to find Crispus awake and chafing because the Jews had not yet returned in headlong flight.

But the Jews did not return that day; no, nor yet the next! A whole week passed, a week filled with strange rumors of Roman defeat and Jewish success.

On the eighth day the Jewish multitude reappeared, chanting songs of victory.

Their entry into the city took the shape of a triumphal procession, made resplendent with chariots and horses, with arms and standards, all captured from the enemy!

When Simon, the hero of the fight, appeared riding in an ivory car, whose front and sides were decorated with the gory heads of slain Romans, the delighted citizens greeted him with the waving of palm-branches, as though he were the very Messiah. Young maidens flung flowers before his chariot, and men cast down purple mantles.

"Hosanna to the son of Giora!"

"Hail to the Scourge of the Romans!"

It was a great day for the Zealot chief, too great in the eyes of the jealous Eleazar, who was beginning to fear that Simon had ambitions inconsistent with his own supremacy.

"We must clip the wings of this eagle ere he fly too high," he muttered darkly.

As for Crispus, the procession seemed to him like some hideous dream. Could it be that a fine Roman army, commanded by his own father, had suffered defeat at the hands of an undisciplined horde of Oriental barbarians?

It was even so; Vashti that evening told him the whole story as she had gathered it from others.

Simon's followers, keeping to the heights that overhung the Pass of Beth-boron, had followed the Romans day by day, attacking them in front, flank and rear, but never venturing an open engagement. The Roman legionaries, demoralized by the retreat, seemed to lack even the spirit to defend themselves. At last, when more than five thousand of his men had fallen in this guerilla warfare, Cestius, to avoid further disaster, was compelled to resort to a stratagem of despair. Having with studied pomp and display formed and fortified a camp, he stole off quietly in the dead of night, leaving the tents standing and the watch-fires burning, so as to deceive the enemy for a time. The trick answered; and Cestius, gaining a few hours' start, succeeded by forced marches in bringing his panic-stricken troops to Antipatris, behind whose ramparts he was secure from attack. As for the camp with its standards, furniture, and military stores, this was, of course, seized and plundered by the delighted Jews.

Not since the day when the German barbarians, under Arminius, had cut to pieces the legions of Varus in the depths of the Teutoburg forest, had a disaster so great befallen the Roman arms.

Had this defeat happened under any other commander, the shame of it would have touched to the quick the patriotic pride of Crispus, but that this defeat should have been brought about by the bad generalship of his own father——!

Filial affection seemed for the moment to die within Crispus.

"Doth my father still live?" he muttered moodily. "Had he no sword to fall upon? He hath made the name of Cestius synonymous with coward."

That day, the first time for several weeks, Crispus was able to rise from his bed and assume his Roman garb.

And now came the momentous question as to how he should get safely out of Jerusalem, a question that was settled in a very remarkable manner.

Miriam's house, like all the larger houses in Jerusalem, was built around a square court paved with tiles, and adorned in the middle with a fountain.

One afternoon, Vashti was sitting alone in this court, and thinking, as she was always thinking, of Crispus, when a heavy footstep caused her to look up. The thing that she had been fearing during many weeks had come to pass at last. There, a few paces distant, stood Simon of Gerasa! Only by a great effort was she able to keep herself from fainting at sight of the dark and terrible Zealot.

"Interpret me this riddle," said he. "Into the house was seen to go that which never came forth again."

She knew that he was alluding to Crispus, and her heart almost ceased beating.

"To be more plain, doth not Crispus the Roman abide here?"

In defiance of the teaching of Simeon the bishop, that a falsehood is never justifiable even when its purpose is to save human life, Vashti was tempted to deny all knowledge of Crispus.

"Why should you think that?" she replied in a trembling voice.

"You do not deny it? Take me to him."

Vashti did not stir.

"Come, girl," exclaimed Simon, growing impatient, "delay not, or I summon my Zealots to search the house, and if these patriots once enter," he continued with a grim smile, "they'll leave little of value behind. I seek the Roman to do him not evil but good. I swear it."

"*You* swear!" flashed out Vashti, her indignation getting the better of her fear. "You, who broke your oath and massacred the Roman garrison! What is *your* word worth?"

The Zealot laughed unashamedly.

"When a man, desirous of hanging a dog, lures the creature to him by a tempting bait, do you call him wicked? And what are the Romans but dogs, unfit to live."

"Then Crispus, being a Roman, is a dog?"

"He is; but he is the best of the dogs, and therefore am I minded to do him a service."

Compelled to yield, Vashti led the way, wondering what Crispus would think of her action in bringing the Zealot upon him.

She found him in an upper chamber, sitting at a table, reading a Greek scroll of one of the gospels, and frowning at what he considered its bizarre style. Upon the same table lay a drawn sword.

"'*And they shall lay thee even with the ground,*'" read Crispus. "Now, I trust that this man may prove a true prophet, for—ah! who comes here?"

His eye, lifting, had caught sight of Simon. Familiarized with sudden perils, Crispus kept an unmoved countenance.

"How fares the noble patient?" said Simon, sardonically.

"Why, as to that, you may test his strength, if you will," replied Crispus, laying his hand upon the sword.

But though he spoke thus boldly, and longed to slay

the man who had helped to massacre his fellow-Romans, he felt himself, in his present state of convalescence, to be as weak as a babe. It was all over with him if the Zealot took him at his word.

"Tush!" responded Simon, with folded arms. "Do you not see that I am unarmed. I come as a friend. Were I thy enemy and desired thy death should I have sought to save thee from the hand of Eleazar?"

"And why that attempted grace on your part?" asked Crispus, laying down his weapon.

"Were you not the first to rise at my trial and condemn the dastardly Florus?"

"My condemnation of Florus was not meant as the justification of Simon."

"Be that as it may. Let me state my errand. You are surrounded by enemies, who, if they did but know that you are abiding here, would break in and slay you. Be it mine to save you. I am here secretly to offer you a safe conduct to your Roman friends at Antipatris."

"'Tis scarcely credible," said Crispus.

He was amazed, as well he might be, at the offer. Why should Simon be willing to undertake this enterprise, which, if detected, would put him at feud with Eleazar and the whole body of the Zealots?

"My reason for this course I reserve till to-night," was the only answer Simon would give to Crispus' questioning.

"But if you are willing that I should get safely from Jerusalem, why not let me arrange my departure in my own way?"

"Do so, and die. You cannot escape in the daytime, and at night no one can leave the city without a signed order from Eleazar. But should you succeed in evading the sentinels at the gates you will find the public roads leading from Jerusalem patrolled by armed Zealots, who slay all whom they detect escaping from the city. 'Jerusalem,' they say, and rightly, 'hath need of all her sons, and he who deserts her at this crisis shall receive a traitor's doom."

How Vashti rejoiced that the Christians had seized the first opportunity to escape!

"Your safety," continued Simon, addressing Crispus, "lies in my escorting you; apart from me you will be stopped, interrogated, slain."

"I will avail myself of your offer," said Crispus. "But I forewarn you that when the Roman army comes again from Cæsarea, as come it will, I shall be found within its ranks, and if we meet in battle look to no sparing from me."

"Be it so," said Simon coldly. "To-night at the sixth hour be ready for the journey. I will bring two steeds with me. But a word of caution. Exchange that Roman costume for the Hebrew caftan and abba, if you would be safe."

With that Simon took his departure, directing his steps to the temple, where he found to his surprise that the Sanhedrim were holding a meeting in the hall Gazith, a meeting to which they had not thought fit to invite him.

The object of their deliberations, so it seemed, was to appoint military governors for the various toparchies or districts, of not only Judæa, but also of Galilee, Idumæa, and Peræa, these three provinces having decided to throw in their lot with the Jewish cause.

As the Sanhedrim, having dispatched this business, were departing, Simon encountered Eleazar on the threshold of the hall.

"A council, and I not invited?" he said in an injured tone. "But there, let be! How have matters sped?"

"Joseph ben Gorion and Ananus have been appointed rulers of Jerusalem."

"Priests both," commented Simon.

"*I* am a priest," returned the other.

"Were these two like thee I would rejoice," replied the Zealot, who recognized the military abilities of Eleazar.

"Rejoice, then, that I am made ruler of Idumæa."

"Why, so I do. What more?"

"Josephus hath rule over the two Galilees."

"Another priest, and a smooth-tongued, double-faced Pharisee; not to be trusted."

Eleazar proceeded to enumerate other appointments, few of which met with Simon's approval.

"It seems," said the Zealot, when the other had finished his list, "that the Sanhedrim hath no need for my services."

"Your name was not brought forward in connection with any office."

"Not even by you?" Eleazar was silent. "Who was the first to enter Antonia? Not a Sanhedrist, I trow. Who promised to free Jerusalem from its siege, and did so? Not a Sanhedrist. Who was foremost in the attack on the retreating legions of Cestius? Not a Sanhedrist. And now do they pass me by, and distribute the rewards of victory among themselves? Verily, you have not done well, Eleazar, son of Ananias."

And Simon stalked wrathfully away.

As night drew on Crispus' feelings became a curious mingling of pleasure and regret—pleasure at the thought of freedom, regret at having to part from Vashti, whose companionship had grown dear to him.

In this hour of parting as they sat in the upper chamber by the light of a silver lamp, Vashti gently sought, as she had frequently sought before, to bring him over to her faith.

Crispus shook his head.

"Your creed is an impossible one," said he. "A religion that tells us to love our enemies would be the ruin of states. Where would the Roman empire have been had we followed that doctrine? The world will never be ruled by love, but by *this*." Taking his sword by the point he held it aloft.

"Look!" said Vashti, gently.

Crispus looked where she pointed, and lo! upon the chamber wall was a shadow cast by the light of the lamp, and that shadow had *the shape of a cross!*

He who had not started at Simon's sudden advent started now. He lowered the sword and sheathed it with a thoughtful air. Upon him who was so much disposed to catch at omens that little incident made more impression than all Vashti's discourses.

"The time of your departure is at hand," she said sorrowfully. "You must kiss little Arad before you go, and say farewell to my mother."

When the sixth hour of the night had come, Crispus, disguised in Jewish garb, descended to the door of Miriam's dwelling. Vashti was with him, and looked cautiously forth. Under the radiance of the full moon the street of Millo was half in silver light and half in ebon shadow. Out of the latter emerged the tall form of Simon leading two horses by the bridle.

As Crispus beheld Vashti's eyes eloquent with the sorrow of parting, he longed to take her within his arms and press her lips to his. He knew that this maiden loved him, as well as he knew that he loved her. But between them there lay the shadow of the unknown Athenaïs; and even should Crispus, invoking the law, repudiate his consort, he would be no better off as regards Vashti, whose Christian faith, dearer to her than earthly love, forbade her to marry one that had put away his wife.

With the words "Farewell, sweet Vashti; may we soon meet again!" he mounted the horse, and, in company with Simon, rode slowly away, pausing for a moment at the street corner to wave with his hand a final adieu.

They drew nigh to the gate Gennath, where a guard

## The Triumph of Simon

was stationed. Simon's well-known face procured a ready passport both for himself and his companion.

"Who is he that rides with thee?" asked the captain of Simon.

"In his way as good a patriot as myself," was the answer.

The two passed through the gate and galloped off in the moonlight, the sense of freedom and the rapid motion through the night air causing Crispus to tingle with exhilaration.

It was well that Simon remained with him. Twice they were stopped by bands of Zealots, who speedily withdrew on recognizing the " Scourge of the Romans."

Crispus, though in a way grateful for Simon's protection, did not feel much disposed to talk with him; the Zealot, on his part, was moody and taciturn, and so the strangely-assorted pair rode side by side with scarce a word till in the first faint light of an Eastern dawn the distant towers of Antipatris rose to view.

At about a hundred yards from the gate Simon drew rein.

"We part here."

"Good! And now why this friendly act on your part?"

"My bringing you here is a proof that Simon the Black can sometimes keep faith. I pledged my word to your father, Cestius, to conduct you safely to Antipatris. He will tell you the story," added the Zealot, turning as if about to ride off.

"I prefer to hear it now, and from you," said Crispus, a suspicion of the truth beginning to dawn upon his mind.

"Well, since thou art curious, listen. On the night following Cestius' investment of the city, a youth was seen descending the wall by a rope. I dispatched a party, who brought him back. Upon him I found a letter, whose contents I kept to myself. On the sixth night of the siege our affairs being, as you may remember, a little desperate, I went to the Roman camp, and was admitted to the presence of Cestius. 'Your son is alive,' I said, 'as this letter plainly shows; but he shall die, unless you immediately withdraw your troops.' He threatened to hang me for daring to come with such a message. 'As you will,' I answered, 'but know this, I have left behind me the order that if I am not back in the city within three hours Crispus is to be brought forth upon the battlements and crucified.'

"That stayed his hand. He fell to thinking, and the end of it was that love for his son triumphed over his duty to the state. But I made it my condition not to surrender you till he had entirely withdrawn to Cæsarea."

"And you broke your promise. My father pledged his word to retreat, and you attacked him during that retreat."

"Nay, I broke no promise, for I warned Cestius that if he retired I should be unable to check the Zealots from following. 'Let them follow,' were his words. He welcomed the idea of pursuit, thinking to give us over to the sword, but he found he had to deal with men that could fight."

"Aye, from the safe covert of the hill-tops. Your courage stopped with the open plain."

"I may not talk longer with you, for I see soldiers issuing from the city-gate, and I have no desire that my head shall decorate the battlements of Antipatris. I have fulfilled my word to Cestius, and now I return. We shall meet again under the walls of Jerusalem."

So saying, Simon turned his steed and galloped off by the way he had come.

Looking towards Antipatris, Crispus saw a small body of foot soldiers advancing from the gate; at their head was a mounted officer, none other than Terentius Rufus, who came spurring forward with all speed, as if bent on learning the business of the two Jewish-looking horsemen.

"Hold, fellow!" he cried, reining in his steed, as he drew abreast of Crispus. "Who art——?" And then, his voice suddenly changing, he exclaimed, "By the gods, 'tis Crispus."

His quick look of delight was instantly succeeded by one of gravity.

"Turn from the city," said he, "and ride back a little way, lest you should be recognized by my men. Five thousand aurei are a strong temptation to mercenary natures."

"How mean you?"

"There is a price on your head."

"Ah! what have I been doing to deserve it."

"'Tis said that when Cestius had invested Jerusalem you wrote a craven letter imploring him to raise the siege, or your life would be forfeit."

"I would that I had my hand on the throat of the man that invented that lie."

"Think not that *I* ever believed it. Unfortunately, however, this slander hath reached the ears of Nero, who, in his rage, hath decreed that the lives of the two Cestii, father and son, are forfeit to the state."

Confounded by this tidings, Crispus could do nothing for a few moments but stare blankly at his friend.

"What has become of my father?" said he, finding his voice.

Rufus' hesitation told its own tale.

"Speak!" said Crispus, growing pale. "How did he die?"

"Like a Roman; he fell on his sword."

Crispus paid to his father's memory the tribute of a brief and pitying silence. It was a bitter thought to him that if he had not written that letter Cestius might now be living, the conqueror of Jerusalem, to be greeted at Rome like a second Pompey with the title, "Noster Hierosolymarius."

"Go not to Antipatris, or to any town where you are known," said Rufus, " since any man may lawfully slay you. The streets of Cæsarea are posted with tablets offering five thousand aurei for the head of Crispus."

" I need scarcely ask what has become of my father's estates? "

" Confiscated," replied Rufus, laconically.

That he had toppled down in a moment from his high office of Secretary to the Legate of Syria; that he had lost his patrimonial estates—nay, even the fact that he had been doomed to death—was to Crispus as nothing in comparison with the thought that he was now deprived of all opportunity of returning to Jerusalem in company with legions to avenge the massacre of the Roman garrisons.

Gone, too, was his hope of a kingdom. The doom pronounced upon him was a proof that Nero had revoked his purpose of ratifying Polemo's intended disposal of his crown. And his wife, the mysterious Athenaïs? Was it likely that she would remain faithful to him on learning that the Roman noble whom she had wedded was now a pauper, and that a proscribed one?

" Who commands in this war, now that my father has gone? "

" Old Flavius Vespasian, with his son Titus as second in command. Titus," continued Rufus, with a wry mouth, " our equal once. Now he'll hold his head high above us both. Perhaps my lady Berenice will smile on him now, seeing what a great man he has become."

" Berenice? ah! " said Crispus in a curious tone. " Of course she hath heard of my disgrace. How doth she take it? "

" One of the proscriptive tablets directed against you hangs upon her palace-wall at Cæsarea, whence it may be inferred that your fall is not a matter of much concern to her."

## The Triumph of Simon

Crispus wondered whether Vashti would suffer a placard dooming him to death to remain upon the wall of *her* house.

"You must live in concealment," advised Rufus, "till Nero be persuaded to revoke his unjust decree; or, it may be, that your freedom will come in another way, for if all the rumors circulated be true, our present Cæsar is like ere long to lose his throne, if not his life, so outrageously doth he shock public sentiment; in which case all his acts will be annulled by his successor, and thus your patrimonial estates may return to you. The question is, where will you hide in the meantime?"

"I will go," replied Crispus, his mind still under the singular impression evoked by the shadow of the cross, "I will go to a people that will suffer death rather than betray a suppliant; I will go to the Christians of Pella."

# CHAPTER XVI

#### THE AMBITION OF BERENICE

MORE than two years and a half had now passed since the disastrous retreat of Cestius, and during all that time no Roman legion had come within sight of Jerusalem.

Vespasian, the successor of Cestius, had first directed his arms against Galilee, almost every city of which was in a state of rebellion.

Thanks to the spirit and activity displayed by the warrior-historian Josephus, as well as to the situation of the Galilean cities, most of which were built upon hill-tops and almost inaccessible crags, the campaign was prolonged for more than a year.

Then came a long interval of inactivity, due to a series of revolutions taking place at Rome, the seat of the government. Within the space of a single year the throne of the Cæsars was occupied in turn by a series of ambitious generals, the self-murdered Nero having been succeeded by Galba, by Otho, and by Vitellius.

During these political crises Vespasian was under the necessity of having his position as commandant in Judæa successively recognized and confirmed by each new Cæsar, and as this was a matter requiring much time, it led to frequent pauses in the campaign, a state of affairs very much to the advantage of the revolutionary factions in Jerusalem.

The Roman army destined to act against the holy city had formed a huge camp upon the seashore at a point a few miles to the north of Cæsarea, and here day by day with unfailing regularity the iron warriors of Rome went through those evolutions and exercises that had made them the masters of the world.

This similitude of war naturally attracted crowds from the neighboring region. It became quite a custom with the fashionable Greeks of Cæsarea to take their morning promenade along the seashore for the purpose of witnessing a spectacle as thrilling almost as the contests at Olympia or the combats of the amphitheater.

One fair, sunny morning in the month of June, just as the legions were beginning their daily drill, under the personal inspection of Vespasian and his son Titus, there drove up a magnificent chariot, which, by the grace of the lictors, was given a place considerably nearer to the exercising troops than was allowed to the ordinary spectator, for the occupant of the chariot was none other than the fair princess Berenice, who was paying her first visit to the Roman camp.

No sooner had Titus detected her presence upon the field than he at once made his way to her side. His look and voice alike told how much he was enamored of the fascinating princess, who at the age of forty had, like Cleopatra, all the grace and beauty of youth.

"Princess, you seem sad to-day," said he, after an interval of silence. "Of what are you thinking?"

"Perhaps," she replied, with a tantalizing little sigh, "perhaps of Crispus."

"Why do you torment me with the name of a rival who is dead?"

"*Is* he dead?" said Berenice. "True, nothing has been heard of him since he parted from Terentius Rufus at Antipatris."

"And that is more than two years ago. The ban put upon him by Nero has been revoked. If he be alive why does he not show himself, since he has nothing now to fear?"

"Except the being claimed by a wife whom he does not like," said Berenice with a silvery laugh, and a glance at the house called Beth-tamar, which, seated on a lofty crag, was plainly visible from the camp.

"Princess," said Titus, with a tender look, "if Crispus should ever return it will mean to me——"

Berenice raised her finger with a witching smile.

"Ah me! Now you are going to make love again. We shall never be friends, if you do that. Let me watch your Romans. They interest me."

The air at that moment was all alive with the crisp, sharp commands of tribune, and centurion, and decurion.

The exercises performed by the Romans comprehended feats in running, leaping, wrestling, swimming, sword-play, hurling the pilum—everything in short that could add strength to the body or tend to success in war.

Here, Cretan archers, having set up their targets, were demonstrating the deadly accuracy of their aim. There, Balearic slingers were discharging their leaden bullets, which not infrequently melted with the heat engendered by the swift rush of the missile through the air; here, a body of soldiers was busily engaged in bridging within a given time a broad sheet of water; there, a group were vigorously occupied in storming a wooden fortress, whose defense was as vigorously maintained by a garrison of fellow-Romans.

"Why, it is like war itself," said Berenice, fascinated by the spectacle.

"So like, that it is the fashion of the soldiers to call the exercise a bloodless battle, and the battle a bloody exercise."

"Where are these men going?" she asked as a certain cohort tramped past at full speed.

"They are marching to Dora and back."

"That is not very hard work."

"You think so, princess. But mark that each soldier is carrying the full equipment customary in war time, consisting of various utensils, as well as victuals for fifteen days, the whole amounting to sixty pounds' weight, not including arms, for the Roman soldier considers these, not as a burden, but as a part of himself. Weighted thus, he is to march in this burning sunlight to Dora and back, the double journey being a distance of twenty miles, and he is to do it within five hours. If this be not hard work, what is?"

"And supposing they should take more than five hours?"

"Terentius Rufus, who rides at their head, will see to that."

"But if they should fail?"

"He will punish them."

"And what will the punishment be?"

"It takes various shapes. Yon cohort, as is shown by the carrying of the eagle, is the First Cohort of the legion. They may be degraded by being compelled to resign the eagle, and to take the second place; or their diet for the week may be barley bread instead of wheaten; or they may be excluded from their tents, and made to sleep at a distance from the camp."

"How often do the troops practice these exercises?"

"Every day of the year."

"But when a soldier has learned his work?"

"He goes on practicing just the same. Let a man have been forty years in the army, that fact will not exempt him from the daily exercise. And mark this: every weapon you see in use now, every helmet, breastplate, and shield, is double the weight of those used in actual warfare."

Berenice opened her eyes in wonder.

"Why, a battle must be an easier matter than the daily exercise!"

Titus laughed.

"The soldier would much prefer a battle," said he.

Berenice spoke no more for a long time; so long that Titus began to see from her rapt expression that some momentous thought was occupying her mind.

"I am thinking," said she, in reply to his questioning, " I am thinking what *I* would do with these troops, were they mine."

"And what *would* you do with them, princess?" asked Titus with a smile.

Instead of replying directly to this, Berenice put a question.

" Is not your father Vespasian a skillful general? "

" He hath no equal in the art of war; it is not I only who say this, but others."

" And he is liked by all the legions, near and far? "

" Liked is but a feeble word to express his hold over them."

" But he is somewhat lacking in ambition? "

" Ambition is apt to die with the sixtieth year."

" But his son Titus is ambitious, and being so, and having great influence over his father, should act as a spur to his mind."

" Princess," said the puzzled Titus, " to what does all this tend? "

" I am thinking," said Berenice, watching him keenly from beneath the dark fringe of her half-closed eyelids, " I am thinking what a pity it is that the great Vespasian should be serving Cæsar, when he might be Cæsar himself. The present emperor Vitellius can show no hereditary title to the imperial throne; an ambitious general, he gained the purple by fighting for it. Why should Vespasian not do the like? "

It was a startling suggestion, so startling as almost to deprive Titus of breath. He glanced at the charioteer, who stood by the horses' heads—glanced in fear lest the man should have overhead Berenice's treasonable remarks, despite the low tone in which they were spoken.

" When Titus can call himself Cæsar's son," she whispered, " then will Berenice listen to his love—not till then. Go," she added, with a little peremptory wave of her hand. " Ponder it well! "

Left to herself, the princess, sinking back upon the silken cushions of her chariot, indulged in a pleasing reverie.

"The idea is new, and it frightens him," she murmured with a somewhat contemptuous smile. "But he will grow used to it. I have sown the seed in his mind, and it will grow and bear fruit."

Daringly original in all her ways, Berenice had often embarked upon some political enterprise which, pronounced by her more sober-minded brother Agrippa to be impracticable, had nevertheless met with brilliant success. Would she succeed in this, a more daring venture than any she had hitherto dreamed of? Why not? All things are possible to the brave, and why should not the brave Vespasian, the idol of the legions, prevail against the feeble-minded Vitellius, whose follies were daily alienating the loyalty of the nations?

The chief obstacle in the way was honest old Vespasian himself; he might refuse to listen to the voice of the charmers, Berenice and Titus, charm they never so wisely. But, if otherwise, and if the enterprise succeeded, what glory would be hers!

Even now it filled her with pride to think that she was, in a manner, the mistress of all the troops she saw exercising before her. Recover Jerusalem they might, and would; but destroy it—never! Thanks to her influence over Titus, the holy city would be spared from dilapidation, the temple preserved from the torch. She was the new Esther destined to save the Hebrew nation from destruction—destined, too, if Titus would but exercise his ambition, to be the empress of the world, the mother, it might be, of a line of Cæsars, all adherents of the Jewish faith!

And if Cæsar were once the disciple of Moses, the conversion of the world would follow.

In the midst of these brilliant dreams her ear caught the sound of a quiet footfall; and, turning her head, she saw—Crispus!

She gave a start, as was natural in one who supposed him dead, or at the least to be hundreds of miles away. Crispus, keenly attentive, fancied he could detect on her face an expression akin to dismay; at any rate it was an expression very different from her tender, lovable look in the Prætorium when she had avowed her wish to stay and die with him.

"I have startled you, princess."

"You are as one returning from the dead," she said with a faint smile.

"And the dead are not always welcome visitors."

Then for a brief space there was a silence, during which both seemed to be reflecting.

"What do you here?" she asked.

"Would it surprise you, princess, were I to say that I am seeking my wife?"

"Your wife?" repeated Berenice, in her eyes an odd look as of fear, at least that is how Crispus interpreted it. "Your wife?"

"You did not perhaps know that I had a wife?"

"If you keep the matter a secret from the world how is one to know it? What is her name?"

"You do not know it?"

"How should I?" replied Berenice with a touch of impatience in her voice.

"I cannot tell you her name, seeing that it is unknown to me." This answer seemed to afford some satisfaction to Berenice. "Nay, I have never yet seen my wife's face."

"You are telling me strange things," laughed Berenice. "I pray you, my lord Crispus, mystify me no farther, but speak plainly."

"Why, so I will."

Leaning with folded arms upon the broad brim of the chariot, and looking directly into the eyes of Berenice, who seemed helplessly fascinated by his gaze, Crispus proceeded to relate the story of his marriage.

"As," concluded he, with a glance at the distant Beth-tamar, "as it was in this neighborhood that I first met Athenaïs, I naturally turn to this neighborhood in the hope of again meeting her here."

"And you do not really know who this Athenaïs is?"

"I do not. As you doubtless know, King Polemo died suddenly, a year ago; and, unfortunately for me, died without revealing the secret. But the three years' limit is now past, and it is therefore permissible for Athenaïs to reveal herself by sending me the ring."

"And if she chooses *not* to reveal herself, you may never know whom you wedded."

"That is so."

"I greatly fear," said Berenice with a grave shake of her head, "that your unknown bride will prefer to keep herself hidden from you."

"Why should she so act? She was not coerced into the match. She accepted me of her own free will."

"True, but reflect that you are not the great Crispus of her anticipation. She wedded you in the hope of sharing the crown of Pontus, and that hope is now extinguished, Pontus having become annexed to the empire."

"Your opinion then is that a woman should take for her husband one well endowed with material advantages, and that should he, through misfortune, lose these advantages, the woman is justified in discarding him?"

"Though woman may not profess that doctrine with her lips," smiled Berenice, "she'll carry it out in practice. But answer me this: should you, by happy chance, discover your wife, would you keep her against her will? Would you not grant her a divorce, if such were her desire?"

Crispus gravely shook his head.

"She cannot part from me, nor I from her, for be it known to you, O princess, that I am a Christian, and a Christian can be separated from his wife by death only."

Tidings so unexpected caused Berenice to draw a sharp breath. Her look of horror could not have been greater if Crispus had suddenly announced himself as a deadly leper.

"*You, a Christian!*" she gasped.

"The name is displeasing to you, I know; so it was once to me. If you will hear me———"

She cut him short with an imperative gesture.

"I have had the chief exponent of Christianity, Paul of Tarsus, lecturing in chains before me; where *he* failed, *you* can hardly hope to succeed. Go!" she exclaimed, disdainfully waving him away with her hand as though he were a slave or some other inferior creature. "Yet stay! one question I will ask," she continued with a certain uneasiness of manner that did not escape Crispus' notice. "In what light do you, as a Christian, regard the holy temple?"

"As an obstacle to the progress of Christianity," he replied significantly, as he turned on his heel and walked quietly away. "Veni, vidi, *non* vici," he murmured sorrowfully.

Berenice watched him with a strange fear at her heart.

"A Christian," she murmured; "and one who hates the temple! Now, if he should accompany the legions to Jerusalem how easy for him, when they are camping against the holy house, to fulfill his dream by throwing a lighted torch through its windows. If *that* be his aim, I will foil it. He shall not be permitted to take part in the siege. Titus shall prevent him from joining the army. I have but to say the word and Vespasian will banish him from Palestine."

Meanwhile, Crispus, suspecting something of Berenice's intentions towards him, and resolving to forestall her, walked along the shore intent upon finding Vespasian, with whom he had always been a great favorite.

He found that general joining in the exercises like a common soldier, one of the ways by which he maintained his popularity with the troops.

A burly, bluff, red-faced man he looked less like a warrior than some honest old farmer who had just for sport's sake put on the scarlet paludamentum of a general.

He greeted Crispus right heartily, and wanted to know where he had been hiding himself so long, a question which by the way Berenice had not thought of asking. So Crispus related how upon his proscription he had taken refuge with the Christians first at Pella and then at Antioch, and how, whenever he was in danger of being detected by the minions of Nero, the brethren would convey him by devious routes to some other Christian community; and how, in the end, convinced by infallible argument that theirs was the true and only religion, he himself had joined the sect.

"A good soldier marred!" growled Vespasian, on hearing this last. "My cousin Flavius Clemens is a Christian. An excellent character once, but now look at him! Takes no interest in state affairs or military matters. This world is nothing to him. A woman and no man! mild-mannered, lacking in spirit and backbone."

"There is no reason, sire, why a Christian should not be a good soldier. As a matter of fact, I have come hither to ask for a place in the army that is to be sent against Jerusalem; I care not how humble the post so long as it puts me in the forefront of the battle."

"Now, that's the way to talk," cried Vespasian delightedly. "A place in the army? You shall have it. There's a post waiting for you. The First Cohort of the Twelfth Legion hath lost its tribune."

"Dead?" asked Crispus.

"Dead! No! Degraded! 'Twas but a few days ago he received his baton. Yesterday he came to me, reeking with perfumes. Ye gods! is it a soldier's business to be perfuming himself. 'I would rather you had smelled of garlic,' I cried. 'Return to the ranks.' —You shall captain that cohort. You have heard of the Twelfth Legion before, eh? 'Twas one of those that fled at Beth-horon. They are longing to redeem their lost character. You shall show them how. You accept the post? Good!. Come with me and let me show the First Cohort its new tribune."

As they made their way along the shore two figures came walking slowly towards them. One was a legionary, wearing an armlet to which was attached a chain, two cubits in length, its other end being fastened to a similar armlet clasped round the wrist of a somewhat distinguished-looking personage.

It was a Jewish captive and his Roman guard.

The prisoner saluted Vespasian; and, as if well acquainted with Crispus, gave him a friendly smile.

Crispus gazed, and then suddenly recognizing the captive he there and then tendered him a warm thanksgiving; for the captive was none other than Josephus, the man who had been instrumental in saving his life by begging his supposed corpse from Eleazar.

When Josephus had resumed his walking, Vespasian remarked:

"Of all the rebels who fought against us in Galilee that man was the most valiant. When he was taken prisoner I had much ado at first to keep our soldiers from killing him."

"I deemed him to be more of a scholar than a warrior."

"He can handle both pen and sword, and he hath also prophetical gifts."

Crispus was naturally somewhat surprised at this last observation.

"What prophecy hath he made?"

"Why, this. Though he so bravely defended Jotapata against us, he nevertheless told its inhabitants that the city was destined to be taken on the forty-seventh day of the siege, and so it came to pass. Oh!" he continued in answer to Crispus' look of skepticism, "I know it to be true, for I made careful inquiry among the captives, and all testified that from the very beginning Josephus had foretold that Jotapata would fall on the forty-seventh day."

What was very wonderful to Vespasian seemed simple enough to Crispus. If Josephus, as was very likely, had formed the secret purpose of going over to the Roman side, it would not be difficult for him to prolong the defense of such a rock-fortress as Jotapata till the forty-seventh day. The character gained as prophet on this occasion might stand him in good stead with the Roman general; in point of fact it had already so served him. Crispus could not help thinking that the man to whom he had so much reason to be grateful, was, nevertheless, a somewhat ambiguous character.

Glancing along the shore, Crispus saw that the "prophet" had halted in his walk by the chariot of Berenice, and was now conversing both with that princess and with Titus. As the three were holding their heads close together it may be inferred that the conversation was a very important one.

Its purport became apparent to Crispus ere many hours were past.

# CHAPTER XVII

#### THE MAKING OF AN EMPEROR

CRISPUS had the high honor of dining that night in the tent of Vespasian with a select company of tribunes, Terentius Rufus being of the number.

Titus was, of course, present. His office of second in command, added to the glory gained by him in the Galilæan campaign, had disposed him to adopt a somewhat lofty air towards his former friends and acquaintanecs; but Crispus had acquired the Christian grace of humility, and the patronage that he might have resented in his pagan days now afforded him matter only for a little quiet amusement.

Let Titus receive his just due, however; though Berenice had earnestly pressed him to persuade Vespasian to exclude Crispus from the army intended to act against Jerusalem, he had declined the task as an ungenerous one. "If Crispus wishes to play the soldier, I am not the man to prevent him," he said, an answer that considerably mortified the proud princess, as showing that Titus was not quite the plastic clay she had thought him.

The fare provided by Vespasian for his guests was simple, as became the tastes of the general, and they sat to it.

"I hate the effeminate habit of reclining at meals," said he.

The conversation at table naturally turned upon the war, and Crispus, who knew little of the then state of Jerusalem, received some enlightenment from Vespasian.

"True is the saying," said he, "that those whom the gods wish to destroy they first make mad. Listen to what is happening at Jerusalem.

## The Making of an Emperor

"Simon of Gerasa, disgusted that his great services should be passed over by the Sanhedrim while Eleazar was rewarded with the government of a province, retired from Jerusalem; and, collecting a numerous body of followers, took to brigandage again.

"Whilst Eleazar was administering the affairs of Idumæa, a certain ambitious Zealot seized the opportunity to make himself master of the temple; by a singular confusion of names this new captain is called Eleazar.

"In the meantime that fierce Zealot, John of Giscala, defeated by us in Galilee, fled to Jerusalem, where, becoming powerful, he played the tyrant, putting the rich to death, and seizing their wealth.

"The high priest Matthias sought to free the miserable people by calling in the aid of Simon; he came, but was unable to expel John.

"The result is that the city is now groaning beneath the tyranny of three factions.

"Simon rules in Zion, with the Tower of Phasaelus for his palace; John holds the Lower City, and the outer courts of the temple; Eleazar keeps jealous guard over the Sanctuary.

"These three Zealots, each aiming at sovereignty, wage war with one another by night and by day.

"Titus would have me march to Jerusalem at once, but why should I, when they are doing our work so effectually? At sight of us, faction would disappear; they would unite their arms against the common enemy. No; let them go on with their internecine warfare till two of the factions are exterminated, and then we will deal with the survivor."

"Sound policy!" commented Rufus.

Crispus, with his Christianized way of thinking, could not help seeing in the terrible state of the city the working out of a Divine retribution. The people that had cried, "Not this man, but Barabbas," desiring that a murderer might be granted to them, were now delivered over to the rule of murderers. "The assassin's dagger was to sway the last councils of their dying nationality."

Rufus now added *his* contribution to the story of Israel's degradation.

"And, that they might not have a moralist perpetually rebuking them for their misdoings, the Zealots of Eleazar's party deposed the high priest Matthias; and, calling for the register of priests, they broke through all precedent by casting lots for the office. The lot fell upon an obscurity named Phannias, a rustic so illiterate as scarcely to know what the high priesthood meant. Yet, they brought him from his native village; and, putting the sacred vestments upon him, instructed him how to act, finding matter for laughter and sport in the many blunders that he made."

Again the finger of Divine retribution! The high priesthood, that had mocked at the Crucifixion, had itself become a subject for mockery, a thing of scorn.

Somewhat to his surprise, Crispus discovered that Vespasian at the end of his day's labor would sometimes find relaxation in listening to the discourses of Josephus upon Jewish history and Jewish philosophy. He chose to do so on this present occasion; and, accordingly, after the repast was over, a centurion was dispatched to bring in the captive.

He came, linked as usual to the guardian soldier, and advanced with an air meant to be solemn and dignified, but which in Crispus' view was pompous only; nay, contradictory as it may seem, beneath this air of importance there was lurking an undercurrent of obsequiousness and servility that set Crispus against him. If ever man was sycophant this man was!

"We have sent for you," began Vespasian, "to hear you discourse for a time upon the history and laws of your nation."

"Sire, thou honorest our holy books by wishing to

derive instruction from them. But, to-night—to-night, I would speak, not of the past, but of the future."

"Of which he knows no more than you or I," whispered Rufus to Crispus.

"Sire, when the Almighty created the seventy nations of the earth he gave to each its peculiar gift; to the Roman, sovereignty in war, and to the Greek, supremacy in art; to the Egyptian, depth in wisdom, and to the Hebrew, the power of prophecy. To us are granted at times glimpses of the future, prevision denied to other races. Did I not show the knowledge of the seer by declaring that Jotapata would fall on the forty-seventh day of the siege? And now again do I lift the veil that hides the future. The God of our fathers hath revealed to me that great thing which shall come to pass."

He advanced a step, accompanied necessarily by the soldier; and, falling on his knees before Vespasian, he touched the ground with his forehead, saying, as he made this Oriental salutation:

"HAIL, CÆSAR THAT IS TO BE!"

As if a chasm had suddenly yawned at his feet, Vespasian started back in an amazement so obviously genuine as to show plainly that this treasonable notion was being sprung upon him for the first time.

Crispus shared in Vespasian's amazement, as did most of the other officers present. Titus was the only one that showed no surprise; one might have thought that he had been expecting something of this kind; he sat with his eyes keenly attentive to his father's face.

Crispus could not help thinking that this little tableau was not a spontaneous ebullition on the part of Josephus, but a premeditated piece of acting, primarily due to the scheming brain of Berenice, and seconded by the ambitious hopes of Titus.

The deep silence was broken by the voice of Vespasian, who spoke with stern indignation.

"No more of this. Thou talkest treason—treason to the reigning emperor."

Titus' face became clouded.

"If it be treason to declare the will of God, then am I talking treason," said Josephus.

"Peace! I and the legions have sworn to uphold the throne of Vitellius."

"They took the oath with great reluctance, however," observed Titus, "and are repenting of it. Their dissatisfaction grows from day to day."

"Their dissatisfaction shall not divert me from the path of duty."

"Seek not," said Josephus, "to resist your destiny. Cæsar you will be, in spite of yourself. For so is it written in our sacred scriptures, that one arising in Judæa shall obtain the empire of the world."[20]

Crispus, in spite of the debt he owed Josephus, could not conceal his scorn at this amazing perversion of Messianic prophecy, a perversion that showed to what depth of sycophancy the soul of this priest and Pharisee could descend. That the sacred predictions of Isaiah should receive their fulfillment in the elevation of a heathen soldier to the throne of the Cæsars was to the Hebrew mind an interpretation so blasphemous that if Josephus had ventured to assert it among a circle of his own countrymen he would most assuredly have been torn to pieces.

On the present occasion, however, he was safe from such a fate; and if he himself did not believe in his own statement what mattered, if the lie could but accomplish his purpose?

"Rise," said Vespasian sternly, for during all this time Josephus had been kneeling. The captive arose; and Vespasian, turning to his officers, asked in a tone of pleasantry: "How shall I punish this knave for urging me to treason?"

Rufus answered him.

"Give him his freedom on the day that you become

Cæsar. If he hath prophesied truly his freedom is bound to come, and if not——"

Vespasian slapped his thigh with a hearty laugh.

"By Castor, a just sentence! As thou sayest, so shall it be."

A close observer might have detected in the "prophet's" expression a certain uneasiness suggestive of the idea that he was by no means confident of the fulfillment of his words.

"Retire," said Vespasian, whose desire for Hebrew history had vanished. "I will hear thee no more to-night."

So Josephus departed; but when Titus began to comment upon his vaticination, Vespasian forbade him with so stern an air that Titus at once dropped the subject; and when, later, a centurion looked in to ask the watchword for the night, Vespasian wrote upon the tessera the word "FIDELITAS."

The throne of the Cæsars!

Despite Vespasian's repudiation—a repudiation made at the time in all sincerity—it became evident within the space of a few days that the seed sown in his mind by Josephus was beginning to germinate.

Under the haunting spell of a new and splendid ambition, he became moody, restless, uneasy. Shunning the daily exercises of the army he took long walks, communing with himself in lonely woods. Deep in thought, he would stare vacantly when addressed; one had to speak twice or thrice ere he understood. At times he was heard to murmur, "I will not do this thing," and his officers would look at each other, well knowing what thing was meant.

One morning, as if wishful to escape from his vexing thoughts, he mounted a horse and rode mile after mile along the shore towards the point where the long ridge of Carmel, intercepting the maritime road, thrusts a rocky bluff into the sea. In this wild gallop he was attended by his staff-officers, Crispus and Rufus being of the number.

Arrived at the foot of the mount, Vespasian, either as wishing to take a survey of the country around, or moved perhaps by a desire to show what the agility of a man of sixty could accomplish, resolved to make the ascent; and soon he and his staff were toiling on foot up the craggy path that wound through forests of pine, oak, and olive to the point

*" Where Carmel's flowery top perfumes the skies."*

The glorious panorama presented by the mountainous landscape and the dark-blue sea well rewarded them for their climb. The officers were particularly interested in pointing out to Crispus the various hill-fortresses of Galilee—Giscala, Tabor, Jotapata—subdued by their arms in the campaign of the previous year.

As the staff moved first this way and then that, following the steps of Vespasian, they turned the corner of a crag, and came suddenly upon a stately figure in a flowing white robe, who with folded arms was gazing silently and pensively seaward. Obviously, he was a priest, since there was in attendance upon him a young boy holding in his hands what seemed an acerra, or box containing incense. Near by, formed from a number of rough unhewn stones, was an altar, upon which lay a few dried shavings of cedar-wood.

The man was not quite a stranger to Crispus; he had seen him, or rather had caught a fleeting glimpse of him, on the previous evening, holding converse with Titus in a lonely spot at some distance from the camp. Crispus had come upon the pair unawares, and it seemed to him that Titus was not altogether pleased at being detected in company with this priest, though what there was to be vexed at it would be hard to say.

On hearing footsteps the priest turned, and caught sight of the armed men.

## The Making of an Emperor

"Who art thou?" he asked of Vespasian, as being evidently the chief of the band.

"I am Flavius Vespasian."

"I know not the name."

"And this is fame?" smiled Vespasian. "To be unknown after so many victories in this Galilæan province!"

"Hast thou dropped from the moon," asked Rufus, "not to have heard the name of the great Vespasian?"

"Content with my grotto," said the priest, pointing to a cave in the face of the rock, "and with this altar, I stir not from Carmel,"—Crispus, remembering where he had seen him last, wondered at this speech, but held his peace,—"hence I know nothing of the affairs of men. If thou art some great one of the earth, the gods teach thee to use thy power well."

"To what deity is this altar erected?" asked Vespasian.

"To the god Carmelus, the tutelary genius of this mountain."

"Hath he no image nor temple?"

"None. This altar—'tis composed of twelve stones—is alone acceptable to him. Such hath been his worship from ancient days."

"Thou art about to offer incense to thy god, I perceive. We will join in thy worship. Offer on our behalf as well as on thine own."

And with that the superstitiously devout Vespasian doffed his helmet, in which act he was imitated by the rest, save Crispus, who drew aside from a ceremony incompatible with his Christian faith.

Rufus, observing that the priest apparently lacked the means of kindling a fire, offered him his own flint and steel, but they were waved aside by the priest.

"Our rites forbid such method," said he. "The wood must be kindled not by ordinary means, but by the pure fire of heaven."

So saying, he produced a thick glass lens, with which

he proceeded to focus the sun's rays upon the cedarwood.

Crispus, whose Christian training among the learned brethren of Tarsus and Ephesus had embraced the study of the Greek Septuagint, murmured to himself:

"Mount Carmel? an altar of twelve stones? fire from heaven? This deity Carmelus is none other than Elijah in a heathen guise!"

It was not long ere the wood began first to smolder and then to break into a flame. The feat was one as common in that age as in this, but being new to Vespasian, he looked on as though it were a miracle.

The attendant boy now held forth the acerra, and the priest, taking from it some grains of incense, cast them upon the fire.

As the strong fragrance became diffused around the priest began the chanting of an invocation which fell with a somewhat weird effect upon the ears of the Romans, being delivered in the Phœnician, a tongue not understood by them.

"Now, how know we that this fellow is not cursing us?" muttered Rufus.

From time to time the priest continued to cast fresh incense upon the altar. It seemed that the sacrifice was scarcely acceptable to the god Carmelus, for the fire was dull and smoky, always deemed a bad omen.

Then, all in a moment, there was a change.

A tongue of flame sprang up, high and brilliant, and lasting for several moments.

At the first leap of the fire the priest turned and stared hard at Vespasian, as though that general had become suddenly invested with a new and strange interest.

"Vespasian—if that be thy name—whatever project thou now hast in thy mind, whether it be the enlargement of thy house, the augmentation of thy lands, or the increase of thy slaves, the Fates are preparing for thee a splendid seat, a large territory, a multitude of men." [21]

The Roman officers, aware of the thought that was then paramount in the mind of their general, looked significantly at each other.

"What is thy name?" asked Vespasian.

"What thine shalt be—Basilides."

Now this name is, by interpretation, a king; and therefore Vespasian was not a little startled to find this Phœnician seer hinting, and that not obscurely, at the same high destiny assured him by Josephus. Surely, since there had been no previous concert between them, that must be true which was prophesied by Hebrew priest and by Phœnician priest alike?

During the course of the long ride back to camp, Crispus had ample time to review the incident that had just happened, and he saw in it not the hand of the gods, but the trickery of man, the man in this case being Titus, who by subtle devices was luring his father on to make an attempt for the imperial throne.

Vespasian on the previous evening had announced his intention of visiting Carmel on the morrow, and it had therefore been a very easy matter for Titus to obtain the collusion of the priest Basilides for the purpose of playing upon the superstitious feelings of Vespasian. The sudden springing up of the flame upon the altar was a result easily obtainable by concealing a grain of fat among the incense. Titus was the real source of this "divine sign," as well as of the ambiguous but significant oracle delivered by Basilides.

Crispus hesitated whether to enlighten Vespasian as to how he was being duped into believing himself to be a recipient of divine signs, but finally resolved to hold his peace. What mattered it how Vespasian was induced to revolt, whether by necessity, reason, or superstition, so long as he *did* revolt? The rule of Vespasian would be infinitely preferable to that of the bestial Vitellius. And when Crispus, further refleeting that should a Flavian dynasty be established, and should Titus and Domitian—both at present childless—die without issue, the next heir to the throne would be Flavius Clemens, an adherent of the faith, he began to wonder whether a Christian Cæsar might not be among the possibilities of the near future.

So here was Crispus wishing, like Berenice, to see Vespasian upon the throne, though for a different reason—*she* hoping to promote the cause of Judaism, *he* hoping to promote the cause of Christianity.

The course of the next few days furnished additional proof that subtle art was being employed to make Vespasian accept a position almost akin to that foretold of the Messiah.

"Do I look like a god?" said he with a caustic smile, entering the tent of Rufus, who chanced to be alone.

Truth to tell there was little in the homely, and even vulgar, aspect of Vespasian to suggest kinship with the Olympian divinities, but naturally Rufus did not say so, contenting himself with asking the general to explain his meaning. Then Vespasian, sitting down, proceeded to tell a strange story.

"There hath been wont to sit at the fountain beside the gate of Cæsarea a blind man. This morning as I was passing by the gate I saw a little crowd gathered there, and among them this blind man. Guided by two friends, he drew near, and, kneeling at my feet, implored me to cure his blindness, declaring—and the two that were with him said the same—that if I would but anoint clay with my spittle, and put the clay upon his eyes, he would there and then recover his sight.

"I held my laughter and tried to reason him out of this belief, but the more I argued the more earnest he became, and so I left him still kneeling. But as I walked away, the poor fellow's lamentations became so pitiful that I could not help turning back, determined by making the actual experiment to convince the man of his folly. But, lo! as soon as the clay was washed from his eyes and I had pronounced the Hebrew word '*Ephphatha!*'—for it seems these spells are more efficacious when spoken in a barbarous language—the man cried out in an ecstasy of delight that he could see!"

"'A miracle! a miracle!' cried the crowd.

"'So shalt thou give light to a dark world, O Vespasian,' cried a voice which I recognized as that of the priest Theomantes.

"As for me, I doubted whether the man *had* recovered his sight, but he gave proof of it by telling what number of coins lay on my palm, and though I changed the number several times he did not once err.

"There must be some divine efficacy in my touch became the opinion of the crowd. The news flew from mouth to mouth, and as I stood amazed at my own deed, there came to me a man whose right arm, as if paralyzed, hung stiff and motionless at his side.

"'I was a mason,' said he, 'earning my livelihood by my hands. I pray thee that thou wouldest make this arm whole like the other, that I may not basely beg my bread.'

"Compliant with his will I clasped his right hand firmly in my own, and after a few moments he cried out that he had recovered the use of the withered limb, and gave evidence of his words by freely gesticulating with it. Now, Rufus, how explainest thou these marvels?"

These feats of healing, so analogous to those recorded in the gospel, as to suggest to the mind of more than one historian the suspicion that they were purposely counterfeited with a view of investing Vespasian with a sort of Messianic character, offered no difficulty whatever to the pagan mind of Rufus.

"It is clear to me, sire," said he, fully believing in the truth of his own words, "that the gods wish to point you out to mankind as one distinguished by their special favor and destined to attain a dignity and splendor beyond that of ordinary mortals."

And the perplexed Vespasian, though the least conceited of men, was gradually driven to adopt this opinion in view of these strange happenings.

A few days afterwards, Mucianus, the Legate of Syria, arrived at Cæsarea, having come direct thither from a brief visit paid to Rome.

He was accompanied by Tiberius Alexander, the prefect of Egypt. A Jew by birth, a nephew, in fact, of the brilliant theologian Philo Judæus, Tiberius Alexander had deserted his ancestral faith for Grecian paganism, a conversion unique in the annals of Judaism.

Vespasian at once hastened from the camp to Cæsarea to pay his respects to Mucianus, who, besides being his life-long friend, was also his superior in office.

The two illustrious visitors had accepted the hospitality of Berenice, and it was in the palace of that intriguing princess that Vespasian and Titus met them in a consultation upon which hung the destiny of an empire.

"The senate of Rome," began Mucianus, "loathes the rule of the bestial Vitellius and his brutal soldiery. Shall I tell you what are likewise the secret whisperings of the people in the forum? 'Would to the gods that Vespasian would deliver us from this glutton, who has already spent seven million sesterces upon his stomach!' Vespasian, you have but to proclaim yourself Cæsar here in Judæa, and Rome—yea, and all the provinces, will rise in your favor. I have here a list, and 'tis a long one, of Roman patricians who have sworn to me that they are willing to risk their lives and fortunes in your cause."

Vespasian, having listened to all this, and much more of like import, showed his indifference to the imperial throne by offering it to Mucianus! A plain, sensible man, and a born soldier, Vespasian cared little who was

Cæsar so long as he himself should hold the chief military command.

But however much Mucianus may have desired the purple he knew that his chances of obtaining it were infinitely small, and he therefore continued to press its acceptance upon Vespasian.

"Syria and its four legions are with you," said he.

"And I can promise you Egypt," observed Tiberius Alexander. "As soon as you are proclaimed Cæsar I will cause the legions of Alexandria to take the oath of allegiance to you."

"And then your first act must be to stop the corn-ships from sailing," said Berenice, who was taking part in these deliberations.

"A wise policy!" commented Titus.

The possession of Egypt, as the conspirators well knew, was extremely important from a political point of view, the populace of Rome being almost dependent for their existence upon the supplies of grain exported from Alexandria. Famine at the heart of the empire would not be favorable to the cause of Vitellius.

"With Syria, Palestine, and Egypt on your side," pursued Mucianus, "you will occupy a continuous and united territory. Your rear you must secure by an alliance with the Parthians. As to your front, by land it is accessible only by way of the Taurus mountains; occupy the Syrian and Cilician Gates, and you can bid defiance to any attack coming from that quarter. As to your sea-front we have in Phœnicia the finest race of seamen in the world, and in the cedars of Libanus an inexhaustible supply of timber for shipbuilding. Phœnicia falls within my province. Bid me do it, and ere two months be out you shall have a fleet of triremes that shall guard all coasts from Cilicia to Cyrene. Thus secure, we may advance to attack Vitellius, or await him here, as may best seem convenient to us."

But Vespasian, prudent and cautious, still delayed his final answer.

Accordingly, after his withdrawal the remaining conclave, at Berenice's suggestion, determined to force the hand of the reluctant general, that princess propounding an ingenious scheme for the purpose.

"You, Titus," said she, "must persuade all the soldiers in the camp to salute Vespasian with the title of Cæsar."

"They want no persuading. The difficulty is that he'll refuse to listen to them."

"He will be compelled."

"How so?"

"Vitellius will hear of it. He cannot with dignity pass over such treason. He'll demand that these disloyal legions be punished. In declining this task—for how can he punish a whole army?—Vespasian will become an object of suspicion to Vitellius. He'll be summoned to Rome; to go will be certain death. Therefore, if the legions here persist in crying 'Hail, Cæsar!' whenever Vespasian appears, he must either accept the title or be prepared for immediate ruin."

"Princess, you have it," cried Mucianus admiringly. "The plan cannot fail. Now, Titus, do your part, whilst Alexander and I hasten to set our provinces in order."

The conspirators departed to put their plan into operation.

It succeeded admirably.

On the third of July A.D. 69 Vespasian was proclaimed emperor by the legions of Cæsarea. His elevation was everywhere received with delight. Embassies from various cities and provinces hurried to Cæsarea, bringing addresses of congratulation and crowns of honor; within a month Vespasian had received the submission of all the East, with the exception of Jerusalem and its immediate neighborhood.

And the prophecy, long current in the East, not only among the Jews, but likewise among other nations, that one coming from Judæa should obtain the empire

## The Making of an Emperor

of the world, was thought to have received its fulfillment at last!

It was decided at a council composed of Eastern statesmen and Roman warriors that Mucianus should proceed by land against Italy, that Titus should carry on the war against Jerusalem, and that Vespasian should retire to Alexandria, and there await the issue of events.

"And now, O father," said Titus, delighted at having attained the rank of Cæsar—for to be scrupulously exact that was his title as heir-apparent, the reigning emperor being called Augustus—" now, O father, remember your promise and release Josephus from his bonds, else will it be a shameful thing that the man who told beforehand of your coming to empire, and hath been the minister of a divine message to you, should still be retained in the condition of a captive."

It was in the camp at Cæsarea that these words were spoken. So Vespasian sent for Josephus, who came still wearing the chain that bound him to the guardian soldier.

The new emperor gave orders that the captive should be set at liberty; and accordingly the soldier was about to loose the chain when Titus intervened, suggesting that the chain should be *cut* from him, this being the Roman method with such as were bound without just cause.

This advice being agreeable to Vespasian, a smith was sent for, a fellow strong and dexterous of arm, who cut the chain to pieces.

"Josephus, thou art free," exclaimed Vespasian, "and the citizenship of Rome is thine."

"Call me no more Josephus," said the liberated one, boldly venturing to assume the name of his imperial patron. "Henceforth let all men know me as Titus Flavius."

"Titus," said Vespasian, referring to his son,

"Titus has the glory of being Cæsar. Josephus has——"

"Flavius, sire," murmured the adopter of that name, remonstratingly.

"Flavius, then, to please you. Flavius has received the honor of the citizenship. What honor," he continued, turning to Crispus, "what honor shall we confer upon you?"

On the point of replying that the emperor's friendship was of itself a sufficient honor, Crispus paused, suddenly seized by a happy idea.

"There is one favor I would ask, sire—a very simple one."

"Name it."

"'Tis of a private nature. I prefer to state it before you and Titus only."

Vespasian looked surprised. He gave a nod, and Josephus and the others withdrew from the tent.

"Now, Crispus, for what do you make request?"

"It may not be known to you, sire, that I have a wife."

It certainly was news to Vespasian, as his looks plainly showed. Crispus proceeded to relate in as few words as possible the story of his wedding at Bethtamar.

"Eh! what is this?" said the old general, turning with a chiding air to Titus. "You were Crispus' paranymph, and yet you have never told me of it. Fie on you! But what has this to do with the favor you would ask?" continued he, addressing Crispus.

"You, sire, as emperor, are supreme in matters of the law. 'Tis yours to see that the terms of a contract be fulfilled. Therefore I ask that when I discover this woman she shall be made to keep her nuptial pledge."

"Find her, and if you want her, you shall have her, be she never so reluctant," said Vespasian, smiling grimly. "Who is *she* to refuse my bravest tribune?"

In that immoral age fidelity to a wife was a rare

virtue, and one that commended itself to honest old Vespasian.

"You swear it, sire, that no man shall be permitted to take her from me?"

Vespasian was painfully impressed by the tense, earnest look of Crispus.

"By the gods, it shall go ill with the man, if any such there be. He who dares to take your wife from you shall be hanged on high—yea, though he were my own son."

"Take it not amiss, sire, if I ask for that promise in writing."

While Vespasian, surprised yet compliant, was putting his promise into documentary form, Titus stood silent in the background.

His face at that moment was a study, and confirmed Crispus in the suspicion he had long entertained.

# CHAPTER XVIII

#### THE PRELIMINARIES OF A GREAT SIEGE

It was the spring of the year A.D. 70, nearly nine months after the elevation of Vespasian to the imperial throne, and still the Roman legions, now under the sole command of Titus, tarried in their encampment at Cæsarea-by-the-sea.

The self-confident Zealots of Jerusalem began to doubt whether the enemy ever *would* come within sight of the city again.

In the intervals of their internecine warfare they were much interested in watching the progress of a new planet or comet, fiery red in color.

It first appeared in Pisces, the constellation which, in the astral lore of that age, was supposed to be connected with the fortunes of Judæa. Night after night it mounted higher, and ever higher, in the sky, seeming to be making for a point directly above the holy city.

At the very first sight of it the multitude had cried with one voice, "*The star of the Messiah!*" Ere long it became so distinct and bright as to be plainly discernible in the daytime, and crowds gathered at street corners to stare at what they devoutly believed to be a heaven-sent sign.

The glorious day foretold by the prophets was at hand when the Jews, with the assistance of the heavenly powers, should reign supreme over all the nations of the earth. And when the star, growing more plain, was seen to take the shape of a sword [24] with its blade pointing in the direction of the Roman Camp at Cæsarea, who could doubt that it portended the doom of those who were threatening the holy city?

## Preliminaries of a Great Siege

" There shall come a star out of Jacob, and a scepter shall rise out of Israel."

Such was the text upon which Rabbi Simeon ben Gamaliel proposed to give a midrash or sermon, an announcement that attracted to the Royal Synagogue a congregation larger than any previously seen within its walls.

Devout joy was at first the prevailing keynote of the assembly; but, after the preliminary prayers, a strange uneasiness fell upon them when it was discovered that the prescribed parashoth or lesson for the day—and there could be no omitting it!—was that section of the Pentateuch containing the solemn and thrilling words addressed to the nation by the great Hebrew lawgiver on the eve of his death.

As the chazan began his reading the sunlight without became clouded, and a gloom pervaded the edifice, a gloom that seemed to deepen with each successive moment.

It was, of course, customary to receive the reading of the Law in reverential silence, but a silence so tense as the present had never been known in this synagogue. With bated breath and with eyes fastened on the chazan's face they listened to the voice of the divine lawgiver sounding down to them through the corridors of time.

" The LORD shall bring a nation against thee from far, from the end of the earth, as swift as the eagle flieth; a nation whose tongue thou shalt not understand. A nation of fierce countenance, which shall not regard the person of the old, nor show favor to the young. . . . And he shall besiege thee in all thy gates, until thy high and fenced walls come down, wherein thou trustedst. . . . And thou shalt eat the fruit of thine own body, the flesh of thy sons and of thy daughters, in the siege and in the straitness, wherewith thine enemies shall distress thee. . . . In the morning thou shalt say, Would God it were even! and at even thou shalt say, Would God it were morning! for the fear of thine heart wherewith thou shalt fear, and for the sight of thine eyes which thou shalt see."

At this point the assembly, hitherto as motionless and as silent as the dead, impulsively started to their feet, with fear stamped upon their faces.

It was not, however, the words of the Law, awful though they were, that had moved the worshipers, but a tumult coming from the streets in the vicinity of the synagogue.

During the previous few moments the air had resounded with the running of feet intermingled with the sound of voices.

Those voices, confused at first, had now become clearly audible. Rolling upward to the skies in accents of surprise and fear there pealed again and again the startling cry:

"THE ROMANS! THE ROMANS!"

The sight of the Roman vanguard, glittering upon the northern heights of Scopus, though it might put fear into the hearts of the common people, served only to evoke the scorn of the Zealots. Their astonishing victory over Cestius, and the fact that for three years no attempt had been made to recover the city, had given them an exaggerated notion of their own prowess.

The Zealots of Galilee might yield; those of Jerusalem were invincible!

"They are the same sheep," scoffed Simon, "but with a new shepherd."

For a long time the Zealots and the people, massed upon the northern wall of the city, continued to watch the distant host, who seemed to be occupied in forming an encampment. Suddenly a shout arose. Something was seen to separate itself from the common body, and to move forward quickly towards the city amid a cloud of dust. That something on a nearer approach proved to be a detachment of cavalry, six hundred strong, led by Titus in person, who, coming not to fight but

## Preliminaries of a Great Siege

merely to reconnoiter, rode bareheaded, having left both helmet and breastplate behind. By his side rode that Jewish apostate, Tiberius Alexander, who, having at one time been procurator of Judæa, was in a position to explain to Titus the topography of the city.

A sea of faces glared at them along the whole extent of the northern wall; the battlements of Antonia, the porticoes of the temple, the distant ramparts of Mount Zion were similarly crowded; in all the wide city there was neither wall nor tower, neither roof nor window, but showed a cluster of human beings. Their excited cries blending together came to the ears of Titus like the restless murmur of the sea.

" How many people doth the city hold, think you? " he asked of Alexander.

" My spies report the number to be a million—yea, and a hundred thousand beyond that. 'Tis the eve of the passover, and Jews from every province of the empire have come up to worship."

" A million? Ye gods! Has this nation appointed a rendezvous for its own destruction? But as to the fighting men? "

" All will fight, even children, if it be to defend their city and their religion. The women and girls will weave their hair into ropes, if ropes be needed. The priests themselves will arm should the war approach the temple."

" Little care I for such foes. My concern is with those who have any knowledge of actual warfare."

" Why, as to that, Eleazar guards the holy house with 2,400 Zealots; John, your old opponent in Galilee, keeps the cloisters with 6,000. But Simon, who holds Mount Zion, is the man to be feared. He hath 15,000 fierce spirits, so fanatically devoted to him, that each would fall on his own sword did he but command it."

" Twenty-three thousand fighting men? Well, we have more than double that number with us."

" Your number may be tenfold theirs, but such superiority avails nothing in view of their impregnable position.—As you see, O Cæsar," he continued, pointing first to the city, and then to a map that he carried, a map drawn by the hand of Josephus, "Jerusalem occupies the southern tongue of a rocky plateau; on the east, on the west, on the south, its walls look down upon ravines and valleys whose slopes are too steep to be scaled by an army; it is from this quarter only that the attack can be made."

Titus recognized the fact at a glance. The city, the real city—namely, the stronghold of Zion—was assailable only from the north, but the way to it was barred by huge ramparts.

Three gigantic lines of masonry were drawn east and west across the plateau.

First, there was the wall directly facing them, called by the Jews the Third Wall, as being the latest built.

This, when breached or surmounted, opened the way into the northern suburb of Bezetha or New-town. Marching through Bezetha, the Romans would come to the Second or Middle Wall, which, when taken, would admit them to Acra or the Lower City; passing through Acra, they would find themselves staring helplessly up at the scarped cliff of Mount Zion or the Upper City, whose edge was surmounted by a wall so lofty that the Titans themselves might have despaired of scaling it.

But ere any attempt could be made upon Zion, it would be necessary first to take the towering rock-citadel of Antonia, and, secondly, the lofty temple-fortress, otherwise while besieging Zion they would be continually exposed to a flank attack from these two strongholds.

"You have to deal," said Tiberius Alexander, "not with one city, but with five cities. A fivefold siege lies before us."

As Titus glanced with the eye of a trained soldier from point to point, and took in the nature of the de-

## Preliminaries of a Great Siege

fenses, natural and artificial, he began to realize the stupendous nature of the task imposed upon him.

Haughtily enthroned upon its mountain-rock, this Oriental city with its girdling *enciente* of walls, towers and bastions, seemed as if built with set purpose to triumph over every device that could be brought against it by the military science of the West.

There was no doubt about it: it was THE STRONGEST CITY IN THE WORLD, and if adequately provisioned, and defended with due care, was absolutely impregnable.

" And I have wagered Mucianus," said Titus grimly, " that I'll take it within seven weeks."

Alexander gravely shook his head.

" Twice seven weeks will pass—yea, and three times seven weeks—ere the eagles fly over Zion."

In the midst of this reconnoitering, a gate by the Women's Tower opened, and the Zealots poured forth in such numbers that the little Roman band, after holding their ground for a time, deemed it prudent to beat a retreat.

Great was the delight of the Jews. Cæsar himself had been seen to fly! It was the promise and presage of more glorious victories.

Early next day the Roman army advanced to within a mile of the northern wall of the city, and there began the construction of two huge camps.

The forces of Titus consisted of four legions, the fifth or *Macedonia*, the tenth or *Fretensis*, the twelfth or *Fulminata* (memorable for its flight under Cestius), and the fifteenth or *Apollinaris*.

In imperial times the legion usually consisted of 6,000 men, all Roman citizens, none other being admitted to its proud ranks; but as each legion was always accompanied by an equal number of auxiliaries, levied from the subject nations, together with 300 cavalry; and as several petty kings of the East (including Agrippa) had joined in the expedition, each bringing with him his own little army, the forces arrayed against Jerusalem must be stated at a figure considerably in excess of 50,000.

Flashing in the morning sunlight, the various squadrons of this vast host, horse and foot, heavy-armed and light-armed, deployed into never-ending lines upon the brow of Olivet and upon the descent of Scopus; and as the Jews gazed from their walls upon the long array of eagles and standards bearing the letters S.P.Q.R., they realized the full meaning of the expression " terrible as an army with banners."

As the battering-rams and other ponderous machines used in sieging were mounted upon wheels, whose revolution required a comparatively even surface, the first work of the legionaries, after forming their camp, was to level the ground between their lines and the foot of the northern wall.

This fore-suburb, ere the Roman engineers set to work, was a scene of sylvan beauty, consisting of groves and watercourses, gardens and fair mansions.

Now all was ruthlessly swept away: the trees fell before the ax; the watercourses were destroyed; the houses demolished; even the deep and shady glens were no more, being filled up with the picturesque crags that were wont to overshadow them.

While some of the troops labored at the rocky ground with iron instruments, others were employed in bringing up from the valley of Cedron countless baskets laden with pebbles and earth; these were used in filling up the inequalities of the surface, the soldiers stamping the materials firmly with their feet.

In spite of a cloud of missiles discharged at them from the ramparts, in spite of the sudden and daring sallies made by Simon and his men, the Romans contrived, in the course of a few days, to transform the picturesque fore-suburb into a dreary, uniform level.

While the Roman operations were proceeding without, the Jews within the city were preparing to celebrate the passover, memorable as being THE LAST IN

## Preliminaries of a Great Siege    235

THEIR HISTORY as a nation; memorable, too, for the armed fray that accompanied it.

On the fourteenth of Nisan, Eleazar and his party opened the gates of the upper temple to admit those bringing the paschal lambs. The cautions previously exercised by him to exclude the Zealots of the other two factions seem to have been wanting on this occasion. Members of John's party, with weapons concealed beneath their garments, contrived to enter in company with the multitude of foreign pilgrims, and drawing together in a compact body, they suddenly flung off their outer robes and appeared in the panoply of war. At this sight Eleazar's faction flew to arms, and a fierce mêlée took place around the golden house, innocent pilgrim and guilty Zealot alike falling fast. When the fray ended, John of Giscala was master of all the temple. Eleazar having fallen, the survivors of his party consented to be absorbed in that of the victor; and thus the three factions in the city were now reduced to two, the Johanneans and the Simonians.

To these Johanneans Simon now made appeal.

Standing on the bridge that connected Mount Zion with the temple-hill, he called for John, and when that chief appeared he thus addressed him:

" Shall a house stand that is divided against itself? Why do we fight each other, making fine sport for the foe? We are, it seems, valiant against ourselves only, content to let the city be taken by our love of faction. Let us lay aside our enmity, and join in opposing the common foe."

" Thou art a subtle knave, Simon," replied John. " Thou desirest me and my forces to go with thee to the Wall of Agrippa that thy men in my absence may seize upon the temple, for all know of thy desire to make thyself tyrant of the city. However, I will so far assist thee that such of my men as are so minded may go with thee, but as to myself and certain other, we will remain behind to defend the temple."

Availing themselves of the permission thus given, hundreds of John's men came forth from the temple to join with the Simonians in the defense of the city.

The Romans, having cleared the ground from all obstructions, were now occupied in erecting opposite the northern wall a series of lofty banks, upon which to set the engines used in discharging missile-weapons, for the higher the position of these engines the more accurate and the more deadly their aim.

Each bank or agger was made of earth strengthened by beams of timber. During the erection of these banks, the Zealots were not content to look idly on. Preceded by a veritable rain of stones discharged from the ramparts, they poured forth by hundreds, armed with long poles terminating in iron hooks; with these they sought to pull apart the beams composing the agger, with intent to bring down the whole mass.

In these sallies the Zealots came on with the rush of a whirlwind, each man ready to sacrifice his life provided only he could kill one of the enemy, or do but the least damage to the agger.

Not for a moment, however, could they stay the progress of the work. The Roman guard stationed in front of the banks drove back every onset; and at last the Jews, despairing of accomplishing their object, kept within their walls, and sallied forth no more.

Each embankment, when finished, presented a vertical front to the city, but the other side was inclined at a very low angle, in order to facilitate the mounting of the military engines: and gaps were purposely left in it to permit the passage of the battering-rams and the movable towers.

The shrill réveille pealed through the Roman camp, rousing the legionaries from their slumber.

Every man on waking turned his eyes towards the tent of Titus, and every face gleamed with a grim

## Preliminaries of a Great Siege

satisfaction at sight of the scarlet mantle hoisted above it, the sign that the day was to be one of battle.

As the Roman host gazed upon the holy city rising fair and stately in the golden light of an Eastern dawn, they were fain to confess that it was a city worth fighting for.

From its walls the tocsin of war was sounding in the shape of a six-foot brazen gong, whose deep, sullen tone reverberated monotonously on the morning air.

The whole northern rampart was alive with a multitude of Zealot warriors moving to and fro, their shining armor obscured at times by faint columns of blue smoke.

The Romans knew well what that smoke meant.

Behind those battlements burned fires, over which were slung cauldrons hissing with scalding water, boiling pitch, and molten lead!

At sight of this smoke the Romans merely smiled; but at sight of the military engines, disposed at due intervals along the wall, they burned with secret rage, being reminded of their tarnished honor, for these engines represented a triumph over Romans, having been captured, some from the camp of Cestius, and others from the Tower of Antonia and the Prætorium of Florus.

Moving everywhere along the ramparts, now giving an order here, and now a caution there, was seen the form of that brawny Titan, Simon the Black, the very soul of battle, hatred of the Roman looking out from his wild, dark eye. Over his armor he wore a wolf-skin mantle with the shaggy side turned outwards, a mantle that suggested to his followers the prophecy (for he came of the " little " tribe), " Benjamin shall ravin as a wolf."

Even those among the Romans that were most given to the despising of Hebrew valor, were obliged to admit that in Simon they had a warrior worthy of their steel.

It was a lovely morning, giving promise of a sultry noontide; a dazzling sun shone from a sky of deepest blue; far away on the horizon hung a pall of pearly white mist.

As a hush precedes the desert sandstorm, so upon the two armies there lay a strange stillness.

It was a sublime and thrilling spectacle this, of two nations facing each other in arms—nay, an act in a Divine drama, the true significance of which was understood by none present, except by Crispus and the very few that were of like faith with him. The struggle was more than it appeared upon the surface; it was not merely the subjugation of a revolted city, but a battle betwixt two religions; the religions, not, as might be thought, Judaism and Paganism, but Judaism and Christianity. The legions of Titus, though they knew it not, were truly soldiers of the Cross, continuing the work to which they had been divinely pre-ordained— *the work of the Church!*

For the Romans, by uniting the nations of the civilized world under one government, by establishing a universal peace—the " *Romana pax* " that was the just boast of their orators; by clearing the sea of corsairs, and the land from banditti; by linking all parts of their empire with a series of splendid roads; by diffusing among their provinces a knowledge of the Greek language; had created conditions such as had never before existed in the world's history: conditions that were absolutely essential, if the Church were to make quick progress; conditions that enabled the evangelist, knowing one language only, to travel in safety and preach the faith from the banks of the Euphrates to the Pillars of Hercules.

The Roman legionaries, paradoxical as it may sound, were the coadjutors of the apostles. They were now about to put the final touches to their work by demolishing the temple, whose further existence was an obstacle to the free development of Christianity; and

## Preliminaries of a Great Siege 239

by acting as the sword of the Lord against those who had cried, " His blood be on us and on our children."

A.D. 70 was the necessary sequel of A.D. 29; and he who refuses to see a Divine Judgment in the fall of Jerusalem has yet to learn the elements of history.

Ignorant of the high mission assigned to him, Titus, distinguished by a purple mantle and by the splendor of his gilded arms, had taken up his station upon the central agger. Beside him, and clothed in a magnificent white robe, gold-embroidered, stood Theomantes, the priest of Jupiter Cæsarius, presiding at an altar of unhewn stones, upon which there flamed a sacrificial ox. Titus and the Romans in the immediate vicinity of this altar were standing bareheaded in reverential attitude.

The Zealots upon the wall, keenly attentive to this religious ceremony, noticed that Theomantes, as he stood with his arms raised in prayer to some deity, kept his eyes fixed throughout upon their holy temple.

A sudden suspicion fell upon them. They strained their ears in the hope of catching his utterance, though distance might well forbid that hope. Fortune favored them, however. A breeze blowing from the north at that moment wafted to their ears the word—JEHOVAH! —a word so sacred that it was seldom uttered even by the Jews themselves, and never in the presence of a Gentile.

How came this pagan priest to know the true name of God, and why was he praying to Him?

Then the full meaning of the scene was borne in upon them. It was the ceremony called by the Romans the Evocation.[25] It was the custom of that people at the beginning of a siege to invoke the tutelary deity of the invested city, inviting him not to be made a prisoner, but to come forth and take up his abode among the divinities of the Roman Capitol. Without such ceremony they would be fighting against the gods —an impious deed!

The ceremony, ludicrous or blasphemous, according as one may view it, was at all events unnecessary on the present occasion. The tutelary angels *had* quitted the city, and Crispus was of those who had heard their departing voice.

To the Jews upon the wall, the affair was as blasphemy. Jehovah was their own peculiar heritage! That the heathen should dare pray to Him, above all that they should call upon Him to quit the place where He had chosen to put His name forever, was a thing not to be borne.

Calling for their most expert archer, they bade him shoot down the impious Theomantes.

But the action was observed by the quick-eyed Rufus, who interposed his shield between the priest and the oncoming arrow.

A moment afterwards Titus tossed his baton high in air.

At that sight—the signal for battle—there rolled down the Roman lines a shout that seemed to shake the very towers of the city, the thrilling war-cry of "ROMA! ROMA!" and with that each man flew to his appointed work.

The greatest siege in the world's history had begun!

# CHAPTER XIX

#### THE FIRST DAY'S FIGHT

ON the very edge of each agger there leaped up, as if by magic, a cloud of archers and slingers, who, setting up iron screens in front of themselves, proceeded to direct their missiles upon the defenders of the battlements.

Expert as were these archers—Cretans all, a nation famed from Homeric times in the use of the bow—they were surpassed in accuracy of aim by the slingers. These, natives of the Balearic Isles, had been trained to their work from very childhood, when their daily meal, set upon some high point, could not be obtained, unless brought down by themselves with the sling. Hence a force of Baleares formed an adjunct to every Roman legion. Their missiles, consisting both of stones and leaden plummets, were discharged by a triple whirl of the sling; with a force so powerful that headpiece, breastplate, and buckler afforded little protection; with a motion so swift that the leaden plummet, glowing in the air, sometimes melted; with an aim so true that the slinger could not only hit the face of a distant enemy, but could even hit whatever part of the face he chose. Not infrequently the missile bore some insulting inscription; and Simon, picking up a stone that had very nearly brained him, found it marked with the message: "ΔΕΞΑΙ—Take this!"

The slingers and archers were aided in their death-dealing business by the workers of the catapults, machines which, framed somewhat upon the principle of the medieval crossbow, discharged gigantic javelins and beams headed with iron.

The Jews did not remain passive under this attack. In the use of the bow and the sling they were almost as well skilled as their opponents, and returned the fire of the besiegers with a fire equally brisk.

The fray became more deadly as soon as the Romans had got their balistæ into action.

These were huge machines, whose working part consisted of an arrangement of levers and ropes, which, when forcibly drawn back and let go, produced a tremendous recoil, sufficient to hurl ponderous stones to a distance of three furlongs, and farther.

These stones were discharged mainly for the purpose of carrying away the battlements, turrets and parapet of the wall, so that, deprived of cover, the defenders would be compelled to quit the ramparts, since to remain there open and exposed would mean certain death at the hands of the archers and slingers. The withdrawal of the defenders would be the signal for the escalade.

More than fifty of these balistæ were now at work, making terrible havoc, not only with battlement and parapet, but also with the lives of the Jewish people. Some of the stones hurled aloft exceeded three hundred pounds in weight, and had force sufficient to kill six men, if taken in file. Josephus describes how he saw a man's head struck clean from his shoulders and carried to a distance of three furlongs! Anyone standing within a yard of such stone as it swept past was certain to be flung to earth by the accompanying rush of air.

Such was the effect of the ponderous rocks that now went whirling over the ramparts, fifteen or twenty at a time, into the suburb of Bezetha, crashing through the roof and wall of many a private dwelling, and tumbling it into ruins amid the wild shrieking of its hapless occupants.

To this artillery Simon sought to reply with the captured Roman balistæ; but the Zealots, for lack of

## The First Day's Fight

skill and practice, bungled so miserably at the task as to evoke the laughter of the enemy.

While this terrific fusillade was going on, a party of Romans began to push forward a pluteus—a sort of iron shed open at both ends and running upon wheels. As it moved along, the Romans walked beneath its roof, and were thus effectually screened against the missiles showered at them from the battlements.

As soon as the pluteus touched the foot of the wall, the party within, kneeling down upon the ground, set to work vigorously with lever and crow, endeavoring to loosen the lower courses of the masonry.

Stones and darts were powerless against a machine of this kind. But Simon's fertile brain had devised a plan for defeating its operations. Liquid bitumen, in immense quantities, was flung upon the pluteus, and when all the ground beneath it and around it was flowing with the liquid, lighted torches were thrown down. In a flash the interior of the pluteus as well as the air above and around became a flaming fire. With terrible howlings the miserable Romans, their hair, beard, and garments alight, rushed forth into the open, only to be shot dead by the Jewish archers.

What Simon had done once he was likely to do again. Titus, therefore, when informed of this incident gave orders to keep the plutei in reserve and to push forward the battering-rams.

One of these, by reason of its hugeness, excited the wonder, if not the fears, of the Zealots.

It was a wheeled tower, consisting of several stages, the topmost one rising high above the city wall. Through an opening in the lower story there projected the gigantic brazen head of a ram, forming the forepart of a wooden beam, 120 feet in length, a beam poised upon ropes, and of a weight so great as to require the united strength of two hundred men to put it in motion. The different stages in the tower were for the use of archers, whose business it was to clear the enemy from that part of the wall directly facing the ram. A little turret at the top of the structure afforded a coign of vantage for a sentinel to observe and report to those below the doings of the besieged.

This structure, which was under the charge of Rufus, bore the Greek name of Nico, or the Conqueror, for although its powers had not yet been tested, it was confidently believed that no wall, however strong, could long withstand the repeated shocks of the ram.

As soon as this heavy machine was brought within striking distance of the wall, two hundred brawny legionaries, grasping a multiplicity of ropes, began slowly to draw the gigantic beam as far back as it would go; then, at a given signal, every man simultaneously relinquished his hold, and the released beam, darting forward with lightning speed, came with terrific impact full tilt against the wall.

At that mighty stroke the masonry shivered from parapet to foundation. But more appalling than the shock itself was the thunder-boom accompanying it. The sound ran through the length and breadth of the city, terrifying Vashti in her distant home on Mount Zion; it was echoed and re-echoed from all the hills around; it filled the breasts of even the most stouthearted of the Zealots with fear; while from every quarter of Bezetha there came shrieks of terror from women and children, for all who were not near the spot made sure that the wall had fallen in, and that the enemy were entering the breach.

Again that terrifying boom! and yet again!

Dreadful as was the sound, the agony of waiting for it was even more dreadful. Some women, unable to bear the strain, stopped their ears with their fingers; others fled to cellars and underground places to escape from the terror.

The whole Roman army was now in working order; forty thousand troops arrayed against the northern wall, and not a man idle among them.

## The First Day's Fight

It was a terrific spectacle, both within and without the city. The groaning of the wounded, and the shrieking of the women; the twanging of the catapults, and the whizzing of darts and arrows; the peculiar hum of the swift-flying stones slung from the balistæ; the crash of falling masonry; the shout of the combatants hurling defiance at each other; and, above all, the thunder-boom of the brazen rams, as they smote against the wall—all contributed to form a scene that transcends the power of the pen to describe.

All in a moment there was on the part of the Jews a simultaneous cessation of activity; their archers stopped firing; their engines ceased playing; the whole force stood mute and motionless. A sight so surprising caused a temporary suspension of hostilities on the part of the Romans, who were wondering whether this Jewish attitude implied the wish to surrender.

The mystery was soon explained.

From the temple—that temple where priests were falling dead or wounded from the stones cast by the engines of the Tenth Legion, stationed upon Mount Olivet, there came the piercing clangor of the silver trumpets. It was the time of the morning sacrifice.

The trumpet-peal was followed by the lifting of every Jewish sword, and along the whole length of the ramparts there rolled one sublime shout, a shout flung in defiance at the polytheism of their opponents, a shout expressive of the grandest truth ever proclaimed to mankind:

" HEAR, O ISRAEL, THE LORD OUR GOD IS ONE LORD."

With that they flew to the fight with renewed ardor. And now in the occasional lulls of the fray could be heard a voice, far off at first, but drawing gradually nearer, a voice that by the space of eight years had never ceased its melancholy ditty:

" Woe, woe, to Jerusalem!"

Along the rampart, winding in and out among the

ranks of the fighting Zealots, who received him with black looks and angry murmurs, came the weird form of Jesus, the son of Hanan, clad, not as was his wont in a garment of camel's hair, but in a long robe of white linen, such as might be used to enshroud the dead.

"A voice from the East, a voice from the West, a voice against Jerusalem and the holy house!"

"Now, what doeth this madman here, putting fear into the hearts of brave men?" muttered Simon, eying the other darkly. But, as Jesus approached, there was in his looks something so awe-inspiring that the Zealot chief, who was minded to do the "madman" hurt, lowered his weapon and let him pass on.

The wild figure, with its lifted arms outlined against the sky, was plainly visible to the enemy.

Now, there prevailed in those days the belief that it was possible for a soothsayer to paralyze the efforts of a hostile army by the utterance of magical spells; and hence, the Romans being too far off to catch his words, even if they had been able to understand his Hebrew language, mistook him for a priest engaged in the task of cursing them.

"His curses shall fall upon his own pate," muttered an angry balistarius, directing his assistants to slew the head of the machine round so as to bring its aim to bear athwart the line of the moving figure.

"Woe to the city! Woe to the people! Woe to the holy house! *Woe, woe, to myself also!*"

Scarcely had this last utterance left his mouth when the stone prepared from all eternity for the purpose, smote him so that he fell to rise no more.

The Zealots gazed at the horribly mangled form in fear and awe. This man, who had prophesied the moment of his own doom, had prophesied likewise the doom of the city; since his word was true in the one case, why should it not be true in the other?

Leave musing for the night; the day is for action,

## The First Day's Fight

and the Zealots flew to obey the orders of Simon, who was growing somewhat concerned at the shaking of the masonry caused by the strokes of the ram Nico.

He directed that gabions or huge sacks stuffed with chaff, should be lowered in front of the ram in order to weaken the effect of its blows.

But the simple device was defeated by one equally simple. Projecting horizontally from each side of the tower in which the ram hung were iron mantelets or screens, under cover of which stood a number of Romans armed with long poles ending in sharp scythes, and with these they severed the ropes from which the gabion hung, and when the defenders substituted a chain for the rope, the Romans fell upon the gabion instead, so that through a score of rents the chaff came pouring out, leaving the gabion to flap emptily against the wall.

"Why this waste?" said Rufus sarcastically. "They'll be glad of this chaff for food before the war be over."

A third gabion was lowered. This time a soldier bolder than his fellows, breaking cover, ran forward, and with a lighted torch fired the lower end of the gabion. Instantly there shot upwards a column of blinding smoke and dazzling flame, whose heat drove the holders of the gabion backwards; in their confusion they let go the chain, which thus fell into the hands of the Romans, who punctuated their capture with an extra loud boom of the ram.

"No more burnable stuff. Fill the sacks with earth," said Simon. For a few moments he looked on, watching the destruction of gabion after gabion. His brow frowning at first began gradually to clear.

"What will you say, Ananus," said he, turning to one of his fifty captains, "if I prophesy that within a little space the brazen head of yon ram shall be hanging over the gate of the temple, an offering to Jehovah?"

"If Simon says it, 'twill be so," replied the other, who had unbounded faith in his chief.

"Tie one end of this rope round my waist," said Simon; "securely—for hereby hangs my life."

It was done.

"Now bring levers."

When they were brought Simon directed the attention of his followers to a block of masonry which formed part of the battlement that directly overhung the head of the charging ram.

"When I lift my hand heave the stone over, and lower me with all speed."

Like a watchful lion waiting to swoop upon its quarry stood Simon, his eye upon the ram, which at that moment was being drawn back by four hundred arms fresh to the task, for the Romans wisely worked in relays and a new body of men had just been put on.

The released beam shot forward, humming through the air.

Simon gave the signal, and the huge stone was instantly levered over and fell plump upon the forepart of the ram with such good effect that the brazen head snapped clean off amid a mighty splintering of woodwork, and lay on the ground beside the fallen stone.

But it lay there for a moment only.

A figure suspended at the end of a rope shot down with lightning speed, grasped the great brazen head in both arms, and was drawn up again; and, almost before the astonished Romans could realize what had happened, there was Simon on the ramparts above triumphantly holding aloft the trophy he had so daringly won.

"Simon, thou art a lion, and the son of a lion," said Ananus admiringly.

A flood of curses broke from the Romans; the ram was useless till the damage had been repaired, and as this repairing could be effectively done only at a distance from the walls, there remained nothing for it

## The First Day's Fight

but to drag the machine away amid the mocking laughter of the Jews.

Simon now turned his attention to a terrible danger approaching the wall in the shape of a *turris ambulatoria* or movable tower, seventy-five feet in height, made of wood, mounted upon wheels, and provided with a drawbridge by which when lowered the besiegers hoped to leap upon the battlements.

This great tower was under the charge of Crispus.

It would go ill with the Zealots, as Simon well knew, if Crispus and a body of well-disciplined Romans should succeed in establishing themselves upon the ramparts.

Projecting from the rear of the tower, and at a height of about four feet from the ground, were six long beams, each provided with crossbars; one hundred and twenty men had their shoulders set hard against these crossbars, but in spite of their efforts the rate of progression was infinitely slow, owing to the ponderous weight of the tower.

The Zealots made vigorous attempts to set the structure on fire by means of flaming darts; these were wooden shafts, a cubit in length, the head being armed with a triangular steel barb to which was affixed a lump of bitumen or other combustible matter; the dart, when set alight, was hurled with great force into the side of the tower; wherever it fixed itself in the woodwork little jets of flame spurted forth.

The interior of the tower presented at this moment a scene of excitement. At every window of every story were seen soldiers repelling the attack, some by discharging javelins at the casters of the fiery darts, others by pouring water upon the hissing flames, which as fast as they died out in one part leaped to life in another.

Crispus, moving from story to story, directed the operations.

"Water, here!" he cried, on seeing a dense volume of smoke ascending from one side of the tower.

"The supply has run out," replied the decurion in charge of the water department.

Had Crispus not left his pagan days behind him he would have run the fellow through for his supposed negligence.

"With six water-carts, and the Serpent's Pool but a furlong distant, you dare to say——?"

"The Serpent's Pool hath been so well drawn upon by us and by others that it has become exhausted."

"Ha! sayest thou so?" exclaimed Crispus, relenting somewhat at this explanation. "Well, since water be denied us, hang out the raw hides," he cried, for every tower carried a supply of these to be used as a protection against fire. "And bring up sand and earth to drop upon the flames."

By these means Crispus contrived, not indeed to quench the fire, but to keep it somewhat under control.

As soon as the giant tower had been pushed to a point sufficiently near for the lowering of the drawbridge, the toiling troops, letting go the beams, grasped their weapons; and, losing for the moment something of their Roman discipline, scrambled pell-mell into the tower, all eager to be foremost in the attack, for among the Romans the soldier that was first to mount the ramparts of an enemy's city received—if he survived—the gift of a Mural Crown, a prize that shed a glory over the recipient to the end of his days.

The way out upon the drawbridge, when it should be lowered, led from the fifth story; it was into this chamber, therefore, that the storming-party was now crowding. The drawbridge, standing bolt upright before the doorway, acted as a screen, but when it fell they would be facing a storm of arrows and javelins. It was almost certain death to the men who should be foremost to run out upon the drawbridge; yet, despite the peril, each soldier was striving with his fellow for the honor of being second, the first place being claimed by Crispus himself.

"A Cestius lost the city; a Cestius shall recover it," said he. "Stand by me," he continued, addressing the aquilifer, "we'll plant the eagle on the ramparts, or die in the attempt."

For the eagle, though no longer an object of worship with Crispus, was still sacred in his eyes as the emblem of a glorious empire.

It was a thrilling moment. As they stood there in a mass so dense that each could scarce lift his arms, they could hear the never-ceasing thud-thud of the fiery darts falling upon the outer walls.

At each side of the doorway, awaiting the signal to lower, stood two brawny legionaries, their hands upon the ropes that worked the drawbridge.

"All ready, men?" said Crispus, with a glance at the set faces behind him.

The question met with an eager response.

"Guard your faces well. Now!"

Up went the ropes, and as they swirled fast over the creaking pulleys, the upper end of the drawbridge falling away from the tower began a rapid descent upon the city wall.

The sight was seen from near and from far, and both armies set up a simultaneous roar, the one in dismay, the other in exultation, a roar so tremendous as to drown even the thunder-boom of the battering-rams.

Titus, who knew that Crispus was in charge of this tower, slapped his thigh with a fierce joy.

"By the gods, Crispus hath opened a way into the city!" he cried.

Thousands on both sides paused in the fray to watch the contest upon the drawbridge. Of what use was it to continue the fight elsewhere, if once this part of the wall should be seized and held by Crispus and his band?

The fate of Bezetha at least, if not of all Jerusalem, hung upon the issue of the next few moments.

As the drawbridge fell with a mighty thud upon the ramparts, Crispus, sword in hand, and with buckler held before his face, leaped out upon the shivering timbers, followed by a crowd of warriors.

The sequel was appalling!

They found themselves amid a blinding, whirling hurricane of arrows and darts, javelins and stones, coming from the front, from the left, from the right. Obedient to Simon's orders every Jewish marksman, far and near, from turret, battlement and loophole, shot thick and fast at the devoted band upon the drawbridge. In such numbers and with such fury did the missiles smite upon helmet and breastplate, shield and greave, that the little band were absolutely unable to advance; they staggered to and fro as though struck by lightning; they fell, dead and dying from the bridge.

Crispus, preserved from death by the superior temper of his armor, took several wounds, nevertheless; three arrows were quivering in his sword-arm; two hung from the calf of his leg, though the fierce excitement of the moment prevented him from feeling them.

For one bewildering moment he stood irresolute; then, gathering himself up for a mighty effort, he darted forward all alone across the bridge. Twenty missiles striking him at one and the same time, caused him to reel like a drunken man.

Then came the end!

Simon had not seen the advance of the ambulatory tower without making due preparation for its reception.

The moment the drawbridge touched the battlement there sprang up before it four of his strongest captains, each armed with a mighty ax; and, while Simon with the keen edge of his scimitar severed the ropes by which the drawbridge had been lowered, his four captains plied their axes with such good effect that ere the Romans could come rushing across to prevent it, the whole bridge, cut clean off from the battlement,

## The First Day's Fight

swung downwards, and its living freight were hurled precipitately through forty feet of air to the rocky ground below, where they lay a struggling, helpless mound of heads, arms, and legs, which in the next moment bristled all over with arrows shot at them by the delighted Jewish archers.

"Bring on your next tower," cried Simon mockingly, "and we'll deal with it in like fashion."

Among the few who contrived to limp painfully away to a place beyond reach of the enemy's fire was Crispus, bruised, dizzy, white-faced, with a dozen arrowheads embedded in his flesh.

Sitting down, he proceeded to extract these barbs, and, the means being at hand, he anointed his wounds and bound them with linen swathings, in which task he was engaged when Titus came up.

"Now, the gods be praised, you live. But you are wounded; there must be no more fighting for you to-day. Hither, two of you! Lay the noble Crispus upon a buckler, and carry him back to camp."

But Crispus vowed he was not so hurt as to necessitate his immediate removal.

"Mere flesh-wounds, though I confess I am somewhat dazed by my fall. Let me rest for an hour in this cool shade, and I'll be ready for the fray again."

"Well, as thou wilt. Farewell awhile. I am beginning to like this Simon; he is a foe worth fighting."

Simon's admirable tactics seemed to have a discouraging effect upon the legionaries. At any rate the attack began to languish. The noontide sun was now streaming directly upon the faces of the Romans, dazzling the eyes of the archers and slingers, and marring the accuracy of their aim. The heat of the day, the clouds of dust, the toil of war had produced among the besiegers the agony of a raging thirst, a thirst which they had no means of quenching. The *posca* —the water, sharpened with vinegar—which every soldier was wont to carry with him in a leathern bottle, had long since been drained to the last drop, and no further supply was at hand.

Crispus, still faint and dazed, reclined against the agger.

"O, for water!" he murmured.

"There is none in all the host," remarked a soldier standing by. "Men are offering a gold piece for a cup of water."

"And the enemy have become aware of our want," said a second soldier. "See! they are holding up vessels of water, and wastefully spilling it in mockery at our distress."

Titus with a troubled face came up at that moment.

"We are in rueful strait," said he. "Our men are fainting for lack of water. The Serpent's Pool is exhansted; Cedron hath run dry. Our engineers cannot sink a well, the rocky ground forbidding it. Where are we to look for water?"

"There is a pool called Siloam, on the south side of the city," replied Crispus. "It may not be dry."

"Ha!" exclaimed Titus, with new hope. "But," he added doubtfully, "whoever goes thither must pass under the eastern wall exposed to the fire of the enemy."

"But is not the Tenth Legion stationed on Olivet ready to repel any sortie from that quarter? Give me the water-carts and a convoy of two hundred horsemen, and I'll engage to return with water enough for the whole host."

"Take three hundred, and good fortune go with you."

Ere many minutes were past there went clattering down the Vale of Cedron a long train of wagons, whose drivers were escorted by a detachment of mounted soldiers, three hundred strong.

High above their heads hummed and whizzed volleys of stones and darts slung from Olivet by the balistæ

## The First Day's Fight

and catapults of the Tenth Legion, who sought in this way to protect the movements of the water-seekers.

Looking forth from the eastern wall, John of Giscala and his Zealots caught sight of the Roman horsemen, and vainly tried to stay their progress by flights of arrows.

On dashed the convoy, past the olive grove of Gethsemane, and now they were in the deepest part of the Black Glen; far above them on their right was the temple, towering aloft in the sunlight to the height of nearly five hundred feet; on, past the wall of Ophel, and, rounding its southern end, they swung westward. Here, where the glen of Tyropæon opens out into the Vale of Cedron, was a picturesque spot known from of old as the King's Garden, and watered by a streamlet from Siloam.

To his great joy, Crispus found that the Pool of Siloam—a long, rectangular basin, excavated in the solid rock for the reception of the outflow of a spring —was full of cool, limpid water.

By a coincidence, too timely to be regarded as fortuitous, Siloam, whose waters had been "sealed" for nearly four years, *had started flowing again upon the coming of the Roman army!*[26] To the Jews the Messianic fountain seemed to be playing the part of a traitor. The water, so long withheld from them, was now flowing for the enemy. What did it mean? they darkly asked, failing to see in this acted parable that the Divine kingdom was being taken from them and given to the Gentiles.

The thirsting Roman band, springing from their steeds, first refreshed themselves, and proceeded next with all speed to the filling of the water-carts.

When the Jews, who were looking on from the wall of Ophel, realized the object of this sudden dash on the part of the Romans, they gave vent to indignant and wrathful cries.

What? Must the unclean and uncircumcized heathen

be permitted to carry away for his profane use the water used in the sacred rites of the temple? In the name of Elohim—no!

Wide clanged the Fountain Gate, and out poured a tumultuous crowd of fierce-shouting saber-brandishing Zealots, led on by John of Giscala.

"To horse!" sang out the Roman trumpet; and instantly the troops mounted and swung into line. Crispus' question, "Shall we give them battle?" met with an eager affirmative. Not a man among them but thrilled with joy at the prospect of a hand-to-hand engagement with the enemy. For many hours they had been waging an unsatisfactory warfare against flying missiles, but here was something more substantial, something they could flesh their steel upon!

With the spirit of his fighting ancestors dancing in his veins, Crispus cried, "Why wait we here? We'll go to meet them. *Charge!*"

He put his steed to the gallop, and the whole three hundred, knee to knee and sword in air, went racing after him up the valley of Tyropæon.

Faster and faster they whirled towards the foe, gathering momentum with every yard. The thundering hoofs and flashing steel made a sight so nerve-shaking that the crowd of onrushing Zealots came to a dead halt.

"Stand fast!" yelled John to his followers.

The next moment he was hurled to the earth, as the head of the Roman column went crashing with irresistible force into the midst of the Zealots.

The contest was short and sharp. John's men lacked the fire of Simon's; for a moment only they fought, then turned tail and fled; and the delighted Romans chased and slew up to the very gate of the city, all but entering with the foe.

"John of Giscala hath escaped us," growled a centurion, as he turned away from the gate at which he had been savagely kicking.

"He is reserved for another day," answered Crispus.

Laughing over their easy victory the little band galloped back to their water-carts, and, as they clattered again up the valley of the Cedron, they cast gibes at the discomfited Zealots upon the wall.

With the arrival of the water the thirsting Roman army imbibed fresh energy, but though they toiled hard till nightfall they failed to open a way into the city.

Thus ended the first day's fight.

# CHAPTER XX

CIRCUMVALLATION

On the fourteenth day of the siege the repaired ram Nico, or the Conqueror, justified its name by effecting a breach in the northern wall; and Simon, seeing his position no longer tenable, fell back upon his second line of defense.

This was the first great step in the siege.

The Romans, entering Bezetha on the fifteenth day, proceeded to demolish the greater part of this suburb, the demolition being necessary in order to clear the way for the advance of the battering-train.

Nine days more, and the Romans had penetrated the second wall, and were now masters of the suburb of Acra, which they proceeded to treat in like fashion with that of Bezetha.

This was the second great step in the siege.

" Bezetha taken in fifteen days, Acra in nine," exulted Titus. " We are getting on."

Tiberius Alexander, to whom the remark was addressed, shrugged his shoulders.

" Mere outworks, Cæsar. What we have done is child's play compared with what remains to be done."

Titus began to be of the same opinion as he stood amid the fast dismantling Acra, and surveyed a long chain of defiant fortresses.

Before him as he looked southwards rose the rugged escarpment of Mount Zion, forty feet high, its edge surmounted by a lofty wall, whose circuit included those magnificent towers, Hippicus, Phasaelus, and Mariamne, each a citadel in itself. Above him, on his left hand, soared the temple-fortress, and adjacent to it the Turris Antonia, this last standing on a rock, which rock was not only seventy-five feet high, but had its perpendicular sides cased with smooth marble!

After deliberating with his staff Titus resolved to make a simultaneous attack on Mount Zion and on Antonia.

But how to reach these strongholds elevated in mid-air?

There was but one way, by the raising of banks— a stupendous operation! But the Romans were familiarized with such tasks, and, animated by the same resolute spirit as their general, they set to work with a fiery energy that nothing could daunt. Owing to the scarcity of earth, timber and fascines were largely used in the erection of these works, to such an extent indeed, that not a tree remained within sight of Jerusalem. The sylvan beauty of the landscape vanished; the Jewish people, looking far and wide from the city walls, could see around them nothing but a treeless and desolate waste. On the seventeenth day a huge embankment faced the northern side of Antonia, but just when the engines planted upon it were beginning to play, the Romans, to their consternation and dismay, found the whole mound slowly beginning to sink. As the rate of subsidence varied in different parts, chasms began to yawn, the rams and towers rolled this way and that, crashing into each other with destructive effect; men found themselves entangled among the machines, overwhelmed with earth, suffocated with dust; a prodigious quantity of smoke burst forth from the embankment, followed by darting tongues of flame. It was death to remain longer upon it, and the amazed and affrighted Romans, running in all directions, leaped from the mound.

The cause of it all soon became clear. John of Giscala and his Zealot crew, toiling underground with an energy almost superhuman, had driven a vast mine beneath the Roman agger, a mine whose roof and supports were formed of timber, daubed with bitumen, sulphur, and other combustibles. The ignition of these supports caused the engulfing of the bank, and the complete destruction of the engines.

"Seest thou what John hath wrought?" cried Simon to his followers. "Shall we be outdone by him?"

Now a similar bank was facing Zion, and two days later, at eventide, just when the Romans had retired to their camp, leaving the customary force to guard this bank, the gates of Zion opened, and from each issued a crowd of Zealots, every one carrying either a lighted torch or a vessel flaming with combustibles, and every one under a *cherem* or curse, not to return till he had seen the Roman engines and the Roman bank in a blaze.

Coming forth, not by hundreds, but by thousands, they poured down the craggy descent like a flood, wave upon wave, and swept up to the embankment; some, fighting like fiends, impaled themselves upon the points of the Roman spears, and so died; others, equally brave but more fortunate, broke through the guard, scaled the embankment, and, running hither and thither, set the engines alight, and finished the work of destruction by firing the embankment itself, so that by the time Titus and the rest of the army came up, the huge platform of earth and timber was a roaring sea of unquenchable flame!

Now, for the first time during the siege, the spirit of despair fell upon Titus. He began to think with the murmuring and superstitious legionaries that the fiery comet which, in the shape of a sword, shed a red gleam nightly over Jerusalem, was directing its malignant influence not against the Jews but against the Romans.

His mood was shown by the letter directed jointly to his father Vespasian and the Roman Senate; the dispatch omitted the customary formula: "I rejoice

## Circumvallation

if all is well with you and your children; with myself and the army all is well."

All was *not* well with him and the army. The tactics of Simon and John had caused the entire disappearance of his battering-train.

Was there no other course left him than to order the Greek engineers of Cæsarea to construct a new set of military machines, an order that would require several weeks for its fulfillment?

Many and various were the suggestions put forth at the council held in the tent of Titus.

The plan of massing the whole strength of the legions against a selected part of the wall, and of continuing the assault night and day with testudo and scaling-ladder, regardless of the loss of life, till the place should be finally stormed, was rejected as impracticable, as was also the proposition to tunnel a way through the rock into the heart of the city.

Tiberius Alexander rose to speak.

"By all means send to Cæsarea for new engines," said he. "In the meantime we'll turn the siege into a blockade, and make famine our chief weapon. Food within the city is already running short, even among the Zealots themselves, so much so that, if the stories of deserters be true, these same Zealots are robbing the people of their bread, and torturing those whom they suspect of concealing it.

"But if the city is to be effectually starved, we must close up every avenue of access. Now, hitherto, we have kept but an ill watch upon the western and southern sides of the city, with the result that certain merchants, despising the Roman power, and eager to coin wealth out of Jewish necessities, are in the habit of stealing nightly to the city to supply its wants. Tyrians bring fish, and Egyptians corn; Arabs purvey dates, and the Nabatæans supplies of bitumen from the Dead Sea, that fiery bitumen whose effects we know so well. Unless these doings be stopped, the siege will be prolonged indefinitely. Now, my counsel is that we encircle the city with a wall to be patrolled night and day; so shall we cut off the enemy from all outside help.

"And since the more mouths there are in the city the more quickly will food vanish, do you, O Cæsar, who have hitherto dealt kindly with deserters, make it known that henceforth crucifixion shall be the lot of those who come to us for pity.

"In six weeks' time they will be eating each other, and victory will be ours; for we shall be contending, not with strong men, but with gaunt and famished weaklings, scarce able to lift spear or shield.

"Fasting is a part of their religion," this renegade Hebrew concluded, with a sneer. "Let them be made to keep such a fast as they never before kept in all their history."

The counsel of Tiberius Alexander prevailed, as Crispus knew that it would prevail, even before the prefect had made an end of speaking. Vain was it for others to propose a different plan, when, forty years previously, a Divine voice had said: "*Thine enemies shall cast a trench about thee, and compass thee around, and keep thee in on every side.*"

The next day witnessed the beginning of the fatal circuit.

Around the doomed city was drawn, over high hill and down deep ravine, a double wall; one, the contravallation, designed to repel sorties from the city; the other, the circumvallation, to repel attacks coming from without.

Each of these investing lines was defended on its outer side by a deep trench, and at every third furlong rose a castellum or fort, the station of a garrison.

The whole of the army, 50,000 strong, was employed upon the work, which was completed at the end of three days; a marvelously quick feat, even for Romans, accustomed, as they were, to trenching and embanking.

The Zealots affected to view these operations with unconcern, casting gibes at Titus, whenever he came within earshot.

Some of these gibes had reference to Berenice, who was known to be the object of his adoration.

"The fair one at Cæsarea is lonely," they cried. "The daughter of Agrippa looketh out at a window, and crieth through the lattice, 'Why is his chariot so long in coming? why tarry the wheels of his chariot?'"

Other gibes were directed at Titus' plebeian origin.

"Thy father was once a horse-doctor," cried one. "Why not return to the old trade, Titus? for plainly thou art no warrior. Depart, seeing that thou canst not take this city."

At this, Terentius Rufus, growing fierce for the honor of Cæsar, lifted up a plow that by chance was lying near, and swore a memorable oath.

"Hear now the vow I make, O ye rebels! With this will I plow Zion as one ploweth a field!"

A flight of arrows caused him to retreat, but he kept to his plow.

"Take this to my tent," said he to a soldier, "and there let it be till the day when I call for it. Terentius Rufus will keep his word."

On the first night after the completion of the investing lines Titus himself, accompanied by Crispus, went the round of the watch. Often did the eyes of Crispus turn towards the city, now sleeping peacefully beneath the light of the stars. The reduction of the place by famine was doubtless justifiable from a military point of view, but he could not help thinking of the fearful anguish that would fill ten thousand homes; above all, he thought of Vashti. He pictured her, tormented by all the agonies of slow starvation, dying by inches, her sweet and graceful beauty all gone, a hollow-eyed thing of skin and bone, with brain crazed for the lack of food, and he scarcely a mile distant with bread and to spare, yet unable to pass her so little as a crust.

When the city should be taken, would she be living or dead? It was a point which, strangely enough, had not occurred to him before that, if living, she would be, according to the rights of war as practiced in a brutal age, a captive doomed to slavery. He resolved there and then to claim her freedom from the only man capable of granting it.

"When you take the city, Cæsar, there is one whose life and freedom I would fain crave."

"'Tis granted, provided that the object of your request be not a descendant of David."

"Why that exception?" asked Crispus in great surprise.

"The orders of my sire Vespasian are that I am to make search for all that are of David's line with a view to their extirpation." The Jew is convinced that a descendant of this ancient royal house is destined to attain universal empire, a belief which has given rise to this present revolt; therefore, destroy all that are of David's line, and you extinguish this vain Jewish dream."

How Crispus rejoiced in the thought that the saintly bishop Simeon, and the remaining Desposyni—relatives of the Master—were at that moment in distant Pella!

"She for whom I would make request," said he, "is one Vashti, daughter of Hyrcanus."

Titus gave a start of surprise.

"She to whom you gave the golden zone at Cæsarea?"

"The same," replied Crispus, conjecturing that Titus' knowledge of this incident was derived from Berenice.

"What is this maiden to you?" asked Titus with a keen glance.

"Much, seeing that but for her I should no longer

be living," replied Crispus, relating the circumstances of his recovery from Eleazar's sword-thrust.

Titus seemed genuinely troubled. Crispus had distinguished himself so well in the siege that it was hard to refuse him this favor.

"Gladly would I grant your request, but that it comes too late. The Princess Berenice is desirous of obtaining possession of that damsel."

Crispus at that moment looked more dazed than when he fell from the drawbridge.

"Berenice!" he murmured. "What would *she* with Vashti?"

"The princess likes to have pretty and graceful maidens about her. She made me promise that out of the spoils of the city I would give her this Vashti."

"And you will?"

Titus shrugged his shoulders.

"She was not content with an oral promise. She holds a parchment signed by my hand empowering her to claim Vashti as her slave."

In Crispus' opinion it would be better, far better, for Vashti to die of slow starvation than to fall into the hands of the jealous Berenice, whose only object in this enslavement was to gratify her spirit of revenge.

He said no more, knowing the uselessness of interceding, but he had quite made up his mind what he would do; and he could do it, too, in all good conscience.

"Let Cæsar's parchment bond say what it will," said he within himself. "I will save Vashti from the doom intended for her, though it cost me my life."

# CHAPTER XXI

#### THE DYING CITY

The gaunt specter of famine was stalking through Jerusalem.

On the very first day of the siege the price of food had mounted so high that a bushel of wheat could not be had for less than a talent of gold,[28] but as soon as the Roman wall had cut off the Jews from all external supplies ten times ten talents could not purchase even a handful of grain.

Then from ten thousand homes there rose up the cry for bread; but the heaven above was as brass; the God that had shed down manna upon their forefathers remained cold to all the wild wailings in the synagogues.

He who had laid up food for himself was not certain of benefiting by his forethought, for the Zealots broke into whatsoever house they pleased, and upon those suspected of concealing food they inflicted torments so horrible as to seem rather the invention of fiends than of men.

Among those hitherto preserved from the visits of the Zealots, though living in daily dread of such visits, were Vashti and her mother.

The two dwelt all alone, since Miriam, in expectation of famine, had dismissed her handmaids at the beginning of the siege.

Vashti had never known a more unhappy time than the present, and she had begun to doubt whether it would not have been wiser to have followed the counsel of the holy Simeon by escaping while it was possible from the doomed city.

It was not the gnawing pangs of hunger that distressed her so much as the knowledge that she had altogether lost her mother's love. Miriam treated her with an unkindliness that seemed to increase with each succeeding day. She was forever reproaching Vashti as being a Christian and a lover of the Romans.

"But I love you, too, dear mother, more than all the Christians, or would I have remained here with you, when I might have retired safely to Pella?"

Her mother took no notice of this pertinent argument, but began to inveigh against Crispus, whose conspicuous valor during the siege had inspired the Jews with a hatred almost equal to that felt for Titus himself.

"Why did you nurse him back to life? He is a serpent repaying our kindness by doing all the hurt he can to the holy city."

Not wishing to vex her mother, Vashti refrained from argument, and went with aching heart to survey their fast diminishing store of provisions. The slender stock of meal, figs, and dried grapes would last but a few days more, and then——?

The two women contented themselves with a few mouthfuls a day in order that little Arad might have sufficient for his wants. He was now between five and six years of age, and was idolized at least by his sister, if not by his mother. The child could not help observing how little they ate.

"It is all through the Romans," answered his mother fiercely, adding, say, 'God curse the Romans!'"

The little fellow repeated the words.

"Now you say it, Vashti," said he.

But Vashti, believing that the Romans were God's ministers, tearfully shook her head, and this produced a fresh outburst of wrath on the part of Miriam, who seemed to take an unholy pleasure in setting the child against Vashti, saying so many bitter things that Vashti withdrew weeping.

At last came the time of starvation.

For two days the women fasted, giving to Arad what remained of their store; and, as Miriam watched him eating, there was in her eyes a look that Vashti did not like to see, a look as if she were begrudging the child its food.

On the third day he, too, had to fast.

His pitiful questionings and sobbings gave additional pangs to Vashti's own anguish. But where was she to look for relief? To solicit food from her friends and neighbors would but provoke them to mocking laughter, if indeed the power to laugh remained in them. If they had food, would they part with it, when such act would be but to hasten their own end? What was Arad to them? they would say. Had they not dying children of their own? Why prolong Arad's sufferings? The quicker death came to him the better. Such were the answers Vashti would receive, as she very well knew.

As for Miriam, she had grown neglectful of the boy; faint and dizzy, she restlessly tottered with feeble step from room to room, looking into every corner, probing behind every piece of furniture, emptying every chest of its contents, in the hope of lighting upon something —anything—that could satisfy for a time the gnawing pangs of hunger. But vain was her search.

The two women passed the third night foodless. Arad cried himself to sleep. Vashti spent the dark hours in a state between slumbering and waking; when she dreamed, it was of delicious banquets, from which with a sudden start she would wake to the dreadful realities of her position.

And now dawned the fourth day of her fast, and Arad, waking again, set up his piteous cry for food, a cry that went to the heart of Vashti. Must she sit idly by, and watch the child die?

A sudden thought set all her nerves thrilling with joy. Looking around and finding her mother absent, she knelt beside his pallet, and whispered to him, " Don't cry, Arad. Lie still, and be good, and I'll bring you something to eat."

Pacified somewhat by this announcement the little fellow became quiet.

On passing into the next chamber Vashti saw her mother crouching in a corner upon the floor, her head bowed down upon her knees. She seemed, as if having once sat down, to lack all power to rise again. As Vashti drew near, Miriam feebly raised her head, and stared in moody and dull despair at her daughter. She made no inquiries as to Arad; not a word passed her lips; she had reached the stage when speaking becomes painful and irritating, the stage when all interest in outward things ceases, the stage where one sits on the ground silently brooding, waiting for the slow approach of death.

Vashti's youthful frame contained more life and energy than her mother's, but soon she, too, unable to drag her limbs along, must sit, brooding, silent, dying.

Vashti said nothing to her mother. What could she say? Cheering words would be but a mockery.

She climbed the stairway, and passed out upon the roof.

A few weeks previously Arad had taken there a large cake of bread with a view of amusing himself by tossing crumbs up into the air in order to attract the attention of pigeons and sparrows. For some reason or other he had not carried out his purpose, and the bread instead of being carried down again was placed by him within a hollow under a tile to be reserved for the sport of some other day. That day had never come, however; and there it had lain forgotten by Vashti till this moment. Was it still there? she wondered. Yes, there it was, large enough to serve little Arad for one meal. A great temptation came upon Vashti to fix her teeth into it there and then, and gnaw away till nothing remained; but the thought of Arad controlled this selfish prompting.

The bread was as hard as iron, but a little soaking in water would soon render it soft and palatable.

Concealing the precious fragment within her bosom, Vashti descended the stairway, passing by her mother again, who looked at her with the same listless, mechanical stare as before. Under that dreadful look Vashti felt like a traitress. A struggle began in her breast. Was it right to conceal this discovery from her mother? Was she not entitled to a share of the crust? Yes, if she would be content with a share, but supposing in her fierce hunger she should seize upon the whole? *There* was Vashti's fear. Affection bade her choose between her mother and Arad, and the latter prevailed. It went to her heart to leave her mother dying there, but it would go to her heart still more to see little Arad robbed of his last morsel by the mother who bore him.

As Vashti entered the chamber the little fellow turned his eyes eagerly upon her.

She stole to his pallet.

"See! here is a large cake of bread; but it is hard, and must be softened before you can eat it." And then, dreading lest her mother's ears should be caught by these doings, she added in a whisper, "Hush! do not talk, darling. Lie still, and you shall have it soon."

Having rendered the bread eatable by moistening it with water, tormented the while by a fearful longing to devour it herself, she handed the whole to Arad.

There were many fathers among the besieging Romans outside, men of humane disposition, despite their warlike calling. Could they have witnessed the joy with which the little fellow swallowed the not very palatable morsels, they would surely have loaded their balistæ, not with stones, but with loaves, and have rained them upon the roof of Miriam's dwelling.

"Eat slowly," said Vashti, "or 'twill do you hurt."

She had scarcely said this when a scream broke from her. Between her and Arad there had suddenly dropped a skinny hand, a hand that clutched greedily at the bread, a hand belonging to the figure whom Vashti had thought to be still crouching upon the floor of the next apartment.

Arad, instinctively divining that he was about to be robbed of his meal, crammed one end of the crust into his mouth.

"Give it to me," shrieked Miriam, tugging at the other end with such force as to drag the child from off his pallet.

Arad hung with his teeth upon the crust; it suddenly parted, and Miriam, securing her own piece, swallowed it with a wolfish gusto dreadful to witness, while Vashti looked on in fear and trembling.

"Oh, mother! mother!" she gasped. "How could you do it?"

Arad, frightened almost to death by his mother's deed and look, clung to his sister, who strove to soothe his grief.

"It is as I have suspected," said Miriam. "You are hiding food from me to satisfy yourself and Arad, while I, your mother, may starve."

"Not so, mother."

"Will you deny what mine eyes have seen? Show me the way to your secret store."

"I have no secret store."

"Whence, then, did you obtain this bread?"

Vashti explained, but all to no purpose. Miriam persisted in declaring that Vashti had secreted provisions somewhere in the house, and announced her intention of watching henceforth all her daughter's movements.

Vashti, weak before, was now almost ready to collapse under the shock of this rude encounter, but for Arad's sake she bravely bore up.

Her indignation against her mother passed away

after a time, giving place to pity; in taking Arad's food Miriam had been doing only what she herself had been terribly tempted to do. Though tormented within by a gnawing pain that grew greater with each hour, Vashti, hiding it all under a cheerful mien, sought to make Arad forget his sorrows; she brought out his toys (for children had toys in those days as in these) and played with him; she procured parchment, ink and pens, and drew letters and objects and little pictures for his diversion; she told him simple stories and sang some of the psalms known to him that he might chime in with his little voice. Those psalms recalled the happy twilight hours spent with Crispus, and she sang with a quaver in her voice and tears welling from her eyes, till at last she broke down entirely and sobbed aloud. Seeing his sister cry, Arad naturally cried, too; and, the pangs of hunger asserting themselves, he began his piteous wail for something to eat.

"Give us of your store," said Miriam.

"Mother, I have no store."

"Then, find us food," returned Miriam, raising her voice to a shriek. "You see me and the child starving, and yet you sit idly by doing nothing to prevent it. Are we to die? I am too weak to stir abroad, but you have strength left. There must be food somewhere in the city. Go and find it. Take money, your jewels, your golden zone. Buy—beg—steal, if need be, but bring us food."

In Vashti's opinion Miriam's words were mere raving. Of what use was it to wander through the city offering to buy food from a starving populace? He who had bread, would he not keep it?

Suddenly she bethought herself of one with whom she had always been a favorite, the benevolent Johanan ben Zacchai, whose two daughters had been her life-long friends.

She would go to their home in Ophel, and, if they should be the happy possessors of food, beg a little

## The Dying City

of it for the sake of Arad. Kissing him passionately she laid him down, and went forth on this dubious errand.

The setting sun was tingeing with a golden glow the higher parts of the city as Vashti unbarred the gate of her dwelling, a gate that had not opened for many weeks.

The first thing that impressed her was the strange stillness that prevailed around, "*a deep silence and a kind of deadly night*," to use the language of the contemporary historian. The street was empty; every house, like her own, was shut and barred.

Significant fact! What silent tragedies, what scenes of anguish, were taking place behind those closed doors and latticed windows?

As she stepped out into the street her eye was caught by a startling object. Hanging by a rope from a hook fixed into an adjacent wall was a shriveled and mummified corpse, that of a man, who, doubtless unable longer to endure the agonies of slow starvation, had chosen to hasten his end by suicide. The thought that before her journey's end she was likely to see other sights like this, or even more ghastly, almost drove her within the house again, but her mother's wrath and Arad's hunger spurred her on, and she walked away as quickly as her weakness would let her.

A few paces, and she saw lying within the entrance of a narrow archway the body of a woman but recently dead, a woman with a frame emaciated by famine, the skin tightly drawn over her bones, the veins on her shriveled neck showing like sinews. Pillowed upon her arm lay an infant whose hand convulsively grasped his mother's withered breast, twisting it with his fingers, and uttering feeble little cries of anger at finding himself deprived of sustenance. Pity for the mother, a greater pity for the babe, put Vashti in a state of hesitation. To leave the infant dying there was an unnatural act; on the other hand, where was the good in taking it to her own home? Neither she nor her mother had the means of preserving its life. It might as well die under the open sky as under a roof; and so, steeling her heart, Vashti went slowly on. But she got no further than the end of the street; beginning to feel like a murderess, she turned back, only to find the infant breathing its last.

Leaving mother and babe Vashti went on her way, seeing with a pitying heart other sights equally grim. The Apocalypse, but recently written, had not yet come to her knowledge, or she might have recalled the passage, "*Their dead bodies shall lie in the streets of the great city.*"

She entered a silent square, seemingly empty, but a second glance around showed her on its southern side a group of human figures—perhaps twenty in all—men, women, and children, clustered in various attitudes upon the steps of the Royal Synagogue. They took no notice of her approach, though her footsteps sounded unnaturally loud in the strange stillness.

Vashti stopped short, absolutely appalled at their aspect. Though terribly wasted herself, Vashti was plump compared with these figures. With limbs attenuated to those of a skeleton; with eyes deep sunken in their orbit; with cheek-bones projecting hideously; with complexions darkened by famine, they looked like weird beings from another world. More dreadful than all was the look of unspeakable anguish stamped upon their features; it was the look of men who would never smile more in this world. They had come to this spot because from it their beloved temple could be seen; and they would fain die with their glazing eyes fixed to the last upon the lofty golden pinnacles of the white marble shrine that stood out in all its loveliness against the calm blue sky of evening.

Dead and dying they lay, stretched athwart the steps. "Those who were just going to die looked upon

## The Dying City

those that were gone to their rest before them with dry eyes and open mouths."[29]

Suddenly a sound became audible; distant at first, it grew painfully loud, and at last, with a rattle and a clang, a dozen armed Zealots, belonging to John's party, came marching into the square, their well-preserved physique affording a striking contrast to the ghastly group on the synagogue steps. Famine had not yet laid its finger upon *them*.

Seemingly in the best of spirits they talked and laughed in rude fashion, indifferent to the suffering that met them at every point. As a matter of fact, they had come out purposely to add to the city's sufferings. Four of their number carried a small battering-ram, intended to force open the doors of such obstinate citizens as were bent on keeping their own provisions.

Vashti noticed that these Zealots were taking the way that led past the synagogue. Not wishing to attract their attention, she crept to the side of the building, and hid herself behind a buttress, contriving the while, however, to keep watch upon the approaching group.

As they drew nearer she saw to her surprise that the more youthful of them were *dressed as women* in all the bravery of finely dyed garments and golden anklets that tinkled as they walked; their long, flowing hair was decked with the *suffa*, a gauzy network, that, attached to the headdress, hung down over the shoulders as far as the waist; red coloring glowed on their cheeks, while their eyes, to make them appear larger and more lustrous, were painted round with *kohl*, and their eyebrows arched and darkened with the same preparation.

Their appearance thrilled Vashti with a mysterious and nameless horror; she wondered what this feminine garb should mean, not knowing in her innocence that the temple had become, under John of Giscala, the seat of infamies that caused the seer of Patmos to brand the once holy city with a fearful name.

The Zealots in passing glanced at the silent throng, whose dying anguish provoked only their savage mirth.

"More victims for the dead-cart," laughed one. "Aha!" he continued, stopping in his walk, and pointing to a ghastly stiffened figure lying supine upon the stairs, "whom have we here? Asenath the harlot, as I live. One can scarce recognize in her the one-time favorite of old Ananias. How she stares! Is she living or dead?"

"Dead!" replied another Zealot.

"I'll wager ten shekels she's living," cried he who had spoken first.

"And I'll wager the same that she's dead," answered the second.

"Good! you hear," said the first, addressing the rest as desiring them to be witnesses of the wager.

The Zealots had a way of their own—and for sport often practiced it—of ascertaining whether a body were dead.

Drawing his blade the first ruffian pulled aside the woman's robe and pierced her breast with the point of the weapon, an act followed by a faint moan, and a slight writhing of the figure.

"Thou hast lost thy bet, Malchus," laughed the first ruffian. "She's living."

"She's dead now, at any rate," answered the second; and, furious at losing the wager, he drew his sword and stabbed the woman to the heart.

At this a dying man beside her spoke in hollow tones.

"In the name of God be merciful, and do the like by me. Thrust me through that my anguish may have an end."

"Thou wishest to die? Then thou shalt live," replied Malchus; and, sheathing his blade, he moved off with the rest of the Zealots, who laughed as though the affair were a merry jest.

When silence had descended upon the square again Vashti crept fearfully forth, and, after hesitating whether or not to return home, she resumed her slow and trembling way to Ophel, and arrived without further adventure at the house of Johanan ben Zacchai. It was a humble dwelling situated in a street that, like all others in the city, was as quiet as the tomb.

Vashti found the gate, as she expected, barred.

Before knocking she listened, and detected coming from within a sound that caused her heart to leap with hope, for it was a sound like that produced when corn is ground between two millstones.

Even in her dazed and frightened state of mind Vashti could not but think it imprudent to be grinding corn within hearing of the street, a street that might be traversed at any moment by ruffianly, food-seeking Zealots.

The household of Johanan were evidently not without grain; surely they would spare her just a little from their store?

She knocked at the gate, and the sound of the grinding, if such it were, instantly ceased.

"They think I am a Zealot," she said with a wild little laugh.

She knocked a second and a third time, but received no reply; she called out her name so loudly that those within must have heard who the visitor was, but they made no response. A dead silence prevailed within.

Vashti withdrew to the middle of the street, and turned her despairing eyes towards the lattice over the gateway. No friendly face looked down at her; no face at all.

She turned sorrowfully away, but came again presently, and this she continued to do at intervals, beating piteously upon the gate, but all to no purpose.

Then did hope die within her. If Johanan ben Zacchai would not listen to the voice of a suppliant, there was none other in the city that would.

Nothing remained for her but to return home; but how could she, empty-handed, face the despairing gaze of her dying mother, the fearful, famishing eyes of little Arad, who quite expected to see his sister come back laden with food.

Loth to return home she wandered slowly and aimlessly through the streets and squares of the star-lit city.

In the Xystus that faced the half-burned palace of Agrippa she came upon a group of men, all bearing the signet-mark of famine—the skeleton limbs, the dark complexion, the sunken eyes of unnatural luster with the scared look in them.

Leaning upon staves they were listening to one of those self-deluded fanatics, so numerous at that time in Jerusalem—fanatics whose dream no reverses could destroy, the dream namely of a coming universal empire for the Jews; the darker and the more hopeless the situation seemed, the more fervent and enthusiastic became the faith of these false prophets, who did not relinquish their hopes till they saw the temple sink into everlasting night, and the plow drawn over the soil where once the palace of Zion had stood.

Vashti paused for a moment to listen to his wild harangue.

" Think you that Jehovah will let the place in which He has chosen to put His name fall into the hands of the uncircumcized heathen? Men, brethren, there is no contradiction in the Divine nature, and therefore He who decreed that the temple should be built can never decree that it shall be destroyed. Take heart and rejoice! The time foretold by the prophets is at hand: the heavens shall open, and the Messiah shall descend therefrom—yea! it is but a matter of a few hours now—to avenge His people. His feet shall stand upon Olivet, and with the breath of His mouth will He slay the host of Titus even as He slew the host of Sennacherib."

## The Dying City

And so speciously did he argue by texts drawn from the prophetical scriptures that his famishing auditors, with scarcely strength to stand, became as hopeful as the orator himself; they forgot their present sufferings; their faces brightened, and they turned their glance upward to the comet gleaming red in the sky, half-expecting to see it launch forth fiery death at the girdling hostile line that, "hushed in grim repose," was patiently waiting the slow but certain doom of the city.

With a sigh Vashti passed on, and coming to a street corner beheld the emaciated figure of a man kneeling, in his hand a drawn bow with an arrow fitted thereto. Never had she seen eyes so fiercely wild, or an expression so painfully eager and expectant. Following the direction of his glance she saw that he was aiming at a pigeon which had just alighted upon the ground only a few yards distant. "Food, food! Life, life!" was the thought that frenzied his brain.

But Vashti could see what he could not, namely, that much nearer to the bird, and crouching down within a gateway was the skeleton figure of a woman, whose manner showed that she was waiting to snatch the prize from the archer. And so it proved. As the shaft flew true to the mark the woman tottered feebly from her hiding-place; her eyes sparkled with wild glee; she gave a demoniacal chuckle as she pounced upon the slain pigeon, and ghoul-like tore greedily at the raw flesh with her teeth.

At that sight there broke from the man a cry of surprise and despair, of agony and rage, a cry horrible yet pitiable to hear. "Thief! bitch! accursed!" he screamed. "Give me what is mine. Ah! she would devour it all! In the name of God give me a mouthful, a morsel, that I may live, and not die."

As the speaker lurched forward in the endeavor to get at the thief his legs gave way beneath him, and he fell heavily to the ground; feebly struggling to his feet he staggered on again with intent to wreak vengeance upon the spoiler.

Outraged nature did the work for him.

The eater gorging herself to the full, and being long unused to the taking of so great an amount of sustenance, became suddenly convulsed, dropped to the ground in horrible contortions, and there and then died, her end being greeted with mocking laughter by the weakling pursuer, who, seemingly undeterred by her fate, knelt down, and plucking the remnant of the bird from the dead woman's teeth began to gnaw it with his own.

Vashti, shuddering, turned away, and retracing her steps to Ophel, sought once more the house of Johanan ben Zacchai. But she stopped aghast ere reaching it.

Its gate was wide open now, hanging wrecked upon its hinges, with the battering-ram that had done the work lying within the entrance.

From the house came the cries as of an old man in pain.

" Give his limb another twist," cried a voice that she recognized as that of Malchus the Zealot. " We'll soon make the old graybeard tell where he has concealed his corn."

At the same moment there broke forth from an upper chamber the thrilling screams of Johanan's two daughters, painly calling upon their aged father to deliver them from the hands of the lewd and laughing Zealots; for John's followers made it their boast that if there were a virgin in any house they entered there would be none there when they left.

With the blood about her heart congealing to ice Vashti fled, lest a like fate should befall her; fled, not knowing whither she went, not caring; fled, till she suddenly found herself facing a great black mass that rose up into the starry night. It was the wall of Zion, the huge rampart of masonry that lay between the Romans and victory, that lay, alas! betwixt herself

*The Dying City* 281

and Crispus. She was near the Valley Gate, whose approaches as she saw were guarded by a small party of Zealots, while on the battlements above them slow-pacing sentinels kept their watch. Hastily Vashti retreated within the shadows ere she should be seen.

By the gate stood Simon the Black. An unpleasant odor, so palpable that one could almost taste it, hung in the air; and this was doubtless his reason for holding in his hand a perfume box whose fragrance he inhaled from time to time.

At intervals there came from beyond the city walls weird, plaintive cries, mysterious voices as of human creatures in pain; the sounds, borne on the wings of the night, seemed to come like arrows to the heart of Vashti, thrilling her with an unknown fear. The strange odor and the eerie sounds—what did they mean? The apparent unconcern of the men about the gate showed that to them at least these were familiar things.

Conversing apart with Simon was a somewhat sad-eyed man, by name Mannens, the scribe appointed to take note of all the dead carried forth through the Valley Gate; for be it known that the bodies of the dead as being like to create a plague if allowed to remain in the city were collected at night by paid agents of the Sanhedrim, thrown upon carts, and carried out to be promiscuously flung, without funeral rites and without burial, into the ravines that surrounded Jerusalem; all which matters were as yet unknown to Vashti.

"How many, think you, up to yester even have been borne forth from this gate?" asked Mannens of Simon.

"Twenty thousand, perhaps," replied the Zealot, hazarding a guess.

"*One hundred and fifteen thousand, eight hundred and eighty,*"[20] returned Mannens, consulting his tablets.

Even Simon, little prone to emotion, was staggered by these figures.

"Fire of Gehenna!" he muttered. "And this is but one gate! How many from each of the other gates? Our Jewish brethren from foreign lands whose wish it is to be buried at Jerusalem seem to be having their wish," he added grimly. "But, ah! whom have we here?"

This last question was caused by the action of Vashti, who, moved by some uncontrollable impulse, came tremblingly forward, and addressed to him a pitiful plaint for bread.

"Bread?" repeated the Zealot. "Why comest thou to me?"

"Because you are as a king in this city."

"Captain," said one of the Zealots, recognizing Vashti, "this damsel is of the Nazarenes, who were forever preaching the doom of the city. She is, moreover, the ward of Josephus, that traitor, who is high in the councils of the enemy."

"A Nazarene, true. Yet," answered Vashti, eager to seize upon any argument that might influence the Zealot chief in her favor, "yet did I not quit the city, when the Nazarenes left it, but have remained behind to share the fate of my fellow-citizens. In the name of God," she continued, addressing Simon, "give me bread. I ask not for myself, but for a dying child. Give me but one loaf, and on the resurrection morning, when all deeds will be brought to light, this shall be counted to you for righteousness."

"You shall have a loaf," said Simon, moved strangely by her words, "you shall have a basket . . . a basket filled with bread." The bewildered Vashti could scarcely trust her hearing. "But ere you return home you must eat a morsel yourself, or you will faint by the way. Come with me."

Vashti, loth to go with him, yet not daring to refuse, accompanied Simon to the tower adjacent to the Valley Gate. Entering the first room that he came to, the Zealot chief peremptorily ordered out of it three or four of his followers who were sitting there occupied with dice and wine.

"Here," said he, addressing Vashti, when the men had withdrawn, "here are six dried grapes, a fig, and a morsel of bread. No more at present. Put a curb upon your appetite, if you would live."

To Vashti's mind there was something selfish in eating while thousands of her fellow-citizens were dying of want—doubly selfish, when she reflected that this food had perhaps been wrung by violence from the famishing people. Natural appetite, however, prevailed over sentiment; and with a strange feeling towards Simon, a feeling compounded of gratitude and repulsion, Vashti began the slow eating of what was to her a repast more delicious than that in the banquet-hall of Florus, though her enjoyment was somewhat marred by the unpleasant odor that seemed to cling around everything in this vicinity. That she did not know its cause seemed to surprise Simon. Perceiving that her ignorance was real and not feigned, he rose, and said, "Come with me, if you would learn."

Vashti began to regret her curiosity, being all-anxious now to return home with the promised loaves. Not wishing, however, to offend the Zealot she followed him up a stone staircase, and through a doorway that opened upon the ramparts.

Simon, first handing her his perfume box, bade her look down over the battlements.

And Vashti looked.

It was a moonless night, but the sky was jeweled with stars whose faint light was just sufficient to give her a glimmering of what lay below. It was the light required for such a scene: the full blaze of the noonday sun would have made it a horror too great to be endured by human nerves.

"*They shall look upon the carcasses of the men that have transgressed against me!*"

Vashti, peering down, could dimly see that the deep

and shadowy ravine of Hinnom—that ravine already regarded in Hebrew theology as the type of hell—was filled with the remains of the dead, who were to be counted not by hundreds, but by tens of thousands. The bodies lay, piled promiscuously, some clothed, some naked, in every possible stage of decay, from that of the newly dead to that of the whitened skeleton glimmering ghastly through the gloom.

The air that hung above and around the ravine was tainted with an effluvium so gross as to be all but palpable to the touch, and so loathsome that but for the perfume box Vashti would have sunk to the ground overpowered.

More dreadful still, from every part of the gloom came significant and horrid rustlings, intermingled with sounds like to the tearing of flesh by some sharp instrument.

" Mark! " said Simon.

He flung over a stone; at its sudden and startling descent a black cloud of ravens and vultures, gorged with human flesh, rose on the wing, high above the battlements, their slow-sailing shadows darkening the face of the sky.

Vashti, as they passed, drew back with a shudder, and as she did so, her eyes fell upon a sight still more startling and awful. *Now* she knew the origin of the weird and midnight cries!

There, beyond the ravine, under the cold light of the pitiless stars, were rows upon rows of crosses; and to every cross was nailed a naked human form!

The number of these crosses was past all counting; they circled the whole city, extending as far back as the Roman wall, whose castellated outline was dimly visible from the battlements. How many of the crucified victims were dead; how many were bearing their sufferings in heroic silence; how many had reached the sullen stupor that is the immediate precursor of death, it was impossible to tell. Vashti might have thought

## The Dying City

all dead, but that every now and then some poor wretch, now in this quarter and now in that, lifting his hitherto bowed head would shiver convulsively, and would break the stillness of the night by a long-drawn mournful cry of pain, a cry that might have caused the coldest, sternest nature to weep, but seemed to have no effect upon Simon.

"In God's name, who are these?" gasped Vashti.

"Jewish deserters. It is thus that Titus receives those that come to him from the city, nor do I pity them. Let them die; they deserve their doom. Mark," he continued, "mark the ill-fortune that has attended all who have deserted the holy cause! In the early days of the siege Titus was wont to receive such renegades with favor, a favor, however, that proved the doom of many, who, eating too freely of the food given to them, burst, and so died." He paused, with a vindictive smile, and then resumed. "They were succeeded by other deserters, who, ere leaving the city, swallowed gold pieces and precious stones, thinking to recover them after they had passed the Roman lines. Fatal avarice! The secret became known to the Syrian and Arabian allies deputed to take charge of these deserters; they slew them and cut open their bodies to get at the treasures. In this way were two thousand of them killed in one night." Again he smiled vindictively. "At last Titus, growing stern, as he saw the little progress made by his arms, sent to our walls a herald to proclaim that he would receive no more deserters; let the whole body of the people come forth, or none. Regardless of this decree, fresh parties made their way to the Roman camp, to be sent back to the city, a shrieking train of victims, with their hands lopped off." Again that vindictive smile. "And now," added Simon, pointing to the ghastly scene before them, "now he hath taken to this way of dealing with them. *They are crucified to the number of five hundred a day!*"

The vengeance of history!

These were the men, and the sons of the men, who forty years earlier had cried " Crucify Him! crucify Him!" And now they themselves were crucified—some on the very site of Golgotha itself!—in such numbers that, in the language of Josephus, " room was wanting for the crosses, and crosses wanting for the bodies." And the victims, if they but chose to look, could see overhead in the sky the red gleam of the heavenly sword. Stay! was it the figure of a sword, or was it not rather *the likeness of a cross*, intended to remind them of the greatest and most awful tragedy in the world's history?

Vashti's head swam with horror; a mist obscured her vision; air and landscape seemed slowly turning to one universal blood-red hue. Her wild wail went forth upon the night air:

" O God, have mercy upon this hapless city!"

It was past the sixth hour of the night when Vashti, with her basket of bread upon her arm, reached home.

Closing and barring the gate behind her, she went along the short passage, and crossed the little court.

Entering a chamber upon the ground floor she paused for a moment and stood in the attitude of listening. She had so expected to hear Arad's plaintive cry for food that it was almost a disappointment to find the house as silent as the tomb. Evidently Arad was sleeping, unless indeed——! Her heart almost stood still at the dread thought that suddenly smote her. But no! she was alarming herself without cause. A two days' fast, though it might very much weaken a child, would not kill him. Arad must be sleeping.

She smiled lovingly as she pictured his delight when he should awake and see what his sister had brought him.

If mother and son were sleeping it could not be otherwise that the house should be without sound; yet in the prevailing stillness that hung about the place like a tangible veil there was something so strange and oppressive as to fill Vashti with vague fears. Her tread on entering had sounded so hollow that she had paused, almost fearing to take a second step. For the first time in her life she feared the darkness.

Plucking up her courage, she moved through the gloom towards the stairway that stood in one corner of the room. When she was half-way across the floor her foot touched some object; moved by curiosity she stooped, and picking the thing up found it to be— *a long knife!*

Now when Vashti had last gone through this room there was no knife lying upon the floor; her sandal had become loose upon this very spot; she had knelt to tie the string, and the knife, had it been lying there at that time, could scarcely have failed to come within the ken of her vision. Evidently someone must have entered this room during her absence; doubtless Miriam.

There was nothing strange in the fact that her mother, if so minded, should leave the upper story and descend to the court, yet Vashti could not help wondering why Miriam should have removed the knife from its customary place upon the shelf, since it was the one used only in the culinary operations, this room being the kitchen of the little household. But that existing circumstances forbade the hypothesis, the knife might have been taken as evidence almost of the preparation of a meal.

As if expecting the darkness to furnish some clew Vashti looked vacantly around, and there upon the floor distant but a few feet, and scintillating through the gloom, was a something that had the semblance of an eye, an eye intently watching all her movements.

It stared at her a while, blinked, glittered again, then the eyelid seemed to close, and there was darkness where the thing had been.

Vashti gave a little insane laugh of relief, perceiving that what had frightened her was no eye at all, but a faint point of light upon the hearth, the last spark of some dying embers. It was clear that during her absence a fire had been kindled in this room, and by whom, if not by her mother? and this fact when taken with the knife would seem to point to the preparation of food. If so, by what means had Miriam become so fortunate? After what Vashti had seen that night it was scarcely credible that, Zealots excepted, there could be anyone in this famishing city so well provided as to be capable of giving relief to others. Such being the case, then, what was the meaning to be put upon the fire and the knife?

Instead of hastening at once to her mother's room Vashti lingered in this chamber, impressed somehow by the belief that here was to be found the key to the mystery. Though entirely ignorant as to its nature, she nevertheless felt certain that she was on the verge of some startling discovery, and she trembled all over.

Slowly she drew near the hearth; over it the air still hung warm. Her feet pressed upon some light yielding material like cloth. Cloth it was, a little woollen garment belonging to Arad; nay more, certain fringes upon it told her that it was the little caftan he had been wearing when she last parted from him. What strange whim had induced her mother to deprive the child of his one and only garment? Had it been exchanged for another? If so, it was not easy to see the reason, or why the old one should have been brought down, and left lying by the hearth.

Wondering whether there were anything else here belonging to Arad she put forth her hands, and grasped a little girdle and two sandals.

A moment she stood in bewilderment: then, as the ghastly truth came rushing upon her mind, there broke from her a cry so awful as to seem scarcely human; the fear of the thing caused her hair to bristle, and the cold drops to start from every pore.

All the appalling tragedies she had seen that night —what were they compared with this?

She turned and ran up the staircase, her frenzy of grief giving her a strength so great that armed men could scarcely have had the power to stay her.

With a quick tread she entered the upper chamber. It was dark, yet not quite dark: the light of the stars seen through the open lattice sufficed to make the nearer objects faintly visible. Miriam lay in the middle of the apartment asleep upon her pallet. It was not to her that Vashti first turned. Though knowing well that she would not find him there, she nevertheless ran at once to Arad's pallet.

It was empty!

She flew to her mother's side, knelt, and peered shudderingly into the somnolent face, a face that wore at this moment the dull heavy air as of one whose animal wants are satisfied. Her mother actually *sleeping*, as if this were merely some ordinary night! sleeping, after such a deed as hers! Sleeping—she who ought never to sleep again!

There was little of the daughter left in Vashti as she fiercely shook the slumbering woman by the shoulder.

And the soul of the unhappy Miriam starting from blissful dreams to the dread reality of earthly things awoke to hear sounding through the gloom of night a voice that, like the voice of the accusing archangel, addressed her with the awful question:

"WHAT HAVE YOU DONE WITH ARAD?"

# CHAPTER XXII

#### THE RESCUE OF VASHTI

TIBERIUS ALEXANDER, the apostate Jew, and Crispus, with four legionaries attending on them, stood at the foot of the city wall at the point where masonry, carried aloft to an amazing height, supported the Colonnade of Solomon.

The night, bright and starry in its earlier part, had now become clouded and dark, an event that seemed to give satisfaction to Alexander.

"The darker the night, the more likely am I to discover something," he observed, from which remark it was clear to Crispus that Alexander had some special reason for bringing him to this spot, a spot that was a sore trial to the olfactory sense, owing to the effluvium arising from the dead bodies in the ravine of Cedron.

Into that ravine Alexander was now gazing. He could quote the Hebrew prophets on occasion; usually, however, to ridicule them.

"'Son of man,'" said he mockingly to Crispus, "'can these dry bones live?'"

"My answer is that of the scribes whose teaching you have deserted," retorted Crispus. "That which was not, came into being; how much more, then, that which has been already?"

Tiberius Alexander might perhaps have replied to this celebrated, rabbinical argument but that his attention was attracted at that moment by the sudden appearance of a light at a window in one of the castella or forts on the Roman line of contravallation.

Three times did the light flash, and then it vanished.

"You saw it?" said he to Crispus. "So, too, have I seen it, on other nights than this. There can be no doubt that it is a signal to the Jews in the city. We have a traitor in our camp. By remaining here we shall, if I err not, discover who he is. Keep we in the shadow of this crag."

"Is not yon castellum the one in which King Agrippa is quartered?" whispered Crispus.

"Thou hast said," replied Alexander.

For a long time the little party remained silent and expectant. At last a sound was heard above their heads like the clanking of metal against masonry, and looking up they saw coming down through the darkness a very large basket of strong wicker-work attached to the end of an iron chain. It touched the ground and there remained.

"Empty," remarked Alexander, taking a peep into it. "It is as I suspected. This is lowered by the priests for the reception of something to be put into it by the man who signaled with the light. And here comes the traitor himself."

As he spoke there came stealing along at the foot of the city wall a man whose garb showed him to be a soldier belonging to King Agrippa's troops. He was leading a file of lambs attached to one another by a cord. Having arrived at his destination the man was about to lift one of the animals into the basket when he stopped short in guilty confusion upon seeing Alexander, who chose that very moment for making his presence known.

"Are you not Sadas, the freedman of the Princess Berenice?"

The soldier admitted that he was. Then did Crispus recognize in him the man who had denounced Vashti in the Royal Synagogue.

"Ah! that puts a different complexion on this affair, which is not so grave as I had thought it. These lambs, presumably from Bethlehem, none others being permissible on the temple-altar, are sent by the Princess Berenice in order that the morning and the evening sacrifices may not cease for want of victims. Is it not so, my Sadas? The supply above is running short, I ween. Now I have a great regard for the princess, but it seems to me that the fair lady's zeal for her religion borders closely upon treason to us Romans. It were foolish of us to permit sacrifices to Jehovah here, after Theomantes hath so kindly invited him to take up his dwelling in the Capitol. Therefore, as my men, not to speak of myself, are very fond of roast lamb, do you, Quintus, lead these animals to my tent, and place this fellow under ward. To-morrow we'll inquire further into the matter."

The soldiers proceeded to do as bidden.

"I would we had a dozen swine to put into this basket," continued Alexander, giving it a contemptuous kick.

At that moment the priests on the cloister above observing that the lambs were being taken back to the Roman camp by a party of soldiers, saw that the affair had somehow miscarried and began to haul up the basket again.

While Tiberius Alexander followed close upon the heels of the soldiers, Crispus lingered in the vicinity of the walls, his mind tortured almost to madness at the thought of what might be happening to Vashti in this long and cruel process of starving the obstinate city into submission. For all he knew to the contrary, she might be lying at that very moment among the festering horrors of the glen of Cedron, her body torn by the beak and claw of obscene birds of prey, to be seen no more by him till the resurrection morning, when these " dry bones " would live again, to shame the doctrine of the mocking Alexander.

The air grew darker, so dark that a circle of a few yards only was the limit of Crispus' vision; all beyond was blackness.

## The Rescue of Vashti

An ideal night for the enemy if they were minded to attack the Roman entrenchments!

Scarcely had this thought occurred to Crispus when he heard, or fancied he heard, a sound proceeding from a point not many yards distant. He listened intently. Footsteps, not loud, but quiet footsteps; not of one man but, so it seemed to Crispus, of three or four men, all walking in a stealthy sort of way, as if wishing to keep their movements a secret. They were coming slowly through the darkness right towards the place where he stood. In another moment they would be upon him.

Romans on some errand of espial? or a party of Jewish deserters?

Bracing his buckler upon his arm and drawing his sword Crispus awaited their approach.

As the men—they were three in number—came into view he bade them halt, which they did with surprising promptitude. Questioning on the part of Crispus elicited the fact that they were Jews, passover pilgrims from Asia, detained by the war: appointed to guard a portion of the wall in Ophel they had, through despair of the city's salvation, resolved to desert; and so, tying a rope to a battlement, they had let themselves down.

The madness of these men! Though the crucifixions of Jewish fugitives amounted to five hundred a day, the stream of defection from the city never ceased, the deserters hoping, in spite of failure on the part of their predecessors, to steal secretly through the Roman lines, or, if need be, force a way at the sword's point.

"How long is it since ye fled?"

"Less than the fourth part of an hour," replied one whose name was Asaph.

"Is the rope still hanging there?"

"Surely. How could we, when on the ground, detach it from the battlement?"

"Think you that your flight is known?"

"We purposely waited till the night-watch had gone by, and left the moment afterwards; therefore our flight will not be discovered for some time yet."

"Is it yours to watch the same part of the wall every night?"

"Till the next Sabbath."

These questions of Crispus were inspired by a daring idea that had suddenly darted into his mind.

A rope hanging from the city wall at a part deserted by its watchers!

Why should he not enter the city by the same means as that by which these men had left it? His object in this enterprise was to find Vashti, and having found her to bring her out of this city of death, and to put her into some safe place of concealment, thereby defeating the wicked scheme of Berenice. But his plan, as he rapidly conceived it, required the co-operation of these three Jews, and there lay the difficulty: they might refuse to join him, or, deceiving him by a pretended assent, turn traitors at the very moment of his seeming success. Nevertheless, desperate as the plan was, he determined to take the risks.

"Hearken unto me, Asaph, and ye two," said Crispus, adopting a Hebrew phraseology, to make his address the more impressive. "As the Lord liveth, before whom I stand, if ye attempt to pass the Roman lines without me ye are dead men. But fear not, I will go with you and save you. Yet will I not go with you to-night, but to-morrow night. Ye must return, and resume your post upon the wall. I will go with you, not to betray the city, but to seek therein a damsel, whose life I would save. 'Tis an easy matter for me to mount the wall by the rope ye have left, but how am I to return, unless the wall be held by those friendly to me? Therefore ye must delay your flight by twenty-four hours. To-morrow night about this time when ye are again playing the part of sentinels I will come to you bringing the damsel, and that hour shall be the hour of your departure.

"Know that I am Crispus the Tribune, high in the favor of Titus, and therefore capable of fulfilling my word. Now, if ye will aid me in this, my soul's desire, I will conduct you to the Roman camp, and send you away in safety; but if ye will not do this thing, then go on your way alone to meet whatever doom befall you. Now, delay not your answer, for the success of my scheme depends upon your speedy return to the city."

The three men whispered together. They were not long in coming to a decision.

"Swear in the name of the Lord that you will save our soul alive," said Asaph, "and we will aid thee in this matter."

Under the black sky the strange compact was made, the three men taking Crispus to be a Hebrew proselyte, a belief in which he did not undeceive them.

"Let us return at once," said Asaph, "ere our flight be discovered."

Accompanied by his new-sworn allies Crispus began the steep ascent of Ophel, climbing with all silence and caution, and grateful to the darkness that hid them from the view of the sentinel Zealots above.

Arrived at the foot of the ramparts they crept along, Asaph leading the way, till a point was reached where the semicircular base of a huge projecting tower made an angle with the wall. Within this angle, and scarcely discernible in the dark, hung a rope attached to a battlement above.

"A good sign, this," said Crispus in a whisper. "Had these battlements been visited in your absence this rope would surely have been detected and drawn up."

Clambering up hand over hand the three Jews ascended the rope, and disappearing over the battlements proceeded to haul up their new ally.

The portion of wall allotted to their care proved to be about twenty yards in length, terminated at each end by two circular towers—the tower in Siloam, and " the tower that lieth out "—which effectually screened them from the observation of the sentinels disposed along the rest of the wall.

" Can you not bring the damsel here within the hour, and so make an end of the matter this night? " asked Asaph anxiously.

" Right gladly would I do so, but that I fear the finding of her will be a work of time, and within an hour from now day will be dawning. Can you hide this, my crested helmet, or 'twill betray me? and if you can find me a cloak——"

Asaph entered one of the towers and returned with a Jewish cap, and with a gabardine, beneath which Crispus found effectual concealment for his military garb.

" At what hour of the night do you begin your vigil? "

" Ours is the third watch and lasts from the sixth hour till the ninth."

" Look for me a little after the sixth hour. As a sign that all is well fix a spear erect upon the middle of the rampart. Unless I see it standing out clear against the sky I will not draw near. And now farewell for a time. Keep to your oath, and it shall go well with you."

As Crispus descended the stone stairway that led to the ground he congratulated himself upon the ease with which he had contrived to enter the city. Would he be able, however, to quit it with similar ease? That depended chiefly upon the fidelity of his new associates, and since they could hardly betray him without betraying themselves he felt somewhat assured. Turning from the wall of Ophel he set off for the street of Millo on Mount Zion.

When lying convalescent upon the roof of Miriam's

dwelling Crispus had had ample leisure to study the topography both of Ophel and Zion; this knowledge stood him now in good stead, and though, owing to the darkness, he once or twice missed his way, he finally found himself in the gray light of dawn before the gate of the house he sought.

He was about to knock at the gate when it suddenly opened, and there appeared in the entrance the figure of a young woman terribly emaciated by famine. She was habited as if for a journey.

"Is Vashti, daughter of Hyrcanus, within?" asked Crispus.

The figure gave a smile. *Such* a smile! One more fearful and weird he had never seen.

"Don't you know me, Crispus?"

He started, looked at her again, and could scarcely recognize her, so fearfully had she changed from the beautiful maiden of other days.

"Vashti, my poor girl, can this be you?"

To see her looking thus caused the tears to come welling to his eyes. His weeping caused her likewise to weep. Then ever mindful of others, rather than of herself, she suddenly said, amid her tears:

"Crispus, what do you here in this city of your enemies? Oh, if you should be discovered!"

"What do I here?" he repeated. "This is the answer to that question," he continued, tenderly lifting her hand that she might see how thin it was. "You are slowly dying of starvation, and yet you ask what do I here. I have come to snatch you from death by carrying you away to the Roman camp."

Vashti looked at him with a fearful joy in her eyes.

"Oh! if you could! if you could! I was just going to Simon of Gerasa to implore him to let me leave the city——"

"You shall not ask Simon's leave. That I have entered the city safely, you can see for yourself. By what means I have entered by that same means shall you leave." He smiled cheerfully as he closed and barred the gate. "To-morrow about this time," he added, "you shall be feasting in the Roman camp, you, and your mother, and little Arad."

But at the mention of this last name Vashti wept like one heartbroken.

"Arad," she said, "Arad—is—is——"

Crispus guessed the cause of her emotion.

"What! is the poor little fellow dead?"

"If you had but come yesterday!" she sobbed. "Oh! if you had but come yesterday, my brother might be living."

Seeing that she had scarcely strength to stand, Crispus lifted her in his arms, and carried her into the court.

"No, not that side!" said she, shivering, as he was about to enter the house by way of the room where her dreadful discovery had taken place. "Not that side!"

So Crispus carried her to a chamber that opened from a different part of the court, and producing the leathern wallet carried by every Roman soldier, he drew from it figs and bread and made her eat before he would let her say another word.

When she had finished the simple repast she told him the terrible story of a child slain by a famishing mother to satisfy her appetite; and Crispus listened, knowing from deserters' tales that deeds equally dark had been perpetrated in other households besides this.

"And because I have reproached her—was I wrong in so doing?—my mother has cursed me, and has bidden me leave her and go to my friends, the Romans. I call her mother," she added, "for I cannot easily rid myself of the familiar word."

"Is she not really your mother, then?" asked Crispus, receiving the news with the same satisfaction that Vashti herself had felt at the discovery.

"She has told me—and there was in her manner

something that convinces me she is speaking the truth —that I am her daughter by adoption only."

"And I believe it," said Crispus emphatically, "if only for this reason, that you are so different from her in every way; and you have another proof of it in this, that your name does not appear in the public genealogical rolls as the daughter of Hyrcanus. What were Miriam's words to you?"

"When I cried, for I could not help crying it, 'Would to God you were not my mother!' she laughed and said, 'You have your wish; I am not your mother. You were brought to me when you were a babe of about twelve months by my husband Hyrcanus, who found you one winter's night crying among the crags of Mount Hermon, where you had been purposely left to perish, and where, but for him, you would have perished. That is all I know of your origin, save this, that since there hath never been aught of the Jewess in you, I doubt not that you come of Greekish parents —nay, it would not surprise me to learn that your mother was a Samaritan, and hence your perverse nature.'"

A few years earlier the doubt that she was not of the chosen race would have troubled Vashti, but now baptized into a faith in which there is neither Greek nor Jew, neither barbarian nor Scythian, neither bond nor free, she viewed the question of her nationality as a matter of no moment.

The two for a while talked of Miriam's revelation; and then, quitting this theme, Crispus proceeded to tell Vashti of an event that he knew would interest her, an event the most momentous in his life—namely, how, during the time of his proscription, the Christians of Pella had given him harboring, and how he had become a catechumen, receiving instruction in the faith from the holy bishop Simeon, and from others who had seen the Lord.

"And when," concluded Crispus, "I learned that it

was Simeon who had baptized you, I would not let any other perform that rite for me."

Night and day for nearly four years had Vashti prayed for the conversion of Crispus, and now came the sweet realization of her prayer! His words seemed to lift her from earth to heaven—but for a moment only; like a swift, painful dart came the memory of little Arad, and she wept. How happy would she now be but for that black deed!

Knowing the cause of her sadness, Crispus tried to divert the course of her thoughts by talking of the way in which he hoped to remove her from the city; he made her eat again; and then, learning from her that she had been out all the previous night, he bade her sleep. So Vashti, compliant with his will, lay down upon a divan, and though sweet oblivion was a long time in coming, it came at last.

Miriam remained invisible throughout the day, a fact for which Crispus felt extremely grateful, since it was not at all unlikely that, if he were seen by her, she might, in her hatred of Romans, raise an alarm, and bring the Zealots upon him.

It was much past noon when Vashti awoke. She smiled on learning how long she had slept; but it was a wan, sad smile; Arad's end was ever present to her memory.

That day was the longest Vashti had ever known, but it came to an end in due course, and shortly before the sixth hour of the night she got ready for her departure. With tears in her eyes she took a last, lingering look at the silent starlit court of the dwelling that had been her home since childhood, knowing that she would see the place no more; the flaming torch and the iron crow of the Roman were destined ere many weeks had passed to bring this and ten thousand other houses crashing to the ground.

The two closed the gate behind them, and made their way through the dark streets.

## The Rescue of Vashti 301

As Vashti drew nigh to the great black wall of Ophel, she looked up and saw a sight that made her shudder.

Was she never to get away from the sight of death?

There upon the battlements and standing out in ghastly relief against the dark blue sky of night was a line of lofty posts, twenty-one in number, to each of which was nailed a naked human body!

Pacing to and fro upon the rampart was the Jewish trio, Asaph and his two comrades.

Having caught sight of the pre-arranged sign, the spear set erect, Crispus, exercising a spirit of caution, bade Vashti remain where she was while he went forward to reconnoiter.

Having found all satisfactory, Asaph and his companions receiving him with unfeigned joy, he returned and assisted Vashti to mount the stairway ascending to the battlements, where he threw off his Jewish gabardine, and resumed his crested helmet.

"Who are these?" asked Vashti, shrinking at the sight of the dead bodies.

"Matthias, alas! the one-time high priest, his three sons, and others of the priesthood. Accused by Simon of corresponding with the Romans they were slain to-day by Ananus,[31] the most savage of Simon's fifty captains, and their bodies hung here on high for Titus to see."

Of all the events that had occurred since the beginning of the siege, there was in Crispus' opinion scarcely any more mournful or more significant than this, the death of Matthias, THE LAST OF THE HIGH PRIESTS— for the irregularly chosen Phannias must be excluded from the catalogue—stabbed by the hand of a brutal ruffian, his body denied sepulture, and exposed naked upon the ramparts of the holy city to become the prey of the fowls of the air.

"*Non hunc, sed Barabbam!*" had been the cry of

the chief priests. And this was how Barabbas had rewarded them!

While thinking thus, Crispus made a sudden dash forward, and then stood disappointedly peering down the flight of steps.

"What is amiss?" asked Asaph, seeing excitement written on Crispus' face.

"I saw a black shape rise, and run down these stairs."

As Crispus spoke, the deep silence of the night was suddenly broken by the startling scream of a trumpet coming from beneath the very part of the wall on which he stood. It was the Jewish call to arms.

There was an immediate murmur of voices, swelling into a babel of excited cries, accompanied by a sudden blazing up of torches in all directions. By the ruddy light the little party on the ramparts could see hundreds of dark figures racing towards the wall of Ophel, all in a tempest of Eastern fury.

"We are lost!" gasped Vashti, her skin, darkened by famine, becoming white now.

"Have no fear," responded Crispus cheerily; and, addressing the three Jews, he said in a rapid, staccato utterance, "Make for the rope—lower the damsel first—descend yourselves—when the last man is down blow your trumpet—AWAY!"

With this, Crispus drew his blade; and, taking his station at the head of the steps, glared down like an eagle upon the coming foe.

In the full belief that Crispus' end was at hand Vashti would fain have stayed to die with him, but, heeding not her protests, the three Jews whirled her off her feet and ran like madmen towards the suspended rope, their sole means of escape. It was woe to them if they were caught!

The torch-carrying, saber-brandishing multitude halted at the foot of the steps, surprised to see but a single armed Roman, surprised still more that that Roman should be preparing to offer resistance.

## The Rescue of Vashti

The stair at the head of which Crispus stood formed the sole access to the battlements; of narrow width it did not permit two men to stand abreast; and, moreover, neither on the one side nor on the other was it provided with a hand-rail. Strong therefore in his position, Crispus felt that he could hold the foe in play for a space of time sufficiently long to enable his confederates to descend the wall; after which it would be a race between himself and the enemy as to which would first reach the rope-encircled battlement.

"A Roman! How came he there?" exclaimed one.

"Asaph is playing the traitor," cried a second. "He is admitting the enemy into the city."

"Why, 'tis Crispus the Tribune," said a third.

*Crispus!*

At the sound of that name, a man—the foremost of the crowd—who had just put his foot upon the lowest step, immediately withdrew it in favor of anyone else that chose to mount.

Crispus, during the siege, had added to his former fame gained by his defense of the Prætorium of Florus; so quick of limb and eye, so deadly dexterous in fence was he known to be, that it was the confident belief of almost every Zealot present that the first of their number to reach the topmost stair would be a dead man the moment afterwards. Their state of hesitancy was highly favorable to the escaping fugitives. A quick, backward glance on the part of Crispus showed him that the three Jews, having lowered Vashti, were themselves preparing to descend.

"Way there!" cried a powerful voice from among the crowd. The throng parted, and a tall, red-bearded figure, armed with sword and shield, mounted the lowest stair and began a wary ascent. His example inspired others to follow.

Crispus looked calmly down upon the first of the ascending file.

"Who art thou?" he asked.

"Ananus, Simon's chief captain," was the proud answer.

"Ah! And are all Simon's captains as ugly as thou?"

With a snarl of rage—for he knew himself to be ill-favored, and nothing touched his vanity more than to be reminded of the fact—the slayer of the last high priest leaped fiercely up the stairs towards Crispus, who, at that moment, caught the welcome peal of Asaph's trumpet.

Then, to the amazement of the gazing crowd, Crispus, stepping backwards, actually sheathed his sword.

They saw the reason a moment afterwards.

At his feet lay a huge post, similar to those upon which Simon's crucified victims hung. Crispus lifted this long beam in his arms, carefully adjusting its balance; and, as soon as Ananus appeared at the top of the stairs, he sent the head of this improvised battering-ram full tilt into the Zealot's stomach with so tremendous an impact that not only did Ananus fly backwards, gasping and helpless, but in his fall he also carried with him the rest of the file that were coming up behind. The indignant howls of the bruised crew were as music to the ears of Crispus. Dropping the log, he instantly turned and fled, an act that naturally made the crowd below dash at once up the stairway in pursuit.

But never did Grecian runner skim over the Olympic stadium more fleetly than did the Roman Crispus along that wall of Ophel. Ere the foremost of the Zealots had come tumbling over the top stair, he had reached the place where the rope hung, and, pausing for a moment to fling a gesture of defiance at his pursuers, he swung himself over the battlement, and made a rapid hand-over-hand descent to the foot of the ramparts, where stood the three Jews and the trembling Vashti.

"Are you hurt?" she asked.

"No, but I warrant Ananus is," laughed Crispus.

"For some days to come he'll have no stomach for the fight. And now, away! See, they are opening a gate on our left."

Lifting Vashti—how thin and light she was!—he sped down the slope of Ophel with her, and succeeded in safely reaching the Roman lines.

Determined to forestall any attempt on the part of Titus to detain her he dispatched Vashti that same hour of the night, under the care of two Christian soldiers, to the saints that dwelt at Pella.

# CHAPTER XXIII

### CLOSING IN

THE long blockade had failed to bring about the surrender of the city; and Titus was beginning to grow weary of the delay; in fancy he could hear the patricians of Rome laughing at the plebeian-born general, and declaring that a city taken by famine was not a very brilliant way of inaugurating the new dynasty of Flavian emperors.

So it came to pass that on the day following Vashti's departure for Pella, the mighty Roman host at a word from Titus roused itself to toil again like a giant refreshed by a long sleep.

As the fortress Antonia was the key to the temple, Titus began by raising opposite this fortress four huge aggeres.

The construction of the former banks had cleared all the timber from the immediate vicinity of Jerusalem, so that the Romans were compelled to go farther afield, and at the end of twenty-one days—the time taken in raising these new aggeres—there was not a tree left within ten miles of the city!

Meanwhile, long teams of oxen, bellowing under the lash, were toiling up the rugged pass of Beth-horon, drawing endless files of wagons roped to each other, upon which were mounted the new military machines, huge and terrible, constructed by the Greek engineers of Cæsarea.

On the twenty-second day, the artillery (this word is long anterior to the use of firearms) was placed in position, and the legions, massing all their strength, directed a fierce attack upon the northern wall of Antonia, the stronghold of John of Giscala.

Now this wall happened to stand upon that part which had been undermined by John at the time when the Romans made their former attack; and the hollow ground, weakened by the shaking caused by the battering-rams, gave way during the first night, hurling down a portion of the wall with all the sentinels upon it.

The Romans, startled from their sleep by the appalling crash and by the thrilling shrieks of the doomed victims, knew not at first what had happened, but when the morning light revealed the nature of the disaster, they grasped their weapons, clambered over the ruins, and poured through the breach.

But Antonia was not yet taken. John, exercising a military foresight that moved his enemies to surprise, if not to admiration, had previously raised a second wall within.

As it was impossible to advance the engines through the breach, the Romans, in order to overcome this new barrier, were compelled to resort to other means.

Having failed to surmount it by boldly climbing up in the very face of the enemy, they lay down at last at the foot of the wall, and, forming a testudo, or roof of shields, they sought to loosen with iron crows the lower courses of the masonry, a process attended with little hurt to the wall, but with considerable loss of life to the Romans.

Now Crispus, having taken due note that a certain part of this wall declined backwards, and that the stones at this said part projected in such a manner as to afford some slight foothold, resolved to attempt a nocturnal surprise on his own account. At the dead of night he assembled fifteen of his bravest troops, including a trumpeter and an eagle-bearer.

Creeping forward with soundless tread, the little band, favored by the gloom, gained the foot of the wall unseen by the Jewish sentinels above. Then Crispus silently and cautiously began the ascent; his men followed like a file of grim specters. One javelin hurled from above would have sufficed to send the whole party thundering down. No such disaster occurred, however. Whether the sentinels were sleeping, or whether they were keeping careless watch, is a matter that will never be known: certain it is that the heroic sixteen safely gained the top of the wall.

A whispered word from Crispus, and then on the still night air the trumpet rang out the call to arms; long, shrill, and piercing, the summons startled the Romans from sleep; it startled still more the Jewish sentinels close at hand. Even now it would have been a comparatively easy matter to repel the attack; but, as Crispus and his party, their lifted blades glinting through the gloom, dashed forward with a mighty shout, the Zealot sentinels, without waiting to ascertain the number of their assailants, turned tail and fled, fully convinced that the whole of the Roman army was pouring over the battlements.

Their shouts awoke their fellows. Roused thus in the dead of night the entire garrison became the victims of one of those panics which have been known to fall sometimes upon even the hardiest veterans. From above, from below, from every hall and chamber, there came running wild-eyed Zealots, whose only object was to save their lives; in mad confusion they made for the south side of the fortress, where lay the only available exit—a narrow causeway over the deep ravine that separated Antonia from the temple.

Meantime, Titus and the rest of the Romans in the camp, guided by the continuous pealing of the trumpet, hurried forward, scaled the wall, and found to their surprise and delight that the enemy had vacated the fortress without striking a blow.

Now the surrender of Antonia had opened the way to the temple, and Crispus, thinking in one night and by the same stroke, to capture both places was pursuing the retreating Zealots across the connecting causeway.

But now the Zealots, cursing themselves for their cowardly folly, turned and made a stand upon this same causeway.

Then began a battle, perhaps the fiercest and bloodiest in the whole course of the siege. Spears and javelins being useless, both sides drew their swords and fought it out hand to hand. In the gloom of night the troops of both parties were so intermingled that no man knew where he was; more often than not Roman slew Roman, and Jew slew Jew. Crispus, stunned by a blow on the head, was dragged forth from the fray by a faithful legionary.

With the dawn Simon came to the aid of his Zealot rival; and then indeed the fighting, and the shouting, and the clangor, grew fiercer and louder than ever. On that narrow viaduct there was no room either to advance or retreat; scores of the combatants were forced over the parapet, and shrieking, fell, to be dashed to pieces in the rocky ravine below. The passage became so crowded with dead that the living to get at each other were obliged to mount upon piles of bodies and of armor.

At last, when it became clear that the Romans could make no headway, Titus, after ten hours of this fighting, gave the signal for recall.

Thanks to Crispus, however, the great fortress of Antonia was now in Roman hands, and as Simon beheld the standard inscribed S.P.Q.R. floating proudly again from its lofty battlements, he wept tears of grief and rage, and cursed John to his face saying—somewhat unjustly—that none but a fool or a coward or a traitor could have lost such a stronghold.

Later that same day Rufus and Crispus stood on the battlements of Antonia; and of all the Romans, who more pleased than Rufus at finding himself once more in his old familiar fortress?

The two, looking down from their lofty position, watched the preparations that were being made for the defense of the temple. The marble courts and gilded pinnacles were assuming the appearance of a warlike citadel. Thousands of Zealots, under the direction of Simon and John, were hauling their huge military engines over the tesselated pavement, till the northern porticoes facing Antonia fairly bristled with balistæ and catapults. The clang of arms and the creaking of the machines, the shouting of men and the ceaseless hurrying hither and thither, made a scene difficult to reconcile with the belief that the place was the house of God.

"What is the day of the month?" asked Rufus, suddenly.

"The seventeenth of July," replied Crispus.

"I venture to prophesy that in the years to come the Jews—if there be any of them left after this war—will keep this day as a day of mourning."

"Why so?"

"The answer is to be found *there!*" remarked Rufus, pointing to the court of the priests. "It is the hour of the evening sacrifice," he continued, glancing at a sun-dial near by, "but where is the smoke ascending from the altar? 'Twas absent, too, this morning, so I am told. *The daily sacrifice hath ceased* for lack of victims. If I rightly foresee the fate of the temple, they made their last sacrifice yester even."

To the mind of the pagan Rufus the matter was one of little moment, but to Crispus, with his Christian way of thinking, this cessation of a sacrifice that had taken place twice a day for a space of thirteen hundred years was full of a profound significance; he knew that to the pious Hebrew, if not to the fighting Zealot, it must appear an event as grave almost as a stoppage in the progress of the universe, for had not the scribes said, "The world was made for the sake of the temple," and what was the temple without its sacrifices?

Titus, made aware of the event, sought to conciliate the religious sentiment of the foe by a very remarkable offer.

Josephus, covered by the shield of a legionary, walked along the causeway; and, halting in the middle, lifted up his voice, and addressed the Jewish people in the Hebrew tongue.

"Simon Bar-gioras and John of Giscala, hear now the words of Titus Cæsar. He hath a reverence for your temple, and would fain save it from the destruction which ye, by converting it into a citadel, are bringing upon it. If ye will remove your men of war, he will meet you in battle at Mount Zion or in whatever place you choose; he, too, will withdraw his arms from the temple, leaving it sacred and inviolate. And as a token of his good will towards you, he offers you this day a gift of threescore rams that ye may continue the daily sacrifice as heretofore."

"Ha! mark you that?" said Rufus to Crispus. "There speaks not Titus but Berenice."

There were among the Jewish people thousands that would gladly have seen the war removed from the temple and its precincts, but they were overawed by the Zealots, who, by the mouth of Simon, thus made answer:

"Titus, knowing that he cannot take the temple by force of arms, whereof the fight of this morning is a witness, speaks thus, hoping to lure us from our stronghold, that he may the more easily enter it. But in vain is the net spread in the sight of the bird. His threescore rams we will not take, for never shall it be said that the sacrifices to the Eternal One have become dependent upon the polluted offerings of an uncircumcized heathen. And to him and to the whole Roman empire do we offer an everlasting defiance. Now, renegade, carry back in thy detestable Greek or Latin the answer of Simon Bar-gioras."

This haughty reply, and especially its boastful note as to the fight on the causeway, so provoked Titus that he determined to make a second attempt that very night. As the whole army were unable to join in the assault owing to the narrowness of the approach, there were picked out from each century the thirty bravest and strongest men; tribunes were appointed over each thousand, and one Cerealis, an officer of rare valor, was chosen to command the whole. In the great hall of Antonia the storming party consecrated themselves, as it were, to the work by offering, under the presidency of Theomantes, a solemn sacrifice to Mars.

An hour before dawn Cerealis at the head of his men, advanced over the causeway with swift silent tread, but failed to effect a surprise. Simon, if not John, was on the alert. Then began a battle similar in all respects to that of the preceding night. After eight hours of desperate fighting the Romans had not gained a foot of ground, and the battle ceased, as it were, by mutual consent.

Now no more could the Romans boast that, man for man, they were superior to the Jews, when the picked soldiers of their army, the very flower of the legions, had suffered repulse at the hands of the Zealots.

The iron warriors, who had carried their eagles triumphantly over all nations from the Euphrates to the Atlantic, leaned moodily upon their spears, and stared up with dark and sullen faces at the laughing Zealots, who, clustering upon the roof of the northern cloisters, pointed with their swords at the causeway and mockingly asked the foe why they did not come into the temple.

"Give counsel what we shall do," said Titus to Tiberius Alexander.

"Raze Antonia to the ground, and with the materials fill up this intervening glen so as to make a broad level way, over which we may haul our engines to batter the northern cloisters."

Titus without delay adopted this suggestion.

The Roman soldiers, burning to retrieve their tarnished honor, had no sooner received the new command than they flew with ardor to its execution. All along the sky-line, on every tower, turret and battlement, were seen groups of men furnished with lever and crow, by whose means blocks of masonry were lifted up to be sent whirling and crashing into the valley below; far into the night the soldiers toiled by the ruddy glare of a thousand torches, and as the mighty fortress sank lower and lower so did the débris accumulated in the valley rise higher and higher.

The Zealots no longer mocked, but looked on in silent wonder at this display of almost superhuman energy. There was something sublime in this demolition of a magnificent citadel merely for the purpose of filling up a trench.

At last a broad and level way was successfully carried across the ravine right up to the very foot of the northern cloisters.

On the evening of the day that saw its completion Crispus, walking meditatively upon the crest of Olivet, came suddenly upon a figure standing solitary, silent, motionless. It was the woman who was steadfastly refusing to acknowledge herself as his wife, the Princess Berenice. Not far off, in the background, stood two attendants with a chariot. Evidently she had come to take a look, perhaps her last look, at her native city.

Crispus had leisure to observe her, for she was so wrapped in contemplation that she did not hear his tread.

Her face was pale, and anguish looked from her eyes as she surveyed the ruin wrought by man against his fellow-man.

The country, swept of all its timber to supply materials for the Roman banks and for camp fires, had lost all its sylvan charm and beauty.

To this denudation must be added the ravages of the Arabian and Syrian allies, who, haters of the Jews, had diffused their devastating frenzy so far around that, from the summit of Olivet, neither village nor house, neither tower nor wall, could be seen to break the dreary monotony of the landscape. So mournful a change had passed over the country that in the striking language of Josephus, "*Anyone that had previously known the place, coming on a sudden to it now, would have failed to recognize it!*"

It was a scene of utter desolation, a howling wilderness, made more awful by the light of the setting sun, which, half sunk below the horizon, shot a sinister red glare athwart the melancholy waste.

In all the wide extent of landscape there was no vestige of life or movement, save at one spot only, where the grim and ever-narrowing circle of fire and steel was slowly extinguishing the life of a once great nation.

Berenice set her eyes upon the city, or rather upon what was left of it. Was this the place that the Psalmist had called, " The joy of the whole earth "?

Gone was the suburb of Bezetha! Gone was the suburb of Acra! Gone was the citadel of Antonia! Zion and Ophel remained, but woefully wrecked and dilapidated; and the temple—shorn, alas! of its divine sacrifices—still rose as fair as ever, its marble porticoes and golden pinnacles dyed in the blood-red hues of sunset. But how long would it stand? Ah! there was her fear, and she pressed her hand to her throbbing heart.

Turning suddenly she caught sight of Crispus, and started. There was a proud trembling of her lip as if she were trying to subdue some emotion—anger probably—that was rising to the surface.

"So it was *you*," said she, taking no notice of his greeting, "who prevented my weekly gift of rams from reaching the temple?"

"Nay, it was Tiberius Alexander, though I freely admit that his deed has my approval."

"Why so?"

"The Law, princess, was but a shadow of things to come. There is now no need for typical sacrifices when the True Sacrifice has been offered, once and for all. And since the Jew refuses to acknowledge the temporal character of the Law, there is but one way of teaching him the lesson—a stern and terrible way!"

It is doubtful whether Berenice, not being versed in Pauline theology, quite comprehended the import of these words; at any rate, she did not reply to them.

"They tell me you are great at slaughter," she said, with a sort of sneer, "and that, as being the first to mount the battlements of Antonia, you have gained a Mural Crown. And now, grown more bold, you seek to take God himself captive."

"Princess, you talk as do the heathen. The Most High dwelleth not in temples made with hands."

"Yet your master Paul was wont to worship in yon edifice."

"I doubt whether he would do so to-day, were he living, seeing that there is now no holiness in yon temple. The spirit of true religion has fled from the place. The high priest Phannias is a village rustic, unlawfully chosen by lot, so ignorant that he knows not how to perform the duties of his office. The temple has become a slaughter-house, reeking with innocent blood shed by the wicked Zealots, who have held therein mock trials of the rich, condemning them to death that they may seize upon their wealth. The place is no longer a temple but a citadel. The holy vessels have been melted down to form instruments of war. Assassins pile their arms around the altar, and revelers make themselves drunk in the Sanctuary. It were a shame to speak of the things that have been done there. John's men, tricked out in feminine garb, have imitated the infamies of the guilty Cities of the Plain. And you would bid us deal tenderly with this place, forsooth!

Nay, verily, its stones cry out for the avenging, purifying fire of heaven."

"Or the flaming torch of Crispus," sneered Berenice. "You think to see the temple destroyed, but it shall not be so. Titus has pledged me his solemn word to preserve it."

"Titus may promise what he will; he cannot overturn the counsels of the Most High."

"Whose instrument you deem yourself to be," returned Berenice, disdainfully. "I know the secret thought of your heart. A vision sent, not as you vainly think by God, but by Beelzebub, the prince of the devils, is luring you on to a wicked deed. You have desired to take part in the siege for this end only, that when the attack on the temple shall begin you may be able in the confusion to apply an incendiary torch. Do so, and the act shall bring death upon her whom you hold most dear."

"And who is that?" asked Crispus quickly.

"Vashti, who, instead of being safe at Pella, as you intended her to be, is a captive at my mercy—my slave to do with as I list. Your act in bringing her forth from Jerusalem has had this result only—to deliver her into my hands the sooner."

Though Crispus tried to receive this startling news with outward calmness, something of the fear felt by him looked from his eyes, and drew a triumphant smile from Berenice.

Mistress of Vashti, she was mistress of his action, so she thought, and his action must be the sparing of the temple.

"It was by accident I discovered that your Vashti was at Pella. Armed with the written authority granted me by Titus I immediately arrested my slave, and conveyed her to—to——"—No! she would keep the name of the place a secret—"to where you will not find her. Now, mark my words, Crispus Cestius Gallus. If by your hand yon temple burns, so too shall Vashti burn; she shall die, shrieking in a flaming vesture of pitch, even as the Christians died in the gardens of Nero."

"Princess, if yours be the heart of a woman, I am glad to possess the heart of a man."

Berenice laughed, a cold, hard laugh.

"I care not how vile I be in your sight so long as I can but save the temple. Retire this night from the army—Titus will permit it—have no more to do with the siege, and I will set Vashti at liberty. What is your answer?"

"This. Your threat supplies an additional argument for the destruction of the temple, since it is clear that its dead ritual and external formalities have no power to purify the heart or quicken the conscience. As to your menace against Vashti, forget not that it is written, 'Whoso sheddeth man's blood, by man shall his blood be shed.'"

Berenice laughed scornfully.

"Who will venture to punish a princess and the friend of Titus merely for putting her own slave to death?"

"The Christians."

"The Christians!" repeated Berenice, disdainfully.

"I have said it, princess. If Vashti dies, you die also. Trust not to the power of Titus to save you. There are in yon army Christians who, in the execution of what they deem to be right, fear neither kings nor Cæsars. You shall be secretly seized and carried off to a conclave of Christians there to be judged of the deed by your own Law, which has said: 'Eye for eye, tooth for tooth, burning for burning'; Berenice's death for Vashti's death. If you are found guilty, be sure of this, princess, *they'll not lack an executioner!*"

As Berenice beheld the set, stern look on his face, she had no need to ask who that executioner would be.

Without another word he turned and left her.

She had sought to frighten him, but it was *she* who

was the frightened one. She stood in fear and trembling, knowing that her threat instead of acting as a deterrent had but made him the more resolved to carry out his purpose.

Next day the toiling legions pushing forward their military engines directed a fierce attack along the line of cloisters—more than a thousand feet in length—that formed the northern side of the great temple-platform.

Now that the battle had reached the very seat of their religion the Jews fought with a fury they had never before shown; the priests themselves were under arms, rivaling the Zealots in deeds of valor; Simon, with bare arm and flashing scimitar, was seen at every point along the line, urging on to fresh exertions men who required but little urging.

Let Jewish valor do what it would, however, it could not prevail; each day marked an advance on the part of the Romans, who at last became masters of the whole northern gallery, which they proceeded at once to destroy by fire, ax, and crow, in order to facilitate the advance of the battering-train.

The victors had now gained the summit of the lofty temple-platform, a vast square open to the sky save at the sides which were adorned with cloisters. In the midst of this square towered the Sanctuary or temple proper, a structure 360 feet in length and 270 in breadth. Its exterior wall, formed of gigantic blocks of marble, and nearly 40 feet in height, was pierced by nine gateways, there being three upon each side save the western, that side being without gates.

It was within this fortress—for such it was—that the defeated Jews had taken refuge, and here they prepared to make their final, and, as they believed, triumphal stand.

Strange and incredible fact!

In spite of their numerous defeats, hope was stronger than ever in the breast of the Jews, who still dreamed of seeing the scepter of empire transferred from the Capitol to Zion. They were fully convinced that the temple which God Himself had ordered to be built could never be trodden by the foot of pagan conqueror. The deity would be certain to work a miracle in their favor; at the least, something would happen to astonish and disperse the enemy. And they talked of Sennacherib and the burning simoon, but forgot Nebuchadnezzar and the Chaldeans.

And now the sacred precincts of the temple echoed with the clang of horse-hoofs. Roman cavalry clattered on the marble pavement of the Court of the Gentiles, and with leveled spears swept round and round the Sanctuary, driving in every sortie made from the gates, and acting as a cover to the Roman infantry, who, with tremendous toil and difficulty, were hauling along a train of battering-rams.

The Sanctuary was surrounded by a low balustrade, bearing tablets—one has survived to the present time—inscribed in Greek and Latin letters with notices prohibiting the Gentiles on pain of death from entering the edifice—notices that evoked the mocking laughter of the Roman soldiery as they set their engines in array against the building.

The " middle wall of partition," which the Law had set up betwixt Jew and Gentile, was now breaking down in no figurative sense!

The temple-platform had a circuit so ample as to contain within it a synagogue, and it was from the roof of this structure, as from a throne, that Titus directed the military operations against the Sanctuary.

It was not without an expectant thrill that the Jews awaited Titus' signal for the assault, there being a half belief among them that fire from heaven would descend upon the impious band that first ventured to swing a beam against the sacred wall of God's house; and therefore something like a sigh of disappointment went up when nothing marvelous followed upon the first stroke of the ram.

Relying upon the strength of the masonry the Jews did little fighting, content to watch amid laughter and gibes the futile labors of the enemy.

For six days the battering-rams swung, and thundered, and pounded against the walls of the Sanctuary; yet not a stone was pushed from its place, so marvelously compacted was the masonry.

"Bring scaling-ladders and storm the walls!" cried Titus on the seventh day.

The legionaries, relinquishing the battering-rams, flew to execute this new order.

The Jews made no resistance to the Romans while mounting, but as soon as each man had reached the top, they either hurled him down headlong or slew him before he had time to cover himself with his shield.

Now here, and now there, a ladder crowded with ascending legionaries, would be toppled backwards and the men dashed to pieces upon the marble pavement.

The fierce shouts of the active combatants intermingled with the cries and groans of the wounded and the dying.

After two hours of this deadly game there came a lull. Despairing of taking the place by escalade the Romans withdrew to a distance, and stared up in moody silence at the Zealots, who, brandishing their weapons, shouted, "Ye cannot take this place; it is the abode of God."

The superstitious legionaries were beginning to think the same. They no longer laughed at the words, "Let no Gentile enter here on pain of death." The dead and dying strewn around on the pavement were a significant commentary on that interdict.

Vainly did the trumpets peal out a call to renew the charge. Not a man would move.

## Closing In

Titus sought to stimulate their courage by a new expedient. Pointing to that part of the wall where stood the Zealot chief, he shouted:

"Ten thousand gold pieces to the man who brings me Simon's head."

No one seemed willing to earn this rich reward.

Simon laughed.

"Titus knows my value. Now to him who brings me the head of Titus I shall give ten shekels only, it not being worth more."

Suddenly a standard-bearer, darting forward, mounted a ladder, and when three-fourths of the way up, he deliberately flung the eagle into the midst of the foe, crying as he waved his sword, "Romans, will you see your standard taken by the enemy? Follow me."

Lose an eagle? Never!

Amid a wild, shrill clangor of trumpets, the legionaries, with the flame of battle in their blood, swept forward, wave upon wave, determined this time to carry the fortress. But, alas! for them, this attack fared no better than the others. The bold standard-bearer was struck down; those following him were either slain or repulsed; and the eagle remained in the hands of the foe.

Simon viewed the idolatrous image with loathing.

"An abomination brought into the place where it ought not to be," said he. "Bring ax and hammer."

And with his own strong arm he hewed the golden eagle to pieces, and cast them down at the feet of the Romans contemptuously, crying: "Behold your god!"

If a yell could have brought down the walls of the Sanctuary they would most assuredly have fallen at that moment before the terrific yell of concentrated hatred and fury that burst from the Romans, when they beheld the destruction of what was to them not merely a patriotic emblem but a darling object of worship, a worship far more real and fervent than they ever paid to Jove or Mars!

Simon's studied affront goaded Titus to a course from which he had hitherto refrained.

"*Fire the gates!*" he cried.

To this command the legionaries responded with a huge roar of delight. Vast quantities of timber were quickly brought and piled high against the metal-plated doors of the nine gateways.

Of these, the most splendid was the one facing the east, and known as the Corinthian Gate, for, whereas, the other doors were crusted all over with gold and silver, the eastern door was a marvel of richly chased Corinthian bronze.

It was Alexander, the wealthy Alabarch of Alexandria, who had adorned the gate in this fashion; and, by a singular turn of destiny, it was his apostate son Tiberius who wrought its destruction—a deed surprising to the Romans themselves, who could not but regard it as an act of filial impiety. With buckler held over his head to protect himself from the arrows that came whizzing obliquely from above, the ex-procurator of Judæa ascended the stately flight of fifteen stairs, and, with his own hand, applied a lighted torch to the pile of timber.

Nine huge fires were now smoking, and crackling, and flaming, and roaring, at the nine gates of the temple. As the metallic platings became red-hot the fire, carried to the woodwork behind, began to consume the entire gate.

The sight produced a strange and stupefying effect upon the Jews, who had never thought such an event to be possible; at one stroke their courage seemed to vanish; they made no attempt to quench the flames, but stood mute spectators of the scene.

It was Titus himself, who, not wishing the conflagration to extend too far, gave orders to fling water upon the burning gates; and when this had been done, the

## Closing In

besieged realized that their defense was all but at an end; the charred timber of the doors would yield at the first stroke of the battering-ram, and the enemy would enter by nine different ways.

"The day is far spent and the soldiers are faint," said Titus. "We will defer our final attack till the morrow."

With a view of cutting off the retreat of Simon and John, who might seek during the night to make their escape to Mount Zion, Titus caused a great part of his army to camp round about in the cloisters of the Court of the Gentiles.

Leaving Crispus and Rufus in charge of these forces Titus retired to Antonia, or rather to a corner of it that had been spared in the general demolition in order to furnish a lodging for himself and his chief officers.

And here, that same night, there sat that memorable council, assembled to decide the great question (as if it were in *their* power to decide!) whether the Jewish temple should be preserved or destroyed.

Tiberius Alexander was the first to speak; more pagan than the pagans themselves he brought forward several reasons, all tending to show that the existence of the temple was a menace to the safety of the empire. He ended with a religious argument:

"If you spare this edifice, O Cæsar, the Jews will boast that their God has put His fear in your heart and that you dare not destroy it. They will see in your leniency both a proof of the divine origin of their temple and an augury of its eternal existence; its preservation will more than ever convince them that they are the favorites of heaven, and are therefore under no obligation to obey an earthly power.

"It must be ours to show that Jupiter of the Capitol is supreme over Jehovah of Jerusalem.

"Two superstitions, equally fatal to the empire, depend for their existence upon yon temple, that of the Jews and that of the Christians!"[32] These two superstitions, although contrary to each other, have the same origin: the Christians come from the Jews; destroy the root, and the shoot will quickly perish. Wherefore," concluded he, with reminiscences of the psalms, " my counsel is, ' Down with it; down with it, even to the ground!' "

But Titus, secretly moved by his infatuation for Berenice, was, of course, disposed to take a milder view.

" We ought not," said he, " from hatred of our enemies to take revenge upon inanimate things. To burn so vast and splendid a fabric is to do hurt to ourselves, seeing that it is an ornament to our empire." [13]

And, perceiving on which side of the question the mind of their general lay a certain minority, who had been disposed to favor the views of Alexander, dropped their opposition.

" This, then, is our decree," said Titus solemnly, " and let the whole army know it—the temple shall be preserved."

He that sitteth in the heavens shall laugh; the Lord shall have them in derision!

For scarcely had Titus made an end of speaking when from without there came a cry, distant and faint; it was repeated in a louder key; caught up by a thousand tongues, alike by the startled Romans in the camp and by the terrified Jews in the city, the wild tidings came rolling louder, and ever louder, upon the night air, to the mockery and confusion of the military council:

" THE TEMPLE IS ON FIRE!"

# CHAPTER XXIV

## " WATCHMAN, WHAT OF THE NIGHT? "

NIGHT, still and beautiful, rested upon the temple-courts; in the immeasurable depths of a purple sky the stars were burning with the brilliancy peculiar to southern latitudes.

The battle-toil of the day had given place to a strange quiet; both sides seemed bent on taking rest as a preparation for the greater struggle of the morrow.

No sound came from the Sanctuary; its unseen sentinels moved with silent tread.

Within the circumjacent cloisters, and hidden by the shadows, lay the Roman troops, sleeping on their arms, yet ready at the first blast of the trumpet to spring into life and action.

Crispus and Rufus paced softly to and fro over the pavement of the Court of the Gentiles, seldom, if ever, removing their eyes from the Sanctuary, lest a sudden rush on the part of the enemy should take their troops by surprise.

Crispus was thinking of the fate of the Roman Capitol which, nine months previously, in the civil war between the Vespasians and the Vitellians, had been destroyed by fire.

Now the Capitol was the temple of sovereign Jupiter, and hence its fall had sent a profound sensation through the pagan world. It would be a fact more significant still, if, within the same year and by similar means, the great Jewish temple should fall. To minds intent on studying the signs of the times, the two events would seem as if foreshadowing the doom of two religions, that of heathendom, and that of Jewry.

And doomed they were! They had played their preparatory part in the history of human progress, and were now to give place to a loftier and more spiritual faith.

"Titus holds high council to-night," remarked Rufus, suddenly breaking in upon Crispus' thoughts. "He is for preserving the temple. Every man knows why. He is moved by love for the new Cleopatra. She and her brother Agrippa visited his quarters yesterday, and remained there for some time. We can guess what their talk was about. Now if this temple be permitted to stand, we shall continue to have the annual gatherings of treasonable Jews breathing defiance to Roman rule. The result will be another war, and we shall have all our work over again. And what a work it has been! Was there ever in all history a siege like this?"

"And it is by no means over yet," commented Crispus. "All our previous work will appear but as child's play when we come to deal with the taking of Zion."

"My fear, too," responded Rufus moodily. "This stubborn people, refusing to see that they are beaten, will go on fighting to the end. But as to this temple, my opinion is that since the Jews choose to turn it into a fortress it should be treated as such, and razed to the ground. If I were Titus," he added emphatically, "I would destroy both city and temple, exclude all Jews from Jndæa, and colonize it with Romans. Thus only shall we have peace."

Crispus fell into a reverie.

He had, when a pagan, seen reasons to wish the temple at an end, and now, as a Christian, he could add to his reasons.

It was thus that he argued within himself.

The existence of the temple was a perpetual affront to the living Christ, since its daily sacrifices were a tacit denial of the great fact that the True Sacrifice had been offered once and for all. With the death of Christ Judaism had come to an end, but what Jew would ever believe this until he saw that the God who had ordered the temple to be built now permitted it to be destroyed? Add to this, that the sure word of prophecy had said that the Messiah would come while the Second Temple was standing; if this—the Second Temple—should fall, it would be a proof to the Jewish nation that the Messiah *had* come—and gone!—and that those were wrong who looked for Him in the future.

Another point worth noting: so long as the temple stood—that temple in which the apostles themselves were wont to meet for worship—so long would there be on the part of Christianity a temptation to revert to the precepts and rites of the Law. As a matter of fact, in spite of all the writings and labors of Saint Paul to the contrary, a hybrid belief, a Christianized form of Judaism, the heresy called at a later day Ebionism, was already in existence, threatening the purity of the Church's faith. The development of Christianity required that it should be freed from the bondage of the Law, and how could that freedom be more effectively attained than by the fall of the edifice, which was, as it were, the actual embodiment of that Law?

Moreover, had not the Saviour said that some of His own generation should not taste of death till they had seen the fall of the temple? Forty years had now passed since that utterance. If its fall were delayed much longer, would not the Saviour appear as a false prophet? But, unless a miracle were going to happen, must not the destruction of the temple be brought about by human instrumentality? Why not by his own? Was it impious to imagine that he was the agent foreordained to carry out the Divine purpose?

He thought of the vision of the flaming torch, and of the Divine voice, crying, "*Burn!*" and he doubted no longer.

Rufus put the finishing touch to his determination by a significant remark.

"Now if Titus could be persuaded to destroy the temple, to-day would be an appropriate date for it."

"How so?"

"By the Jewish calendar to-day is the ninth of the month Ab. On this very day exactly 658 years ago the Chaldeans burnt the first temple."

The very date seemed to be inviting him to the deed!

Scarcely had this thought passed through his mind when Rufus exclaimed:

"Ah! what light is that? By the gods, a sortie!"

His remark was caused by the sight of an immense body of Jews, who, having opened one of the half-burned gates, were issuing noiselessly forth.

They were seen, however, not only by Crispus and Rufus, but by the vigilant Roman sentinels. Instantly, the shrill trumpet blast rang out the call to arms, and the legionaries, starting from sleep, grasped their weapons and stood ready for the conflict.

Heedless of the fact that they were discovered the Jews poured down the steps of the gateway and raced across the court towards the wooden synagogue, from whose roof Titus had directed his operations against the Sanctuary. They ran amid a blaze of light cast by torches, the object of the Jews being evidently to fire the synagogue in the hope of burning such of the enemy as lay sleeping within.

They failed in their purpose, however. Both from the nearer synagogue itself and from the more distant cloisters, the Romans poured forth with clanging buckler and flashing broadsword; a desperate hand-to-hand combat took place, lasting for a brief space only, inasmuch as the Zealots, seeing the number of their foes

Moved by a Divine impulse

increasing moment by moment, turned tail and fled, pursued by the shouting, triumphant legionaries.

Crispus and Rufus, who had taken an active part in the fray, joined also in the pursuit.

Suddenly, while Rufus ran on, Crispus stopped, attracted by the sight of a flaming torch dropped probably by a flying Zealot. Moved by some unaccountable prompting he picked it up, and as he did so he caught sight of something above that sent a strange thrill through him; all unconsciously he had checked his footsteps beneath the golden window of the room Gazith, that judgment-hall in which the Saviour of the world had received His sentence of condemnation at the mouth of the Sanhedrim.

Something light and cool stirred the hair of Crispus; it was a faint wind coming from the north, the very direction required to carry the flames throughout the building!

Let others regard these things as mere coincidences; to Crispus they were signs that the hour, long predestined, had come.

"Marcus," said he, stopping one of his own soldiers who was running past at that moment, "lift me up to yon window."

Without a word the man clasping his tribune's ankles, reared him aloft, and set his feet upon his own shoulders.

For a moment Crispus hesitated; then, as the historian of the event testifies, "MOVED BY A DIVINE IMPULSE," he thrust the flambeau through the golden lattices, and, having effectively kindled the woodwork of the interior, sprang to the ground again.

So little time had he taken that it was doubtful whether any other Roman besides Marcus had witnessed his act; certain it was that none of the Zealots suspected that there was kindling a fire whose flames were destined to sweep the temple from end to end.

Crispus glanced at the gate from which the Zealots

had issued but a few minutes previously; having retreated to it they were now endeavoring with might and main to stay the entering of the Romans.

He turned his eyes again to the golden window, and laughed to see that the light within was increasing in brightness; the whole room must soon be in a blaze, and the hall that had once reverberated with the unjust cry, " He is guilty of death," would be the first of the temple-chambers to perish.

As yet no one either within or without the building seemed to be aware of what was going on; so much the better! the fire would gain such a hold that human efforts must fail to extinguish it.

The room above the hall Gazith was now burning, burning with a hidden glow. Then, all in a moment, with a snap and a crackle, there leaped skywards a dazzling sheet of flame accompanied by a wave of black smoke and a fierce shower of red sparks that, carried by the northern wind, swept southwards over the Sanctuary.

That startling glare, lighting up the dusk of night with the sudden brightness of noontide, caused the fighting at the gate to cease for a moment; Roman and Zealot alike turned their eyes to ascertain the cause.

A moment afterwards there ran through the length and breadth of the Sanctuary one thrilling simultaneous shout:

" *The temple is on fire!* "

By this time the whole Roman force that had lain within the cloisters had gathered round the Sanctuary. Their feeling was one of dismay, for the fire was destroying their hopes of plunder. Behind those walls there lay stores of wealth greater far than were ever contained in the palace of the Cæsars; the gold and silver utensils used in the sacrifices; the rich offerings —accumulations of centuries—made by pious Jews throughout the world; the jeweled vestments of the priests; the hoards of costly spices; the countless shekels plundered from the citizens by the Zealots.

For several days previously the Roman soldiery had talked of little else but the temple-treasures with which they were hoping to enrich themselves as a recompense after their many weeks of toil.

And now must they lose their reward?

If they should wait till the morning, the time fixed by Titus for the final assault upon the Sanctuary, the riches would be consumed. Why tarry?

A moment they stood, irresolute, murmuring; then, with a simultaneous shout, "On to the gold of the temple!" each soldier firmly grasping blade and shield, and disregarding the remonstrations of his officer, rushed forward to whichever gate of the nine happened to be nearest.

The Zealots, massed in dense bodies at each entrance, fought with fanatical fury, animated by no other desire than that of revenging themselves upon their enemies and of perishing amid the blazing ruins of the temple.

Those Romans who attacked the great Corinthian Gate were the first to fight their way in. Headed by Terentius Rufus, who, finding himself unable to check his men, determined to lead them, they entered the quadrangle known as the Court of the Women, so called because thus far women might enter to worship, but not farther.

This court contained, among other things, the twelve chests with funnel-shaped openings into which pious Jews were wont to drop their free-will offerings.

While some of the Romans were breaking open these treasury boxes and others were dispersing into the chambers around in search of plunder, a third and more numerous party, led by Rufus, continued the fight, driving the Zealots before them across the Court of the Women, and up the semicircular ascent of twelve stairs that fronted the great brazen gate of Nicanor, which led to the inner court, or Court of Israel. Twining around the sides and above the entablature of this entrance was an object attractive to the eyes of plunderers—the celebrated vine whose branches, leaves, and grape-clusters were all of pure gold.

"Close the gate!" shouted Simon.

Vain the command!

Like some moving wall of bronze, buckler touching buckler, the front rank of the legionaries pushed its way forward inch by inch up the stairs and into the interior court.

"Way there for Cæsar!" shouted Rufus as, standing on the topmost of the twelve stairs, he caught sight of Titus, who, surrounded by his chief officers, was seeking to clear a path through the throng of surging, shouting Romans.

Consternation was written on the face of Titus. Though not troubling to communicate the fact to his council, he had pledged his word both to Berenice and to Agrippa that the temple should be preserved; and now, to his confusion, there was fast spreading along the northern cloister of the Sanctuary a fire that, unless immediately checked, would consume the whole edifice.

Many of the soldiers, possessed by the frenzy for destruction that is apt to come upon man at such wild times, were helping to spread the conflagration by hurling lighted joists into the surrounding chambers and cloisters.

Standing on the stairs of the Nicanor Gate so that he might the more plainly be seen, Titus, shouting his loudest and making signals with his hand, gave orders to the soldiers to extinguish the fire.

But so great was the roaring of the flames and the din of the combat that few could hear him, and those that did affected not to understand, but went on with the double work of carnage and plunder.

"'Tis useless to restrain them," said Tiberius Alexander. "They are drunk with delight at having come as they think to the end of their labors. Discipline is at an end for this night at least. The soldier will acknowledge no master but his own will."

"Must we let the temple burn to the ground?" asked Titus in despair.

Alexander shrugged his shoulders. Secretly he was not at all displeased by the turn events were taking.

"Let us try at least to save the Golden House," said Titus, commanding his bodyguard to open a way for him into the inner court.

The Sanctuary formed a series of terraces, and upon the highest of all, within the Court of the Priests, stood the world-famed Golden House—the shrine containing the Holy Place and the Holy of Holies—now lovely in the firelight and flashing with a splendor that dazzled the eyes.

Driven from all other parts of the Sanctuary the Zealots gathered about this golden shrine, determined that it should not be profaned by the foot of the heathen Gentile.

The triumphant Romans followed to the attack, and a desperate fight ensued.

Sword in hand the furious Zealots fell by hundreds, and at last Simon and John, seeing that all was lost, massed the survivors at one point, and charging at their head, succeeded in cutting their way through the Roman ranks out into the Court of the Gentiles, and thence by the bridge that spanned the Tyropæon they made their way into the Upper City.

The flight of the Zealots was followed by a terrible carnage around the great brazen altar of sacrifice, a sort of truncated pyramid, forty-eight feet square at the base, standing directly in front of the Golden House. Hither, upon the first entering of the Romans, had fled a helpless, trembling crowd of children, women, and aged men, thinking that the sanctity of the spot would stay the sword of the conqueror.

Vain hope! The foe, made cruel by the long duration of the siege, stabbed and slew without distinction of age or sex; the bodies of the dead lay piled like hecatombs upon the sacrificial altar; upon the pavement around the red blood spread in a quickly widening circle, till, reaching the marble stairs, it rolled in sullen streams into the courts below.

Though isolated groups of desperate Jews continued here and there to fight Titus was now practically master of the temple, but the victory gave him little pleasure when he noticed the progress made by the fire, which, fanned by the wind, had reached one end of the northern cloister, and, having turned the angle, was now fast advancing along the western cloister, and would soon be on a line parallel with the western wall of the Golden House; true, a space separated the cloister from the shrine, but the space was, perhaps, not too wide for the flames to leap across; already sparks and fragments of fiery matter, floated by the wind, were beginning to patter upon the fretted and pinnacled roof.

Moved by Titus' look of despair, Alexander put forth a suggestion.

" We can perhaps preserve it by drenching its roof with water."

" But whence the water? "

" There is a draw-well on the southern side of the Sanctuary."

Springing upon one of the many marble tables where sacrificial victims were laid prior to their being offered upon the brazen altar, Titus, trying to make his voice heard above the noise of fire and vociferation, shouted that the soldiers should bring water for the preserving of the Golden House.

But none would put hand to the work, for the sides and western end of this house were set about with treasury vaults, and the fool who spent his time like a slave in fetching water would lose the chance of enriching himself.

"Urge them to the work, Liberalis!" cried Titus, addressing a centurion. "Threaten them! Strike them with your staff!"

Liberalis did so, but all in vain; respect for Cæsar gave way to the insatiable desire for plunder.

"Let us see the interior of the Golden House, ere it perish forever," said Alexander.

Speaking thus, he led the way; Titus and his staff followed, walking ankle-deep in blood.

Entering the Propyleon, a magnificent porch with wings on each hand extending far beyond the width of the shrine, they stood before the great golden gate, and found it barred from within.

"'Twill require a battering-ram to force it," said Titus, hesitating at such a measure. There came into his mind tales told him by Berenice of Gentiles who had fallen dead for profaning a place sacred to the Jewish priesthood only.

"There is a little wicket at the side by which the priest enters to unbar the door in the morning," said Alexander. "The noble Agrippa will perhaps lead the way?" he added, addressing that king, who stood beside Titus.

But Agrippa declined the honor.

"Nay, I'll give thee the precedency," he answered.

"Thy face is pale, Agrippa. Thou fearest," sneered Alexander.

What no orthodox Jew durst do, and what even the Roman hesitated at, was done by the apostate Alexander.

Putting his shoulder to the little wicket he forced it wide, passed boldly within, and, having first drawn aside the Babylonian curtain, he unbarred the double doors, and flung open the Holy Place to the profane gaze of the Romans, who saw what they had never before seen, what no man would ever see again.

A low murmur of admiration broke from Titus and his staff at the beauty of the golden interior all radiant in the wild light of the leaping flames.

On the right or north side was seen the golden table, but without the twelve loaves of shewbread; on the left the seven-branched golden candlestick, unlighted; at the far end rose the golden altar of incense, standing in front of the solemn " veil," a curtain of linen finely twined; in color an admirable mingling of blue, and scarlet, and purple, and wrought in golden thread with the figures of cherubim.

" Let these things be brought forth and kept against the day of my triumph," said Titus.

Emboldened by the example of Alexander he passed into the Holy Place and came to the veil that hung at its far end.

This Alexander lifted, and Titus gazed with curious eye upon the Holy of Holies, the place where the Shechinah had once dwelt. But the Divine Presence had long since departed; the place was empty save for an oblong stone upon which rested a golden ark with two golden cherubim, one on each side, having their faces bent downwards and their wings expanded. The stone itself was not without interest, seeing that, in Hebrew opinion, it marked the very center of the earth's surface.

Directing that the ark and the cherubim, with the other sacred furniture, should be carried to his own quarters, Titus came forth again.

The imagination of Dante could scarcely conceive a scene more wild and weird than that now taking place.

A wind blowing from the north carried into the temple-courts whirling clouds of smoke and intermittent gusts of heat that came and went like the breath of a fiery furnace.

Amid the roaring of the flames could be heard the shrieks of victims cut off from escape, intermingled with the crackling of cedar roofs and the crash of falling masonry.

The shouting legionaries, fierce with the lust for gold, were running hither and thither like madmen, ransacking first this chamber and then that. Here and there some priest, detected in hiding, would find himself surrounded by fierce-eyed soldiers, and with the keen edge of a sword laid across his windpipe, he would be addressed with the cry, " Show us gold, and you shall live!" And wild were scenes that occurred when some new vault was discovered glittering with treasure, the plunderers trampling each other down in their eagerness to be first at the spoil.

On all sides were to be seen men carrying off vessels of gold and silver, ingots of the same precious metals, bags of shekels, jewel-hilted weapons, myrrhine vases, caskets of ivory, ebony, and alabaster filled with spices, ointments, and perfumes, costly vestments, and ten thousand other objects of spoil. Never in all the world's history did riches so vast fall to the lot of a conquering army as fell to those who plundered the temple—riches that were destined within a week to send down the price of gold in the markets of Syria to one-half of its former value!

The attention of Titus was attracted by two men who were dragging along a heavy cedar chest which they had just rescued from the flames; but on breaking it open, they found within, not gold, as they had hoped, but books merely—historic writings, temple records, genealogical rolls, and the like. In their disappointment the two were about to set fire to the whole, but were checked by Titus.

"Hold! Let these be kept for Josephus. I doubt not that he will esteem them more highly than gold. Carry this chest to my tent."

But though Titus might save the sacred books of the temple, the Golden House he could not save.

Unperceived by him a soldier, moved by a frenzy to

destroy, held a lighted torch between the hinges of the golden door; a flame sprang up which, from lack of water to quench it, spread rapidly over the whole, a sight viewed with satisfaction by the soldiery.

" Where is now the God of the Jews? " they cried.

Numerous figures, clad in priestly vestments, now appeared upon the burning roof.

" Who are these? " asked Titus.

" Priests," replied Alexander, " forced by the heat from the secret chambers, of which there are many about the Golden House."

" Surrender, and your lives shall be spared," shouted Titus.

But to this invitation the priests replied by a flood of curses. Wrenching from the roof the gilded spikes, with their leaden sockets, they hurled them as missiles against the foe.

The eddying flames, the blinding smoke, the overpowering heat, now forced Titus and every other Roman, not only from the vicinity of the Golden House, but from the Sanctuary itself; for the outer circle of fire, having traversed both the western and eastern cloisters, had now seized upon the southern side, threatening to cut off the retreat of all who lingered within.

As there was still abundant pillage left, the soldiers quitted the burning building with reluctance; some lingering too long were overtaken by the flames, and did not quit it at all, while others by their scorched clothing, singed eyebrows, and half-burnt beards showed how narrowly they had escaped death.

Withdrawing to a safe distance Titus and his staff continued to watch the appalling spectacle, the like of which they had not seen since the burning of Rome by Nero.

" The whole summit of the hill blazed like a volcano. One after another the buildings fell in with a tremendous crash, and were swallowed up in the fiery abyss. The roofs of cedar were like sheets of flame; the gilded pinnacles shone like spikes of red light. The gate towers sent up tall columns of flame and smoke."

But if it were an appalling spectacle to the Roman what was it to the Jew?

All along the northern ramparts of Mount Zion was gathered a vast multitude (for though myriads had died of famine, there were still myriads left)—a countless host of gaunt, famishing specters, who looked fearfully into each other's eyes as if asking whether what they saw could be real.

Must they let go the great hope that had so long sustained them? During the space of four years, ever since the outbreak of the war, they had lived in hope of the immediate advent of the Messiah, who should overturn the empire of the wicked Romans and establish a glorious kingdom for Israel.

And this was the end of it all—to know that the fiery star in the sky had been but mocking them all this time; to learn that their own Jehovah had taken the side of the heathen enemy! to see the temple, which they had supposed eternal, sinking in the flames! to be so near the realization of the grandest of visions, and to be forced to renounce it when their tutelary angel had already partially withdrawn the cloud! to be compelled to accept the soul-shaking alternative that either their holy scriptures had lied in stating that the Messiah should come during the time of the Second Temple, or that He must have already appeared, only to be rejected by them! to see all their bright hopes vanish into space! Was ever nation so fearfully deceived as this nation?

They gazed again and again in doubt and bewilderment; and when, at last, they were forced to realize that the temple was actually blazing, and that angelic powers would NOT descend from the skies to help them, there pealed forth into the infinity of night long shrieks, terrible in their pathos and despair; the shrieks of a dying nation; shrieks so piercingly loud that they were echoed and re-echoed from all the hills that surrounded the city.

Slowly the leaping flames sank and died out, to be followed here and there by intermittent flashes and flickerings; and then, at last, the darkness of night fell over the smoking, smoldering, blackened ruins.

Three centuries later the heathen emperor Julian, resolving to show that Christ was a false prophet, called upon the Jews to rebuild their temple.

The supernatural circumstances attending the defeat of this project on the part of him, whose last, dying cry was, "Thou hast conquered, O Galilæan!" are attested alike by pagan and by Christian writer. The lesson of history is clear: THE ABOLITION OF THE TEMPLE WAS THE ACT OF GOD!

# CHAPTER XXV

## " JUDÆA CAPTA!"

THUS was the temple burnt, and when Titus learned —for the matter was secretly reported to him—whose was the hand that had kindled the first flame, he swore by all his gods that Crispus should suffer death; and, in so resolving, he tried to think that he was actuated by a spirit of justice, and not by the wish of removing one who was a hindrance to his union with Berenice. That princess had often spoken of Crispus' purpose as touching the temple, but at her fears Titus had laughed, never thinking that Crispus would so far transcend all rules of military discipline as to dare to fire a magnificent edifice without due orders from his commander-in-chief. But Crispus *had* dared so to act, and fiercely did Titus express his wrath to those of his officers with whom he breakfasted next morning.

Tiberius Alexander tried to placate his angry chief.

"What command did Crispus disobey? He fired the building ere he learned of your decree."

"Is Crispus, forsooth, commander-in-chief? By whose orders did he act?"

"By those of the immortal gods, I verily believe," replied Alexander. "Josephus, whom you regard so highly, will tell you that it is the Divine will that the temple should perish. Crispus could not resist his destiny. It was fated that he should so act."

"Very like. And 'twas fated, too, that I should behead him."

Alexander's face darkened.

"By so treating the bravest soldier in your army you will incense the legions to the verge of mutiny."

"Be that as it may," retorted Titus, frowning, for he well knew that there was truth in what the other had said.

"And you will lose my services, for I shall immediately return to Alexandria."

"And I shall resign my tribuneship," said Rufus.

"And I!"—"And I!" came from many others.

As he beheld the stern faces of his staff Titus saw the imperative necessity of revoking his too hasty judgment upon Crispus. He could not afford to lose his bravest officers with that terrible stronghold of Zion—the goal of all his labors—still untaken. Moreover, there was Vespasian to think of; he would not be pleased at the execution of one for whom he had always entertained a fatherly affection.

"Summon Crispus to our presence," said he moodily, addressing a centurion.

The messenger departed, and presently returned with a grave face. Crispus, it seemed, had been carried forth from the previous night's battle so slashed with wounds that his recovery was a matter of doubt.

"He was endeavoring," stated the centurion, "to save from slaughter an aged widow, named Miriam, who had taken refuge at the altar—an action on his part that so incensed some of those Syrian allies who, if Cæsar will pardon me for saying it, are the curse of our army, that they dared to turn their arms against him—a Roman tribune!"

"By Castor, if he can point them out, they shall be crucified!" exclaimed Titus. "Well, since he cannot come to me, I must go to him. O, fear not, brave captains," he added, observing their dubious looks, "my resentment is over. You have my word for it that Crispus shall come to no hurt through me."

So saying, he followed the centurion, and came to the castellum, or fort, where upon a pallet lay Crispus, swathed in bandages, and looking more dead than alive.

The sight of the pallid figure disarmed all Titus' anger, and in sympathetic tones he expressed his sorrow at seeing Crispus in such state.

"It is better thus," said Crispus, believing his end to be at hand. "Berenice will be free."

"Now by the gods!" exclaimed Titus, his better nature flashing out, "a plague on these women who set friend and friend at variance. If Berenice is to be won only at the cost of your life, may she never be won, say I. But as to this matter, do you know that Berenice denies that she was the veiled lady of Bethtamar?"

"But you do not believe her?"

Titus' silence would seem to show that he was of the same opinion as Crispus.

He spoke a few more cheering words, and then took his departure. Making his way to the ruins of the temple, he was hailed with loud cries of "*Ave, Imperator!*" by the soldiery, who, assembled before the blackened eastern gate, were offering incense and prayers to the eagles, the gods that, in their superstitious fancy, had given them the victory.

"'Imperator!'" said Titus scornfully, recalling their disobedience of the previous night. "Very much imperator, when ye let the temple burn contrary to my will."

It was customary among the Roman troops to honor the victorious general with a new title drawn from the name of the people subdued by him—Scipio *Africanus* and Metellus *Creticus* are cases in point—but when some of the soldiery proceeded further to salute Titus with the epithet "*Judaicus*," he sternly forbade them to use an appellation that he knew would be a perpetual reminder to Berenice of the fall of her nation.

Though the ordinary soldier was left to cure his wounds as best he might, with the aid of his sympathizing comrades, Titus himself was attended in this campaign by a Greek physician, whom he now sent to watch over Crispus, and great was the satisfaction throughout the camp when it became known that the state of the patient was such as to afford good ground for hope.

A week later Titus, when paying a second visit to Crispus, dwelt again on the subject of Berenice.

"No man," said he, "would risk his life, as you did, in rescuing a damsel from a beleaguered city—you see I know the story—unless he were madly enamored of her. Since your heart is set, not upon Berenice but upon this Vashti, what is to prevent you from repudiating the one and taking the other?"

"Firstly, I have not said that my heart *is* set upon Vashti; secondly, even if it were so, my Christian creed forbids me acting in the way your prescribe. With Christians marriage is a perpetual obligation."

"Crispus, don't deny it; you love this Vashti, and yet you are going to allow your foolish religion—for such must I call it—to stand in the way of your desires. But I doubt whether you fully understand your own creed. I have been conversing with some of your faith, for it appears that you are not the only Christian in our army, and their saying is that if a wife takes a lover, her husband is justified in obtaining a divorce. It is Berenice's intention," added Titus significantly, " to supply you with the grounds for one."

In his pagan days Crispus would have readily availed himself of this way of escaping from a union that was hateful to him, but being no longer a pagan, he would not consent to Berenice's doing evil that thereby good might come to him.

"Cæsar," said he, "I will be no party to this scheme, which I look upon as an infamous one. Nay, more; if you so act, I will have justice upon you. Forget not the oath of your sire, Vespasian, that he would hang the man who takes my wife from me, though that man were his own son. Do this thing, and I will accuse you at the foot of the imperial throne, and demand that he keep his word."

Titus laughed pleasantly.

"I'll take the risk," said he.

And with that he withdrew, bent on fulfilling his purpose, as Crispus was equally bent on fulfilling his.

Among others that visited Crispus during his illness was Josephus, who, as intending to write a history of the war, was naturally desirous of obtaining all the information he could respecting the burning of the temple.

Crispus complied with this request, but as he had no particular desire for worldly fame, he added:

"Keep my name out of the history."

"Is it possible," smiled Josephus, "in view of your great deeds?"

"Quite possible. You can allude to me as 'a certain captain tribune,' or 'one of the soldiers.'" And then, turning to a matter of far more interest to him than future fame, he said, "Do you know that your ward Vashti is a slave in the household of the Princess Berenice?"

"Yea, I know it," said Josephus with a queer smile, the meaning of which was not at all apparent to Crispus, "and I am this day setting off for Cæsarea, carrying to the princess a letter from Titus enjoining her to deal tenderly with my ward."

"That is good, but it would be better were he sending an order that she must be set at liberty. However, that will perhaps come in time," he continued, resolving to petition Vespasian on behalf of Vashti. "But let me not delay you. Go, and heaven prosper your mission."

Crispus had ordered that his bed should be placed by a window from which he could watch the preparations that were being made to storm Mount Zion, where the implacable Zealots were making their last stand. With the capture of that stronghold, the long siege would be brought to an end.

Titus had offered, by the mouth of Josephus, to spare the lives of all the insurgents on the condition of instant surrender. But Simon and John still talked big. They demanded a free passage for themselves and their followers, together with their wives and children, promising to depart to some far-off spot in the wilderness. Titus rejected these terms, and in his anger vowed to slay every man, woman, and child, and to level the city to the ground.

Then did Crispus rejoice that Vashti was delivered from the possibility of such doom.

The Roman banks were completed in eighteen days, and on the nineteenth morning Titus began his attack upon the northern wall of Zion.

Even now it was within the power of the Zealots to prolong the siege for many weeks in virtue of their almost impregnable position in those three magnificent fortresses, Hippicus, Phasaelus, and Mariamne. But the steady and triumphant progress of the Roman arms through the suburb of Bezetha and the suburb of Acra, over the ruins of Antonia and the ruins of the temple, had put a secret fear into the heart of the Zealots, so that as soon as they heard the terrible rams swinging and pounding against the walls of Zion they quitted their fortifications, and fled. Some sought the catacombs with which the sub-soil of Jerusalem is everywhere honeycombed; others, opening the southern gates, made a wild and futile attempt to force the Roman line of circumvallation.

With a fierce shouting that seemed to shake the very towers, the triumphant legionaries poured over the walls, and proceeded to carry fire and sword through the length and breadth of the city. Enraged by the long opposition of the Zealots, the Romans made no distinction between the innocent and the guilty, but wreaked upon all alike, man, woman, and child, the accumulated vengeance of a long term of weeks.

The flames of night lit up wild scenes of carnage, lust, and rapine, scenes that have scarcely any parallel in history. One significant fact attests the extent of the slaughter—the fires on the lower parts of Zion were extinguished by the rivers of blood that poured down from the higher!

The Romans only ceased from slaying when their arms had become weary of striking; the surviving Jews —still to be counted by myriads—were driven like sheep across the Tyropæon bridge to the ruined cloisters of the temple, where they were put under guard. Scores of them, sullen and defiant to the last, refused to taste food prepared by Gentile hands, and so died.

When Titus entered the city and beheld the massy towers which the Zealots had so cravenly relinquished, he was filled with wonder.

"Truly," he murmured, "unless the gods had put it into the hearts of these men to flee, we should never by our own strength have taken these towers."

But however much Titus may have thought himself indebted to Divine power, he showed little of the Divine in his treatment of the captive multitude, who, if the figures of Josephus are to be trusted, amounted to ninety-seven thousand!

For many days a sorting process went on in the temple-courts. Those who were convicted of having borne arms against the Romans were executed at once. Seven hundred others, the tallest and most handsome, were set aside to grace the triumph of Titus. Of the rest, those under seventeen years of age were sold into slavery; all who had passed that age were either sent in fetters to Egypt, there to work in the mines, or were distributed among the provinces, to die in the amphitheater by the sword of the gladiator or by the fangs of wild beasts. As for the aged and infirm, these, as being useless and unsaleable, were simply put to death in cold blood. Thus were weeping families parted to meet no more on earth; never were such heart-rending scenes as those that took place in the temple-courts upon the closing days of September in the year A.D. 70, and all under the sanction of the Cæsar who was called by his sycophantic contemporaries, "*Amor et deliciæ generis humani*—the love and darling of mankind!"

As Crispus heard the nightly wailings of the captive multitude he longed for the day when the progress of Christianity should temper warfare with a spirit more humane and merciful.

Josephus received the privilege of setting free from among the prisoners all his former friends, of whom he must have possessed a remarkable number, seeing that, after setting aside his father and mother, he contrived to liberate nearly two hundred more of the throng.

There were two faces, however, he looked for in vain.

"What hath become of Simeon ben Gamaliel?" he asked.

"Slain at the taking of Zion," was the reply.

"And Johanan ben Zacchai?"

That rabbi, it appeared, was now at Jamnia in southern Judæa, having escaped from the holy city in a very singular manner.[15] Feigning to be dead, he was placed in a coffin, which the Zealot sentinels at the gate permitted to be carried forth for burial within his father's sepulcher in the glen of Cedron. When once outside the city Johanan made his way to the Roman lines; and being permitted to pass by the good will of Crispus before whom he happened to be brought, he retired to Jamnia. And here, in subsequent years, he established the celebrated rabbinical school whose teaching was destined ultimately to develop into that strange system of Jewish scholasticism known as the Talmud.

Titus ordered the city to be razed to the ground

with the exception of the three great towers—Hippicus, Phasaelus, and Mariamne. These were spared partly for the accommodation of a garrison to be stationed there with a view of preventing any attempt at rebuilding by the Jews, but mainly to demonstrate to posterity what kind of a city it was that Roman valor had subdued.

Terentius Rufus was appointed to superintend this work of demolition, and his first care was to remove Crispus to the splendid apartments in the tower Hippicus, as being more conducive to the patient's recovery than the close and squalid quarters of the castellum, in which he had hitherto lain.

It was a matter of vexation to Titus that Simon the Black and John of Giscala were not to be found among the captive multitude. It turned out that the two Zealot chiefs had taken refuge in the catacombs beneath the city, and though the dauntless Simon contrived for a while to elude pursuit, John, reduced by stress of famine, came forth from his hiding place to meet, by a singular leniency on the part of the conqueror, with the sentence of perpetual imprisonment.

And now, the Roman troops, having done the work they had set out to do, broke up their camp and commenced a slow and stately march to Cæsarea-by-the-sea, leading with them a long train of melancholy captives, the remnants of a once great nation, together with the spoils of the temple.

Terentius Rufus was left behind with the Legio Fretensis—bricks stamped with the name of this legion are still found in the sub-soil of Zion—and he proceeded to execute the work of demolition with a thoroughness that has made his memory forever hated by the Jews. The Talmud has no more fearful curses than those laid upon the head of him whom, with the Oriental peculiarity for disfiguring Western names, it miscalls *Turnus* Rufus.

Over the site of what had once been a splendid and

populous city he drew a plow in accordance with the oath which he had sworn to the Jews.

"Where is now their God?" he laughed, in scornful ignorance that his own action was a striking confirmation to the truth of the Hebrew religion, for had not the prophet written, "*Zion shall be plowed as a field*"?

For the accommodation of the garrison, however, a few houses were left standing upon the western side of the city, and among them the celebrated *Cænaculum*,[36] or House of the Last Supper, destined in the age of Constantine to be transformed into a Christian church.

For more than a month that fugitive of the catacombs, Simon, continued to evade arrest. Attended by a small but faithful band of miners and hewers of stone, well provided with cutting tools, he had been essaying the gigantic feat of boring his way through the solid rock to a point that should be beyond the ken of the Roman garrison, but the difficulty of the work and the failure of provisions compelled him to relinquish the enterprise.

He then took a singular step.

Assuming a white robe and a mantle of purple he emerged unexpectedly from the ground in the very place where the temple had stood, thinking perhaps by this act to impress the Romans with the belief that he was a new Messiah resuscitated from the dead.[37] As a matter of fact, the soldiers in the vicinity were not a little awe-struck at sight of this strange apparition rising from the ground. Their first amazement over, they drew near, formed a circle round him, and demanded who he was.

But Simon declared that his name was not for vulgar ears.

"Call your commandant," said he with a mysterious air.

But when that commandant proved to be one well

acquainted with the features and figure of Simon, the Zealot chief saw that deception was at an end.

Rufus received him with a pitying smile.

"Simon, if thou art attempting to imitate the God of my friend Crispus, thou art playing the part to no purpose. I know thee to be mortal man. Thou art my prisoner. This is a sorry ending for thee. Why didst not thou, Roman fashion, fall on thy blade, and so round off thy wild life?"

"'Tis forbidden by our law to slay one's self," returned Simon. "Now tell me what will be my doom?"

"Titus hath already decreed it. With a rope round thy neck thou wilt march through Rome in Cæsar's great triumphal procession that all the citizens may see what manner of man it was that kept their soldiers at bay so long. As thou walkest, attendant lictors will beat thee with rods, for such is the custom. If it will give thee any pleasure thou wilt see borne aloft before thee the holy vessels of thy temple. But while these will be carried on to the journey's end to be laid up in the temple of Peace, thou, at a certain point in the procession, wilt be led aside to the Tarpeian Rock, precipitated therefrom and slain. And a mighty shout of joy will go up from the multitude, for it is not till thy death has been announced that the sacrifices and the feasting will begin. Now, I might pity thee, but that the memory of the massacred Roman garrisons hardens my heart."

"Better to fall with Israel than to triumph with Rome," retorted the Zealot.

Rufus had no further parley with his prisoner, but dispatched him at once to Titus, who was then at Cæsarea. What must have been the feelings of Simon, when he found himself journeying along the same road as that on which he had gained his memorable victory over Cestius? Verily, the fortune of war had indeed changed!

It was not till three months after the burning of

the temple that Crispus was strong enough to leave his chamber in Hippicus, and walk with halting step among the shapeless heaps of stones which represented all that was left of the once proud city.

Accompanied by Rufus he ascended the temple-hill. Its columns and cloisters, chambers and courts, had vanished, but the Legio Fretensis with all their toil had been unable to pull apart the masonry of the vast basement on which the temple structures had rested.

It remained, and remains to this day, a part of it forming the celebrated "Wailing-place" of the Jews.

Now as Crispus and Rufus stood there, they were surprised to see a band of men and women, quiet and orderly, ascending Mount Moriah from the Vale of Cedron.

As they drew near, Crispus recognized in them his friends of Pella. There was the saintly bishop Simeon, who had baptized both him and Vashti; and there, too, were the two youthful grandsons of the apostle Jude, destined on account of their Davidic descent to be haled one day before the jealous tyrant Domitian, and by him to be dismissed again as innocent and foolish visionaries.

"Now, who be ye?" asked Rufus, casting a suspicions glance at the throng.

"We are natives of Jerusalem, who, four years ago, quitted the city, rather than take up arms against the Romans."

"That's a point in your favor."

"These," explained Crispus, "are the Christians who befriended me during the time of my proscription by Nero."

"And what would ye here?" asked Rufus, addressing them.

"We seek to inhabit this place again, and to carry on our worship as heretofore."

"What! Think ye that Titus has destroyed this city merely to see it built again?"

"Titus destroyed the city as being a center of Jewish sedition," remarked Crispus. "But these persons repudiate the Jewish religion. They are Christians with no wish for an independent kingdom. Acknowledging the authority of Rome, they will be a hindrance to rebellion, and a source of strength to us."

"Humph! I doubt whether Titus will agree to their settling here."

"His cousin, Flavius Clemens, would. Thou knowest that he is a Christian."

"Flavius Clemens is not Cæsar."

"But his two sons may become Cæsars, seeing that Vespasian has nominated them as his heirs next after Titus and Domitian, who, as you know, are both childless. You and I may yet live, Rufus, to see a Christian Cæsar on the throne, and a Cæsar who will know how to reward any favor shown to this little community here." [15]

There was something in this argument, and Rufus thought he might as well have an eye to the future. To him, personally, it was a matter of indifference whether the Christians remained or withdrew; his only wish was not to be embroiled with Titus.

"Christians," said Rufus meditatively. "Humph! well," he added, turning to Crispus, "since you warrant them to be orderly, and innocent of any innovation against Rome, let them, if they will, remain and build. Titus hath not actually said aught to the contrary."

Thus had the saints returning from Pella good cause to bless the day when they received among them the heathen and proscribed fugitive Crispus; for, thanks to his good offices, they were permitted to remain, and by their daily worship in the Cænaculum to carry on the historic continuity of the Church of Jerusalem.

# CHAPTER XXVI

#### JUSTICE THE AVENGER

IT was a lovely sunny morning in April as Crispus and Rufus strolled along the sands in the vicinity of Cæsarea-by-the-sea.

" Have you seen the new coin struck by Titus to commemorate his conquest? " asked Rufus; and, being answered in the negative, he drew forth a sesterce, and exhibited it to the gaze of Crispus.

The obverse of the coin bore the laureated head of Titus; the reverse, a graceful palm-tree, at the foot of which sat the weeping figure of a woman, emblematic of Judæa; behind the palm stood Titus in a military uniform, with his foot on a helmet, holding in his right hand a lance, and in his left a sword. The words JUDÆA CAPTA formed the legend.

" This weeping figure is obviously intended as a portrait of Berenice," remarked Crispus in some surprise.

" Just so. 'Tis said that Titus, happening to see Berenice sitting beneath a palm weeping, or pretending to weep, for her country, was so struck by the sight that he ordered the Master of the Mint at Cæsarea to immortalize her figure and attitude in the issue of commemorative coins."

" Did Berenice have aught to say on the matter? "

" She was not averse to it."

No; doubtless it suited her taste for emotional display to see herself set forth to the Roman world in the character of a devout patriot weeping for the fall of her country. The hollowness both of her grief and of her religion, in fact her entire lack of womanly feeling, was shown by her presence at the games held at Cæsarea Philippi in honor of Domitian's birthday, when she could calmly sit in the amphitheater there and see 2,500 hapless Jews slaughtered, either in combats with wild beasts, or in fighting with each other as gladiators; for Titus, prevented from sailing to Rome by reason of the advanced season at which the war ended—navigation being usually suspended during the winter months—had spent his time in giving a series of fêtes in various cities of the East, fêtes that were seldom celebrated without the butchery of Jews in the arena.

"Berenice has been with Titus at all these festivities," remarked Rufus. "She has become his mistress, as I thought she would. So amorous are they that they all but fondle each other in public. It is Antony and Cleopatra over again. Will he marry her, I wonder?"

"Not till I have divorced her," responded Crispus, quietly.

Rufus stared in amazement at this intimation of a secret hitherto kept from him. Crispus proceeded to tell the story of the wedding at Beth-tamar, giving his reasons for supposing Berenice to be the veiled lady.

"The Princess Berenice your wife?" murmured Rufus, scarcely able to credit the statement. "Humph! and when Cæsar takes a man's wife, where shall the man look for redress?"

"He's welcome to her. She is my wife no longer. I shall repudiate her."

"No, not yet," exclaimed Rufus, his face suddenly lighting up with excitement. "You must not do so just yet. You must delay your purpose for a while in order to save Vashti."

"Ha! what mean you? How can the delay serve Vashti?"

Rufus laughed with a sort of good-humored contempt at what he conceived to be a sad lack of discernment on the part of Crispus.

"Was there any stipulation made at this marriage that the wife was to retain the separate possession of her property?"

"None."

"Then Vashti may be set free."

"How?" asked Crispus eagerly.

"By you, of course. O, dullard! All you have to do now is to walk into the presence of Titus and Berenice, and to say, 'Woman, you are my wife. The law gives you to me, as doth also this document signed by Vespasian.' Titus dare not oppose you, if you are determined to assert your legal rights. Then you lead the proud princess home, by force if she will not come by persuasion, and you address her thus: 'You are mine, and all that you have is mine, including your household slaves. Therefore, in the exercise of my lawful right, I declare this maiden Vashti to be free.' That's the plan you must adopt, Crispus. Afterwards, repudiate her, if you will; but—liberate Vashti first."

Crispus, with the fire of hope coursing through his veins, resolved to follow the daring suggestion of Rufus.

"The sooner this business be done, the better," said he.

"There I agree with you. What more appropriate time than to-morrow night when Berenice gives a grand banquet in the Prætorium, that edifice being graciously lent for the occasion by the new procurator, Antonius Julianus, who, by the way, talks of writing a history of the war, thereby entering into rivalry with Josephus. You and I are invited to this entertainment; in truth, if you are absent, Berenice will suffer sore disappointment, seeing that she hath prepared a little mortification for you. She hath decreed that her slave Vashti shall wait as cup-bearer upon the chief guests."

"May the intended humiliation fall upon Berenice's own head!"

"So say I. What hath our pretty Vashti done that

she should be thus shamed? I confess I am beginning to dislike the princess, whom I once so much admired. You must certainly put your plan into operation tomorrow night. In the face of all the company claim Berenice as your wife, and assert your authority over her, to the confusion of Titus. She is desirous, so 'tis said, of providing her guests with a rare entertainment; it's very likely she'll succeed."

Crispus, determined to adopt this scheme—he blinked its difficulties—impatiently awaited the moment for putting it into execution.

When the time fixed for the banquet drew near, Crispus, assuming his whitest and handsomest toga, with its broad purple border, went, accompanied by Rufus, to that palace, still called, though its founder had been seventy years dead, Herod's Prætorium.

Upon entering he found that the scene of the feast was the same as that in which Florus had held *his* banquet.

It was malice that made Berenice choose this hall; the very place that had seen Vashti hailed as the queen of beauty was now to see her degraded to the condition of a slave, compelled to wait upon the princess whose charms had been slighted by Crispus, while Crispus himself was invited to look on and behold her humiliation.

He smiled within himself. The sequel would show whose was to be the humiliation.

The banquet-hall presented a brilliant scene, thronged as it was with all the brave captains who had taken part in the war, and with fair ladies whose richly dyed robes afforded a perpetual feast of color.

Crispus and his companion arrived just as the guests were preparing to take their places at the various triclinia.

Berenice was there, moving with a proud and stately step, and, as though she were already an empress, wearing an Eastern diadem upon her dark hair.

By her side walked the laureled Titus, clad in imperial purple, and seemingly in excellent spirits, though he suddenly started as he caught sight of Crispus, and over his face came a guilty look which Rufus interpreted in his own way.

"Ashamed of himself at stealing his friend's wife. Though he be Cæsar, and my commander, I shall rejoice if he meet by and by with deserved discomfiture."

Crispus and Rufus were allotted places next each other, not, however, at the chief triclinium where were Titus, Berenice, Agrippa, Alexander, and others, but at an adjacent triclinium, an arrangement that suited the two friends, who were thus enabled to talk with more freedom than they could have enjoyed at Cæsar's table.

At the same triclinium with Crispus was Josephus, who had his place next to the Roman.

"Do you know the humiliation intended for Vashti?" asked Crispus.

Josephus signified assent, adding:

"Aware that your presence here will save her, I can await the issue with a serene mind."

"Rufus," whispered Crispus to his friend, "you have been communicating our plan to Josephus."

But as Rufus gave an emphatic denial to this, Crispus was not a little puzzled by the words of Josephus.

By the side of the historian sat a stately and venerable dame.

"My mother," remarked Josephus, "and her purpose in being here is the same as mine," he added with a mysterious smile, "to obtain Vashti's freedom."

It seemed from this that Josephus, too, had some plan for delivering his ward from Berenice's hands. What was the nature of the plan, and was it likely to succeed? But to all questioning Josephus remained provokingly evasive, so that Crispus was fain to hold his soul in patience.

It soon became clear, however, from the conversation of Josephus, that he was animated by a spirit of bitter hostility to Berenice, caused by her patronage of those amphitheatrical games in which Jews were pitilessly butchered. Titus, too, came in for a share of his animadversions.

"He hath ordered that the didrachmas which every adult Jew is accustomed to pay annually into the temple treasury, shall now be paid into the temple of the Capitoline Jupiter. You, as a Christian, can understand the feeling of the Jew in this matter. And the golden cherubim that overshadowed the mercy seat he hath given to the heathen; the sacred figures which none but the high priest was permitted to see are now profanely placed as a trophy over the eastern gate of Antioch, so that it is beginning to be known as the Gate of the Cherubim. And nigh to it he hath dedicated a chariot to the Moon, for the help which she hath given him during the siege. The moon, forsooth!"

The signal for the feast was now given, and richly clad slaves, both male and female, moved to and fro, attentive to the wants of the guests.

"I do not see Vashti," whispered Crispus to Josephus.

"She will not enter till the drinking begins."

Gay conversation went on all around, but Crispus took little or no part in it. Vashti! Vashti! was the one thought of his mind.

At last repletion came to the guests; both the heavier and the lighter dishes were removed from the tables to make way for the wines.

"And now, my lords," cried Berenice, addressing those at her own triclinium, but speaking sufficiently loud for Crispus to hear, "I have a rare vintage for you, to be offered by a cup-bearer as graceful as Hebe herself."

Among a crowd of wine-bearing slaves that now entered the hall Crispus distinguished the form of

Vashti. Quickly the slaves spread themselves to right and left, each going to his appointed place.

Of the thousand persons in the banquet-hall Crispus saw but one only—the fair girl that was moving with a light, graceful step towards the chief triclinium.

Vashti, but how different from her appearance when last seen by him! The disfigurement wrought by the famine had vanished; she was her own sweet self once more.

The charming grace and beauty of her figure were set off by a clinging robe of pure white silk, richly embroidered with gold, and girt at the waist with a broad, silver-sparkling zone. A necklace of pearls encircled her fair throat, and a wreath of violets rested upon her golden ringlets.

She was the living picture of beauty; from the crown of her head to her dainty, gold-embroidered sandals there was not a flaw to mar her radiant loveliness.

The eyes of Josephus' mother glistened with pleasure at the success of the toilet for which she was responsible, the good dame having resolved that Vashti should appear at her fairest before the guests.

As Vashti caught Crispus' look she gave him a smile that sent the blood coursing like liquid fire through his veins; it was a smile that showed she had no fear; a smile that seemed to say she knew that he could and would save her. Was she aware of his intentions? he wondered, or was she relying upon the aid of Josephus?

Berenice, with a sudden uneasiness at her heart, began all too late to wish that she had kept her slave from appearing at this banquet, for Vashti's beauty drew murmurs of admiration from the men, if not from the women.

"Ye gods! who is this?" said Tiberius Alexander. "I did not know, princess, that you had invited Venus to be a guest."

"'Tis only one of my slaves," replied Berenice, outwardly calm, inwardly thrilling with jealousy.

"A slave!" said Alexander, with the light of amatory desire leaping into his eyes. "I'll give you ten thousand aurei for her—fifteen thousand," he added, breathlessly.

"I would not take a hundred myriads," replied Berenice, coldly. "She is not for sale."

At this moment the murmur of tongues ceased throughout the hall. The guests, catching sight of Berenice's dark face, became suddenly silent, desirous of discovering what was amiss.

The princess rose to her feet, and angrily faced the slave who was disobeying her on two points—she was wearing a costume different from that enjoined her, and she lacked the flagon of wine that it was her duty to bear.

"By whose leave do you wear that dress?"

"By my own," replied Vashti, with a sweet smile that maddened the other. "Why should I consult *you*, princess, as to what manner of raiment I must wear?"

It was a revelation to Crispus to hear the hitherto submissive and gentle Vashti taking this bold stand, and he loved her the more for it. There was no tremor in her voice, nor did she shrink in the least from the fierce gaze of the princess. Indeed, Vashti, in her proud fearlessness, looked at that moment far more of a princess than did Berenice. What wonderful power was it that enabled her thus to brave a mistress who, if she chose, could order her off to instant scourging?

"You dare speak thus to *me?*" exclaimed Berenice amazedly. "O, I see. A freewoman all these years, you cannot yet realize that you are a slave. I will overlook your offense. Go! Bring hither the flagon of wine that you were bidden to pour out for my guests."

But Vashti shook her pretty golden tresses, and cast an arch smile at those reclining at Berenice's triclinium.

"Nay, verily, if they desire the wine let them wait

upon themselves; or perhaps *you*, princess, will play the part of cup-bearer."

Berenice stood completely dumfounded at these audacious words from one who had hitherto behaved as her submissive slave. The men looked on with smiles of wonder and amusement; the women were more disposed to side with the princess.

"The slave claims to be a Christian," sneered Agrippa to a fair lady by his side.

"That explains her insolence," replied his partner. "I once had one of those creatures among my household, and know the trouble they give. Were I the princess, I would whip the new religion out of her."

"The girl must be mad," exclaimed Berenice. "On your knees and cry pardon, or——"

Vashti turned disdainfully away.

"It has pleased me for a time to abide in your house as a slave," said she. "It pleases me now to resume my freedom. Give your commands to others. There is but one person here who shall have my obedience, and that is my lord Crispus."

She walked to where Crispus stood—for he had risen to his feet—laid an appealing hand upon his arm, and looked with trusting eyes into his. The supreme moment had come! But how was he to save her? His plan had melted into thin air. It was all very well to claim Berenice as his wife, but the cold conviction suddenly struck him that his claim was based not upon proof, but upon conjecture merely. If Berenice chose to deny his statement, as she undoubtedly would, how could he make his word good? He turned his eyes upon Josephus, but that priest made no movement, uttered no word. "Not yet," he seemed to be saying.

"Guards!" cried Berenice, addressing some of her own soldiers, who were stationed at intervals along the wall of the banqueting chamber. "Drag yon girl away, and bring whips hither. Since her defiance of me is public, so, too, shall her scourging be."

## Justice the Avenger

Even these words did not disturb Vashti's serenity. Her pitying smile, implying as it did that she was secure from the threatened punishment, lashed Berenice into a secret fury.

During all this time the greatest man at the feast, Titus, had remained silent, looking on perplexed and uneasy. The redemption of Vashti, though he had often asked for it, was a favor Berenice would not grant him. He was sorry for Crispus, and secretly sympathized with the daring maid who was seeking to assert her liberty, but under the influence of his passion for Berenice he hesitated to do the right thing, namely, to declare Vashti free.

As the soldiers came forward to execute Berenice's command, Vashti turned to Titus and addressed him.

"Cæsar, bid these men stay their hand till I have spoken. I have that to say which will show the justice of my cause."

At a sign from Titus the advancing guards paused.

"Say on," he commanded, hoping that Vashti might somehow be able to furnish him with a plausible pretext for delivering her from the power of Berenice.

Verily, Vashti seemed to be doing the work from which Crispus shrank; for she began to address Titus with a catechism very similar to what Crispus himself would have employed had he carried out his plan as originally intended.

"Have you forgotten, sire, a brief visit made by you and my lord Crispus to a house called Beth-tamar on a certain night more than four years ago?"

Titus started; he guessed what was coming, and frowned.

"I have not forgotten it," said he, with a side glance at Berenice, whose lip curved with the scornful smile as of one who should say, "That silly story!"

"You can testify that my lord Crispus wedded at Beth-tamar a woman unknown to him?—unknown, because she was veiled and spake never a word."

This strange and romantic statement caused a murmur of surprise and wonder to run around the banquet-hall.

"I can testify to that," said Titus, with the air of one who would fain deny what he was affirming.

"Do you know the name of the woman?"

"I do not," replied Titus, with another side glance at Berenice, which set some of the guests wondering as to whether *she* were the mysterious bride.

At this point Berenice, with a gesture of impatience, addressed Titus.

"What hath all this to do with the question of punishing an insolent slave?"

"Everything, as you will see," returned Vashti quietly, continuing her questions to Titus. "Did not Crispus give his bride a ring, saying that when the unknown lady should come to him with the said ring he would acknowledge her as his wife?"

"That is so."

Vashti, with eyes shining with love, and with a tender smile that made her face the more beautiful, turned to Crispus, and, withdrawing her hand from a fold of her dress where it had lain concealed, she held it forth, and there, sparkling on her finger, was the very ring that he had given to his bride at Beth-tamar!

Scarcely able to grasp the momentous truth Crispus stood like one enchanted to stone, silently staring at Vashti and her ring. To think that his marriage with Berenice, the ugly black incubus that had so long oppressed him, was the mere figment of his own imagination! that the sweet Christian maiden, whom he had loved from the first hour of seeing her, should be his wife, was a revelation so astounding that it was no wonder that at first he could not give it credence.

Vashti gave a low, sweet laugh at his bewilderment.

"I am your wife, Crispus. Won't you protect me?"

Protect her?

He put his arm about her waist—a dozen men could

not have torn her from his grasp!—and turned to face Berenice, who for the moment was almost as much bewildered and amazed as Crispus himself.

"Prettily acted!" sneered she. "A scheme, artfully preconcerted, for the purpose of robbing me of my slave. But it shall not succeed. That Crispus wedded someone at Beth-tamar we must believe, since Cæsar himself affirms it; but I require something more than this girl's word, ere I shall believe her to be the wife of Crispus."

"I can confirm her statement," said Josephus, intervening at this point, "since it was I who conducted Vashti to Beth-tamar, and from behind a curtain saw her wedded to the lord Crispus. And the woman who attended Vashti during the ceremony was my mother, who is here present to bear her testimony, if need be."

"And in the mouth of two or three witnesses shall every word be established, princess," remarked Alexander.

Berenice though striving to maintain a calm exterior, was nevertheless full of a secret rage at finding her intended victim slipping from her hands.

"What if she be the wife of Crispus? She is none the less my slave."

"What? Rob a Roman noble of his wife?" interjected Alexander. "O, too bad!"

"At the time I made the gift I knew not that she was the wife of Crispus," remarked Titus, not at all displeased with the turn events were taking.

"That matters not," returned Berenice. "The gift, if made in due legal form, as this was, can be revoked neither by you nor by a court of law."

Crispus smiled pityingly at the baffled princess.

"I have here," said he, drawing forth a papyrus-scroll, "a document that bears a date long anterior to the time when Vashti was made a slave, a document that threatens death to those who seek to take the wife of Crispus from him. It bears the autograph signature of one whose authority not even Titus Cæsar himself will venture to dispute, for the signature is that of his august sire, Flavius Vespasian."

"That is so," observed Tiberius Alexander, who had drawn near, and was inspecting the document, "and, therefore, it seems to me," he added, jocularly, "that both Cæsar and the princess, by enslaving the wife of Crispus, have made themselves liable to the death penalty. Doubtless Vespasian will pardon the offenders, as they acted in ignorance. At any rate, Crispus is entitled to lead away his wife; and may good fortune attend him! The bravest man in the war has obtained the fairest woman for his bride; that is what I say, and who will controvert it?" he added, looking round upon the guests.

"None! None!" was the answer that came from every side. Vashti's romantic story appealed to every heart, save *one;* even those ladies who, a few minutes before, had been most opposed to her, now joined in the acclamations that greeted the happy pair thus strangely reunited.

"Take me away," whispered Vashti. "Anywhere, so that it be from here."

Crispus responded to her appeal. Drawing her arm within his own, he passed smilingly from the hall amid cries of "Long live the brave Crispus and his fair bride!"

Miserable Berenice! Her bitterness of spirit at that moment received but little balm from Titus' gay whisper, "There is now no obstacle to our union," for she had known all along that the obstacle had never existed save in his own imagination.

In the moonlit gardens of the Prætorium Crispus and Vashti, seated in the very same spot where they had sat four years before, were holding a delightful conversation.

Vashti was reclining within his embrace, her little

hand resting within his. The early Christians were very human!

"And to think that during all this time you have been my wife, and I knew it not. Why did you not reveal the truth earlier?"

"Because, like yourself, I was bound to secrecy for three years."

"But that time limit had gone by when I rescued you from Jerusalem."

"True," replied Vashti, the brightness of her face becoming dimmed for a moment by that mournful reminiscence, "but was that a time to be talking love and wedlock? I resolved to keep the secret till the siege should be over."

"I am not sure that you were right in doing so. The making it known would have saved you from the hands of Berenice. Tell me, how has she used you?"

"Not ill, though she would taunt me at times with your name, and threaten to whip the Christianity out of me."

"But why did you not set yourself free earlier, by sending me the ring?"

"Because she was always saying that she would give a grand entertainment at which I should serve as a slave while you should look helplessly on; she seemed to take such delight in the notion that I resolved to await the coming of this feast; it would furnish me with an excellent opportunity of asserting my freedom and of giving her a startling surprise."

"You have certainly succeeded in doing that, my little wife."

"*Am* I your wife, Crispus?" said Vashti gravely. "Was not that ceremony at Beth-tamar somewhat heathenish in character?"

"You speak truth, dearest. We must have the blessing of the Church on our union. To-morrow we will set out for Jerusalem, where the good bishop Simeon shall join our hands."

At this point a centurion made his appearance with a message to the effect that Titus desired the presence of Crispus and his lady.

Responding, though with considerable reluctance, to this summons, the two repaired to the Ivory Hall, where they found Titus seated beside Berenice with Josephus standing near.

"Be seated, noble Crispus and the lady Vashti."

Titus spoke with genuine affability; as for Berenice her disdainful air showed that the presence or the absence of the pair was a matter alike of indifference to her.

"I have asked Josephus," began Titus, when the centurion had withdrawn, leaving the five together, "to tell me the meaning of the strange business at Bethtamar. He is very urgent that you also should be present to hear him. Hence my sending for you."

With that he nodded to the priest as a sign for him to proceed.

"It may be, sire," began Josephus, "that what I have to say will give sharp offense to one of my hearers." Crispus guessed that Berenice was meant. "Therefore, ere I begin, I must receive assurance from you that the utterance shall not bring punishment upon the utterer."

"Say what thou wilt; abuse me, if it please thee; thy tongue shalt have free license to-night."

Assured thus, Josephus began.

"I have but lately returned, O Cæsar, from a visit to Pontus, where it was my fortune to meet with Zeno, the secretary of the royal Polemo, and seemingly a man well acquainted with the secrets of the late king. It is partly from this Zeno, and partly from my own knowledge, that I derive the materials for the story I am about to relate."

At the mention of the names Polemo and Zeno, Berenice, who had hitherto betrayed a languid indifference, began to appear as if keenly interested.

"Many years ago—twenty-three, to give the exact number—the Princess Berenice, then in her twentieth year, married Polemo, king of Pontus, who, after two years, repudiated her, for a reason the princess herself knows."

Here Josephus ceased speaking, checked by Berenice's haughty and indignant stare.

"Is it necessary to bring *my* name into your narration?"

"Absolutely necessary."

"Then I will tell you the reason of our separation. He did not repudiate me; I left him of my own free will, left him because, prior to our marriage, he, himself a proselyte, promised that he would do all in his power to bring the people of Pontus over to Judaism. He failed to redeem his word, however—nay, he actively thwarted my attempts at proselytism, and so I left him."

"Was there not a daughter born of this marriage?"

Berenice's eyes flashed fire.

"I see plainly that your object is to prejudice me in the eyes of Titus by recalling a deed of long ago. What I did then I do not now regret."

"That is a strange thing to say of infanticide."

Berenice gave a cold hard laugh that caused Vashti to shiver.

"The exposure of infants is a custom so common among Romans that Titus will scarcely regard it as a great crime."

"But *our* law, princess, regards it as murder."

"And I regard my deed as a justifiable one, for in destroying the body of the infant I saved its soul. Polemo, who had seceded from Judaism, and had grown to hate both me and my religion, swore that he would bring up the child in his own Hellenic faith, and would teach it to hate the religion of its mother. I resolved to save it from such fate, and took the only possible way—I exposed it one winter's night among the snowy crags of Hermon."

Vashti gave a faint little gasp—inaudible to Berenice—and her heart almost ceased its beating. Not even when coming home on that dreadful night to find Arad gone forever did she feel more horror than she felt at this moment. To learn that she was the daughter of a woman so unnatural as to expose her own child to death! to learn that it was her own mother who had been pursuing her with a malignant aim! to learn that she was a member of that Herodian house that had never ceased persecuting Christianity from its very beginning! to know that her mother was at that very moment living in open sin with the destroyer of her country!—all this rushed with her blood, nearly causing her to shriek aloud.

Josephus continued his narration.

"The loss of the child—for he had loved it as the apple of his eye—threw Polemo into a fever, which, so it seems to me, crazed his brain, for it left him animated by one passion only—a desire to be revenged upon the woman who had wronged him."

"Thou liest," interjected Berenice, "for in due course of time, he and I, as all men can testify, grew to be great friends."

"You were deceived, princess. He masked his hatred under a smiling guise the more effectually to conceal his purpose. Now, mark the result of your deed! It is true that it was decreed in the councils of the Most High that the city and the temple should perish, but the Most High makes use of human instruments to work out His decrees; and yours, princess, has been the hand that has wrought the ruin of Israel."

There was in Josephus' manner something so solemn and convincing, that all Berenice's hauteur and defiance vanished, leaving her nearly as pale and trembling as the daughter that was as yet unknown to her.

"How mean you?" she faltered.

"It was our common religion, so Polemo erroneously argued, that had destroyed his child; he would therefore destroy our religion.

"Nothing was dearer to you, so you had once said to him, than the holy city, and the holy temple; he resolved to bring destruction both upon that city and upon that temple.

"How could he effect it?

"There was but one way; the Jewish people must be goaded into war, a war in which their capital must sink in flames.

"This is the key to Polemo's frequent visits to Judæa; to his friendship with successive procurators—Felix, Festus, Albinus. With these, however, he failed to effect his purpose, but at last in Florus he found the tool he wanted. While you, princess, were on one side of that procurator, winning him to acts of clemency, Polemo was on the other, urging him to deeds of blood; all the provocative acts of Florus were due to the secret, the wicked policy of the Pontic king."

These words caused a deepening of Vashti's horror. To think that she was the daughter of a king so cold-blooded as deliberately to plan the extirpation of a whole nation, and all, so it seemed, on her account!

At this point Titus intervened.

"This secret history is doubtless interesting, but what hath it to do with Beth-tamar?"

"I am coming to it, O Cæsar. It chanced in course of time that the Princess Berenice met my lord Crispus at a banquet at Antioch and became enamored of him."

Berenice gave a scornful laugh; but the statement was true, and her laugh deceived no one. "Polemo suspected this. Now, he had already in mind selected the son of his friend, Cestius the Legate, to be his successor in the sovereignty of Pontus, and it did not suit his policy that Berenice should marry Crispus, and thus again wear the crown that she had once despised. He therefore resolved to thwart her aim. While thinking how he might best succeed in this matter, he happened to pay a visit to Jerusalem, and there, by a singular turn of destiny, he saw one day in the temple-courts a maiden who immediately arrested his attention from the marvelous resemblance she bore to his mother Pythodoris in her youthful days. Avoiding the maiden herself, he made inquiries of others, and learned that her name was Vashti, and that she was the ward of him who now addresses you. He sought me out with eager questionings, and I was forced to admit that the supposed daughter of Hyrcanus was in reality a foundling, nor were proofs wanting to convince him beyond all doubt that in Vashti he had found his daughter Athenaïs, long supposed by him to be dead."

A strange sound broke from Berenice; amazement caused her figure to stiffen into a rigid attitude; for a few moments she sat thus, motionless and wordless; then slowly, mechanically, she turned her head and looked at Vashti. And of all the looks that Vashti had ever received none frightened her more than this; it was a look without a trace of maternal love—cold, disdainful, cruel; a look that said, as plainly as words could say, that she would never acknowledge the Nazarene apostate as a daughter of hers.

"Polemo, for reasons of his own, did not make himself known to his daughter. Whether he now had any affection for her whom, as a babe, he had idolized, it is hard to say; one thing became clear to him; he saw in the daughter an instrument for the humiliation of the mother. If he could persuade Crispus to marry Vashti, and to keep the matter hidden from the world, the fond, enamored Berenice would be pursuing Crispus for months in the vain endeavor to win him to her arms, while he—Polemo—could look on in malicious enjoyment, as knowing that her wiles were foredoomed to failure.

"Such was Polemo's reason for keeping the wedding a secret—a reason unknown to me at the time; I have learned it since from Zeno. Vashti, too, was required to keep the matter hidden, even from her adopted mother, Miriam. Vashti, being my ward, was compelled to take for her husband the man of my choice, and though she long resisted the notion of wedding a heathen Roman, I overcame her scruples at last by persuading her that her intended bridegroom was far more virtuous than many a Jew. She therefore accompanied me by night to Beth-tamar, not knowing that he who presided over these nuptials was her father, not knowing his name even, nor that she had been destined by him to wear the crown of a queen.

" All this was to come upon her later as a delightful surprise.

" My story is all but finished. It was Polemo's intention to stand beside Berenice either upon Mount Olivet when the temple was burning, or at some palace window in Rome when the triumphal procession was sweeping past, carrying the sacred spoils of the temple —to stand beside her and to tell her in fierce, exultant tones that all this was *his* work; he would watch her agony; she was to be the victim of his laughter, of his mockery, of his scorn!

" But this supreme and thrilling moment of revenge —this triumph that he had so long worked for, was not to be his; he died ere the day of his vengeance came.

" Cæsar, my tale is said."

There was a long silence in that chamber after Josephus had finished his narration.

Titus looked at Berenice as if desiring her to say something.

The breast of that princess was the seat of a wild tumult of contending passions, but among them there was neither pity nor love for her newly found daughter.

" It seems," said she, with a superbly disdainful air, " it seems, if the story of Josephus be true, that I am to be presented with a daughter, but I care not for the gift. I should be a hypocrite were I to feign love where love is not. No; I cast her away in infancy that thereby I might save her soul; by becoming a Nazarene she has chosen to destroy her soul; let her still remain a castaway. Let her keep to her own path as I shall keep to mine. I have no daughter; that is my answer to her."

Vashti was willing for reconcilement, but this cold repudiation kept her dumb. With divine pity in her eyes, she looked at her mother, and sighed.

Crispus made reply for her.

"Since such is your decision," said he, "we will not seek to change it. Cæsar, I salute you. Come, Vashti, let us be going."

As the two arose to depart, Titus walked over to them, as if not willing that Berenice should hear what he had to say.

"My sire, Vespasian, knowing that you have been disappointed in the expectation of the crown of Pontus, has offered you the thing that is most like it—namely, the governorship of that province. Its people will be delighted when they know that the wife of the new governor is the granddaughter of the good queen Pythodoris."

But Crispus had little desire for the honor; he would be more happy with Vashti in his beautiful villa among the Sabine hills than in presiding over the destinies of the Pontic people. While thinking thus, however, he received from Vashti a wistful glance which seemed to be urging him to accept the post.

"What, Vashti? Ambitious that I should sit in a curule chair?"

"Yes," whispered she, "for if Crispus be ruler of Pontus there will always be *one* safe asylum for Christians."

"You speak wisely, little woman," replied he; and, turning to Titus, he said, "Cæsar, I accept the post with all thankfulness."

## Justice the Avenger 375

Berenice watched the two as they quitted the Ivory Hall.

She never saw them again!

After a brief visit to Jerusalem, where bishop Simeon joined the hands of the pair, Crispus, accompanied by his bride, set out for his province of Pontus, there to begin a long administration, whose wisdom and justice were to win golden opinions from all men.

And Berenice?

The Roman senate and the Roman people soon made short work of her dream of an imperial throne! Their anger at the thought of a Jewish empress was so fiercely expressed that Titus, albeit with all reluctance, was compelled to banish her from his presence.[40]

Scorned by the Romans because she came of the Jewish people; scorned by the Jewish people because she had allied herself with a Roman; branded with deserved infamy by the poet Juvenal;[41] eating out her heart over the ignominious ending of her splendid ambition, Berenice passed into a state of obscurity and oblivion, History failing to record the time, the place, or the manner of her death.

# NOTES

1 The Talmud.
2 Told by the heathen Plutarch in his *Cessation of Oracles.*
3 Josephus.—*Vita* 2.
4 Acts xxv. 16.
5 Greek Anthology.—I. 77.
6 Acts xxiii. 14.
7 Flaccus, pro-Consul of Asia, for example.—CICERO. *Pro Flacco.*
8 The ancient usage in the Jerusalem synagogues of anathematizing Christ and the Christians is said by some to have originated, not with Simeon, but with his father Gamaliel, a statement scarcely reconcilable with Acts v. 38.
9 A saying of Simeon's, according to the Talmud.
10 The Talmud.
11 Jos.—*Bell. Jud.* vi. 5, 3. Tac.—*Hist.* v. 13. Luke xxi. 11.
12 Zech. xi. 1 was, according to the Talmud, referred by Johanan ben Zacchai to this mysterious opening of the temple doors.
13 Josephus.—*Bell. Jud.* ii. 15.
14 At this point Florus disappears from history, and therefore from these pages. It is not known what became of him.
15 Acts xxiii. 3.
16 Josephus.—*Bell. Jud.* ii. 17, 9.
17 Josephus.—*Bell. Jud.* v. 9, 4.
18 Josephus.—*Bell. Jud.* ii. 19, 7.
19 So writes Hegesippus, an historian almost contemporary with Bishop Simeon.
20 Josephus actually applies the Messianic prophecies to Vespasian!—*Bell. Jud.* vi. 5, 4.
21 Tacitus.—*Hist.* ii. 78.
22 Tacitus.—*Hist.* iv. 81.
23 *Lucem caliganti reddidit mundo*—" he restored light to a dark world," was said of Vespasian.—Jortin—*Eccles. Hist.* i. 4.
24 Josephus.—*Bell. Jud.* vi. 5, 3.
25 It is singular that Josephus, who has described the siege in such detail, should have omitted the ceremony of the Evocation, which must have taken place, unless the Romans departed from all precedent.
26 Josephus.—*Bell. Jud.* v. 9, 4.
27 Eusebius.—*Hist. Eccles.* iii. 12.
28 More than £5,000 in English currency.
29 Josephus.—*Bell Jud.* v. 12.
30 Josephus.—*Bell. Jud.* v. 13, 7.
31 Josephus.—*Bell. Jud.* v. 31, 1.
32 Sulpicius Severus (Chron. xxx. 11), who is believed by competent critics to be quoting from a lost portion of the History of Tacitus.
33 Josephus.—*Bell. Jud.* vi. 4, 3.
34 Dean Milman.—*Hist. of Jews.* Book xvi.
35 The Talmud.
36 Such is the statement of Epiphanius.
37 Such appears to be the belief of Renan.—*Antichrist,* xix.
38 Unfortunately for Crispus' hopes, Domitian, on his accession, put Flavius Clemens to death. The fate of the two sons is unknown.
39 This history, *De Judæis,* has unfortunately, not come down to us.
40 "*Berenicem ab urbe dimisit invitus invitam.*"—*Suet. in Tit.* vii.
41 *Satire* vi. 156.

University of California
SOUTHERN REGIONAL LIBRARY FACILITY
405 Hilgard Avenue, Los Angeles, CA 90024-1388
Return this material to the library
from which it was borrowed.